PENGUIN CLASSICS

BOUVARD AND PÉCUCHET

GUSTAVE FLAUBERT, a doctor's son, was born in Rouen in 1821, and sent at eighteen to study law in Paris. While still a schoolboy, however, he professed himself 'disgusted with life', in romantic scorn of bourgeois society, and he showed no distress when a mysterious nervous disease broke off his professional studies. Flaubert retired to Croisset, near Rouen, on a private income, and devoted himself to his writing.

In his early works, particularly *The Temptation of St Antony* (begun in 1848), Flaubert tended to give free rein to his flamboyant imagination, but on the advice of his friends he later disciplined his romantic exuberance in an attempt to achieve total objectivity and a harmonious prose style. This ambition cost him enormous toil and brought him little success in his lifetime. After the publication of *Madame Bovary* in the *Revue de Paris* (1856–7) he was tried for offending public morals; *Salammbo* (1862) was criticized for the meticulous historical detail surrounding the exotic story; *Sentimental Education* (1869) was misunderstood by the critics; and the political play *The Candidate* (1874) was a disastrous failure. Only *Three Tales* (1877) was an unqualified success with public and critics alike, but it appeared when Flaubert's spirits, health and finances were at their lowest ebb.

After his death in 1880 Flaubert's fame and reputation grew steadily, strengthened by the publication of *Bouvard and Pécuchet* (1881) and his remarkable *Correspondence.*

DR A. J. KRAILSHEIMER was born in 1921 and was Tutor in French at Christ Church, Oxford, from 1957 until retirement in 1988. His publications are *Studies in Self-Interest* (1963), *Rabelais and the Franciscans* (1965), *Three Conteurs of the Sixteenth Century* (1966), *Rabelais* (1967), *A. J. de Rancé, Abbot of La Trappe* (1974), *Pascal* (1980), *Conversion* (1980), *Letters of A. J. de Rancé* (1984), *Rancé and the Trappist Legacy* (1985) and *Correspondance de Rancé* (1991). He has also translated Flaubert's *Salammbo* and Pascal's *The Provincial Letters* and *Pensées* for the Penguin Classic.

Gustave Flaubert

BOUVARD AND PÉCUCHET

TRANSLATED WITH AN INTRODUCTION BY

A. J. KRAILSHEIMER

PENGUIN BOOKS

PENGUIN BOOKS

Published by the Penguin Group
Penguin Books Ltd, 27 Wrights Lane, London W8 5TZ, England
Penguin Putnam Inc., 375 Hudson Street, New York, New York 10014, USA
Penguin Books Australia Ltd, Ringwood, Victoria, Australia
Penguin Books Canada Ltd, 10 Alcorn Avenue, Toronto, Ontario, Canada M4V 3B2
Penguin Books (NZ) Ltd, Private Bag 102902, NSMC, Auckland, New Zealand

Penguin Books Ltd, Registered Offices: Harmondsworth, Middlesex, England

This translation first published 1976

ISBN 978-0-14-044320-2

CONTENTS

Introduction 7

Bouvard and Pécuchet 19

Dictionary of Received Ideas 289

INTRODUCTION

Bouvard and Pécuchet has never enjoyed the wide and immediate popularity of *Madame Bovary*, nor has it come to earn the belated superlatives of an influential minority like *Sentimental Education*. At first sight one might assume that the novel has simply shared the fate of so many other incomplete works of art, and that if death had not for ever obscured Flaubert's intentions, it would now figure in the canon of his famous masterpieces. The more that research reveals, however, about the likely shape of the finished work, the more problematic its eventual impact must appear. Masterpiece it certainly is, but hardly one calculated to become a popular favourite, and in its final form (whatever that might have been) it could hardly have failed to offend the susceptibilities of its clearly designated victims. Now that the targets are more remote, it is easier to judge objectively. As it is, the portion left in virtually complete form by Flaubert, and translated here, can be enjoyed for its own sake, and reveals enough of Flaubert's known intentions to make sense, though not too much to stifle curiosity. The book may be a puzzle, but it is emphatically not a bore.

Flaubert himself attached great importance to writing *Bouvard*, which he regarded as presenting a challenge commensurate with the shattering effect the book was intended to produce. In one form or another the theme of human stupidity in general, and bourgeois stupidity in particular, had fascinated him all his life. As early as 1850 he refers in a letter to his *Dictionary of Received Ideas*, which was to be one of the ways (but not the only one) of illustrating the all-pervading power of stupidity. This collection of clichés, substitutes for critical opinions, was supplemented by a constantly expanding anthology of idiocy, in French 'un sottisier', culled from authors of every period and type, and partly at least compiled for him by friends. In the present, and foreseeable, state of human nature such a collection seems to have no obvious limits, particularly as it includes stylistic absurdities of various kinds, as well as factual errors and foolish opinions.

Concurrently with his absorption in the *sottisier* (on which he drew copiously for his main novels) there began to germinate in Flaubert's mind a growth of more finite proportions: the story of two characters whose lives and attitudes would embody and exemplify the principal features of bourgeois stupidity. A draft going back to 1863 refers to *Les Déux Cloportes* (*The Two Woodlice*), thereby indicating his contempt for the proposed anti-heroes; by 1872 he actually mentions the names Bouvard and Pécuchet in a letter to his niece; and in 1874, after the arduous composition of *Sentimental Education* (1863–9), followed by the reworking of *The Temptation of St Antony*, he was free to start work on the novel as we now have it. There were interruptions, notably for *Three Tales* in 1875–7, but *Bouvard* was his chief occupation until his death on 8 May 1880. In January of his last year he reckoned that it would take another six months to complete his first volume, and only six months after that for the second, which, he explained, was already three-quarters finished, since it consisted almost entirely of quotations. As it turned out his estimate was not too wide of the mark: the skeleton plan for the last part of Chapter 10 is fairly explicit, and he would have concluded his first volume, as far as one can judge, within a week or two if he had lived. As regards the missing second volume, there can never be an end to speculation. It would certainly have included the *Dictionary*, possibly modified before publication, and this self-contained work is therefore added as an appendix to the present translation. Other material, in the form of collections of quotations, is not lacking, and can be found in French critical editions, but is not really suitable for inclusion in a plain text translation.

The story, insofar as there is one, is simple enough: two Parisian copy-clerks, both aged forty-seven, meet by chance one day in 1838 and experience an emotional contact which in other contexts would be called love at first sight. The following year one of them, Bouvard, quite unexpectedly inherits a large sum of money, sufficient to keep them comfortably for the rest of their lives – for it never occurs to Bouvard not to share it with his friend Pécuchet – but they agree to defer a move until Pécuchet reaches retirement age. Accordingly they spend the intervening period looking for the ideal retreat, eventually fixing on Chavignolles, in Normandy, between

Caen and Falaise. At last, in 1841, they take up residence in the small village which is to be the scene of all that happens to them thereafter. The first chapter ends with their first night in their new home, and all the subsequent chapters (including the incomplete Chapter 10) are devoted to their successive explorations into the vast areas of experience and knowledge from which their previous humdrum and economically dependent existence had effectively debarred them.

The organization of these nine chapters is logical, though perhaps not inevitable, and involves an extraordinarily complex interplay between narrative, including characterization, and an encyclopaedic range of facts, theories and phenomena. Because one of the main points of the book is the bottomless pit of knowledge confronting Bouvard and Pécuchet, and because Flaubert went to great lengths, even by his standards, to document himself (he speaks of having read some 1,500 books in preparation for this relatively short novel), there is the constant danger, not always avoided, that the book may degenerate into a mere catalogue or anthology. Flaubert was well aware of this danger, and two of the ways by which he specifically sought to minimize it were by introducing conspicuous bridges between one chapter and the next, so that none should be self-contained, and by emphasizing the role of one or more other characters in each episode to give interest, variety and even continuity to the narrative.

Thus the two friends begin their new life by applying themselves to the reality of living in the country, an ambition revealed in their first conversation in the book, at a time when it seemed no more than an idle dream. Their garden, their farm, such typically rural pursuits as bottling preserves and distilling spirits, are the natural activities for the country gentlemen they have become. Their reasoning is always the same: they are ignorant; the way to dispel ignorance is by acquiring knowledge from authorities; experts who write books must be more authoritative than peasants who merely do what their fathers had done before them. Book in hand (or at least in head) they plant trees, stack hay, treat animals and so on with sovereign disregard for the experience of those around them, whose whole lives have been spent more or less successfully exercising skills quite unsupported by theory. Their delight at the occasional success is almost as pathetic as their dejection at the numerous catastrophes. By the end of the chapter they have come into contact, and often conflict, with all the village notables and the farming community.

The explosion of their still, which concludes the second chapter, provides the bridge to the next. From now on they always explain their failures by their ignorance of first principles. They want to know why things are, and by infinite regress they enlarge the distance between what they are studying at any given moment and their ability to cope with the problems of daily life. If they had known enough chemistry the still would not have blown up, so they study chemistry. Chemistry leads them on to medicine, and the beginning of a long feud with the local doctor, Vaucorbeil. By the end of the chapter on science they have gone right back to palaeontology, geology, creation and, inevitably, conflict with the curé, Monsieur Jeufroy.

Their passion for facts leads them on to archaeology, they set up their bizarre museum, try to master historical method, and start work on their own contribution to scholarship, a life of the ineffable Duc d'Angoulême. Returning from a visit to the library at Caen, they discover that in their absence, while they have been worrying about Angoulême's hairstyle, the most deplorable and unsuspected excesses have been committed in their own household. Their comment, which concludes the chapter, is typical: facts are not everything, psychology is also required, and since history is inadequate without imagination, they will acquire that faculty by plunging into historical novels. The chapter on literature which follows takes them through all the genres; novels, poetry, drama (for which they reveal somewhat special talents), criticism, aesthetic theory. They think of writing a novel themselves, but by a clever twist Flaubert introduces a discussion of the social and moral implications of literature to bring the narrative back to the world of real events. A prediction of forthcoming trouble at the end of Chapter 5 is immediately followed by news of the 1848 Revolution at the opening of Chapter 6.

Up to this point the encyclopaedic element is strongly emphasized, but the treatment of politics in Chapter 6 and love in Chapter 7 marks an important change of direction, as regards both Bouvard and Pécuchet themselves and Flaubert's attitude to them. The events of 1848, even in a small Norman village, aroused the same hopes of a new era as they did in Paris, and the pages in *Bouvard* form an interesting postscript to the detailed and dramatic analysis given in *Sentimental Education*. The two friends actually donate the Chavignolles freedom tree, and for a while their idealistic belief in progress is reinforced by events. It is not long, however, before they are disillusioned, their own brief hopes of a political career are forgotten, and with the return of authoritarian government in 1851 their disgust at the intrigues of leaders and the selfish, stupid apathy of the masses is complete. In one of the most effective scenes they visit Petit, the radical schoolmaster, and see him reduced to collapse by the unctuous but relentless blackmail of the curé. When the chapter ends, a major step in their evolution has been accomplished, for they have revolted against the rottenness of a society which Flaubert himself despised. Instead of isolating themselves through vain attempts to educate themselves beyond their mediocre intellectual capacity, they now do so by a reaction of simple, perhaps simplistic, decency against a state of affairs which everyone else cravenly accepts and, if possible, exploits to his own advantage. The concluding vision of Mélie gracefully drawing water at the pump hints at what is to come.

The whole of Chapter 7 is devoted to sexual passion, and takes Flaubert's plan far beyond a critique of science, or method, into a comprehensive analysis of the human condition. The dates given in the book are not all consistent, and cannot be taken literally, but the political events of 1848–51 are fixed points, so that it is clear when Chapter 7 opens that the friends are now about sixty and have been ten years at Chavignolles. For the first time their age (incidentally that of Flaubert when he died) is directly relevant. We are told at the beginning of the chapter that their solitude is complete, that they have abandoned their studies, that people avoid them, and that they are overwhelmed by the boredom of rural existence. They begin to get on each other's nerves, and without some quite new distraction their future looks bleak and grey. There is, then, no question of their private paradise being invaded by sex; when it comes it is, at first, a release from purgatory.

Only two days after the political riot in the village, Pécuchet accidentally happens upon a highly dramatic meeting between the swashbuckling Gorju and his passionate mistress. The revelation of this unsuspected world of raw emotion turns his head, and he begins to dream of love. In his inexperience (he is still a virgin), he consults his friend about the business of seduction, quite unaware that man-of-the-world Bouvard entertains precisely the same designs on the ample widow Madame Bordin as he does on the deceptively innocent Mélie. The two affairs run their parallel courses, each of the friends disregarding the other in his total absorption with the chase, until the tragi-comic dénouement. Pécuchet's dream of love is indeed consummated with Mélie in the cellar, but at the price of a severe dose of venereal disease, while Bouvard gets his intended bride as far as the notary's office only to discover that her real aim was to gain possession of a long coveted piece of his land. When they finally exchange confidences in a pathetic post-mortem, they recognize that their sexual adventures had momentarily interrupted their friendship, and resolve henceforth to do without women, sealing their reconciliation in a tender embrace. If the events of the chapter reinforce their isolation, they also reinforce their friendship, which can no longer be seen as an inferior compensation for emotional or other disabilities, but as a thing wholly good and worthwhile in itself. There is no need to interpret their sexual mishaps as reflecting any generally negative attitude on Flaubert's part, but the friends unmistakably emerge from the successive trials of politics and love with something real and positive to their credit, which is more than can be said for any of the others involved.

The implications of Flaubert's increasing sympathy for his two heroes would only have been fully revealed in the second volume, but it is clear that their enhanced status decisively affects the reader's estimate of their opinions. The three remaining chapters show their continuing attempts to understand and, if possible, improve themselves and the world in which they live.

After an athletic beginning, Chapter 8 is concerned with different manifestations of the immaterial world. From table-turning, spiritism, mesmerism and necromancy they progress to metaphysics, but such complex studies do them no good. One day, coming upon the hideous corpse of a dog, they carry their meditations to their logical conclusion and decide to commit suicide. At the last moment they desist from execution (because they have forgotten to make their wills) and end the day, not at the end of a rope, but sharing in the common joy of the Christmas Midnight Mass, one of the most splendid passages in the book. Flaubert was always impressed by such ceremonies, and one recalls the loving care with which he had described, in *A Simple Heart*, the similar reactions of the old servant Félicité to the Corpus Christi ceremonies. Bouvard and Pécuchet have narrowly escaped death, and for them the celebration of Christ's Nativity marks the promise of a new life, not a concluding apotheosis. The trouble is, as the next chapter illustrates, that religion, like love, has somehow to be translated into terms of everyday living, and cannot be confined to a single moment of intensity.

Just before they find the dead dog and plan suicide the friends enter upon a period of total despair, and this is introduced by a sentence on which critics have rightly seized as resuming the overall plan of the whole book: 'Then a lamentable faculty developed in their minds, that of noticing stupidity and finding it intolerable' (p. 217). As soon as they seek explanations from others, orally or in books, or look for understanding, they encounter some new form of stupidity and are disappointed yet again. So it is with religion. Chapter 9 shows them reading the Bible and other devotional works, practising various forms of piety, going on a pilgrimage, even making their First Communion, but whenever they leave naïve emotion and blind conformism to seek justification for the Church's teaching they run into a morass of prejudice, inconsistency and plain absurdity. Above all, Christians – or such as they meet – conspicuously fail to practise the charity they preach. It is therefore quite consistent with their convictions that they should, for basically humanitarian reasons, assume responsibility for Victor and Victorine, the wretched waifs adopted by the *bien-pensant* people at the château as an act of visible charity but ruthlessly expelled as soon as they become a liability.

The last chapter deals with their attempts to educate their two recalcitrant pupils and to give them at least the chance of a fuller life than they had known themselves, for want of proper instruction. The process involves numerous trials and massive errors, and is clearly doomed to failure from the start. The most sensible system of education could not have been made to work by two elderly (they must now be about seventy) autodidacts, with no family experience, wrestling with the problems of children from such a deprived and criminal background. Victor's sadistic torture of the cat and Victorine's sexual precocity do not prove or disprove any general thesis, but serve to convince Bouvard and Pécuchet that they have once again been wrong. Similarly, their quixotic defence of the poacher, in the name of justice, only leads to their own punishment and consequent disillusionment with the law. Finally the abortive excursion into the field of adult education, sketched in the plan for the last part of this long chapter, simply completes their isolation, and makes them virtual outcasts, regarded by all as lunatics, and by some as dangerous. It is now, when they seem really to have come to the end of the road, that they independently reach the same conclusion: they will spend their remaining years copying again, and order a double desk to that end. This is the end of Chapter 10 and the first volume, and all critics agree, on the basis of Flaubert's notes, that the bulk of the second volume would have comprised the material they actually copied.

First, it seems, they copy anything that comes to hand, then they introduce their own judgements and end up with some kind of *sottisier* to which they append their comments. There would no doubt have been some narrative to link this copied material, and one draft indicates the eventual fate of the main characters (the notary, Marescot, moves to Le Havre, and then to Paris; Mélie first marries Beljambe, the innkeeper, and then Gorju, and so on). Whatever the final form, it is clear that the later chapters of the existing volume make it possible for Bouvard and Pécuchet to be judges, to some extent, and not mere examples of the stupidity Flaubert wished to denounce. By outlawing and despising the two eccentric old men society has condemned itself. In the event, that society is the very restricted one of a small Norman village, but just after the key sentence describing their new awareness of stupidity comes the statement that even in the Antipodes they would find replicas of the individual idiots of Chavignolles, which thus explicitly becomes a microcosm for mankind.

There can be no single, or simple, conclusion about such a very complex book. Analogies are misleading, and sources are mostly unhelpful. One of the latter should, however, be mentioned, because it suggests that Flaubert may from the start have been attracted to the idea of two more or less evenly balanced friends in preference either to one hero, like Candide or Lemuel Gulliver, or two unequal ones, like Pantagruel and Panurge or Quixote and Sancho Panza. This is the brief tale (some seven pages long) entitled *Les Deux Greffiers* (*The Two Court Clerks*) by Barthélemy Maurice, which first appeared in an obscure review in 1841, but which Flaubert almost certainly saw when it was reprinted in 1858 in another review with which he had connexions. It tells quite simply how two clerks, Andréas and Robert, retire to the country with their wives, but soon get so bored with rustic pursuits that they resume copying as a pastime. The theme is slight enough, but it looks as though Flaubert may have used it for his brilliant variations. Certainly the idea of close companionship stayed in his mind. Foolish as they are, Bouvard and Pécuchet are friends, inseparable, but bound by voluntary ties of choice and loyalty, not compulsion. Though they do not look at all alike, have had different experiences and retain different tastes, they think and act in concert on every major issue. They are incurably naïve, but also, and perhaps therefore, have their own peculiar integrity, a natural kindness and decency which nothing can shake. Moreover, old as they are, they never give up trying for something better. It would be rash to write them off as mere butts for Flaubert's sarcasm and satire: the place of friendship in his own life and his treatment of such characters as Félicité in literature points, possibly, to a more positive role.

Some critics emphasize the excessive intellectual effort which unbalances them and leads to their undoing, and it is true that in the chapter on science, for instance, frenetic study lessens rather than improves their capacity to absorb and discriminate. But their failure is that of two elderly men, quite unfitted by education and experience for such mental strain, whereas the contradictions of the authorities studied, and sometimes their manifest absurdities, recall the sceptical reaction of Montaigne faced with the rival dogmas of his own day. The alchemists and astrologers of the Renaissance were not more absurd than the phrenologists and Swedenborgians of Flaubert's day, nor were post-Tridentine Catholics more dogmatic than those who made up the First Vatican Council. The claims of rationalism, science, industrialization, socialism and all the rest are not dismissed out of hand in *Bouvard*; the reader is invited perhaps to do no more than think again. At one level Flaubert is satirizing the human obsession with 'wanting to conclude' (his phrase) in areas where truth is subject to constant revision and restatement, or is simply unverifiable, but at another he is contrasting the admittedly immoderate appetite of his heroes for certainty and truth with the dishonesty, complacency and selfishness of the supposedly sane and normal people around them. The bourgeois are the worst, but neither the peasants nor the nobles come off much better.

It would be wrong to stress Flaubert's apparent sympathy with his heroes as if he identified with them any more than he did with characters in his other books. His lifelong distrust of cleverness must not be distorted into uncritical support for naïveté. Bouvard and Pécuchet do not become clever, or even intelligent, and the mere fact that they end by sharing their author's awareness of universal stupidity does not make them examples held up for our edification. Moreover, the element of self-parody is always to be reckoned with in Flaubert, and may sometimes be unconscious. The reader who finds Flaubert's attitudes depressingly negative – and many do – may be tempted to look for some positive quality of heart to balance the hopelessly unattractive qualities of mind presented in the book. It is easier to feel sympathy, even respect, for Bouvard and Pécuchet than for any of the others, so satisfied with their cosy materialism and lapped in the security of their received ideas, but this is not really what the book is about. They fail because they try to be what they are not, and never can be, yet they are right to be dissatisfied with what life has made them when the book starts and equally right to reject both the stupidity and the intellectual pretensions which they encounter thereafter. Each reader will come to his own conclusions, but one should realize that the book's many ambiguities can never be resolved because they are part of the irony inseparable from any praise of folly.

A. J. K.

A NOTE ON THE TEXT

The text translated here is taken from the Garnier–Flammarion edition by Jacques Suffel (1966), which incorporates the text established by Alberto Cento for his critical edition of 1964. It varies in places from earlier editions.

BOUVARD AND PÉCUCHET

I

WITH the temperature up in the nineties, the Boulevard Bourdon was absolutely deserted.

Further on, the Canal Saint-Martin, enclosed by the two locks, spread out the straight line of its inky water. In the middle lay a boat loaded with timber, and on the bank two rows of barrels.

Beyond the canal, between the houses separated by various builders' yards, the wide cloudless sky was broken up into bright blue pieces, and, as the sun beat down, the white façades, the slate roofs, the granite quays were dazzling in the glare. A confused murmur rose in the distance into the sultry atmosphere, and everything seemed to hang heavy with sabbath calm and the melancholy of summer days.

Two men appeared.

One came from the Bastille, the other from the Jardin des Plantes. The taller of the two, in a linen costume, walked with his hat pushed back, waistcoat undone and cravat in hand. The smaller one, whose body was enveloped in a brown frock-coat, had a peaked cap on his bent head.

When they came to the middle of the boulevard they both sat down at the same moment on the same seat.

Each took off his hat to mop his brow and put it beside him; and the smaller man noticed, written inside his neighbour's hat, *Bouvard*; while the latter easily made out the word *Pécuchet,* in the cap belonging to the individual in the frock-coat.

'Well, well,' he said, 'we both had the same idea, writing our names inside our headgear.'

'My word, yes! Someone might take mine at the office.'

'The same with me, I work in an office too.'

Then they studied each other.

Bouvard's likeable appearance charmed Pécuchet at once.

His bluish eyes, always half-closed, twinkled in his florid face. His trousers had a broad front flap and fell baggily onto beaver-fur shoes, outlining his stomach, and made his shirt billow out at the waist; and his fair hair, growing naturally in gentle curls, gave him a somewhat childish look.

His lips were pursed in a kind of continuous whistle.

Pécuchet's serious appearance struck Bouvard.

It looked as though he were wearing a wig, so flat and black were the locks adorning his lofty cranium. His whole face looked like a profile, because of the nose which came very far down. His legs, encased in narrow trousers of lasting, were out of proportion with the length of his torso; and he had a loud, booming voice.

He let out the exclamation: 'How good it would be to be in the country!'

But the suburbs, according to Bouvard, were made quite intolerable by the noise from the cheap open-air cafés. Pécuchet thought the same. Nevertheless he was beginning to grow tired of the capital. So was Bouvard.

And their eyes roamed over piles of building stones, the hideous water, with a bale of straw floating in it, the factory chimney rising on the horizon; sewers gave out their stench. They turned to the other side. Then they had facing them the walls of the public storehouse.

Definitely (to Pécuchet's surprise) it was hotter in the street than at home.

Bouvard urged him to take his coat off. He did not care what people might say!

Suddenly a drunkard staggered across the pavement, and speaking of workmen, they began a political discussion. Their views were the same, though Bouvard was possibly the more liberal.

Clattering over the cobbles in a cloud of dust came three hired carriages, going off towards Bercy, carrying a bride with her bouquet, solid citizens in white ties, ladies with petticoats up to their armpits, two or three little girls, a schoolboy. The sight of this wedding led Bouvard and Pécuchet to talk about women, whom they declared to be frivolous, shrewish and obstinate. Despite that, they were often better than men; at other times they were worse. In short it was better to live without them; so Pécuchet had remained a bachelor.

'I am a widower myself,' said Bouvard, 'with no children.'

'Perhaps that is your good luck.' But in the long run it was not much fun to be alone.

Then on the edge of the quay appeared a prostitute with a soldier. Pale, dark-haired and pock-marked, she was leaning on the soldier's arm, slopping along swaying her hips.

When she had moved on, Bouvard allowed himself an obscene comment. Pécuchet went very red, and, no doubt to avoid making any reply, drew his attention to a priest who was approaching.

The ecclesiastic made his way slowly down the avenue of scraggy elms planted regularly along the pavement, and Bouvard, once the tricorn hat was out of sight, expressed his relief, for he execrated the Jesuits. Pécuchet, without absolving them, showed some deference for religion.

Meanwhile darkness was falling, and the shutters opposite had been raised. More people were passing by. It struck seven.

Their words flowed on inexhaustibly, remarks following anecdotes, philosophical insights following individual considerations. They ran down the highways department, the tobacco monopoly, trade, the theatres, our navy and all the human race, like men who have had much to put up with. Each as he listened to the other rediscovered forgotten parts of himself. Though they were no longer at the age of naïve emotions, they felt a novel pleasure, a sort of opening out, the charm of affection in its initial stages.

A score of times they had stood up, sat down again, or walked the length of the boulevard from the lock upstream to the lock downstream, each time intending to go, but incapable of doing so, held back by a certain fascination.

They were however at last saying goodbye, already shaking hands, when Bouvard suddenly said: 'My word, why don't we have dinner together?'

'I had thought of it,' replied Pécuchet, 'but I didn't like to suggest it to you.'

So he let himself be taken to a little restaurant, opposite the Hôtel de Ville, said to be quite good.

Bouvard ordered the meal.

Pécuchet was afraid of spices because they might inflame his body. This was the subject of a medical discussion. They went on to extol the advantages of science: so many things to know, so much research . . . if only one had the time! Alas, earning a living took it all up; and raising their arms in amazement, they all but embraced over the table on discovering that they were both copy-clerks, Bouvard in a business concern, Pécuchet at the Admiralty; which did not stop him devoting a few moments every evening to study. He had noted mistakes in Monsieur Thiers's work, and spoke in terms of the greatest respect about a certain Dumouchel, a teacher.

Bouvard excelled in other directions. His watch-chain of woven hair and the way he beat the remolade sauce revealed an experienced old dog, and as he ate, with the corner of his napkin tucked in under his armpit, he said things that made Pécuchet laugh, on one very low note, always the same, uttered at long intervals. Bouvard's laugh was continuous, resounding, made him show all his teeth and shake his shoulders, so that the customers sitting by the door turned round.

After the meal they went on for coffee somewhere else. As Pécuchet looked at the gas jets he groaned at such extravagant luxury, then, with a scornful gesture, pushed the newspapers away. Bouvard took a more indulgent view of them. He liked all writers in general and when he was young had felt some inclination to go on the stage.

He tried to do balancing tricks with a billiard cue and two ivory balls, like Barberou, a friend of his. Invariably they fell off, rolled over the floor between people's legs and got lost in some remote corner. The waiter, who got up every time and had to crawl under the seats to look for them, finally protested. Pécuchet had a row with him, the proprietor came up, he did not listen to his apologies and even quibbled about their drinks.

Then he suggested finishing the evening quietly at his house, quite near at hand in the Rue Saint-Martin.

As soon as he was inside he put on a kind of cotton print smock and did the honours of his flat.

A pinewood desk, right in the middle of the room, was awkwardly placed because of its corners; all round, on shelves, on the three chairs, on the ancient armchair and in the corners, were heaped pell-mell several volumes of Roret's *Encyclopaedia, The*

Magnetist's Manual, a Fénelon, other books, piles of papers, two coconuts, various medals, a Turkish bonnet and seashells brought back from Le Havre by Dumouchel. A layer of dust coated the walls, which had once been painted yellow. The shoe brush was lying around on the edge of the bed, from which the sheets were trailing. On the ceiling could be seen a large black stain produced by smoke from the lamp.

Bouvard, no doubt because of the smell, asked permission to open the window.

'My papers would blow away,' cried Pécuchet, and he was also afraid of draughts.

However, he was gasping in this small room, heated up since the morning by the roof tiles.

Bouvard said to him: 'If I were you I would take off my flannel waistcoat.'

'What!' cried Pécuchet, with downcast head, terrified at the idea of going without his health waistcoat.

'See me home,' Bouvard went on, 'the fresh air will refresh you.'

Finally Pécuchet put on his boots again, grumbling. 'You are bewitching me, upon my word!' Despite the distance he accompanied him all the way home, on the corner of the Rue de Béthune, opposite the Pont de la Tournelle.

Bouvard's room was well-polished, the curtains were percale and the furniture mahogany, and it had the advantage of a balcony looking onto the river. The two principal ornaments were a liqueur-stand in the middle of the chest of drawers and, along the mirror, daguerrotypes of friends; an oil painting occupied the alcove.

'My uncle,' said Bouvard, and the torch he was holding lit up a gentleman.

Red side-whiskers made his face broad, and he wore a toupet wavy at the crown. His high cravat, with the triple collars of shirt, velvet waistcoat and black jacket, squeezed him in their grip. Diamonds were depicted on the stock. His eyes wrinkled at the edges, his smile was rather sly.

Pécuchet could not help saying: 'He looks more like your father!'

'He is my godfather,' Bouvard replied casually, adding that he had been christened François, Denys, Bartholomée. Pécuchet's names were Juste, Romain, Cyrille – and they were the same age: forty-seven. They were pleased by this coincidence, but surprised, for each had thought the other much younger. Then they marvelled at Providence, whose ways are sometimes wonderful.

'After all, if we had not gone out for a walk earlier on we might have died without meeting each other!'

And after exchanging the addresses of their employers they bade each other good night.

'Don't go off to the ladies!' Bouvard called down the stairs.

Pécuchet went down without answering the quip.

Next day, in the courtyard of Messieurs Descambos Brothers: Alsace Cloth, 92 Rue Hautefeuille, a voice called: 'Bouvard! Monsieur Bouvard!'

Bouvard stuck his head out of the window and recognized Pécuchet, who declared even louder:

'I am not ill! I left it off!'

'What do you mean?'

'It!' said Pécuchet, pointing to his chest.

Everything they had talked about during the day, together with the temperature in the flat and difficulties of digestion, had prevented him sleeping with the result that, at the end of his tether, he had thrown off his flannel waistcoat. In the morning he remembered his action, fortunately without ill effects, and he had come to report it to Bouvard, who thus rose to dizzy heights in his esteem.

He was the son of a small tradesman, and had never known his mother, who died very young. When he was fifteen he was taken away from school, where he boarded out, and put to work with a legal official. The police came on the scene and his employer was sent to the galleys: a frightful tale that still made him shudder. Then he had tried several occupations: apprentice pharmacist, usher in a school, purser on one of the boats on the upper Seine. Finally a departmental head, delighted by his handwriting, had taken him on as a copy-clerk; his educational deficiencies made him self-conscious and caused intellectual frustration, so that he was very touchy: he lived completely alone, without parents, without a mistress. His relaxation was to go on Sundays to inspect public works.

Bouvard's oldest memories took him back to the banks of the Loire, to a farmyard. A man, who was his uncle, had taken him to

Paris to teach him business. When he came of age he was paid about 1,000 francs. Then he married and opened a confectioner's shop. Six months later his wife disappeared with the contents of the till. Friends, good living, and above all indolence had promptly brought about his ruin. But he was inspired to make use of his beautiful handwriting, and for twelve years had been in the same job, with Messieurs Descambos Brothers, Cloths, 92 Rue Hautefeuille. As for his uncle, who had once sent him the famous portrait as a souvenir, Bouvard did not even know where he lived and expected nothing more from him. An income of 1,500 francs and his wages as a copyist enabled him to go every evening and doze in some modest tavern.

Thus their meeting was important enough to be an adventure. They had at once become attached to each other by secret fibres. Besides, how can sympathies be explained? Why does some peculiarity, some imperfection, which would be indifferent or odious in one, seem enchanting in another? What is called the thunderbolt of love at first sight is true for all the passions. Before the end of the week they were on Christian name terms.

They often went to collect each other at the office. As soon as one appeared, the other closed his desk, and they went off together through the streets. Bouvard walked with long strides, while Pécuchet, with short, quick step, his frock-coat catching on his heels, seemed to glide on castors. Similarly their personal tastes were in harmony. Bouvard smoked a pipe, liked cheese, regularly took his cup of black coffee. Pécuchet took snuff, ate nothing but preserves for dessert and dipped a lump of sugar in his coffee. One was confident, thoughtless, generous; the other discreet, thoughtful, thrifty.

To give Pécuchet pleasure Bouvard decided to introduce him to Barberou. He had been a commercial traveller, and was now on the Stock Exchange, a very genial soul, patriotic, fond of women, who affected a vulgar way of speaking. Pécuchet did not like him, and took Bouvard to meet Dumouchel. This author (for he had published a little book on memory training) taught literature in a boarding-school for young ladies, had orthodox opinions and a serious demeanour. He bored Bouvard.

Neither concealed his opinion from the other. Each recognized that it was well-founded. Their habits changed, and giving up their usual boarding-house meals, they finished by dining together every day.

They made observations on the plays that were being talked about, on the government, high food prices, dishonest trading. From time to time the story of the Diamond Necklace[1] or the Fualdes trial[2] came up in their discussions; then they looked for the causes of the Revolution.

They strolled along past curiosity shops. They visited the Conservatory of Arts and Crafts, Saint-Denis, the Gobelins, the Invalides and all the public collections.

When asked for their passports they pretended to have lost them, making out that they were foreigners, English.

In the galleries of the Natural History Museum they passed by the stuffed quadrupeds with astonishment, the butterflies with pleasure, the metals with indifference; fossils made them dreamy, seashells bored them. They examined the hothouses through the glass, and trembled at the thought that all that foliage was distilling poisons. What they found remarkable about the cedar was the fact that it had been brought back in someone's hat.

At the Louvre they tried to be enthusiastic about Raphael. At the National Library they would have liked to know the exact number of volumes.

Once they went into a lecture on Arabic at the Collège de France, and the professor was astonished to see these two strangers trying to take notes. Thanks to Barberou they went behind the scenes in a small theatre. Dumouchel got them tickets for a session of the Academy. They found out about discoveries, read prospectuses and through such curiosity developed their intelligence. Far away on a horizon which receded further every day they perceived things that were both confused and wonderful.

As they admired some old piece of furniture they felt sorry that they had not lived in the period when it was used, though they knew absolutely nothing about the period in question. From the

1. The scandal of the Diamond Necklace, involving Cardinal de Rohan and Marie-Antoinette, raged in 1785–6.

2. The murder in 1817 of the magistrate J-B. Fualdes provoked a famous trial.

sound of certain names, they conjured up visions of lands all the more beautiful for being totally imprecise. Works whose titles they could not understand seemed to contain some mystery.

The more ideas they had the more they suffered. When a mail-coach passed them in the street they felt a need to go away in it. The flower market by the river made them yearn for the country.

One Sunday they started walking in the morning and by way of Meudon, Bellevue, Suresnes, Auteuil, roamed about all day in vineyards, picked poppies from the edge of the fields, slept on the grass, drank milk, ate beneath the acacias of little inns, and came back very late, dusty, exhausted, delighted. They often repeated such excursions. They found the next day so dull that they finally gave them up.

The monotony of the office became odious. Constantly scraping, then making good, the paper, the same inkwell, the same pens and the same companions! They found them stupid and talked to them less and less. They were teased for this. Every day they arrived late, and were rebuked.

They had previously been almost happy, but as their consideration for each other grew, they found their job irritating, and each increased the other's disgust. They stimulated and spoilt each other. Pécuchet contracted Bouvard's brusqueness, Bouvard took on some of Pécuchet's morosity.

'I would like to be a street acrobat!' said one.

'Might as well be a rag-picker!' cried the other.

What an appalling situation! No way out! No hope even!

One afternoon (it was 20th January 1839), Bouvard was at his office when he received a letter, brought by the postman.

His arms went up, his head slowly fell back and he collapsed on the floor in a faint.

The clerks rushed up, someone took off his tie, they sent for the doctor. He opened his eyes; then to his questioners: 'Ah! The fact is . . . the fact is . . . a bit of air will make me better. No! Leave me alone! Please!'

Then, despite his bulk, he ran without stopping for breath all the way to the Admiralty, wiping his brow, thinking he was going mad, trying to calm down.

He asked for Pécuchet.

Pécuchet appeared.

'My uncle is dead! I am his heir!'

'Impossible!'

Bouvard showed the following lines:

Office of Maître Tardivel, Notary. Savigny-en-Septaine, 14th January 39

Sir – Would you kindly come to my office to acquaint yourself with the will of your natural father, Monsieur François Denys Bartholomée Bouvard, sometime merchant in the town of Nantes, deceased in this commune on the 10th instant. This will contains a most important provision in your favour.

I remain, Sir, yours faithfully,
Tardivel, notary.

Pécuchet was obliged to sit down on a bollard in the courtyard. Then he handed back the paper, saying slowly:

'As long as . . . it is not . . . someone joking!'

'You think it is a joke!' replied Bouvard in a strangled voice, like a death rattle.

But the postal stamp, the printed heading of the notary's office, the notary's signature, all proved the authenticity of the news; – and they looked at each other with quivering lips and tears rolling from their staring eyes.

They needed space. They went as far as the Arc de Triomphe, came back along the river, past Notre-Dame. Bouvard was very red. He punched Pécuchet on the back, and for five minutes on end talked absolute nonsense.

They made fun of it despite themselves. This inheritance must, of course, amount to . . . 'Oh, that would be too good to be true! Let's say no more about it!'

They did say more about it. There was nothing to stop one asking for explanations straight away. Bouvard wrote to the lawyer.

The lawyer sent a copy of the will, which ended thus: 'Consequently I give to François Denys Bartholomée Bouvard, acknowledged as my natural son, the portion of my estate disposable by law.'

The old chap had had this son in his youth, but had carefully kept him out of the way, passing him off as a nephew; and the nephew had always called him uncle, although he was well aware of the facts. When he was about forty, Monsieur Bouvard had married, but was then widowed. His two legitimate sons having turned out contrary to his views, he had been seized by remorse over the way he had abandoned his other child for so many years. He would even have brought him into his house but for the influence of his cook. She left him, thanks to the manoeuvres of the family, and in his isolation, approaching his end, he decided to repair the wrong he had done and leave as much of his fortune as he could to the fruit of his first love. It amounted to half a million francs, which left 250,000 francs for the copy-clerk. The elder brother, Monsieur Étienne, had announced that he would respect the will.

Bouvard fell into a kind of stupor. He repeated in a low voice, smiling the placid smile of the drunk: '15,000 francs a year!' – and Pécuchet, though he was more level-headed, could not get over it.

They were rudely shaken by a letter from Tardivel. The other son, Monsieur Alexandre, declared his intention of going to court and even altering the bequest if he could, and as a preliminary demanded seals, inventories, appointment of a sequestrator, etc. This gave Bouvard a bilious attack. No sooner was he convalescent than he set off for Savigny, whence he returned with no conclusions of any kind and bemoaning his travelling expenses.

Then came bouts of insomnia, alternating moods of rage and hope, elation and dejection. Finally, after six months, Monsieur Alexandre calmed down, and Bouvard took possession of the inheritance.

His first cry had been: 'We'll retire to the country!' and Pécuchet had found it perfectly natural that in saying this he should link his friend with his good fortune, for the union of these two men was absolute and profound.

However, as he did not want to be a charge on Bouvard, he would not move until he retired. Another two years; no matter! He remained inflexible and so it was decided.

To resolve the question of where to settle they reviewed the provinces in turn. The North was fertile but too cold; the South was delightful as regards climate, but the mosquitoes made it unsuitable; the Centre was frankly dull. Brittany would have suited them but for the excessive piety of the people. As for the East, because of the Germanic patois, the idea was not to be entertained. There were however other regions. What for instance was Forez, or Bugey, or Roumois like? Maps were uninformative. Besides, whether their home was in this place or that, the important thing was to have one.

They already saw themselves in shirt sleeves, beside a flowerbed, pruning roses, and digging, hoeing, handling the soil, transplanting things. They would awake to the sound of the lark and follow the plough, they would go with a basket to pick apples, they would watch butter-making, grain-threshing, sheep-shearing, bee-keeping, and would revel in the lowing of the cattle and the smell of new-mown hay. No more copying! No more boss! No more rent even! For they would own their own home! And they would eat chickens from their own poultry-run, vegetables from their own garden – and would sit down to dinner with their clogs on! 'We'll do whatever we please! We'll grow beards!'

They bought gardening implements, then a lot of things 'that might come in useful', like a tool-box (every house needs one), scales, a surveyor's chain, a bath-tub in case they fell ill, a thermometer and even a barometer 'Gay-Lussac type' for experiments in physics, should the fancy take them. It would not be a bad idea either (for one cannot always work outside) to have a few good works of literature – and they looked for some – sometimes hard put to it to know whether a given book 'was really a library book'. Bouvard settled the question.

'Well, we won't need a library.'

'Besides, I've always got mine,' said Pécuchet.

They organized themselves in advance. Bouvard would bring his furniture, Pécuchet his big black table; they would use the curtains and with a few pots and pans that would be quite sufficient.

They had sworn to keep quiet about all this, but their faces shone. So their colleagues found them rather odd. Bouvard, who wrote spread out over his desk with his elbows stuck out so that he could more easily round out his copperplate, made a kind of whistling noise and at the same time blinked his heavy eyelids in a sly expression. Pécuchet, perched on a large straw-bottomed stool, still took care over the loops of his spindly writing – but kept puffing out his nostrils, pinching his lips, as if he were afraid of letting out his secret.

After searching for eighteen months they had still found nothing. They travelled everywhere in the vicinity of Paris, from Amiens to Evreux, from Fontainebleau to Le Havre. They wanted country that was really country, without exactly insisting on a picturesque site, but a limited horizon depressed them.

They wanted to be away from other houses and yet were afraid of solitude.

Sometimes they made up their minds, then, fearing that they would regret it later, changed them again, when the place had seemed unhealthy, or too exposed to winds from the sea, or too near some factory or too inaccessible.

Barberou saved them.

He knew about their dream, and one fine day came to tell them that he had heard of an estate, at Chavignolles, between Caen and Falaise. It consisted of a farm of thirty-eight hectares, with a sort of manor house and a garden in full production.

They took themselves off to Calvados and were fired with enthusiasm. Only for the farm and house together (one would not be sold without the other) they were asking 143,000 francs. Bouvard would only give 120,000.

Pécuchet struggled against his obstinacy, begged him to yield, finally declared that he would make up the balance. It was the whole of his fortune, derived from his mother's patrimony and his own savings. He had never breathed a word of it, reserving this capital for a great occasion.

Everything had been paid towards the end of 1840, six months before he retired.

Bouvard was no longer a copy-clerk. At first he had continued his functions out of distrust for the future, but had given them up once the inheritance was certain. However, he went back quite happily to Messieurs Descambos and the day before his departure gave a punch-party to everyone at the office.

Pécuchet on the other hand was sulky with his colleagues and on his last day slammed the door brutally behind him as he left.

He had to supervise the packing, run a lot of errands, buy still more things and take leave of Dumouchel!

The teacher proposed that they should keep up correspondence so that he would keep Pécuchet up to date with the world of literature, and after renewed congratulations he wished him good health.

Barberou showed rather more emotion as Bouvard bade him farewell. He left a game of dominoes specially, promised to come and visit him in the country, ordered two anisettes and embraced him.

Bouvard returned home, stood on his balcony, took a deep breath of air, and said to himself: 'At last.' The lights on the quays shimmered over the water, the distant rumbling of the omnibuses grew quiet. He recalled happy days spent in the great city, picnic meals in restaurants, evenings at the theatre, the gossip retailed by his concierge, all his habits; and he felt a discouragement, a sadness that he did not dare confess.

Pécuchet kept walking round his room until 2 a.m. He would never come back there; so much the better! All the same, to leave something of himself, he traced his name on the plaster of the mantelpiece.

The bulk of the baggage had gone off the previous day. The gardening implements, the bedding, the mattresses, tables, chairs, a stove, the bath-tub and three barrels of Burgundy were to go down the Seine, as far as Le Havre, and would thence be forwarded to Caen, where Bouvard would be waiting and would have them sent on to Chavignolles. But his father's portrait, the armchairs, the liqueur-stand, the books, the clock, all the valuable articles were loaded on to a removal van which would travel via Nonancourt, Verneuil and Falaise. Pécuchet decided to accompany it.

He installed himself beside the driver, on the front seat, and, wrapped in his oldest coat, with a muffler, mittens and the foot-warmer from his office, on Sunday, 20th March, at first light, he left the capital.

The movement and novelty of the journey occupied him during the first few hours. Then the horses slowed down, which led to arguments with the driver and the carter. They chose execrable inns, and though they answered for everything, Pécuchet with excessive caution shared their sleeping quarters. The following day they set off at dawn; and the road, endlessly the same, stretched out uphill to the edge of the horizon. The stones continued yard after yard, the ditches were full of water. The countryside spread out in great expanses of cold, monotonous green, clouds chased across the sky, from time to time rain fell. On the third day squalls blew up. The canvas cover of the wagon was badly fixed and flapped in the wind like the sail of a ship. Pécuchet bowed his head under his cap, and every time he opened his snuff-box had to turn completely round to protect his eyes. During the bumps he heard all his baggage shaking about behind him and issued a stream of suggestions. Seeing that this had no effect, he changed his tactics; he was all good-natured kindness; on the harder climbs he put his shoulder to the wheel with the men; he went so far as to pay for a tot with their coffee after the meal. From then on the pace was more brisk, so much so that near Gauburge the axle broke and the wagon keeled over. Pécuchet at once inspected the inside; the china cups lay in splinters. He threw up his arms, ground his teeth, cursed the two idiots; the following day was lost because the carter got drunk; but he did not have the strength to complain, the cup of bitterness was running over.

Bouvard had only left Paris two days later so as to have one more dinner with Barberou. He arrived at the last moment in the courtyard, then woke up in front of Rouen Cathedral; he had taken the wrong coach. That evening all the seats for Caen had been taken; not knowing what to do he went to the Arts Theatre and smiled at his neighbours, saying that he had retired from business and had recently acquired an estate in the neighbourhood. When he arrived at Caen on the Friday his packages were not there. He received them on the Sunday and sent them off on a cart, warning the farmer that he would be following in a few hours.

At Falaise, on the ninth day of his journey, Pécuchet took on an extra horse, and until sunset progress was good. Beyond Bretteville, leaving the main road, he took a side road, expecting at any moment to see the gable of Chavignolles. However, the ruts grew fainter, then disappeared, and they found themselves in the middle of ploughed fields. Night was falling. What was to be done? In the end Pécuchet abandoned the wagon, and wallowing in the mire went forward to see what he could find. When he approached farms, dogs barked. He cried out with all his might to ask for directions. No one answered. He was afraid and went back into the open country. Suddenly two lanterns shone out. He saw a gig, and ran to meet it. Bouvard was inside.

But wherever could the removal van be? For a good hour they hailed it in the darkness. At last it turned up and they arrived at Chavignolles.

A great fire of brushwood and pine cones blazed in the main room. Two places were laid at the table. The furniture brought by the cart filled the vestibule. Nothing was missing. They sat down to talk.

The dinner prepared for them consisted of onion soup, a chicken, bacon and hard-boiled eggs. The old woman who did the cooking came from time to time to enquire how they found everything. They answered: 'Oh, very good, very good!' and the coarse bread, too hard to cut, the cream, the nuts, everything filled them with delight. There were holes in the flooring, the walls were sticky with damp. Yet they looked around them with a satisfied eye as they ate at the little table on which a candle burned. Their faces were flushed from the open air. They filled their bellies, leaned back on the backs of their chairs, making them crack, and kept saying to each other: 'Well, here we are! Aren't we lucky! It feels like a dream!'

Although it was midnight Pécuchet had the idea of strolling round the garden. Bouvard did not object. They took the candle, and shielding it with an old newspaper, walked along the beds. They enjoyed saying the names of the vegetables out loud: 'Look, carrots! Ah, cabbages!'

Then they inspected the espaliers. Pécuchet tried to discover buds. Sometimes a spider fled suddenly across the wall, and the shadows of their two bodies were thrown onto it, reflecting their gestures in enlargement. The grass dripped with dew. The night was pitch black, and all was still, utterly silent and sweet. In the distance a cock crowed.

Their two bedrooms had a small connecting door disguised by the wallpaper. Someone had banged a chest of drawers into it and made the nails come out. They found it wide open. This was a surprise.

Undressed and in bed they chatted for a while, then fell asleep. Bouvard on his back, mouth open, head bare; Pécuchet on his right side, knees drawn up to his stomach, topped with a cotton nightcap, and both of them snored beneath the moonlight streaming through the windows.

2

WHAT joy when they woke up next morning! Bouvard smoked a pipe and Pécuchet took a pinch of snuff, which they declared to be the best of their whole lives. Then they went to the window to look at the countryside.

Opposite them were the fields, on the right a barn, with the church-tower, and on the left a screen of poplars.

Two main paths, forming a cross, divided the garden into four sections. Vegetables were included in the beds, where here and there dwarf cypresses and fruit-trees grew. On one side an arbour ended at a vine-clad mound, on the other a wall supported espaliers. Beyond the wall there was an orchard, after the clipped hedge, a clump of trees; behind the fence, a little lane.

They were looking at all this when a man with greying hair and wearing a black overcoat came along the lane, rattling his stick against all the bars of the fence. The old servant told them that he was Monsieur Vaucorbeil, a doctor well-known in the district.

The other notables were: the Comte de Faverges, a former Member of Parliament, whose dairy farm was mentioned; the mayor, Monsieur Foureau, who sold wood, plaster, all manner of things; Monsieur Marescot, the lawyer; Monsieur Jeufroy, the priest, and Madame Bordin, a widow of private means. As for herself, she was called La Germaine, because of Germain, her late husband. She was usually a 'daily', but would be willing to be taken on as servant by the gentlemen. They accepted, and set off for their farm, about a kilometre away.

As they entered the yard, the farmer, Gouy, was shouting at a lad, and his wife, on a stool, was clutching between her legs a turkey which she was stuffing with lumps of flour. The man had a low forehead, well-shaped nose, shifty eyes and sturdy shoulders. The woman was very fair, with freckled cheeks, and the look of simplicity one finds in the peasants depicted in stained-glass windows.

In the kitchen bundles of hemp hung from the ceiling. Three old guns were arranged over the high chimney-piece. A dresser full of flowered crockery occupied the middle of the wall and the bottle-glass window-panes cast a pallid light on the tin and copper utensils.

The two Parisians wanted to make a tour of inspection, having seen the property only once before, somewhat cursorily. Farmer Gouy and his wife escorted them, and the litany of complaints began.

All the buildings, from the cart shed to the distillery, needed repairs. They needed to build an outhouse for the cheeses, put new iron-work on the gates, raise the 'edges', dig out the pond and re-plant a lot of the apple-trees in the three yards.

Then they inspected the crops: Farmer Gouy depreciated them. They absorbed too much manure, transport was expensive; it was impossible to clear the stones, weeds were poisoning the meadows; and such denigration of his land diminished the pleasure Bouvard felt at walking over it.

They made their way back by a sunken lane, under an avenue of beeches. From that side the house displayed its forecourt and façade.

It was painted white with yellow trimmings. The outhouse and stillroom, bakehouse and woodshed ran back to make two lower wings. The kitchen gave onto a small living-room. Next came the vestibule, a larger room, and the drawing-room. The four bed-rooms on the first floor opened onto the corridor which overlooked the courtyard. Pécuchet took one of them for his collections; the last was assigned to the library; and as they opened the cupboards they found more books, but did not feel like reading their titles. The most pressing matter was the garden.

Bouvard, passing near the hornbeam bower, discovered beneath the branches a plaster lady. With two fingers she held her skirt aside, her knees were bent and her head was on her shoulder, as if she were afraid of being caught unawares.

'Oh, excuse me! Don't mind me!'

This witticism amused them so much that twenty times a day, for more than three weeks, they repeated it.

Meanwhile the citizens of Chavignolles were eager to know

them, and came to look at them through the fence. They closed the openings with planks, which upset the local people.

As protection against the sun, Bouvard wore a handkerchief tied round his head like a turban, Pécuchet wore his cap, and a large apron with a pocket in front, in which secateurs, scarf and snuff-box bounced about. With bare arms, side by side, they ploughed, weeded, pruned, set themselves tasks, ate as quickly as possible; but went to take coffee on the mound, in order to enjoy the view.

If they met a snail, they went up to it and squashed it, pulling a wry face, as if they were cracking a nut. They never went without their trenching-tool, and cut worms in half so violently that the blade of the implement sank in a good three inches.

To get rid of caterpillars they beat the trees furiously with great cudgel blows.

Bouvard planted a peony in the middle of the lawn and tomatoes, which were meant to hang down like chandeliers, beneath the hoop of the arbour.

Pécuchet had a large hole dug in front of the kitchen, and divided it into three compartments, for making composts which would make a lot of things grow, whose waste matter would bring along other crops, supplying further fertilizer, and so on indefinitely. He went into a reverie at the side of the pit, visualizing future mountains of fruit, floods of flowers, avalanches of vegetables. But he lacked the horse manure so useful for hotbeds. The farmers did not sell it, the innkeepers refused. At last, after much searching, despite Bouvard's pleas, and casting shame to the winds, he decided to go out himself 'on the dung-hunt'.

While he was in the middle of this occupation one day Madame Bordin accosted him on the highway. After paying her compliments, she enquired about his friend. The lady's black eyes, very bright though small, her high colour, her self-confidence (she even had a slight moustache) intimidated Pécuchet. He replied briefly and turned his back – an act of discourtesy criticized by Bouvard.

Then came the bad days, snow, bitter cold. They installed themselves in the kitchen, and made trellises; or perhaps inspected the bedrooms, chatted by the fireside, watched the rain come down.

Once Lent was half-way through they looked for spring, and repeated each morning: 'It's all on the way!' But the season was backward, and they consoled themselves in their impatience by saying: 'It's all going to be on the way!'

At last they saw the peas come up. The asparagus gave a good yield. The vine was promising.

Since they understood about gardening, they were bound to succeed at agriculture, and they were seized with the ambition of cultivating their farm. With good sense and study they would make a good job of it, without the slightest doubt.

First they had to see how others went about it; and they composed a letter requesting Monsieur de Faverges to grant them the honour of visiting his farm. The count at once made an appointment with them.

After an hour's walk they came to the slope of a ridge overlooking the Orne valley. The winding river ran at the bottom. Blocks of red sandstone rose up here and there and larger rocks formed a kind of cliff in the distance, dominating the countryside, covered with ripe cornfields. Opposite, on the other hill, the greenery was so abundant that it concealed the houses. Trees divided it into unequal patches, distinguishable amid the grass by their clearer lines.

The entire estate suddenly came into view. Tiled rooftops indicated the farm. The manor, with its white façade, lay on the right, with a wood beyond, and a lawn ran down to the river, in which a line of plane trees reflected their shadows.

The two friends went into a field of lucerne which was being harvested. Women wearing straw hats, Indian turbans or paper eye-shades were raking up the hay left on the ground, and at the other end of the plain, beside the haystacks, bales of hay were being tossed briskly into a long cart drawn by three horses. Monsieur le Comte came forward followed by his steward.

His suit was of dimity, he carried himself stiffly and wore mutton-chop whiskers, looking like a magistrate and a dandy at the same time. His features, even when he was talking, remained immobile.

After exchanging the initial courtesies, he explained his system regarding fodder; the swathes were turned over without being scattered; the stacks had to be conical and the bales made immediately on the spot, then piled ten at a time. As for a mechanical rake, the meadow was too uneven for such an implement.

A young girl, barefoot in her sandals, and in a dress so torn as to reveal her body, was giving the women drinks, pouring out cider from a pitcher steadied against her hip. The count asked where the child came from; no one knew anything about it. The haymaking women had picked her up to serve them during the harvest. He shrugged his shoulders and, as he went off, made some critical remarks about rural immorality.

Bouvard praised his lucerne. It was indeed quite good, despite the ravages of the dodder; the future agronomists opened their eyes wide at the word 'dodder'. He had so many cattle that he went in for artificial meadows; besides, this was a good precedent for the other crops, which is not always the case with root fodder. 'That at least seems to be beyond dispute.' Bouvard and Pécuchet repeated together: 'Oh, beyond dispute!'

They were on the edge of a field which was quite flat and carefully mellowed: a horse, led by hand, was drawing a large box mounted on three wheels. Seven blades, arranged underneath, were opening up narrow, parallel furrows, into which the seed dropped through pipes coming down to the ground.

'Here,' said the count, 'I am sowing turnips. The turnip is the basis of my four-year cycle of crops.' And he was launching into a demonstration of the seed-machine, when a servant came to look for him. He was wanted at the château.

His steward took his place, weasel-faced and obsequious.

He conducted the 'gentlemen' towards another field, where fourteen harvesters, with bare chests and legs wide apart, were mowing rye. The blades hissed through the straw which was laid on the right. Each man described a broad semi-circle in front of him, and keeping exactly in line they all moved forward at the same time. The two Parisians admired their arms and felt an almost religious awe for the bounty of the land.

They next went along several pieces of ploughland. Dusk was falling and the crows were coming down onto the furrows.

Then they met the flock of sheep. These were grazing here and there and one could hear them continuously cropping the grass. The shepherd was sitting on a tree-trunk, knitting a woollen stocking, with his dog beside him.

The steward helped Bouvard and Pécuchet over a stile, and they crossed two farmyards, where cows ruminated under the apple-trees.

All the farm buildings were contiguous, and took up three sides of the yard. The work was mechanized, using a turbine, driven by a stream which had been diverted specially. Leather bands went from one roof into another, and in the middle of the dung-heap an iron pump was operating.

The steward pointed out to them little openings at ground level in the sheepfolds and in the pigsties, ingenious self-closing doors.

The barn was vaulted like a cathedral with brick arches resting on stone walls.

To amuse the gentlemen a servant threw down handfuls of oats in front of the hens. The shaft of the cider-press seemed enormous to them, and they went up into the pigeon-loft. The dairy specially enthralled them. Taps in the corners provided enough water to flood the stone floor, and when one entered the chill was unexpected. Brown jars, ranged on lattices, were brimful of milk. Shallower basins held cream. Rounds of butter followed one after another, like segments of a copper shaft, and froth spilled out of the pails which had just been set down. But the jewel of the farm was the ox-pen. Perpendicular wooden bars fixed along its entire length divided it into two sections: the first for the animals, the second for service. Hardly anything could be seen inside, because all the shutters were closed. The oxen were eating, fastened by chains, and their bodies gave off a heat which the low ceiling threw back. But someone let in some light, a stream of water suddenly flowed out into the trough alongside the mangers. There was a sudden lowing, the horns made a noise like sticks clashing. All the oxen stuck their muzzles through the bars and drank slowly.

Large carts and other vehicles came into the yard and colts whinnied. On the ground floor two or three lanterns lit up, then disappeared. The farmhands went by dragging their clogs over the stones, and the bell rang for supper.

The two visitors went away.

Everything they had seen enchanted them. They had made up their minds. That very evening they took out from their library the four volumes of the *Country Household*, sent for Gasparin's course and took out a subscription to an agricultural journal.

To get to the fairs more easily they bought a trap which Bouvard drove.

Dressed in blue smocks, with broad-brimmed hats, gaiters up to their knees and a horse-dealer's stick, they prowled round the livestock, interrogated the ploughmen and never missed an agricultural show.

They soon wearied farmer Gouy with their advice, mainly deploring his system of leaving fields fallow. But the farmer stuck to his routine. He asked for a deferment on the pretext of damage by hail. As for his rents and dues, he paid none. His wife met the most justified demands with cries of protest. In the end Bouvard declared his intention of not renewing the lease.

Thereupon farmer Gouy cut down on manuring, let the weeds grow, ruined the property and went away with an angry look, obviously planning revenge.

Bouvard had thought that 20,000 francs, that is more than four times the cost of the lease, would do to start with. His Paris lawyer sent the money.

Their estate comprised fifteen hectares of yards and meadows, twenty-three of arable land and five uncultivated lying on a stony knoll called the Mound.

They procured all the essential implements, four horses, twelve cows, six pigs, 160 sheep and, as farmstaff, two carters, two women, a labourer and a shepherd; in addition, a big dog.

To provide money right away they sold their fodder crops. They received payment at home; the Napoleons counted out onto the oats box seemed to them of brighter gold than any others, extraordinary and better.

In November they brewed cider. It was Bouvard who whipped up the horse while Pécuchet, up in the trough, turned the pulp with a shovel. They panted as they tightened the screw, drew off from the vat, watched the bungs, wore heavy clogs, enjoyed themselves enormously.

On the principle that you can never have too much wheat they did away with about half their artificial meadows; and as they had no fertilizer they used oilcake, which they did not break up before digging it in, so that the yield was pathetic.

Next year they sowed, heavy storms blew up. The sheaves were flattened.

Nevertheless they put all they had into wheat and set about clearing the Mound of stones. A small rubbish cart took away the stones. All through the year from morning till evening, rain or shine, the everlasting cart was to be seen on the little hill, with the same man and the same horse, climbing up, down, and up again. Sometimes Bouvard walked behind, stopping half-way up to mop his brow.

Trusting nobody they treated the animals themselves, and gave them purges and enemas.

Serious disturbances occurred. The girl who looked after the poultry became pregnant. They took on married people; children swarmed, cousins, male and female, uncles, sisters-in-law; a whole horde lived at their expense, and they resolved to sleep at the farm in turn.

But in the evening they were miserable. The squalor of the room upset them and Germaine, who brought along the meals, grumbled at every journey. They were being cheated in all sorts of ways. The threshers in the barn were stuffing wheat into their drinking jugs. Pécuchet caught one at it and drove him out bodily, crying:

'You wretch, you are a disgrace to the village where you were born!'

He inspired no personal respect. Besides, he was feeling sorry about the garden. If he gave up all his time to it, that would not be enough to keep it in good order. Bouvard would look after the farm. They discussed it, and agreed on this arrangement.

The first point was to have good hotbeds. Pécuchet had one built of brick. He painted the frames himself and for fear of damage by the sun daubed chalk over all the cloches.

When he took cuttings he was careful to take off the heads with the leaves. Then he turned himself to layering. He tried several sorts of graft, flute, crown, gem, herbaceous, English. How carefully he adjusted the two libers! How tightly he bound them! What a mass of unguent to cover them!

Twice a day he took his watering-can and swung it over the plants, like a thurifer with a censer. As they became green, under the water descending in a fine rain, he felt his own thirst slaked and seemed to be born again with them. Then, giving way to a kind of intoxication, he took off the rose from the spout and poured out a copious flood.

At the end of the arbour, near the plaster lady, stood a sort of log cabin. Pécuchet locked up his implements there, and spent delightful hours peeling seeds, writing labels, arranging his little pots. To relax he would sit in front of the door on a box, and make plans for further embellishments.

Below the terrace he had created two geranium beds; between the cypresses and the fruit-trees he planted sunflowers; and as the narrow beds were covered with buttercups, and all the paths with fresh sand, the garden was dazzling with its riot of yellow.

But the hotbed swarmed with grubs; and in spite of the warm layers of dead leaves, under the painted frames and chalk-smeared cloches nothing grew but spindly vegetation. The cuttings did not take; the grafts came unstuck, the sap stopped running in the layers, the trees got white rot in their roots; the seedlings were a desolation. The wind enjoyed blowing down the beanpoles. The strawberries were spoilt from too much manure, the tomatoes from not enough pinching.

He failed with the broccoli, aubergines, turnips, and watercress, which he had tried to grow in a tub. After the thaw all the artichokes were lost. The cabbages consoled him. One in particular aroused his hopes. It spread outwards and upwards, finished by being prodigious and absolutely inedible. No matter. Pécuchet was happy to possess a monster.

Then he tried what seemed to him the ultimate in the gardener's art: melon growing.

He sowed seeds of several varieties in dishes filled with compost, which he buried in his hotbed. Then he set up another hotbed, and when it had given out its heat, replanted the best plants with cloches over them. He did all the pruning just as the *Complete Gardener* prescribed, respected the flowers, let the fruit form, chose one from each arm, removed the others, and as soon as they were the size of a walnut he slipped under their skin a piece of wood to prevent them rotting from contact with the manure. He watered them, aired them, wiped steam from the cloches with his handkerchief, and if clouds appeared he hurried to bring up straw mats.

At night he did not sleep. Several times he even got up, and barefoot in his boots, shivering in his nightshirt, he went right across the garden to put his own blanket over the frames.

The cantaloups ripened. At the first Bouvard pulled a face. The second was no better, nor the third. For each one Pécuchet found a new excuse, until it came to the last, which he threw out of the window, saying that he simply could not understand it.

In fact, as he had grown different species side by side, the sweet melons were mixed up with water-melons, large Portuguese with Grand Mogul, and with the proximity of the tomatoes completing the anarchy, the result had been abominable hybrids tasting like pumpkins.

Then Pécuchet turned to flowers. He wrote to Dumouchel for some shrubs and seeds, bought a stock of humus and manfully applied himself to the task.

But he planted passion-flowers in the shade, pansies in the sun, covered the hyacinths with manure, watered the lilies after they had flowered, destroyed the rhododendrons through excessive chopping, stimulated the fuchsias with glue, and roasted a pomegranate tree by exposing it to the kitchen fire.

As the cold weather came on he smothered the honeysuckle beneath paper domes well smeared with tallow: the result looked like sugar loaves held up in the air on sticks.

The props for the dahlias were huge – and one could see among these straight lines the twisted branches of a japonica which remained quite static, neither dying nor growing.

However, since the rarest trees flourished in the gardens of the capital, they must succeed at Chavignolles; so Pécuchet procured Indian lilacs, Chinese roses and eucalyptus, then in the first flush of its reputation. All the experiments were a failure. Each time he was quite amazed.

Bouvard, like him, encountered obstacles. They took each other's advice, opened one book, went over to another, then did not know what to decide when opinions diverged so widely.

Thus, regarding marl, Puvis recommends it; Roret's manual opposes it.

As for plaster, despite Franklin's example, Rieffel and Monsieur Rigaud do not seem very keen.

Fallows, according to Bouvard, were a Gothic prejudice. Yet Leclerc notes cases where they are almost indispensable. Gasparin quotes a Lyonnais farmer who for fifty years grew cereals in the same field: that disproves the theory of rotation of crops. Tull makes much of ploughing at the expense of fertilizer, and here is Major Beetson doing away with fertilizer and ploughing!

To get to know something about weather signs they studied the clouds according to Luke-Howard's classification. They stared at the ones which stuck out like mares' tails, those that look like islands, those that one might take for snow mountains, trying to distinguish nimbus from cirrus, stratus from cumulus, but the shapes changed before they could find the names.

The barometer deceived them, the thermometer taught them nothing; and they resorted to the experiment devised in Louis XV's reign by a priest in Touraine. A leech in a jar should climb up in case of rain, stay at the bottom if it was set fair, and move about if a storm threatened. But the atmosphere almost always contradicted the leech. They put in three more with it. All four behaved differently.

After a lot of hard thinking Bouvard acknowledged that he had been mistaken. His estate required large-scale cultivation, the intensive system, and he risked all that remained of his available capital: 30,000 francs.

Aroused by Pécuchet he went into a frenzy about fertilizer. In the compost pit were heaped up branches, blood, intestines, feathers, anything he could find. He used Belgian liqueur, Swiss 'lizier', washing soda, smoked herrings, seaweed, rags, had guano sent, tried to make it – and, carrying his principles to the limit, did not tolerate any waste of urine; he did away with the lavatories. Dead animals were brought into his yard, and used to fertilize his land. Their disembowelled carrion was strewn over the countryside. Bouvard smiled amid all this infection. A pump fixed up in a farm cart spread out liquid manure over the crops. If people looked disgusted he would say: 'But it is gold! gold!' And he was sorry not to have still more dungheaps. How fortunate are those countries with natural caves full of bird droppings!

The colza was poor, the oats mediocre, the wheat could scarcely be sold on account of its smell. One odd thing was that the Mound, finally cleared of stones, was less productive than before.

He thought it would be a good idea to renew his machinery. He bought a Guillaume hoeing machine, a Valcourt extirpator, an English seed-drill and Mathieu de Dombasle's swing-plough, but the carter scoffed at it.

'Learn to use it!'

'All right, you show me.'

He tried to show him, got it all wrong, and the peasants mocked him.

He could never make them obey when the bell rang. He was always shouting after them, running hither and thither, jotting down notes in a little book, making appointments, then forgetting them, and his head seethed with ideas about industry. He promised himself that he would grow poppies, for the sake of the opium, and especially astragal, which he would sell under the name of 'family coffee'.

To fatten his bullocks more quickly he bled them every two weeks.

He did not kill any of his pigs and stuffed them with salted oats. Soon the pigsty was too cramped. They blocked the yard, knocked down fences, bit people.

During the hottest weather twenty-five sheep began to go round in circles and shortly afterwards died.

The same week three bullocks expired, thanks to Bouvard's blood-letting.

To destroy cockchafer grubs he had the idea of shutting the hens up in a wheeled cage, which two men pushed behind the plough; as a result they inevitably had their legs broken.

He made beer out of germander leaves, and gave it to the harvesters in place of cider. There was an outbreak of intestinal disorders. The children cried, the women groaned, the men were furious. They all threatened to leave and Bouvard gave in.

However, to convince them that his beverage was harmless Bouvard drained several bottles of it in front of them, felt uncomfortable, but concealed his pain beneath a look of delight. He even had the mixture brought to his house. That evening he drank some with Pécuchet, and both tried hard to like the taste. Besides, they must not waste it.

Bouvard's colic became too violent, and Germaine went for the doctor.

He was a serious man, with a bulging forehead, who began by terrifying his patient. The gentleman's dysentery must come from the beer that people were talking about. He wanted to know its ingredients, and condemned it in scientific terms, with much shrugging of shoulders. Pécuchet, who had provided the recipe, was mortified.

Despite pernicious applications of lime, neglected hoeing and untimely campaigns against thistles, Bouvard was confronted next year by a fine wheat crop. He took it into his head to dry it by fermentation, in the Dutch style, by the Clap-Mayer system; that is, he had it cut all in one go and stacked in ricks, which were to be taken down as soon as the gas escaped, and then exposed to the open air; after which Bouvard retired without the slightest misgiving.

Next day, while they were at dinner, they heard a drum beating under the beeches. Germaine went out to see what was going on, but the man was already far away. Almost at once the church bell rang out violently.

Bouvard and Pécuchet were seized with alarm. They stood up and, impatient for information, started off bareheaded towards Chavignolles.

An old woman passed. She knew nothing. They stopped a little boy, who answered: 'I think there is a fire!' And the drum went on beating, the bell rang harder than ever. At last they reached the first houses in the village. The grocer called out to them from a good way off:

'The fire is at your place!'

Pécuchet broke into a run; and he said to Bouvard, running beside him at the same pace: 'One, two; one, two, keep the step! like those light infantrymen at Vincennes!'

The road they were on kept going uphill; the slope of the land hid the horizon from them. They came to the top, near the Mound, and at a glance they could see the disaster.

All the ricks, dotted here and there, were blazing like volcanoes, in the middle of the bare plain, in the still of the evening.

Around the largest there were perhaps 300 persons; and under the orders of Monsieur Foureau, the mayor, in his tricolour sash, lads with poles and hooks were pulling the straw off the top in order to save the rest.

In his haste Bouvard almost knocked over Madame Bordin, who was standing there. Then catching sight of one of his farmhands he swore at him for not letting him know. With excessive zeal the man had instead run first to the house, to the church, then to his master's house, and had come back the other way.

Bouvard lost his head. His servants surrounded him, all speaking at once, and he forbade them to pull down the ricks, begged for help, demanded water, asked for firemen.

'Do we have any?' cried the mayor.

'It's your fault!' replied Bouvard.

He flew into a rage, made unseemly remarks, and everyone admired Monsieur Foureau's patience, though he was a brutal man, as his thick lips and bulldog jaw showed.

The heat from the ricks became so intense that it was no longer possible to come near them. In the devouring flames the straw twisted and crackled, grains of wheat stung one's face like buckshot.

Then the ricks collapsed to the ground in a pile of glowing embers, sending the sparks flying up: and all this mass of red rippled like watered silk with a range of changing colours, some as light as vermilion, others dark as clotted blood. Night had fallen, the wind was blowing; swirls of smoke enveloped the crowd. From time to time a spurt of flame passed across the dark sky.

Bouvard cried softly as he looked at the fire. His eyes disappeared beneath the swollen lids, and his whole face seemed as if it were puffed out with grief. Madame Bordin, toying with the fringes of her green shawl, called him 'Poor Monsieur Bouvard' and tried to console him. Since there was nothing to be done about it, he must simply accept it.

Pécuchet did not cry. Very pale, livid, rather, his mouth agape, his hair plastered down with cold sweat, he stood apart, sunk in thought. But the curé suddenly came up and murmured in an ingratiating voice: 'Oh, what a misfortune, to be sure; most distressing! Believe me, I share your ...!'

The others made no show of gloom. They smiled as they chatted, stretching out their hands to the flames. An old man picked up some burning stalks to light his pipe. Children began to dance. One rascal even cried out what fun it was.

'Yes, it is splendid fun,' replied Pécuchet, who had just heard him.

The fire died down, the heaps grew lower, and an hour later all that remained was ash, making black circles on the plain. Then everyone went home.

Madame Bordin and Abbé Jeufroy accompanied Messieurs Bouvard and Pécuchet as far as their residence.

On the way the widow reproached her neighbour in the nicest way for being so gruff, and the reverend gentleman expressed his surprise at having had to wait until then to make the acquaintance of such a distinguished parishioner.

When they were alone they tried to account for the fire, and instead of recognizing like everyone else that the wet straw had spontaneously ignited, they suspected some attempt at vengeance. No doubt its origin was Farmer Gouy or perhaps the molecatcher. Six months before Bouvard had refused his services, and even maintained before several witnesses that the government ought to prohibit so deadly an industry. Since that time the man had been prowling around the neighbourhood. He wore a full beard and looked frightening to them, especially in the evening, when he appeared at the edge of the farmyards, shaking his long pole strung with moles.

The damage was considerable, and to see where they stood, Pécuchet spent eight full days working over Bouvard's registers, which looked to him like 'an absolute labyrinth'. After collating the daybook, correspondence and ledger covered with pencilled notes and references, he recognized the truth; no goods to sell, no payments due, and nothing in the till. The capital showed a deficit of 33,000 francs.

Bouvard refused to believe it, and they began the calculations more than twenty times over. They always reached the same conclusion. Another two years of such a farming policy and their fortune would all be swallowed up!

The only solution was to sell.

At least a lawyer must be consulted. The approach was too painful; Pécuchet accepted the task.

According to Monsieur Marescot's opinion it would be better not to put up notices. He would speak about the farm to serious clients and leave them to make proposals.

'Very well,' said Bouvard, 'there is plenty of time.' He would take on a farmer, and then they would see. 'We shan't be any worse off than before, it is just that we shall have to economize.'

The economies annoyed Pécuchet because of the gardening and a few days later he said:

'We ought to devote ourselves exclusively to growing fruit trees, not for pleasure, but as a speculation. A pear that costs three sous is sometimes sold in Paris for as much as five or six francs, forty times more! Gardeners can make 25,000 francs a year out of apricots! At St Petersburg, in winter, a bunch of grapes costs a gold piece![1] It is a fine industry, you must agree! And what does it cost? Attention, manure and a bit of pruning!'

He succeeded in firing Bouvard's imagination so much that they went at once to their books to look for the proper names of plants to buy, and when they had chosen some names that sounded marvellous they addressed themselves to a nurseryman at Falaise, who wasted no time in supplying them with 300 saplings for which he had no demand.

They had sent for a locksmith for the props, an ironmonger for the stiffeners, a carpenter for the supports. They first sketched out the shape of the trees. Strips of lath on the wall represented candelabras. Two posts at each end of the flower beds held up the horizontal wires tightly; and in the orchard, hoops showed the structure of vases, cones, pyramids, so that anyone coming to visit them had the impression of looking at the parts of some unknown machine or the frame of a pyrotechnic showpiece.

When they had dug the holes, they trimmed all the roots, good or bad, and stuck them in a compost heap. Six months later the plants were dead. A new order from the nurseryman, new planting in yet deeper holes. But with the rain soaking the ground the grafts buried themselves and the trees grew freely.

With the coming of spring Pécuchet began pruning the pear trees. He did not cut the growing crowns, respected the short fruit-bearing branches, and in his obstinate determination to have the

1. Twenty francs.

duchess pears exactly aligned so that they formed lines on one side only he invariably broke them or tore them off. As for the peach trees, he got tangled up in the upper mother branches, the lower ones, or the secondary lowers. Spaces were always empty or full just where they should not be, and it was impossible to obtain a perfect rectangle or an espalier, with six branches on the right and six on the left, not counting the two main ones, all in a fine fishbone pattern.

Bouvard tried to train the apricot trees. They rebelled. He cut their trunks down to ground level; none of them grew again. The cherry trees, which he had notched, produced gum.

First they trimmed down a long way, which killed the base growth, then too short, which led to suckers; and they often hesitated, unable to distinguish timber buds from flower buds. They had been overjoyed at having flowers; but recognizing their mistake they took off three-quarters of them to strengthen the rest.

They never stopped talking about sap and cambium, paling, fracture, thinning of buds. In the middle of their dining-room they had, in a frame, a list of their saplings, with a number which was repeated in the garden on a little piece of wood at the foot of the tree.

They rose at dawn and worked on into the night, with a rush basket at their waist. In the chilly spring mornings Bouvard kept on his knitted waistcoat under his smock, Pécuchet his old coat under his overall, and people who passed along the fence heard them coughing in the mist.

Sometimes Pécuchet pulled his manual out of his pocket, and studied a paragraph, standing with his spade beside him in the same pose as the gardener adorning the frontispiece of the book. He even felt very flattered by the resemblance, which raised the author in his esteem.

Bouvard was continually perched on top of a high ladder in front of the pyramids. One day he was overcome by dizziness and not daring to come down called out for Pécuchet to come to his rescue.

At last the pears appeared, and there were plums in the orchard. Then they used all the devices recommended for keeping the birds away. But the bits of glass shone blindingly, the clanking of the windmill woke them up at night and sparrows perched on the scarecrow. They made a second, and even a third, in varying dress, but all in vain.

They could however hope for some fruit. Pécuchet had just handed the list to Bouvard when there was a sudden clap of thunder and it began to rain heavily and fiercely. At intervals the wind shook the whole surface of the espalier. The props collapsed one after another, and as the wretched trees swayed their pears crashed together.

Pécuchet had been surprised by the storm and sheltered in the hut. Bouvard stayed in the kitchen. They looked out on a whirlwind of splinters, branches, slates, and the sailors' wives watching the sea on the coast thirty miles away did not have a more intense gaze or a more anxious heart. Then, suddenly, the supports and bars holding up the espalier, with all the trellis-work, collapsed onto the flowerbeds.

What a scene met their inspection! The grass was covered with cherries and plums amid melting hailstones. Of the pears, the Passe-Colmar were lost, like the Bési-des-Vétérans and the Triomphes-de-Jordoigne. As for the apples, there remained a bare handful of *bons-papas* – and twelve Tétons-de-Venus, all the peach crop, rolled about in the puddles at the edge of the uprooted box-shrubs.

After dinner, when they ate very little, Pécuchet said quietly:

'Wouldn't it be a good idea to go and see if anything has happened at the farm?'

'And find still more reasons for being depressed?'

'Perhaps; we are not exactly lucky.'

And they complained about Providence and nature.

Bouvard, with his elbows on the table, was making his little whistling noise, and since all afflictions are connected, their old plans for farming came back into his mind, especially that of producing starch and a new kind of cheese.

Pécuchet was breathing noisily, and while he stuffed pinches of snuff into his nostrils he was thinking that, if fate had been kind, he would now belong to an agricultural society, shine at exhibitions and be quoted in the press.

Bouvard looked around sadly.

'My word! I feel like getting rid of the whole lot and setting ourselves up somewhere else!'

'As you like,' said Pécuchet. Then a moment later:

'The authors recommended suppressing all direct channels. This blocks the sap and the tree inevitably suffers. To grow properly it should not bear fruit. Yet the ones which are never pruned or fertilized produce fruit that is admittedly not so big but tastes better. I demand to know why! It is not just that every species requires special treatment, but each individual as well, according to the climate, temperature, lots of things! Where is the rule then, and what hope can we have of success or profit?'

Bouvard answered:

'You'll see in Gasparin that profit cannot exceed a tenth of the capital. Therefore it would be better to invest this capital in a banking house. At the end of fifteen years with interest accumulating you would have twice as much without having to break your heart over it.'

Pécuchet bent his head.

'Perhaps arboriculture is just a joke!'

'Like agronomy!' replied Bouvard.

Then they accused themselves of having been too ambitious, and resolved from now on to limit their trouble and expense. Periodic pruning would be enough for the orchard. Counter-espaliers were prescribed and they would not replace the dead trees; but there would be some very ugly gaps unless they destroyed all the others that were still standing. What was the solution?

Pécuchet made several sketches, using his geometry box. Bouvard offered advice. They came to no satisfactory conclusion. Fortunately they found in their library Boitard's work, entitled *The Garden Architect.*

The author divides gardens into an infinite number of types. First there is the melancholy and romantic, characterized by immortelles, ruins, tombs and 'an *ex-voto* to the Virgin, marking the place where some lord has been struck down by a murderer's sword'. The terrible sort is composed of hanging rocks, shattered trees, burnt-out huts; the exotic by planting Peruvian torch-thistles 'to evoke memories in a colonist or traveller'. The solemn must provide, like Ermenonville, a temple to philosophy. Obelisks and triumphal arches distinguish the majestic; moss and caves the mysterious; a lane, the meditational. There is even the fantastic, the finest specimen of which could recently be seen in a garden in Wurtemberg – for there one encountered successively a wild boar, a hermit, several sepulchres and a boat which unmoored itself from the bank and took you into a boudoir where jets of water soaked anyone who sat on the sofa.

Faced with this horizon of marvels Bouvard and Pécuchet felt quite dazzled. The fantastic type seemed to them reserved for princes. The temple to philosophy would be a nuisance. The *ex-voto* to the Virgin would be meaningless, given the lack of murderers, and it was too bad for the colonists and travellers, but American plants were too expensive. But the rocks were possible, as were the shattered trees, the immortelles and the moss – and with mounting enthusiasm, after much trial and error, helped by just one servant and at minimal expense they created a residence for themselves without its equal in the whole department.

The arbour was opened up in places to give a view of the copse, which was full of winding paths like a maze. In the espalier wall they had intended to make an archway beneath which the perspective would be revealed. As the coping would not stay up hanging in mid air the result had been a huge gap, with ruins on the ground.

They had sacrificed the asparagus to build in its place an Etruscan tomb, that is a black plaster quadrilateral, six foot high, resembling a dog kennel. Four dwarf firs flanked this monument at its corners, and it was to be surmounted by an urn and embellished with an inscription.

In the other part of the kitchen garden a sort of Rialto straddled a pool, whose edges were decorated with encrusted mussel shells. The earth absorbed the water, no matter! A clay bottom would form and keep the water in.

The hut had been transformed into a rustic cabin, with the help of stained glass.

At the top of the vine-clad mound, six squared trees supported a tin hat with turned up points, and the whole thing represented a Chinese pagoda.

They had been down to the banks of the Orne to select pieces of granite, had broken them up, numbered them, brought them back themselves in a cart, then joined the bits together with cement, piling one on top of another; and in the middle of the lawn rose a rock like a gigantic potato.

Something further was lacking to complete the harmony. They cut down the biggest lime-tree in the arbour (three-quarters dead, in any case) and laid it across the length of the garden, to convey the impression that it had been brought there by a torrent or struck down by lightning.

When the task was done, Bouvard, who was on the terrace, cried from afar:

'Here! You can see better!'

'See better' was repeated in the air.

Pécuchet answered:

'I'm coming!'

'Coming!'

'Well, well, an echo!'

'Echo!'

The lime-tree had hitherto prevented it, and it was helped by the pagoda, opposite the barn, whose gable rose above the arbour.

To try out the echo they amused themselves by calling out comic words; Bouvard shouted rude ones.

He had been to Falaise several times on the pretext of collecting money, and he always came back with little packages which he shut up in his chest of drawers. Pécuchet set off one morning to go to Bretteville, and returned very late, with a basket which he hid under his bed.

Next day when he awoke Bouvard had a surprise. The first two yews of the main path, which as late as the day before had been spherical, were now shaped like peacocks, with a china vase and two buttons representing the beak and eyes. Pécuchet had got up at dawn, and trembling with fear of discovery he had cut the two trees following instructions in appendices sent by Dumouchel.

For six months the yews behind these had more or less imitated pyramids, cubes, cylinders, stags or armchairs, but nothing equalled the peacocks. Bouvard acknowledged this with warm praise.

On the pretext of forgetting his spade, he drew his companion into the maze, for he had profited from Pécuchet's absence to create something sublime himself.

The field gate was covered with a layer of plaster, on which was drawn up a fine array of 500 pipe bowls, representing Abd-el-Kader, negroes, naked women, horses' hooves and snails.

'Do you understand how impatient I have been?'

'Indeed I do!'

And in their emotion they embraced.

Like all artists they needed applause, and Bouvard had the idea of giving a grand dinner-party.

'Be careful!' said Pécuchet, 'You are going to start entertaining. It is a bottomless pit!'

The matter was however decided.

Ever since they had come to live in the area they had kept themselves apart. Everyone, eager to make their acquaintance, accepted their invitation, except the Comte de Faverges, called to Paris on business. They fell back on Monsieur Hurel, his factotum.

Beljambe, the innkeeper, formerly a chef of Lisieux, was to prepare certain dishes. He provided a waiter. Germaine had requested the girl who looked after the hens. Marianne, Madame Bordin's maid, would come too. From 4 p.m. the gate was wide open, and the two proprietors, full of impatience, waited for their guests.

Hurel stopped under the beeches to put on his frock-coat. Then the curé came up, wearing a new cassock, and a moment later Monsieur Foureau, with a velvet waistcoat. The doctor had his wife on his arm, walking painfully and sheltering under her parasol. A stream of pink ribbons waved behind them; it was Madame Bordin's bonnet, which she wore with a beautiful dress of dove-grey silk. Her gold watch-chain swung on her breast, and rings sparkled on both her hands in their black mittens. Finally there appeared the lawyer, a panama hat on his head, a lorgnon in his eye, for the ministry official in him did not keep down the man of the world.

The drawing-room was so highly polished that it was hard to keep one's footing. The eight Utrecht armchairs stood along the wall; a round table in the middle bore the liqueur stand, and above the mantlepiece the portrait of Bouvard's father was to be seen. The dull patches, showing up against the light, made the mouth grimace and the eyes squint, and a spot of mildew on the cheeks added to the illusion of the side-whiskers. The guests detected a resemblance to his son, and Madame Bordin added, looking at Bouvard, that he must have been a very handsome man.

After an hour's wait Pécuchet announced that they could go into dinner.

The white calico curtains, edged with red, were drawn right across the windows, like those in the drawing-room, and the sun came through the fabric to cast a golden light on the panelling, which had no other ornament than a barometer.

Bouvard put the two ladies beside him; Pécuchet had the mayor on his left, the curé on his right, and they started on the oysters. They smelt of mud. Bouvard was very upset, and most apologetic, and Pécuchet left the table to go into the kitchen and make a scene with Beljambe.

During all the first part of the meal, comprising a brill served between a vol-au-vent and a pigeon stew, the conversation turned on cider-making.

After that they came on to food that was digestible or indigestible. The doctor was naturally consulted. He judged things somewhat sceptically, like a man who has seen into the very depths of science, and yet did not admit the slightest contradiction.

At the same time as the sirloin, Burgundy was served. It was cloudy. Bouvard, explaining the accident by the way the bottle had been rinsed, had three others tasted without success, then poured out some Saint-Julien, obviously too young, and all the diners kept quiet. Hurel smiled continually; the waiter's heavy steps rang over the stone floor.

Madame Vaucorbeil, rather dumpy and sulky (she was in fact near the end of her pregnancy), had remained totally silent. Bouvard, not knowing how to engage her in conversation, spoke about the theatre in Caen.

'My wife never goes to the theatre,' replied the doctor.

Monsieur Marescot, when he lived in Paris, only ever went to the Théâtre des Italiens.

'For my part,' said Bouvard, 'I would sometimes treat myself to a place in the pit at the Vaudeville to hear farces!'

Foureau asked Madame Bordin if she liked farce.

'That depends on what kind,' she answered.

The mayor teased her. She joked back. Then she gave a recipe for gherkins. Besides, her domestic talents were well-known, and she had an admirably well-kept little farm.

Foureau addressed Bouvard: 'Do you intend to sell yours?'

'My goodness, so far, I am not too sure...'

'What, not even the bit at Les Écalles?' the lawyer went on; 'It would just suit you, Madame Bordin.'

The widow replied, simpering: 'Monsieur Bouvard might be asking too much.'

'Perhaps he could be softened up.'

'I am not going to try!'

'Oh, supposing you gave him a kiss?'

'Let's try, all the same,' said Bouvard.

And he kissed her on both cheeks, amid general applause.

Almost immediately the champagne was opened, and the popping corks added further to the hilarity. Pécuchet gave a signal, the curtains parted and the garden appeared.

In the half light it was quite dreadful. The rock, like a mountain, occupied the lawn, the tomb formed a cube in the middle of the spinach, the Venetian bridge a circumflex accent over the runner beans – and the cabin beyond made a great black mark, for they had burned its roof to make it more poetic. The yews, trimmed into the shape of stags or armchairs, stretched one after the other as far as the blasted tree, which extended diagonally from the arbour to the bower, where tomatoes hung like stalactites. A sunflower here and there displayed its golden disc. The Chinese pagoda, painted red, looked like a lighthouse on the mound. The peacocks' beaks, caught by the sun, reflected each other brightly, and behind the fence, cleared of its planks, the flat countryside closed the horizon.

The astonishment of their guests filled Bouvard and Pécuchet with genuine delight.

Madame Bordin especially admired the peacocks; but the tomb was not understood, nor the burned cabin, nor the ruined wall. Then each in turn went over the bridge. Bouvard and Pécuchet had carted water all morning to fill the pool. It had run out between the stones on the bottom, which had been badly joined, leaving them covered with mud.

As they walked round they allowed themselves some critical remarks: 'In your place I should have done that – The peas are late – This corner is quite frankly not very nice – The way you prune you will never get any fruit.'

Bouvard was obliged to reply that he did not care about fruit.

As they passed by the arbour he said slyly:

'Ah, we are disturbing someone: I am so sorry!'

No one took up the jest. They all knew the plaster lady.

Finally after several detours through the maze they found themselves before the gateway with the pipes. They all looked at each other dumbfounded. Bouvard watched his guests' faces and eager to know their opinion:

'What do you say to that?'

Madame Bordin burst out laughing. Everyone did the same. The curé made a sort of gurgling noise. Hurel coughed. The doctor wept, his wife was seized with a nervous spasm, and Foureau, completely uninhibited, broke off an Abd-el-Kader and put it in his pocket as a souvenir.

When they had left the arbour Bouvard cried out with all his might, so as to amaze everyone with the echo:

'At your service, ladies!'

Nothing! No echo! This was the result of repairs to the barn, whose gable and roof had been demolished.

Coffee was served on the mound and the gentlemen were about to start a game of bowls when they saw a man looking at them from behind the fence opposite.

He was lean and weatherbeaten, in ragged old trousers, a blue jacket, no shirt, black beard cropped short, and in a raucous voice he uttered the words:

'Give me a glass of wine!'

The mayor and Abbé Jeufroy had recognized him at once. He had formerly been a carpenter at Chavignolles.

'Come along, Gorju! Be off with you,' said Monsieur Foureau, 'no begging here.'

'Me! Begging!' cried the man in annoyance. 'I fought in Africa for seven years. I am just out of hospital. No work! Do I have to kill someone, for God's sake?'

His anger cooled down, and hands on hips he looked at the gentry with an expression of morose mockery. Weariness brought on by camping out, hard drinking and fevers, a whole life of wretchedness and degradation was revealed in his dull eyes. His pale lips trembled and bared his gums. The crimson sky wrapped him in a glow as red as blood, and his insistence on staying there provoked a kind of panic.

To put an end to it, Bouvard went to look for a bottle with some dregs left in it. The tramp greedily swigged it, then disappeared into the field of oats, waving his arms about.

Then Monsieur Bouvard came in for criticism. Pandering to people like that encouraged disorder. But Bouvard, irritated by the scant success of his garden, took up the defence of the people; everyone talked at once.

Foureau praised the government, all Hurel saw in the world was landed property. Abbé Jeufroy complained that religion was not protected. Pécuchet attacked taxes. Madame Bordin cried out at intervals: 'Personally I detest the republic,' and the doctor declared himself on the side of progress. 'For, after all sir, we need reforms.'

'Maybe!' replied Foureau, 'but all these ideas are bad for business.' – 'I don't care about business!' cried Pécuchet.

Vaucorbeil went on: 'At least grant us additional capacity.'

Bouvard did not go so far.

'Is that your opinion?' replied the doctor. 'That sums you up! Good evening! And I wish you a flood so that you can sail on your pool!'

'I must go too,' said Monsieur Foureau a moment later; and pointing to the pocket where the Abd-el-Kader was: 'If I need another I'll be back.'

Before leaving the curé confided to Pécuchet that he found something unseemly in the imitation tomb in the middle of the vegetables. Hurel as he withdrew made a deep bow to the company. Monsieur Marescot had disappeared after dessert.

Madame Bordin started again on the details of her gherkin recipe, promised another for plums in brandy, and went up and down the main path three times more; as she passed the lime-tree the bottom of her dress caught on it, and they heard her murmur: 'My goodness! What a stupid idea that tree is!'

The two Amphitryons stayed until midnight under the bower venting their spleen.

No doubt there were two or three little things here and there in the dinner which might be criticized; and yet the guests had stuffed themselves like ogres, which proved that it was not so bad. But as for the garden, so much belittling arose from the blackest jealousy, and as they both became heated:

'Ah! so there is no water in the pool! Be patient and you'll even see a swan and a fish in it!'

'They hardly noticed the pagoda!'

'Anyone who claims that ruins are out of place must be an idiot!'

'And the tomb unseemly! Why unseemly? Hasn't anyone the right to put one up on his estate? I want to be buried there, in fact!'

'Don't talk about that!' said Pécuchet.

Then they reviewed the guests in turn.

'The doctor looks to me like a fine poseur!'

'Did you notice how Marescot sneered at the portrait?'

'What a cad the mayor is! When you dine with someone, devil take it, you respect the curiosities!'

'Madame Bordin?' said Bouvard.

'Oh, she's a schemer! Leave me in peace.'

Disgusted with society they resolved not to see anyone in future, to live exclusively at home, just for themselves.

So they spent days in the cellar taking tartar off the bottles, re-varnished all the furniture, waxed all the bedrooms; every evening, as they watched the wood burning, they discoursed on the best heating system.

They tried to economize by smoking hams, by making their own soap. They got in Germaine's way, and she shrugged her shoulders. When the jam-making season came she lost her temper, and they settled in the bakehouse.

It had been a wash-house and under the logs stood a great stone vat, excellently suited to their plans, for they had conceived the ambition of making preserves.

Fourteen jars were filled with tomatoes and peas; they luted the stoppers with quicklime and cheese, fastened strips of cloth round the edges, and then plunged them in boiling water. It evaporated; they poured in cold water; the difference in temperature made the jars burst. Only three were saved.

Next they got hold of some old sardine cans, put veal cutlets in them and plunged them into the bain-marie. They came out as round as balloons; they would flatten out as they cooled down. To continue the experiment they filled other cans with eggs, chicory, lobster, a fish-stew, a soup, and congratulated themselves, like Monsieur Appert, 'on having fixed the seasons': such discoveries, according to Pécuchet, were better than the exploits of any conqueror!

They improved on Madame Bordin's pickles by adding pepper to give the vinegar more taste; and their brandied plums were far superior! By maceration they obtained ratafias of raspberries and absinthe. With honey and angelica in a cask of Banyuls they tried to make Malaga wine; and they also undertook the concoction of champagne! The bottles of Chablis, cut with must, exploded of their own accord. So they had no doubts as to their success.

As their studies progressed they came to suspect frauds in every kind of food and drink.

They quibbled with the baker about the colour of his bread. They made an enemy of the grocer by maintaining that he adulterated his chocolates. They went over to Falaise to ask for jujube, and under the very eyes of the chemist put his paste to the water test. It became like bacon rind in appearance, which was a sign of gelatine.

After this triumph their pride swelled. They bought the equipment of a bankrupt distiller and there soon arrived in their house sieves, barrels, funnels, skimmers, filters and scales, not to speak of a pounding bowl and a special still, which needed a reflector furnace with a chimney funnel.

They learned how to clarify sugar, and the different kinds of baking, large and small granulated, puffed, round, runny, caramel. But they longed to use the still; and they set about fine liqueurs, starting with anisette. The liquid almost always brought solids with it, or they stuck to the bottom; at other times they got the dosage wrong. Around them shone great copper pans, the pointed nose of mattrasses protruded, saucepans hung on the wall. Often one was sorting herbs on the table, while the other rolled the cannonball round in the hanging bowl; they stirred spoons, tasted mixtures.

Bouvard was always sweating, and wore only his shirt and

trousers pulled right up to the pit of his stomach by short braces, but completely scatterbrained forgot the diaphragm of the cucurbit, or made the fire too hot.

Pécuchet mumbled calculations, motionless in his long blouse, a sort of child's smock with sleeves; and they considered themselves to be very serious men, doing a useful job.

Finally they dreamed of a creme which would put all the others in the shade. In it they would put coriander as in kummel, kirsch as in maraschino, hyssop as in chartreuse, amberseed as in Vespetro, calamus aromaticus as in Krambambuli, and it would be coloured red with sandalwood. But under what name should they try and sell it to the trade? They needed a name that was easy to remember, and yet unusual. After trying for a long time to find one they decided that it should be called 'Bouvarine'.

Towards the end of autumn spots appeared in the three jars of preserves. The tomatoes and peas were rotten. That must be the result of the sealing? So the problem of sealing tormented them. They did not have the money to try new methods. Their farm was eating up their substance.

Tenants had applied several times; Bouvard had not wanted any of them. But his head man did the farming according to his orders, with dangerous economies, so that the harvests diminished, everything was going to rack and ruin, and they were talking about their troubles when Farmer Gouy came into the laboratory, escorted by his wife, who kept herself timidly in the background.

Thanks to all the dressings it had received, the land had improved, and he had come to take back the farm. Despite all their labours the profits were risky; in short, if he wanted the farm it was because he loved the place and missed such good masters. He was coldly dismissed. He came back that very evening.

Pécuchet had been lecturing Bouvard; they were going to yield. Gouy asked for the rent to be reduced, and as the others protested he began to bellow rather than speak, calling on God as his witness, listing all his tribulations, boasting of all his merits. When bidden to state his price he hung his head instead of answering. Then his wife, who sat by the door with a large basket on her knees, took up the same protestations, clucking in a shrill voice like a wounded hen.

Finally the lease was fixed at 3,000 francs a year, a third less than before.

While they were at it Farmer Gouy proposed to buy the equipment and the dialogues began afresh.

The valuation of the various objects lasted a fortnight. Bouvard was completely worn out, and let everything go for such a derisory sum that Gouy at first stared in amazement, and then cried 'Done', striking hands on the deal.

After which the proprietors, as was customary, invited them to have a bite at the house, and Pécuchet opened one of his bottles of Malaga, prompted not so much by generosity as the hope of winning praise for it.

But the farmer said crossly: 'It's like liquorice syrup,' and his wife, 'to take the taste away', asked for a glass of spirits.

They were concerned with a graver matter! All the ingredients of 'Bouvarine' had at last been collected.

They piled them up in the cucurbit, with some alcohol, lit the fire and waited. Meanwhile Pécuchet, distressed at the unfortunate experience with the Malaga, took the tins out of the cupboard, took the lid off the first, the second, then the third. He threw them away in fury and called Bouvard.

Bouvard turned off the tap in the serpentine and hurried to the preserves. Disillusion was complete. The slices of veal looked like boiled bootsoles. A shiny liquid took the place of the lobster. The fish stew was unrecognizable. Mould had grown over the soup – and a noisome stench filled the laboratory.

Suddenly, with a noise like a shell bursting, the still exploded into twenty pieces which shot up to the ceiling, breaking the saucepans, squashing the skimmers, shattering the glass; the coal scattered everywhere, the furnace was demolished, and next day Germaine found a spatula in the yard.

The pressure of the steam had broken the instrument, because the cucurbit was bolted to the top.

Pécuchet had at once crouched down behind the vat, and Bouvard had collapsed on a stool. For ten minutes they remained in these positions, not daring to move a muscle, pale with terror, amid the shattered fragments. When they were capable of utterance, they asked themselves the cause of so many misfortunes, especially this last one. It was all beyond their comprehension, except that they had nearly died. Pécuchet concluded with these words:

'Perhaps it is because we don't know any chemistry!'

3

To acquire a knowledge of chemistry they procured Regnault's course and first learned that 'simple bodies are perhaps compound'.

Bodies are distinguished as metalloids and metals, a difference which, according to the author, 'is by no means absolute'. Similarly with acids and bases 'since a body may behave like acids or bases according to circumstances'.

They found the notation most fanciful. Multiple proportions worried Pécuchet.

'Since a molecule of A, I suppose, combines with several parts of B, it seems to me that such a molecule ought to divide into as many parts; but if it divides it ceases to be the unit, the original molecule. I don't understand at all!'

'Nor do I!' said Bouvard.

So they resorted to a less difficult work, that of Girardin, where they learned as certain facts that ten litres of air weigh 100 grams, that there is no lead in pencils, that diamonds are nothing but carbon.

What amazed them more than anything was that earth, as an element, does not exist.

They grasped how a blow-lamp works, the facts about gold, silver, washing soda, tinning saucepans; then without the least scruple Bouvard and Pécuchet threw themselves into organic chemistry.

How wonderful to find in living creatures the same substances as those which make up minerals. Nevertheless they felt a sort of humiliation at the idea that their persons contained phosphorus like matches, albumen like white of egg, hydrogen gas like street lamps.

After colours and fats they came on to fermentation.

This led them on to acids, and the law of equivalents upset them once more. They tried to elucidate it with the theory of atoms, and then they were completely lost.

If they were to understand all that, according to Bouvard, they would need instruments.

The expense was considerable, and they had spent too much.

But Dr Vaucorbeil could no doubt enlighten them.

They presented themselves during his consulting hours.

'Yes, gentlemen? What is wrong with you?'

Pécuchet replied that they were not ill, and after explaining the purpose of their visit:

'First we should like to know about superior atomicity.'

The doctor went very red, then criticized them for wanting to learn chemistry.

'I am not denying its importance, make no mistake! But nowadays people bring it into everything! It's having a deplorable effect on medicine.'

The authority of his words was reinforced by the sight of the objects around him.

Sticking plaster and bandages were lying about on the mantelpiece, the surgical box stood in the middle of the desk, probes filled a basin in the corner, and against the wall stood an anatomical figure.

Pécuchet complimented the doctor on it.

'Anatomy must be a fine subject to study!'

Monsieur Vaucorbeil discoursed at length on how much he used to enjoy dissections; and Bouvard asked about the relationship between the inside of a woman and that of a man.

In order to satisfy them the doctor pulled out of his bookshelves a collection of anatomical plates.

'Take them with you! You will be more comfortable looking at them at home!'

The skeleton amazed them by the prominence of the jaw, the eye sockets, the fearful length of the hands. They needed an explanatory text, so they went back to Monsieur Vaucorbeil and, thanks to Alexandre Lauth's manual, they learned the divisions of the bone structure, and were astonished at the spine, sixteen times stronger, it was said, than if the Creator had made it straight. Why sixteen times exactly?

The metacarpal bones distressed Bouvard, and Pécuchet, working on the skull, lost heart at the sphenoid, although it looks like 'a Turkish or Turkic saddle'.

As for articulations, they were concealed by too many ligaments, so they attacked the muscles.

But it was not easy to discover the insertions, and when they reached the vertebral grooves they gave up completely.

Then Pécuchet said:

'Supposing we took up chemistry again, if only to make use of the laboratory?'

Bouvard protested, and seemed to remember that artificial cadavers were manufactured for use in hot countries.

Barberou, to whom he wrote, gave him some information. For ten francs a month one could have one of Monsieur Auzoux's puppets, and the following week the Falaise messenger deposited an oblong box at their gate.

They carried it into the bakehouse, full of excitement. When the nails had been pulled out of the planks, the straw fell away, the tissue paper slipped off, the dummy appeared.

He was brick-coloured, with no hair or skin, striped all over with countless threads of blue, red and white. It did not look like a corpse, but a sort of toy, very ugly, very clean, smelling of varnish.

Then they lifted off the thorax, and saw the two lungs, like two sponges; the heart like a large egg, a little to the side and the rear, the diaphragm, kidneys, the whole mass of entrails.

'To work!' said Pécuchet.

They spent the whole day and evening at it.

They had put on smocks, like medical students in operating theatres, and by the light of three candles they were working on their bits of cardboard when a fist banged on the door: 'Open up!'

It was Monsieur Foureau, followed by the rural constable.

Germaine's employers had been glad to show her the dummy. She had run straight to the grocer to tell him about it, and the whole village now believed that they were concealing in their house a real corpse. Foureau, yielding to public murmurs, had come to assure himself of the facts. Curious onlookers stood in the yard.

When he came in, the dummy was lying on its side, and as they had undone the facial muscles, the eye made a monstrous bulge, and looked rather frightening.

'What have you come for?' said Pécuchet.

Foureau stammered: 'Nothing, nothing at all!' Then, picking up one of the pieces from the table: 'What's this?'

'The buccinator,' answered Bouvard.

Foureau kept quiet, but gave a mocking smile, jealous that they had found a pastime beyond his competence.

The two anatomists pretended to continue their investigations. The people who were tired of waiting at the door had penetrated into the bakehouse, and, as there was some jostling, the table shook.

'Oh, that's too much!' cried Pécuchet, 'clear the public out of here!'

The constable made the spectators leave.

'Good!' said Bouvard, 'we don't need anyone.'

Foureau understood the allusion, and asked if they were entitled to possess such an object, since they were not doctors. He would in any case be writing to the prefect. What a country! The comparison they made between themselves and the rest consoled them; and they became eager to suffer for science.

The doctor came to see them too. He spoke slightingly of the dummy as being too remote from nature, but turned the occasion to good account by giving a lesson.

Bouvard and Pécuchet were delighted, and at their request Monsieur Vaucorbeil lent them several volumes from his library, though he told them flatly that they would never see it through.

They noted down in the *Dictionary of Medical Sciences* extraordinary examples of confinement, longevity, obesity and constipation. Why had they not known the famous Canadian of Beaumont, the polyphagous Tarare and Bijou, the dropsical woman of the Eure, the Piedmontese who went to the toilet every three weeks, Simon de Mirepoix, who was ossified when he died, and the former mayor of Angoulême, whose nose weighed three pounds!

The brain inspired them with philosophical reflections. They were easily able to distinguish inside it the *septum lucidum*, composed of two thin sheets, and the pineal gland, which looks like a small red pea; but there were peduncles and ventricles, arches, pillars, stages, ganglions and all kinds of fibres, and Pacchioni's foramen and Pacini's body, in short an inextricable pile, enough to spend their life on.

Sometimes, in a daze, they completely dismantled the cadaver, then found themselves hard put to it to fit the pieces together again.

It was hard work, especially after lunch, and they very soon fell asleep, Bouvard with sunken chin and protruding stomach, Pécuchet head in hands, both elbows on the table.

Often at that precise moment Monsieur Vaucorbeil, finishing his first round of visits, would put his head round the door.

'Well, colleagues, how's the anatomy going?'

'Splendidly,' they would answer.

Then he would ask them questions for the pleasure of catching them out.

When they were tired of one organ they passed to another, and in this way they successively began and abandoned the heart, stomach, ear, intestines, for the cardboard dummy bored them terribly in spite of their efforts to take an interest in it. Finally the doctor came upon them just as they were nailing it up again in its box.

'Bravo! I was expecting that.' At their age one could not undertake such studies – and the smile which accompanied his words deeply wounded them.

What right had he to judge them incapable? Was science this gentleman's private property? As if he were a very superior person himself!

Then, accepting his challenge, they went in to Bayeux to buy some books.

What they needed was physiology, and a bookseller got them the treatises of Richerand and Adelon, famous at that time.

All the commonplaces about age, sex and temperament seemed of the highest importance to them; they were pleased to know that dental tartar contains three sorts of animalculae, that the seat of taste is in the tongue, and the feeling of hunger in the stomach.

Because it would have helped them to understand its functions they were sorry not to have the faculty of rumination, enjoyed by Montègre, Monsieur Gosse and Bérard's brother, and they chewed slowly, triturated, salivated, mentally accompanying the alimentary mass through their insides, following it right up to its final consequences, methodically and scrupulously, with almost religious attention.

In order to produce artificial digestions they heaped up meat in a phial containing a duck's gastric juices, and carried it under their armpits for a fortnight, with no other result than to make them smell.

They were seen running along the highway, wearing damp clothes in the heat of the sun. This was to check whether thirst is allayed by applying water to the epidermis. They came back panting and both caught a cold.

Hearing, speech, sight were rapidly despatched, but Bouvard spread himself on generation.

Pécuchet's reserve in this matter had always surprised him. His ignorance seemed so complete that he pressed him for an explanation, and Pécuchet, with a red face, made a confession.

Some jokers had once enticed him into a house of ill fame, but he had run away, wanting to keep himself for the woman he would love later on. Circumstances had never turned out right; so that from false shame, financial embarrassment, fear of disease, obstinacy, habit, at the age of fifty-two, and despite living in the capital, he was still a virgin.

Bouvard found it hard to believe, then laughed immoderately, but stopped when he saw tears in Pécuchet's eyes; for he was no stranger to passions, having fallen in love successively with a tight-rope dancer, an architect's sister-in-law, a lady clerk, finally with a little laundrymaid, and the marriage was about to take place when he had discovered that she was pregnant by somebody else.

Bouvard told him:

'There's always a way to make up for lost time. Come now, cheer up. I'll see to it... if you like!'

Pécuchet replied with a sigh that they must give it no more thought; and they went on with their physiology.

Is it true that our body surface constantly gives off a subtle vapour? The proof is that a man's weight decreases every minute. If every day the deficiency is added and the excess subtracted, this will maintain health in perfect equilibrium. Sanctorius, inventor of this law, spent half a century daily weighing his food with all his excretions, and weighed himself, only taking time off to write down his calculations.

They tried imitating Sanctorius, but as their scales would not take both of them, it was Pécuchet who began.

He took off his clothes, to allow free perspiration, and stood on the machine, stark naked, revealing, despite his modesty, his very long torso, like a cylinder, with short legs, flat feet and brown skin. At his side, in a chair, his friend read to him.

Some scientists maintain that animal heat is developed by muscular contractions, and that by moving the thorax and pelvic area one can raise the temperature of a lukewarm bath.

Bouvard went to get their tub, and when all was ready, plunged into it, armed with a thermometer.

The ruins of the distillery, swept to the back of the room, stood out in the shadow like a vague hummock. Periodically the mice could be heard nibbling away; an old smell of aromatic plants filled the air, and feeling very comfortable they chatted serenely.

Bouvard however felt a little chilly.

'Move your limbs about,' said Pécuchet.

He moved them, with no effect on the thermometer.

'It's decidedly cold.'

'I'm not warm either,' replied Pécuchet, shivering himself, 'but shake your pelvic members, shake them!'

Bouvard opened his thighs, twisted his flanks, wobbled his stomach, puffed like a grampus, then looked at the thermometer, which was still falling:

'I don't understand it at all! I am moving though!'

'Not enough!'

And he started up his gymnastics again.

This went on for three hours, when he once more seized he tube.

'What! Twelve degrees! Oh, good night! I'm off!'

A dog came in, half mastiff, half hound, with yellow coat, scabby, tongue hanging out.

What were they to do? They had no bells, and their servant was deaf. They were shivering, but did not dare move for fear of being bitten.

Pécuchet thought it was a good idea to shout threats and roll his eyes.

Then the dog barked, and jumped round the scales, on which Pécuchet, clinging to the ropes and bending his knees, tried to raise himself as high as possible.

'That's the wrong way to go about it,' said Bouvard, and he began to smile at the dog and cajole it.

The dog undoubtedly understood. It tried to lick him, stuck its paws on his shoulders, scratched them with its claws.

'Well now! There he goes with my breeches!'

The dog lay down on them and kept still.

Finally with the greatest caution they risked getting down from the scales and out of the bath respectively; and when Pécuchet was dressed again he could not help exclaiming:

'As for you, my lad, you are going to be useful in our experiments!'

'What experiments?'

They could give him phosphorus injections, then shut him up in a cellar to see if fire would come out of his nostrils. But how could the injections be given? In any case no one would sell them phosphorus.

They thought of shutting him up under a bell-glass, making him breathe gas, giving him poison to drink. Perhaps that would not be much fun! Finally they chose to magnetize steel through contact with the dog's spinal marrow.

Repressing his emotion Bouvard held out some needles on a plate to Pécuchet, who stuck them against the vertebrae. They broke, fell on the floor; he took more and pushed them in hard, at random. The dog broke its bonds, shot like a cannon-ball through the window, across the yard and vestibule, and turned up in the kitchen.

Germaine began to shout when she saw it covered in blood, with strings round its paws.

Her masters in hot pursuit came in at the same moment. The dog disappeared with one bound.

The old servant addressed them:

'This is another of your silly tricks, I'm sure! A nice mess my kitchen is in! Perhaps he'll get rabies! They put people in jail who are not as bad as you!'

They went back to the laboratory to test the needles. Not one of them attracted a single iron filing.

Then Germaine's suggestion worried them. The dog might have rabies, return unexpectedly, turn on them.

Next day they went all round, seeking information, and for

several years they turned off into the countryside as soon as a dog appeared looking like that one.

Other experiments failed. Contrary to what the authors said, the pigeons they bled took exactly the same time to die whether their stomachs were full or empty. Kittens held under water perished in five minutes; and a goose which they had stuffed with madder still had completely white periostea.

Diet obsessed them.

How is it that the same juice produces bones, blood, lymph and excretory matter? But it is not possible to follow the transformations of a given food. A man who only uses one is chemically the same as one who consumes several. When Vauquelin had calculated how much chalk there was in the oats given to a hen, he found that its eggshells contained more. Therefore substance is created. How? No one knows.

No one even knows the strength of the heart. Borelli admits enough to raise a weight of 180,000 pounds, and Keill estimates it at about eight ounces, from which they concluded that physiology is, according to the old saying, the romance of medicine. Unable to understand it, they did not believe it.

A month passed in idleness, then they thought of their garden.

The dead tree, lying spread across the middle, was a nuisance; they cut it up. They found this exercise tiring. Bouvard very frequently had to take his tools to the blacksmith to be seen to.

One day, on his way there, he was accosted by a man carrying a canvas bag on his back, who offered him almanacs, pious books, medals that had been blessed, and finally the *Manual of Health* by François Raspail.

This pamphlet pleased him so much that he wrote to ask Barberou to send him the full work. Barberou despatched it, and in his letter mentioned a chemist for the medicines.

The doctrine delighted them with its clarity. All ailments come from worms. They rot the teeth, sap the lungs, enlarge the liver, ruin the intestines, and cause internal rumblings. The best thing for getting rid of them is camphor. Bouvard and Pécuchet took it up. They took it as snuff, ate it and distributed cigarettes, bottles of sedative water and pills made of aloes. They even undertook to cure a hunchback.

This was a boy they had met one day at the fair. His mother, a beggar woman, brought him along every morning. They rubbed his hump with camphorated grease, put a mustard poultice on it for twenty minutes, then covered it with sticking plaster, and, to ensure that he would come back, gave him something to eat.

Pécuchet, who was on the lookout for helminths, noticed a strange spot on Madame Bordin's cheek. For a long time the doctor had been treating it with bitters. Originally this spot had been the size of a franc piece, but it had grown larger and now formed a pinkish circle. They wanted to cure her. She accepted, but demanded that it should be Bouvard who applied the ointment. She stood in front of the window, undid the top of her dress and extended her cheek, while she gazed at him with a look that would have been dangerous but for the presence of Pécuchet. Keeping within permitted doses, and despite their dread of mercury, they administered calomel. A month later Madame Bordin was saved.

She did propaganda on their behalf, and the tax collector, the secretary at the Town Hall, the mayor himself, everyone in Chavignolles was sucking tubes cut from quills.

However the hunchback did not straighten up. The tax collector gave up his cigarettes, for they only made him choke all the more. Foureau complained of the aloes pills, which gave him piles. Bouvard had stomach ache and Pécuchet frightful headaches. They lost confidence in Raspail, but were careful to say nothing about it for fear of becoming discredited.

They displayed much enthusiasm for vaccines, learned how to let blood on cabbage leaves, even acquired a pair of lancets.

They went with the doctor on his rounds of the poor, then looked up their books.

The symptoms noted by the authors were not those they had just seen. As for the names of ailments, they were Latin, Greek, French, a medley of every language.

The number runs into thousands, and the Linnean classification is very convenient, with its genera and species; but how are the species to be established? Then they lost their way in the philosophy of medicine.

They dreamed about Van Helmont's archeus, vitalism, brownism, organicism; asked the doctor where the scrofula germ comes from, where contagious miasma attacks, and in all cases of morbidity how to distinguish cause and effect.

'Cause and effect are mixed up together,' answered Vaucorbeil.

They were disgusted at his lack of logic, and visited the sick alone, going into their homes on the pretext of philanthropy.

Lying on filthy mattresses in the furthest corner of their rooms were people whose faces drooped on one side, or were swollen and bright red, or pale yellow, or even purple, with pinched nostrils, trembling mouths, death rattles, hiccoughs, sweats, stinking of leather and stale cheese.

They read the doctor's prescriptions, and were very surprised that sedatives are sometimes stimulants, and emetics purgatives, that the same remedy is suitable for various complaints, and that the same ailment may disappear with opposite treatments.

Nevertheless they gave advice, cheered people up, dared to practise auscultation.

Their imagination worked apace. They wrote to the king to ask for the establishment in the Calvados of a nursing institute of which they would be professors.

They went off to the chemist in Bayeux (the one in Falaise was still annoyed with them because of his jujube) and persuaded him to make up *pila purgatoria* like the Ancients, that is medicinal pellets which the individual absorbs by handling them.

On the principle that inflammation can be prevented by lowering temperatures, they treated a woman suffering from meningitis by hanging her from the ceiling in her chair and pushing her to and fro, until her husband arrived and threw them out.

Moreover, to the curé's great scandal, they had adopted the new fashion of inserting thermometers into the rectum.

Typhoid began to spread in the neighbourhood; Bouvard declared that he would have nothing to do with it, but the wife of Gouy, their farmer, came groaning to them. Her husband had been ill for two weeks, and Monsieur Vaucorbeil was neglecting him.

Pécuchet did his duty.

Lenticular spots on the chest, pain in the joints, swollen belly, reddened tongue, all the symptoms of dothienentery. Remembering Raspail's dictum that fever goes when diet is ended, he prescribed broths and a little meat. Suddenly the doctor appeared.

His patient was actually eating, with two pillows at his back, propped up between his wife and Pécuchet.

The doctor went up to the bed, threw the plate out of the window and cried:

'It's downright murder!'

'Why?'

'You will perforate the intestine because typhoid fever is a disorder of the follicular membrane.'

'Not always!'

They began to argue about the nature of fevers. Pécuchet believed in their essence. Vaucorbeil claimed that they depended on the organs. 'So I forbid anything that might over-stimulate!'

'But dieting weakens the vital principle!'

'What's all this nonsense about a vital principle? What's it like? Has anyone seen it?'

Pécuchet became confused.

'Besides,' said the doctor, 'Gouy does not want any food.'

The patient nodded assent under his nightcap.

'No matter! He needs it!'

'Never! His pulse is ninety-eight.'

'What does the pulse rate matter?' and Pécuchet named his authorities.

'Forget about systems!' said the doctor.

Pécuchet folded his arms.

'You are an empiricist then?'

'Not at all! But by observing...'

'And if you observe wrong?'

Vaucorbeil took this remark as an allusion to Madame Bordin's herpes, a story put about maliciously by the widow, of which he did not like to be reminded.

'First of all one needs to have practised.'

'The men who revolutionized medicine never did! Van Helmont, Boerhave, Broussais himself.'

Without answering Vaucorbeil bent over Gouy and asked in a loud voice:

'Which of us do you choose as your doctor?'

The drowsy patient saw the angry faces and began to weep.

His wife did not know what to say either, because one was able; but perhaps the other had a secret?

'Very well!' said Vaucorbeil, 'since you hesitate between a man with a degree . . .' Pécuchet laughed. 'Why are you laughing?'

'Because a degree is not always an argument.'

The doctor was being attacked in his livelihood, in his prerogatives, his social standing. His anger burst out.

'We'll see about that when you find yourself in court for practising medicine illegally!' Then, turning to the farmer's wife: 'Let this gentleman kill him, just as you like, and I'll be damned if I ever set foot in your house again!'

He stormed off under the beeches, brandishing his stick.

When Pécuchet returned Bouvard also was extremely agitated.

He had just had a visit from Foureau, who was irritated by his piles. He had vainly maintained that they are a safeguard against all illnesses. Foureau had not listened to a word, and had threatened to sue him for damages. It was driving him mad.

Pécuchet told him the other story, which he thought was more serious, and was rather shocked at his indifference.

Next day Gouy had a pain in his abdomen. It might be the effect of taking food. Perhaps Vaucorbeil had not been wrong? A doctor after all ought to know something about it!

Pécucher was seized with remorse. He was afraid of causing a man's death.

For safety's sake they sent the hunchback away, but on account of the meal he had missed his mother made loud protests. It was not worth bringing them in every day from Barneval to Chavignolles!

Foureau calmed down and Gouy regained his strength. Cure was now certain; such success emboldened Pécuchet.

'If we worked at confinements, with one of those dummies . . .'

'Enough of dummies!'

'They are half bodies made of skin, invented for student midwives. I think I could turn the foetus round!'

But Bouvard was tired of medicine.

'The springs of life are hidden from us, ailments are too numerous, remedies questionable, and none of the authors offers any reasonable definition of health, sickness, diathesis or even pus!'

However, all this reading had disturbed their brains.

When Bouvard caught a cold he imagined he was starting a pulmonary inflammation. When leeches failed to reduce the pain in his side, he resorted to a vesicant, which affected his kidneys. Then he thought he had an attack of the stone.

Pécuchet became very stiff after trimming the arbour, and was sick after dinner, which gave him a nasty fright; then, noticing that he had gone rather yellow, he suspected liver infection, and asked himself: 'Do I have any pain?' And finished by having some.

They depressed each other, looking at their tongues, feeling their pulse, changing mineral water, taking purges, fearing cold, heat, wind, flies, draughts above all.

Pécuchet took it into his head that taking snuff was dangerous. Besides, a sneeze can sometimes cause an aneurism to burst, and he gave up his snuff-box. Out of habit he dipped his fingers into it, then suddenly remembered how unwise he was.

As black coffee upsets the nerves, Bouvard tried to give up his after-dinner cup, but he went to sleep after meals and was afraid when he woke, because prolonged sleep is a threatening sign of apoplexy.

Their ideal was Cornaro, the Venetian gentleman who, thanks to his diet, reached extreme old age. Without imitating him absolutely one can take the same precautions, and Pécuchet took out of his library a *Manual of Hygiene* by Dr Morin.

However had they managed to live so long? Their favourite dishes were forbidden. Germaine, perplexed, no longer knew what to serve them.

All kinds of meat have disadvantages. Black pudding and cooked meats, pickled herring, lobster and game are 'refractory'. The bigger a fish is, the more gelatine it contains and thus the heavier it is. Vegetables cause acidity, macaroni makes you dream, cheeses are 'in general difficult to digest'. A glass of water in the morning is 'dangerous'. Every food or drink was followed by a similar warning, or by the words: 'Bad! – Be careful not to abuse it! – Does not agree with everyone! –' Why bad? What is abuse? How can one know whether something agrees with one?

What a problem breakfast was! They gave up white coffee, because of its terrible reputation, and then chocolate, for it is 'a mass of indigestible substances'. So there remained tea. But 'nervous people should shun it completely'. However, Decker, in the seventeenth century, prescribed three and a half pints a day to flush out the pancreas.

This information shook their respect for Morin, and all the more so as he condemns all headgear, hats, bonnets, and caps, a requirement that revolted Pécuchet.

Then they bought Becquerel's treatise, in which they saw that pork in itself is 'a good food', tobacco perfectly harmless, coffee 'essential for soldiers'.

Up till then they had believed that damp places are unhealthy. Not at all! Casper asserts that they are less dangerous than others. One should not bathe in the sea without first cooling down one's skin. Bégin thinks it better to plunge in actually sweating. Neat wine after soup is supposed to be good for the stomach. Lévy says it is responsible for rotting the teeth. As for the flannel waistcoat, that safeguard, that health preserver, that palladium dear to Bouvard's heart and inherent to Pécuchet, these authors, quite bluntly and regardless of anyone's opinion, advise against its use by corpulent and sanguine subjects.

What then is hygiene?

'True on one side of the Pyrenees, false on the other,' affirms Monsieur Lévy, and Becquerel adds that it is not a science.

So they ordered for dinner oysters, duck, pork with cabbage, cream, a Pont-l'Évêque and a bottle of Burgundy. It was a liberation, almost a revenge, and they scoffed at Cornaro! How stupid one must be to subject oneself to such tyranny! How ignoble to think all the time of prolonging one's existence! Life is only good if it is enjoyed.

'Another bit?' – 'I don't mind if I do.' – 'Me too!' – 'Your health!' – 'And yours!' – 'And to hell with the rest!'

They were in the highest spirits.

Bouvard announced that he wanted three cups of coffee, although he was not a soldier. Pécuchet, cap pulled down over his ears, took pinch after pinch of snuff, sneezed intrepidly; and feeling the need for a little champagne they ordered Germaine to go at once to the tavern and buy them a bottle. The village was too far. She refused. Pécuchet was indignant.

'I order you, do you hear? I order you to go there!'

She obeyed, but with grumbles, determined to leave her masters soon, so incomprehensible and fanciful had they become.

Then, as they used to, they went to have their glass of spirits on the mound with the vine.

The harvest was just over, and the dark masses of the stacks in the middle of the fields rose up against the soft blue of the night sky. The farms were still. Even the crickets were no longer to be heard. The whole countryside was asleep. They digested their dinner, savouring the breeze, cool on their cheeks.

The sky was very high, and covered with stars; some shone in clusters, others in line, or alone at long intervals. An area of luminous dust, going from north to south, split into two above their heads. Between these bright patches were great empty spaces, and the firmament looked like an azure sea, with archipelagoes and islands.

'What a quantity!' cried Bouvard.

'We can't see everything!' replied Pécuchet. 'Behind the Milky Way are the nebulae; beyond the nebulae, still more stars; the nearest is 300 billion myriameters from us.' He had often looked through the telescope in the Place Vendôme, and remembered the figures. 'The sun is a million times bigger than the earth, Sirius twelve times bigger than the sun, comets are 34,000,000 leagues long!'

'It's enough to drive one mad,' said Bouvard.

He deplored his ignorance, and was even sorry that in his youth he had not been at the École Polytechnique.

Then Pécuchet, turning him towards the Great Bear, showed him the Pole Star, then Cassiopeia, with its Y-shaped constellation, Vega of the Lyre, all sparkling, and low on the horizon, the red Aldebaran.

Bouvard, with head thrown back, had difficulty in following the triangles, quadrilaterals and pentagons which one must picture to oneself in order to find one's way about the sky.

Pécuchet went on:

'The speed of light is 80,000 leagues a second. A ray from the Milky Way takes six centuries to reach us. In fact one can look at a star that has already disappeared. Several are intermittent, others never come back; and they change position; everything is in motion, everything is transitory.'

'But the sun does not move!'

'They used to think so, but nowadays scientists tell us that it is rushing towards the constellation of Hercules!'

That upset Bouvard's ideas, and after a moment's reflection:

'Science is built up of data provided by one corner of the whole expanse. Perhaps it does not apply to all the rest that we do not know, which is much bigger, and can't be discovered!'

They talked like this, standing on the mound, in the starlight, and their remarks were interspersed with long silences.

Then they wondered if there were men in the stars. Why not? And as creation is harmonious, the inhabitants of Sirius ought to be huge, those of Mars middle-sized, those of Venus very small. Unless it is the same everywhere. There are businessmen, police up there; people trade, fight, dethrone their kings.

Some shooting stars suddenly slid past, describing a course in the sky like the parabola of a monstrous rocket.

'My word,' said Bouvard, 'look at those worlds disappearing.'

Pécuchet replied:

'If our world in its turn danced about the citizens of the stars would be no more impressed than we are now. Ideas like that are rather humbling.'

'What is the point of it all?'

'Perhaps there isn't a point.'

'Yet . . .' and Pécuchet repeated the word two or three times, without finding anything more to say.

'It doesn't matter, I should like to know how the universe came about.'

'It must be in Buffon,' answered Bouvard, whose eyes were closing.

'I can't go on any more. I'm going to bed!'

The *Natural Epochs* told them that a comet striking the sun had knocked off a piece, which became the earth. First the poles had cooled down. All the waters had covered the globe; they had withdrawn into hollows, then the continents divided off, animals and man appeared.

The majesty of Creation caused them an awe as infinite as itself.

Their heads expanded. They were proud of reflecting on such grand subjects.

It was not long before minerals wearied them, and they sought distraction in the *Harmonies* of Bernardin de Saint-Pierre.

Harmonies vegetable and terrestrial, aerial, aquatic, human, fraternal, even conjugal, everything was there, not to mention invocation to Venus, the Zephyrs and the Loves. They were amazed that fish have fins, birds wings, seeds a husk – full of that philosophy which discovers virtuous intentions in nature and regards it as a kind of St Vincent de Paul always busy distributing benefits.

Next they admired its prodigies, tornadoes, volcanoes, virgin forests, and they bought Monsieur Depping's book on the *Wonders and Beauties of Nature in France*. Cantal has three, Hérault five, Burgundy two, not more, while Dauphiné has to its credit as many as fifteen wonders. The stalactite grottoes are getting blocked up, burning mountains are going out, natural icehouses are warming up, and the old trees in which services used to be held are falling beneath the levellers' axe or dying off.

Then their curiosity turned to the animals

They opened Buffon again and went into ecstasies at the peculiar tastes of certain animals.

But as all books put together are not as good as personal observation, they went into farmyards and asked the farmhands if they had bulls coupling with mares, pigs going after cows, and male partridges committing acts of moral turpitude together.

'Never in my life.' People even found such questions rather odd for gentlemen of their age.

They wanted to try some abnormal mating.

The least difficult is that of the goat and the ewe. Their farmer did not possess a goat, but a neighbour lent hers, and when the rutting season came round they shut up the two beasts in the cider press, and hid behind the casks so that the event could take place in peace.

Each of the animals first ate its little heap of hay, then ruminated; the ewe lay down, and bleated continuously, while the goat, balanced on his crooked legs, with his great beard and drooping ears, fixed them with his eyes, gleaming in the shadow.

At last, on the evening of the third day, they thought it proper to give Nature some help; but the goat, rounding on Pécuchet, butted him with its horns in the stomach. The ewe, seized with terror, began turning round in the press as if in a roundabout. Bouvard ran after her, leaped on her to hold her back, and fell down with fistfuls of wool in both hands.

They made fresh attempts with hens and a duck, a mastiff and a sow, in the hope that monsters would result, but quite failing to understand anything about the question of species.

This is the word that designates a group of individuals whose descendants reproduce, but animals classified as different species may reproduce, and others, included in the same species, have lost the ability to do so.

They flattered themselves into thinking that they would get a clear idea of all this by studying the development of germs, and Pécuchet wrote to Dumouchel for a microscope.

On the glass plate they placed successively hairs, tobacco, nails, a fly's leg, but had forgotten the indispensable drop of water. At other times it was the small lens, and they jostled each other, upset the instrument, then, seeing nothing but a blur, accused the optician. They came to have doubts about the microscope. The discoveries attributed to it are perhaps not so positive after all.

When Dumouchel sent them the invoice he asked them to collect for him some ammonites and sea urchins, curiosities in which he was always interested and which were common in their part of the world. To arouse their interest in geology he sent them Bertrand's *Letters* and Cuvier's *Discourses on the Revolutions of the Globe*.

After reading these two books they worked things out as follows:

First there was a huge sheet of water, from which emerged promontories spotted with lichens, but not a living creature, not a sound. It was a bare world, silent and still; then long plants began to sway in a mist resembling the steam from a bathhouse. A completely red sun overheated the humid atmosphere. Then volcanoes erupted, igneous rocks spurted from the mountains, and the flowing magma of porphyry and basalt congealed. Third scene: in shallow seas coral islands have arisen; a clump of palm trees dominates them here and there. There are shells like cartwheels, tortoises nine feet long, lizards sixty feet long, through the reeds amphibians stretch their ostrich necks with crocodile jaws; winged serpents take flight.

Finally on the main continents large mammals appeared, with limbs misshapen like badly cut pieces of wood, hide thicker than bronze plates, or perhaps hairy, thick-lipped, with manes and curving tusks. Herds of mammoth grazed over the plains where the Atlantic later came; the paleotherium, half horse, half tapir, used his snout to knock over the ant-hills of Montmartre and the *cervus giganteus* trembled beneath the chestnut trees at the roar of the cave bear, which made the Beaugency dog, three times taller than a wolf, bark in his den.

All these ages had been separated by cataclysms, the last of which was our Flood. It was all like a fairy story in several acts, with man as its apotheosis.

They were stupefied to learn that the traces of dragon-fly and birds' feet can be found on stones, and after leafing through one of the Roret manuals, they went out looking for fossils.

One afternoon as they were turning over flints in the middle of the highway, the curé passed, and addressed them in an unctuous voice:

'You gentlemen have taken up geology? Excellent.'

Because he had a high regard for that science. It confirms the authority of Scripture by proving the Flood.

Bouvard spoke of coprolites, which are petrified animal excrement.

Abbé Jeufroy seemed surprised at the fact; after all, if it was so, that was one more reason for marvelling at Providence.

Pécuchet confessed that so far their investigations had not been fruitful, yet the surroundings of Falaise, like all Jurassic areas, should abound in animal remains.

'I have heard,' replied Abbé Jeufroy, 'that they once found an elephant's jaw at Villers.' Besides, one of his friends, Monsieur Larsonneur, advocate, member of the Lisieux bar and an archaeologist, would perhaps supply them with information! He had written a history of Port-en-Bessin in which the discovery of a crocodile was noted.

Bouvard and Pécuchet exchanged glances, the same hope had struck them, and despite the heat they stood for a long time questioning the ecclesiastic, who was sheltering beneath a blue cotton umbrella. The lower part of his face was rather heavy, he had a pointed nose, and smiled continually, or bent his head and closed his eyes.

The church bell sounded the Angelus.

'A very good evening to you, gentlemen! You don't mind, do you?'

With his recommendation they waited three weeks for Larsonneur's answer. At last it arrived.

The Villers man who had dug up the mastodon tooth was called Louis Bloche; there were no details. As for his history, it took up one of the volumes of the Lisieux Academy, and he did not lend out his copy for fear of breaking the collection. As for the alligator, it had been found in November 1825, under the cliff called les Hachettes, at Sainte-Honorine, near Port-en-Bessin, arrondissement of Bayeux. Followed his compliments.

The obscurity surrounding the mastodon tantalized Pécuchet. He would have liked to go to Villers right away.

Bouvard objected that to save a journey which might be pointless and certainly expensive, it would be advisable to seek information, and they wrote the mayor of the place a letter asking what had become of a certain Louis Bloche. Assuming that he was dead, could his descendants or collaterals tell them anything about his precious discovery? When he made it, whereabouts in the commune was this witness of primitive ages lying? Was there any chance of finding similar ones? What did it cost *per diem* to hire a man and a cart?

In vain they addressed the deputy, then the senior municipal councillor; they had no news from Villers. No doubt the inhabitants were jealous of their fossils? Unless they sold them to the English. The journey to les Hachettes was fixed.

Bouvard and Pécuchet took the coach from Falaise to Caen. Then a gig carried them from Caen to Bayeux; and from Bayeux they went on foot to Port-en-Bessin.

They had not been misled. The coast of les Hachettes offered some strange pebbles, and following the innkeeper's directions they reached the shore.

It was low tide, all the pebbles were uncovered, with a whole meadow of seaweed stretching down to the water's edge.

Grassy hollows divided up the cliff, which was composed of a soft brown earth which, when it hardened, became a wall of grey stone in its lower strata. Streams of water ran down from it constantly, while in the distance the booming of the waves could be heard. Their thunder seemed to be sometimes suspended; and all that could then be heard was the soft sound of the springs.

They stumbled over sticky grass, or had to jump over holes. Bouvard sat by the shore, and gazed at the waves, without a thought, fascinated, inert. Pécuchet took him towards the cliffs to show him an ammonite encrusted in the rock, like a diamond in its gangue. They broke their nails on it, they needed tools, and in any case night was falling. In the west the sky was deep red and the whole beach lay in shadow. In the middle of the almost black seaweed the pools grew wider. The sea was coming up towards them; it was time to go back.

Next day as soon as day broke they attacked their fossil with pick and mattock, and its covering burst. It was an *ammonites nodosus*, eroded at the ends, but weighing a good sixteen pounds, and in his enthusiasm Pécuchet cried: 'We cannot do less than offer it to Dumouchel!'

Then they encountered sponges, terebratulae, orcs, but no crocodiles! Failing this they were hoping for a vertebra from a hippopotamus or ichthyosaurus, any bone from the time of the flood, when they made out against the cliff, as high as a man, contours representing the curve of a gigantic fish.

They discussed the best means of obtaining it.

Bouvard would disengage it from above, while Pécuchet, from below, would demolish the rock to bring it down gently without damage.

As they were getting their breath back they saw above their heads, in the field, a customs officer in a cloak who was beckoning to them in peremptory fashion.

'Well, what is it? Stop pestering us!' And they went on with their task, Bouvard on tiptoe, chipping away with his mattock, Pécuchet, bent double, digging with his pick.

But the customs man appeared lower down, in a valley, signalling more than ever; much they cared! An oval body swelled out beneath the now thin layer of soil, began to lean, was about to slip.

Another individual with a sabre suddenly appeared.

'Your passports?'

It was the rural constable on his rounds, and at the same moment the customs man arrived, running up from a ravine.

'Get hold of them, Morin, old chap! or the cliff will collapse!'

'It is in the interests of science,' answered Pécuchet.

Then a mass fell, brushing so close that the four of them only missed death by inches.

When the dust had cleared away they recognized a ship's mast which crumbled under the customs man's boot.

Bouvard said with a sigh: 'We were not doing any harm!'

'You are not allowed to do anything in an official Engineers' Zone!' replied the constable.

'First of all, who are you, so I can draw up the charge?'

Pécuchet protested, crying against injustice.

'Stop arguing! Follow me!'

As soon as they arrived at the port a crowd of urchins escorted them. Bouvard, red as a poppy, tried to look dignified; Pécuchet, very pale, glared round furiously; and these two strangers, carrying pebbles in their handkerchiefs, did not look very prepossessing. Provisionally they were assigned to the inn, whose proprietor stood at the door, blocking entry. Then the mason asked for his tools back. They paid for them, more expense! And the constable did not come back! Why? At last a gentleman, wearing a decoration, set them free, and they went away, leaving their names, forenames and address, promising to be more careful in future.

Besides a passport they needed a lot of things, and before embarking on fresh explorations they consulted the *Travelling Geologist's Guide* by Boué.

In the first place one must have a good military haversack, then a surveyor's chain, a file, crowbars, a compass, and three hammers stuck in a belt concealed under one's coat 'thus saving you from the conspicuous appearance which travellers should avoid'. For a stick Pécuchet simply adopted a tourist's staff, six feet long, with a long iron tip. Bouvard preferred an umbrella-stick or multi-branched umbrella, with retractable knob for fastening the silk, contained in a separate little bag. They did not forget stout shoes with gaiters, each one had 'two pairs of braces, because of perspiration' and although you cannot 'go everywhere in a cap' they shrank from the expense of 'one of those folding hats, named Gibus after the hatter, their inventor'.

The same work gives rules of behaviour: 'Know the language of the country to be visited'; they knew it. 'Maintain a correct bearing'; they usually did. 'Do not carry too much money'; nothing simpler. Finally to save all kinds of embarrassment, it is a good thing to travel 'as engineers'.

'Very well! We shall do so!'

Thus prepared they began their expeditions, were sometimes away for a week at a time, living out in the open air.

On the banks of the Orne they would notice, in a gap, rocky outcrops rising obliquely among poplars and heather, or be depressed at finding only layers of clay along their path. Faced with a landscape, what impressed them was not the series of perspectives, or the depth of a distance, or the rolling greenery, but what could not be seen, what was beneath, the earth, and all hills were for them 'one more proof of the Flood'. Obsession with the Flood gave way to an obsession with erratic blocks. Large single stones in the fields must originate from vanished glaciers, and they looked for moraine and shell marl.

They were frequently taken for pedlars, because of their attire, and when they answered that they were 'engineers' they had some misgivings; usurpation of such a title might entail disagreeable consequences.

At the end of the day they would be panting under the weight of their samples, but, nothing daunted, brought them home. They had them along the steps, up the stairs, in the bedrooms, the living-room, the kitchen, and Germaine bemoaned the amount of dust.

It was no small task, before sticking on the labels, to know what the rocks were called; the variety of colours and grain made them mix up clay and marl, granite and gneiss, quartz and limestone.

Then the nomenclature irked them. Why Devonian, Cambrian, Jurassic, as though the lands designated by these words existed only in Devon, near Cambridge and in the Jura? It is impossible to find one's way about it; what is system for one is stage for another, a mere course for a third. The sheets of the strata intermingle, become confused; but Omalius d'Halloy warns you not to believe in geological divisions.

This declaration relieved them, and when they had seen limestone with polypiers in the Caen plain, phyllades at Balleroy, kaolin at Saint-Blaise, oolite everywhere, and looked for coal at Cartigny and mercury at La-Chapelle-en-Juger, near Saint-Lô, they decided on a more distant excursion, a journey to Le Havre, to study pyromachous quartz and Kimmeridge clay.

As soon as they left the boat they asked for the road which runs below the lighthouse; it was blocked by landslides, and dangerous to anyone venturing on it.

A carriage hirer accosted them and offered excursions in the neighbourhood: Ingouville, Octeville, Fécamp, Lillebonne, 'Rome if need be'.

His prices were unreasonable, but the name of Fécamp had struck them; with a small detour from the road one could see Étretat, and they took the Fécamp coach to do the greater distance first.

In the coach Bouvard and Pécuchet made conversation with three peasants, two women and a seminarist, and did not hesitate to describe themselves as engineers.

They stopped before the harbour. They made for the cliff, and five minutes later skirted it to avoid a great pool of water advancing like a gulf in the middle of the shore. Then they saw an arcade opening onto a deep cave; it was sonorous, very light, like a church, with columns from top to bottom and a carpet of seaweed all along its floor.

This work of nature astonished them, and gave rise to lofty considerations about the origin of the world.

Bouvard inclined to neptunism, Pécuchet on the other hand was plutonian.

The central fire had broken the global crust, raised up land formations, caused crevasses. It is like an inner sea, with its ebb and flow, its storms; a thin film separates it from us. There would be no sleep for anyone who thought of all that lies underfoot. However the central fire is diminishing and the sun is growing weaker, so that one day the earth will die of cold. It will become sterile; all the wood and all the coal will have been converted into carbonic acid, and no life will be able to survive.

'We are not there yet,' said Bouvard.

'Let's hope so,' replied Pécuchet.

All the same, the end of the world, remote as it might be, made them despondent, and they walked side by side silently over the pebbles.

The cliff, perpendicular, all white, streaked in black here and there by bands of flint, ran off towards the horizon, like the curve of a rampart twelve miles long. A bitter cold east wind was blowing. The sky was grey, the sea greenish and looking almost swollen. From the top of the rocks birds flew up, wheeled, quickly came back to their holes. Sometimes a stone came loose, and bounced from place to place before coming down to them.

Pécuchet continued thinking aloud:

'Unless the earth is annihilated by a cataclysm! No one knows the length of our period. The central fire has only to go out of control.'

'But it is diminishing?'

'That has not stopped eruptions producing the island of Julia, Monte Nuovo, and many others too.' Bouvard remembered reading these details in Bertrand.

'But such cataclysms do not occur in Europe?'

'I'm very sorry, but look at the Lisbon one. As for our part of the world, there are a large number of coal and iron pyrite mines which could easily decompose and form volcanic outlets. In any case volcanoes always erupt near the sea.'

Bouvard looked out over the waves, and thought he could make out a distant plume of smoke going up towards the sky.

'Since the island of Julia,' replied Pécuchet, 'has disappeared, perhaps formations produced by the same cause will go the same way. One of the islands of the Archipelago is as important as Normandy, even Europe.'

Bouvard imagined Europe swallowed up in an abyss.

'Suppose,' said Pécuchet, 'that an earthquake takes place under the Channel; the water rushes into the Atlantic; the coasts of France and England totter on their bases, lean over, join up and presto! Everything between is crushed!'

Instead of answering Bouvard began to walk so fast that he was soon a hundred yards ahead of Pécuchet. Being alone he was disturbed by the idea of a cataclysm. He had not eaten since the morning; there was a throbbing in his temples. Suddenly the soil seemed to shudder and the top of the cliff above his head seemed to lean over. At that moment a shower of gravel rolled down from above.

Pécuchet saw him in headlong flight, understood his terror and cried from afar:

'Stop! Stop! The period is not over!'

Trying to catch him up he took enormous bounds, with his tourist's staff, bellowing the while: 'The period is not over! The period is not over!'

Bouvard, quite beside himself, kept running. The multi-branched umbrella fell, the skirts of his coat went flying, the haversack bounced on his back. He looked like a winged tortoise galloping among the rocks; one of the larger ones hid him from sight.

Pécuchet arrived there out of breath, saw no one, then turned back to reach the fields by a little valley which Bouvard had no doubt taken.

The narrow path was cut out in large steps up the cliff. the width of two men, gleaming like polished alabaster.

When he was fifty feet up Pécuchet wanted to come down. As the tide was on the flood he began scrambling.

At the second turning ,when he saw the void, he froze with fear. As he came nearer the third his legs went limp. The layers of air vibrated round him, he was seized by cramp in the pit of his stomach; he sat down, with his eyes closed, no longer conscious of anything but the heartbeats choking him; then he threw away his tourist staff, and started climbing up again on hands and knees. But the three hammers fastened to his belt stuck into his stomach; the pebbles stuffed into his pockets banged his ribs; the peak of his cap blinded him; the wind became twice as strong. Finally he reached level ground and there found Bouvard, who had come up further along, by a less difficult valley.

A cart picked them up. They forgot about Étretat.

Next evening, at Le Havre, as they were waiting for the boat, they saw at the bottom of a newspaper a serial article entitled: 'On Teaching Geology'.

This article, full of facts, set out the question as it was understood at the time:

There had never been a complete global cataclysm, but a given species does not always last the same length of time, and becomes more quickly extinct in one place than another. Formations of the same age contain different fossils, just as widely distant formations contain similar ones. Ferns of past times are identical with those of the present. Many contemporary zoophytes are to be found in the most ancient strata. In brief, present modifications explain previous upheavals. The same causes always operate, there are no jumps in nature, and periods, Brongniart asserts, are after all only abstractions.

Up till then Cuvier had appeared to them in the radiance of a halo, at the height of an incontrovertible science. This was now sapped. Creation no longer showed the same discipline, and their respect for this great man decreased.

Through biographies and extracts they learned about the doctrines of Lamarck and Geoffroy de Saint-Hilaire.

All this went against received ideas, the authority of the Church.

Bouvard had a sense of relief as though a yoke had been broken.

'I should like to see now how citizen Jeufroy would answer my questions about the Flood!'

They found him in his small garden, where he was waiting for the members of the vestry, due to meet shortly about acquiring a chasuble.

'You gentlemen would like ...?'

'A clarification, if you please.'

And Bouvard began:

What did Genesis mean with 'the fountains of the great deep were broken up' and 'the windows of the heavens'? Because a great deep does not break and the heavens do not have windows!

The priest shut his eyes, then answered: that one must always distinguish between the sense and the letter. Things which begin by shocking us become legitimate as one goes into them more deeply.

'Very well! But how do you explain the rain which rose above the highest mountains, which are five miles high? Just think, five miles! Water as much as five miles deep!'

The mayor, coming up, added: 'Goodness me, what a bath!'

'You must agree,' said Bouvard, 'Moses exaggerates terribly.'

The curé had read Bonald and replied: 'I don't know his reasons; it was partly to give a salutary fright to the people he was leading.'

'But where did this mass of water come from?'

'How do I know? Air changed into rain, it happens every day.'

Through the garden gate came Monsieur Girbal, the tax inspector, with Captain Heurtaux, a landowner, and Beljambe, the innkeeper, gave an arm to Langlois, the grocer who walked with difficulty because of his catarrh.

Pécuchet, disregarding them, took up the discussion:

'Excuse me, Monsieur Jeufroy, the weight of the atmosphere, as science demonstrates, is equal to that of a mass of water covering the globe to a depth of ten metres. Consequently if all the condensed air fell on it in a liquid state it would cause very little increase in the mass of water already in existence.'

The members of the vestry opened their eyes wide and listened.

The curé became impatient.

'Do you deny that seashells have been found on mountains? Who put them there but the Flood? They don't usually, I believe, grow by themselves in the earth like carrots!' This remark made the company laugh, so he added tight-lipped: 'Unless this is yet another scientific discovery?'

Bouvard tried to answer with Élie de Beaumont's theory of how the mountains rose.

'Never heard of him!' replied the abbé.

Foureau hastened to say: 'He is from Caen! I saw him once at the Prefecture!'

'But if your Flood,' Bouvard went on, 'had transported seashells you would find them broken on the surface and not sometimes 300 metres down.'

The priest fell back on the veracity of Scripture, the tradition of the human race, and the animals discovered in the ice, in Siberia.

That does not prove that man lived at the same time as they! The earth, according to Pécuchet, was considerably older. 'The Mississippi delta goes back tens of thousands of years. The present age is 100,000 years old at least. Manéthon's lists...'

The Comte de Faverges came up.

All fell silent at his approach.

'Do go on, please! What were you saying?'

'These gentlemen were having an argument with me,' answered the abbé.

'What about?'

'Holy Scripture, Monsieur le Comte!'

Bouvard at once claimed that they were entitled as geologists to discuss religion.

'Take care,' said the count, 'you know the saying, my dear sir; a little learning takes you away, a lot brings you back.' And in a tone that was both haughty and paternal: 'Believe me! You'll come back! You'll come back!'

Maybe! But what is one to think of a book in which it is claimed that light was created before the sun, as though the sun was not the sole cause of light!

'You forget the so-called Northern Lights,' said the ecclesiastic.

Without answering the objection, Bouvard firmly denied that light can have been on one side and darkness on the other, that there can have been evening and morning when there were as yet no stars, and that the animals appeared suddenly, instead of being formed by crystallization.

The paths were too narrow, so their gesticulations led them to walk over the flowerbeds. Langlois was overcome by a fit of coughing. The captain cried: 'You are revolutionaries!' Girbal: 'Peace! Peace!' The priest: 'What materialism!' Foureau: 'Let's discuss our chasuble instead!'

'No! Let me speak!' and Bouvard in his excitement actually said that man is descended from the ape!

All the vestry looked at one another, quite astonished, and as if to reassure themselves that they were not apes.

Bouvard went on: 'If you compare the foetus of a woman, a bitch, a bird...'

'That will do!'

'Well, I'll go further!' cried Pécuchet: 'Man is descended from the fishes!' There was a burst of laughter which left him unperturbed: 'The *Telliamed*, an Arabic book...'

'Come gentlemen, to our meeting!'

And they went into the sacristy.

The two companions had not got the better of Abbé Jeufroy as they had expected, so Pécuchet found in him the 'mark of Jesuitry'.

The Northern Lights worried them however, and they looked them up in d'Orbigny's manual.

It is a hypothesis to explain how the vegetable fossils of Baffin Bay resemble equatorial plants. Instead of the sun there is supposed to have been a great source of light, now vanished, of which the Aurora Borealis is perhaps just the remnant.

Then they had doubts about the origin of man – and they thought uneasily of Vaucorbeil.

His threats had not produced any effects. As before he went past their gate in the morning, rattling his stick against the bars, one after another.

Bouvard looked out for him, stopped him and said he wanted to put to him a curious point of anthropology.

'Do you believe that the human race is descended from fishes?'

'What nonsense!'

'From apes, rather, don't you think?'

'Directly? Quite impossible!'

Who was to be trusted? For the doctor was not even a Catholic!

They continued their studies, but without enthusiasm, being tired of eocene and miocene, Mount Jorullo, the island of Julia, Siberian mammoths and fossils, invariably compared by all the authors to 'medals which are authentic testimony', so that one day Bouvard threw down his haversack and declared that he would go no further.

Geology is too defective! We hardly know more than a few parts of Europe. As for the rest, including the sea bed, we shall never know about it.

Finally Pécuchet uttered the word 'mineral kingdom'.

'I don't believe in it, this mineral kingdom! Since organic matter contributed to the formation of flint, chalk, perhaps gold! Weren't diamonds once carbon? Coal a collection of vegetable matter? If you heat it up to I forget how many degrees you get sawdust, so that everything decays, crumbles, changes form. Creation is put together in such an elusive and transitory fashion; we should do better to take up something else!'

He lay on his back and began to doze, while Pécuchet with head bowed and one knee clasped in his hands gave himself up to his own reflections.

A border of moss ran along the edges of a sunken lane shaded by ash trees, with gracefully quivering tops; angelica, mint, lavender, gave off warm, spicy smells; the atmosphere was heavy; and Pécuchet in a kind of daze dreamed of the countless beings scattered around him, the buzzing insects, the springs hidden beneath the grass, the sap in the plants, the birds in their nests, the wind, the clouds, the whole of nature, without trying to discover her mysteries, charmed by her strength, lost in her grandeur.

'I'm thirsty!' said Bouvard as he woke up.

'So am I! I should like a drink of something.'

'That's easy,' replied a man passing by, in shirt sleeves, with a plank on his shoulder.

They recognized the tramp to whom Bouvard had once given a glass of wine. He looked ten years younger, wore his hair in kiss-curls, a waxed moustache, and swayed his hips like a Parisian.

After about a hundred yards he opened a gate into a yard, threw his plank against a wall and showed them into a high kitchen.

'Mélie! Are you there, Mélie?'

A girl appeared, was ordered to 'get us something to drink', and came back to the table to serve the gentlemen.

Her corn-coloured headbands showed under a grey linen bonnet. All her poor clothes hung down on her without a crease, and with her straight nose and blue eyes she gave an impression of something delicate, rustic, simple.

'She is nice, isn't she?' said the carpenter, while she was bringing some glasses. 'You could almost swear she was a young lady got up as a peasant! And a hard worker, too! Poor love, when I am rich I'll marry you!'

'You are always talking nonsense, Monsieur Gorju,' she answered in a soft voice, with a drawling accent.

A stable lad came to collect oats from an old chest and dropped the lid so hard that a chip of wood flew off it.

Gorju railed at the clumsiness of all 'these yokels', then kneeling in front of the chest looked to see where the bit had come from. Pécuchet, trying to help him, made out some human figures under the dust.

It was a Renaissance chest, with twisted cord decoration at the bottom, vine branches in the corners, and small columns dividing its front into five compartments. In the middle appeared Venus

Anadyomene standing on a shell, then Hercules and Omphale, Samson and Delilah, Circe and her swine, Lot's daughters getting their father drunk; all dilapidated, moth-eaten and even lacking the right-hand panel. Gorju took a candle to show Pécuchet the left-hand one better; it presented Adam and Eve beneath the tree of Paradise in a highly indecent posture.

Bouvard also admired the chest.

'If you like you could get it cheap.'

They hesitated, in view of the repairs.

Gorju could do them, being a cabinet-maker by trade.

'Come along! This way!'

And he pulled Pécuchet towards the yard, where Madame Castillon, the mistress, was putting out her washing.

When Mélie had washed her hands she took up her lacemaking frame from the window-sill, sat fully in the light and set to work.

She was framed in the lintel of the door, the bobbins went in and out under her fingers with a noise like castanets. She remained bent in profile.

Bouvard asked her about her parents, where she came from, what she was paid.

She was from Ouistreham, had no family left, earned one franc a month; in the end he liked her so much that he wanted to take her into service to help old Germaine.

Pécuchet came back with the farmer's wife, and while they went on bargaining, Bouvard asked Gorju in a very low voice if the little maid would agree to become his servant.

'Bless my soul!'

'But,' said Bouvard, 'I'll have to consult my friend.'

'All right, I'll act accordingly; but don't say anything about it, because of the old girl!'

The deal had just been concluded, for a sum of thirty-five francs. The repairs would be by agreement.

Bouvard had no sooner gone out into the yard before he disclosed his intentions with regard to Mélie.

Pécuchet stopped, so as to think better, opened his snuff-box, took a sniff, blew his nose, and said:

'Indeed, that's an idea! Goodness yes! Why not? Besides, you are in charge!'

Ten minutes later Gorju appeared on the edge of a ditch and hailed them:

'When do you want me to bring the chest?'

'Tomorrow!'

'And have you made up your mind on the other question?'

'Agreed!' answered Pécuchet.

4

SIX months later they had become archaeologists, and their house looked like a museum.

An old wooden beam stood in the vestibule. Geological specimens cluttered up the staircase, and an enormous chain stretched along the floor for the whole length of the corridor.

They had taken out the connecting door between the two spare bedrooms and blocked the outside entrance to the second to make the two rooms into one.

Just inside one bumped into a stone trough (a Gallo-Roman sarcophagus), then a display of ironmongery caught the eye.

Against the opposite wall a warming-pan rose above two firedogs and a hearth-plate representing a monk fondling a shepherdess. On shelves all round stood torches, locks, bolts, screws. Shards of red tiles hid the floor. On a table in the middle were exhibited the rarest curiosities: the frame of a bonnet from Caux, two clay urns, some medals, a phial of opaline glass. Over the back of a tapestry chair lay a triangle of lace. A bit of chain mail adorned the partition on the right, and below it a halberd, a unique piece, was held horizontally on spikes.

The second room, two steps down, contained the old books brought from Paris, and those they had discovered in a cupboard when they arrived. They had taken off the doors and called it the library.

The genealogical tree of the Croixmare family took up the whole back of the door. On the reverse panels the pastel of a lady in Louis XV costume matched the portrait of Bouvard père. The mirror's casing was decorated by a black felt sombrero, and a monstrous clog, still full of leaves, the remains of a bird's nest.

Two coconuts (Pécuchet had had them since boyhood) stood on the mantelpiece, flanking an earthenware barrel with a peasant astride it. Nearby, in a straw basket, was a coin brought up by a duck.

In front of the library stood a chest of drawers made of shells, with plush ornaments. Its lid supported a cat with a mouse in its jaws, a petrification from Saint-Allyre, a work-box also made from shells, and on this box a carafe of spirits contained a bon-chrétien pear.

But the best of all was in the window embrasure, a statue of St Peter! His gloved hand clutched the key to Paradise, coloured apple-green. His chasuble, decorated with fleurs-de-lis, was sky-blue, and his bright yellow tiara was pointed like a pagoda. His cheeks were rouged, he had great round eyes, gaping mouth and a crooked, turned-up nose. Above hung a canopy made of an old carpet on which two cupids in a circle of roses could be made out, and at his feet, like a column, stood a butter jar, with these words in white letters on a chocolate background: 'Executed before H.R.H. the Duc d'Angoulême, at Noron, the 3rd October 1817.'

From his bed Pécuchet could see all this in enfilade and sometimes he even went into Bouvard's room to extend the perspective.

A place remained empty opposite the coat of mail: the one reserved for the Renaissance chest.

It was not finished. Gorju was still working on it, planing the panels in the bakehouse, adjusting them, dismounting them.

At eleven o'clock he had lunch, then chatted to Mélie, and often did not put in another appearance for the rest of the day.

Bouvard and Pécuchet had taken the field in a search for pieces to go with the chest. What they brought back was unsuitable, but they had come across a lot of curious objects. They had acquired a taste for knick-knacks, then a love for the Middle Ages.

First they visited the cathedrals, and the lofty naves reflected in the holy water stoups, the stained glass windows, as dazzling as jewelled hangings, the tombs at the back of the chapels, the dim light of the crypts, everything, even the chill stone walls, gave them a shiver of delight, a religious emotion.

Soon they were able to distinguish the different periods, and scorning the sacristans they would say: 'Ah! A romanesque apse! That is twelfth century! There we are back in the flamboyant!'

They tried to understand the symbols carved on the stone capitals, like the two griffons of Marigny pecking at a tree in blossom; Pécuchet saw satire in the choirmen with grotesque jaws who terminate the strapwork at Feugerolles; and as for the exuberantly obscene man covering one of the mullions of Hérouville, according to Bouvard, that proved that our ancestors were fond of bawdy jokes.

They ended up by finding the least mark of decadence quite intolerable. Everything was decadent, and they deplored vandalism and fulminated against whitewash.

But a monument's style does not always agree with its presumed date. In the thirteenth century the semi-circular arch is still dominant in Provence. The ogive may well be very ancient! And some authors challenge the priority of Romanesque over Gothic. This lack of certainty upset them.

After the churches they studied the castles, those of Domfront and Falaise. Under the gate they admired the grooves for the portcullis, and when they reached the top they first saw all the countryside, then the roofs of the town, the intersecting streets, carts in the square, women at the washplace. The wall dropped straight down to the brushwood in the moats, and they went pale as they thought that men had climbed up there, hanging onto ladders. They would have taken a chance in the underground passage, but Bouvard was impeded by his girth, and Pécuchet from fear of vipers.

They wanted to get to know the old manors, Curcy, Bully, Fontenay-le-Marmion, Argouges. Sometimes in a corner of the buildings, behind the dungheap, a Carolingian tower rises up. The kitchen, furnished with stone benches, evokes thoughts of feudal banquets. Others look wholly forbidding, with their three rings of walls still to be seen, loopholes under the stairway, long turrets with pointed sections. Then one comes into an apartment where a window from Valois times, carved like an ivory, lets in the sun to warm colza seeds spread on the floor. Abbeys are used as barns. Inscriptions on gravestones have been obliterated. In the middle of the fields still stands a gable covered from top to bottom with ivy shaken by the wind.

Numerous objects excited their cupidity, a pewter pot, a strass buckle, cotton fabrics with bold floral patterns. Lack of money held them back.

By some providential chance they unearthed a Gothic window at a tinsmith in Balleroy, and it was big enough to cover the right-hand part of the casement, by the chair, up to the second pane. The church tower of Chavignolles appeared in the distance to splendid effect.

With the bottom of a cupboard Gorju constructed a prie-dieu to put under the window, for he indulged their craze. It was so powerful that they regretted the passing of monuments of which nothing is known, like the country house of the bishops of Séez.

'Bayeux,' says Monsieur de Caumont, 'must have had a theatre.' They looked in vain for its site.

The village of Montrecy contains a meadow famous for the medals that have been found there. They were counting on a fine numismatic harvest from it. The caretaker refused to let them in.

They had no better fortune over the supposed connection between a cistern in Falaise and the outskirts of Caen. Ducks had been put into it and came out again at Vaucelles quacking 'can, can, can', whence the town takes its name.

They did not grudge any effort, any sacrifice.

At the inn in Mesnil-Villement, in 1816, a Monsieur Galeron had eaten for four sous. They had the same meal there and were surprised to note that things were no longer the same!

Who was the founder of the Abbey of Sainte-Anne? Is there any connection between Marin Onfroy, who imported in the twelfth century a new kind of apple, and Onfroy, governor of Hastings at the time of the Conquest? How can one obtain *The Artful Prophetess*, a comedy in verse by a certain Dutrésor, written at Bayeux and now exceedingly rare? Under Louis XIV Hérambert Dupaty, or Dupastis Hérambert, composed a work, which has never appeared, full of anecdotes about Argentan: the problem was to rediscover these anecdotes. What has become of the autograph memoirs of Madame Dubois de la Pierre, consulted for the unpublished history of Laigle by Louis Dasprès, parish priest of Saint-Martin? These were all problems, curious points, to be cleared up.

But often a slender clue points the way to a valuable discovery.

So they put on their smocks to avoid arousing suspicion and in the guise of pedlars presented themselves in private houses, asking to buy old papers. Piles were sold to them; school exercise books, invoices, old newspapers, nothing worthwhile.

Finally Bouvard and Pécuchet turned to Larsonneur.

He was lost in Celticism, answered their questions summarily and asked them more of his own.

Had they noticed around them traces of the dog cult, as can be seen at Montargis; and special details, on Midsummer bonfires, weddings, popular sayings, etc.? He even asked them to collect for him a few of those flint axes, then called *celtae*, used by the Druids in their 'criminal holocausts'.

Through Gorju they procured a dozen, sent him the smallest and enriched their museum with the others.

They walked round it lovingly, swept it themselves, had told all their acquaintances about it.

One afternoon Madame Bordin and Monsieur Marescot arrived to see it.

Bouvard received them, and began the demonstration in the vestibule.

The beam was no less than the former Falaise gibbet, according to the carpenter who had sold it, and who had had the information from his grandfather.

The great chain in the corridor came from the oubliettes of the keep at Torteval. According to the lawyer it looked like the chains that link bollards in front of formal courtyards. Bouvard was convinced that it had once been used to shackle captives, and he opened the door of the first room.

'Why all those tiles?' cried Madame Bordin.

'To heat up bathhouses; but let's have a little order, please. This is a tomb discovered in an inn where it was being used as a drinking trough.'

Then Bouvard took the two urns full of earth which was human ashes, and put his eyes up to the phial to show how the Romans poured tears into it.

'But all the things in your museum are so gloomy!'

Indeed it was a bit serious for a lady, and so he drew several copper coins and a silver denier out of a box.

Madame Bordin asked the lawyer what they might be worth today.

The coat of mail he was examining slipped out of his fingers and some links broke. Bouvard concealed his annoyance.

He was even kind enough to unhook the halberd and, bending

over, raising his arms, stamping his heel, he pretended to slice through a horse's hamstrings, to lunge as if with a bayonet, to strike down an enemy. The widow inwardly found him a tough customer.

She was full of enthusiasm for the shell chest of drawers. The Saint-Allyre cat amazed her. The pear in the carafe rather less, then, as she came to the mantelpiece:

'Ah! There's a hat that needs mending!'

Three holes, where bullets had passed, pierced its brim.

'It belonged to a robber chief under the Directory, David de la Bazoque, caught through treachery and killed immediately.'

'So much the better, that was a good job,' said Madame Bordin.

Marescot smiled contemptuously in front of the objects. He did not understand the clog, which had been the sign of a shoe shop, nor why the earthenware barrel, a common cider-jug, was there, and the St Peter was frankly lamentable with his drunkard's face.

Madame Bordin remarked:

'It must have cost you a bit, all the same?'

'Oh, not too much, not too much.'

A slater had given it for fifteen francs.

Then she criticized as unseemly the décolletage of the lady in the powdered wig.

'Where's the harm,' retorted Bouvard, 'when one owns something beautiful?' And he added in a lower voice: 'Like you, I'm sure.'

The lawyer turned his back on them, studying the branches of the Croixmare family. She did not answer, but began to play with her long watch-chain. Her bosom swelled out the black taffeta of her corsage, and with slightly lowered lashes she bent her chin, like a pouting pigeon; then innocently:

'What was the lady's name?'

'We don't know; she was one of the Regent's mistresses, you know, the one who played about so much.'

'Yes, indeed, memoirs of the time ...'

And the lawyer, without ending his sentence, deplored this example of a prince led astray by his passions.

'But you're all the same!'

The two men protested, and a dialogue ensued on women and

on love. Marescot asserted that there are many happy unions; sometimes even one may have close at hand, without suspecting it, just what one needs to be happy. The allusion was direct. The widow's cheeks flushed, but recovering almost at once:

'We are past the age of follies, are we not, Monsieur Bouvard?'

'Oh, I wouldn't say that!'

And he offered her his arm to go into the other room.

'Mind the steps. That's it. Now look at the stained glass window.'

One could make out a crimson cloak and the two wings of an angel – all the rest was lost under the leading which held the many broken pieces of glass steady. The light was fading, shadows lengthened, Madame Bordin had become grave.

Bouvard went off and came back draped in a woollen blanket. Then he knelt down before the prie-dieu, elbows stuck out, face buried in his hands, the sunshine falling on his bald patch; he was aware of the effect, for he said:

'Don't you think I look like a medieval monk?'

Then he raised his head at an angle, his eyes brimming, setting his face in a mystical expression. From the corridor Pécuchet's grave voice was heard:

'Don't be afraid, it's only me.'

And he came in with his head completely covered by a helmet; an iron pot with pointed earflaps.

Bouvard stayed at the prie-dieu. The two others remained standing. A minute went by in general amazement.

Madame Bordin appeared slightly chilly to Pécuchet, but he asked if she had been shown everything.

'I think so.' Pointing to the wall: 'Oh, forgive me, the object we are going to have there is being restored at the moment.'

The widow and Marescot withdrew.

The two friends had conceived the idea of pretending to compete. They went on expeditions separately, the second one bidding higher than the first. That is how Pécuchet had just acquired the helmet.

Bouvard congratulated him and was praised in return for the blanket.

Mélie, with the aid of cords, had arranged it like a monk's habit. They put it on in turn to receive visits.

Among those who came were Girbal, Foureau, Captain Heurtaux, then lesser people: Langlois, Beljambe, their farmers, even the neighbours' maidservants; and each time they began their explanation once again, showed the place where the chest would go, affected an air of modesty, craved indulgence for the clutter.

On these occasions Pécuchet wore the Zouave cap which he used to have in Paris, judging it more appropriate to the artistic milieu. At a given moment he put on the helmet and tilted it back on his head to leave his face free. Bouvard did not forget the performance with the halberd, finally they exchanged a glance to decide whether the visitor deserved 'the medieval monk' act.

What excitement when Monsieur de Faverges's carriage stopped before their gate! He had only one word to say. It was this:

Hurel, his steward, had told him that, as they looked for documents everywhere, they had bought some old papers at La Aubraye farm.

Perfectly true.

Had they not discovered letters from the Baron de Gonneval, former aide-de-camp to the Duc d'Angoulême, who had stayed at La Aubraye? This correspondence was wanted in the family interests.

They did not have it, but they did possess something of interest to him, if he would deign to follow them as far as their library.

Such highly polished boots had never before cracked along the corridor. They bumped against the sarcophagus. He almost crushed several tiles, turned the chair round, went down two steps, and, when they had reached the second room, beneath the canopy, in front of St Peter, they showed him the butter-jar executed at Noron.

Bouvard and Pécuchet had thought that the date might sometimes be of use.

The nobleman out of politeness inspected their museum. He repeated: 'Charming! Very good!' while tapping his lips with the knob of his cane, and for his own part thanked them for saving these remains of the Middle Ages, age of religious faith and knightly loyalty. He liked progress, and would, like them, have given himself up to these interesting studies, but politics, local council, farming, a real whirlwind of activity kept him from it.

'In any case, after you there would only be the gleanings; because you will have taken all the curiosities in the department.'

'Without conceit, that's what we think,' said Pécuchet.

However, there might still be more to discover. At Chavignolles, for instance, against the cemetery wall, in a lane, lay a holy water stoup buried under the grass from time immemorial.

They were happy to have the information, then exchanged a look which meant 'Is it worth it?', but the count was already opening the door.

Mélie, who was standing behind it, suddenly fled.

As he passed through the yard he noticed Gorju, smoking his pipe, arms crossed.

'So you employ that chap? Hm, if one day trouble were to break out, I wouldn't trust him.'

Monsieur de Faverges got into his tilbury.

Why did their maid seem afraid of him?

They questioned her, and she explained that she had worked at his farm. She was the girl who had been pouring out drink for the harvesters when they had come. Two years later she had been taken on to help in the big house and dismissed because of 'untrue stories'.

As for Gorju, what was there against him? He was very able and showed them enormous respect.

Next day, as soon as dawn broke, they went to the cemetery.

With his stick Bouvard poked about at the spot indicated. It banged on some hard object. They pulled up some nettles and discovered a sandstone basin, a font with plants growing in it.

However, fonts are not usually buried outside churches.

Pécuchet made a drawing of it, Bouvard a description, and they sent it all to Larsonneur.

His reply was immediate.

'Victory, my dear colleagues! Incontrovertibly it is a Druid basin!'

All the same they must be cautious! The axe was doubtful, and for their sakes as much as for his he listed a series of works to consult.

Larsonneur confessed in a postscript that he would like to see this basin, and that would happen one day when he was on his way to Brittany.

So Bouvard and Pécuchet plunged into Celtic archaeology.

According to this science, our ancestors, the ancient Gauls, worshipped Kirk and Kron, Taranis, Esus, Netalemnia, Heaven and Earth, Wind, Waters, and, above all, great Teutates, who is the Saturn of the pagans. For Saturn, when he reigned in Phoenicia, married a nymph called Anobret, by whom he had a son called Jeud, and Anobret has the features of Sarah, Jeud was sacrificed (or nearly so) like Isaac; so Saturn is Abraham, whence it necessarily follows that the Gauls' religion had the same principles as that of the Jews.

Their society was very well organized. The first class of individuals comprised the people, the nobility and the king; the second the lawyers, and in the third, the highest, were ranged, according to Taillepied, 'various kinds of philosophers', that is Druids or Saronides, themselves divided into Eubages, Bards and Prophets.

Some prophesied, others chanted, others again taught botany, medicine, history and literature, in short 'all the arts of their time'. Pythagoras and Plato were their pupils. They taught the Greeks metaphysics, the Persians sorcery, the Etruscans soothsaying, and the Romans copper-tinning and the bacon trade.

But this people, which dominated the ancient world, left nothing but stones, either singly, or in groups of three, or arranged in galleries, or forming enclosures.

Bouvard and Pécuchet, full of zeal, studied successively the Pierre du Post at Ussy, the Pierre Couplée at Le Guest, the Pierre du Darier, near Laigle, and others as well!

All these blocks, all equally insignificant, bored them, and one day, when they had just seen the menhir of Le Passais, they were going to turn back when their guide led them into a beechwood, littered with masses of granite, like pedestals or monstrous tortoises.

The largest is hollowed out like a basin. One of the edges is turned up, and from the bottom two grooves run down to the ground; it was for draining off the blood, there could be no doubt about it! Such things do not come about by chance.

The tree roots intermingled with these steep rocks. It was raining a little; in the distance wisps of mist rose up like giant phantoms.

It was easy to imagine, beneath the foliage, the priests in golden tiara and white robe, with their human victims, arms tied behind their back, and on the edge of the basin the Druidess observing the crimson stream, while around her the crowd yelled, to the din of cymbals and trumpets made of aurochs horn.

At once their plan was decided.

One night by moonlight they took the path to the cemetery, walking stealthily in the shadow of the houses. The shutters were closed and the shabby houses were still; not a dog barked.

Gorju accompanied them; they set to work. All that could be heard was the noise of the spade striking stones as it dug up the turf.

They did not like having the dead so near; the church clock sounded a continuous death-rattle, and the rose-window in the tympanum looked like an eye watching out for sacrilege. Finally they bore the basin away.

Next day they went back to the cemetery to see the traces of their operation.

The priest, who was taking the air at his door, asked them to honour him with a visit. He ushered them into his small parlour and looked at them strangely.

In the middle of the dresser, among the plates, was a soup tureen decorated with yellow bouquets.

Pécuchet praised it, not knowing what to say.

'It is an old piece of Rouen pottery,' replied the curé, 'a family heirloom. Connoisseurs admire it, especially Monsieur Marescot.'

For himself, thank heaven, he was not keen on curiosities; and as they did not seem to understand, he declared that he himself had seen them stealing the font.

The two archaeologists, very crestfallen, began to stammer. The object in question was no longer in use.

No matter! They must return it.

Of course! But let them at least be allowed to bring in a painter to draw it.

'Very well, gentlemen.'

'Between ourselves, don't you agree,' said Bouvard, 'under the seal of the confessional?'

Smiling, the ecclesiastic reassured them with a gesture.

They were not afraid of him, but rather of Larsonneur. When

he came through Chavignolles he would want the basin, and his gossip would reach the ears of the government. Prudently they hid it in the bakehouse, then in the arbour, in the hut, in a cupboard. Gorju was tired of lugging it around.

Ownership of such a piece somehow made them attached to Celticism in Normandy.

Its origins are Egyptian. Séez, in the Orne, is sometimes written Sais, like the town in the delta. The Gauls swore by the bull, an importation of the ox Apis. The Latin name Bellocastes, which is what the people of Bayeux were called, comes from Beli-Casa, dwelling, sanctuary of Belus. Belus and Osiris are the same divinity. 'There is no reason,' says Mangon de la Lande, 'why there should not have been Druidic monuments near Bayeux.' – 'This region,' adds Monsieur Roussel, 'resembles that where the Egyptians built the temple of Jupiter Ammon.' Therefore there was a temple, and one containing riches. All Celtic monuments do.

In 1715, Dom Martin relates, a certain Héribel exhumed in the area of Bayeux several clay vases full of bones and concluded (according to tradition and various authorities) that this place, a necropolis, was Mount Faunus, where the Golden Calf was buried.

Yet the Golden Calf was burned and swallowed up! Unless the Bible is mistaken!

First of all, where is Mount Faunus? The authors give no indication. The natives know nothing about it. Excavations were needed, and to that end they sent Monsieur le Préfet a petition which went unanswered.

Perhaps Mount Faunus has disappeared, and was not a hill but a tumulus? What did tumuli signify?

Several contain skeletons in the foetal position. That means that for them the tomb was like a second gestation in preparation for another life. Therefore the tumulus symbolized the female organ, just as the raised stone is the male organ.

In fact wherever there are menhirs an obscene cult persists. Witness what used to happen at Guérande, Chichebouche, le Croisic, Livarot. In former times towers, pyramids, candles, milestones and even trees had a phallic significance, and for Bouvard and Pécuchet everything became phallic. They collected swing-poles of carriages, chair-legs, cellar bolts, pharmacists' pestles. When people came to see them they would ask: 'What do you think that looks like?' then confided the mystery, and if there were objections, they shrugged their shoulders pityingly.

One evening when they were dreaming about Druid dogmas the abbé discreetly appeared.

They at once showed him the museum, beginning with the stained glass window; but they were impatient to reach a new section, the phallic one. The ecclesiastic stopped them, finding the exhibition indecent. He had come to ask for the return of his font.

Bouvard and Pécuchet begged for another two weeks, time to take a cast of it.

'The sooner the better,' said the curé. Then he chatted about indifferent matters.

Pécuchet, who had gone out for a moment, slipped a gold coin into his hand.

The priest drew back.

'Oh, for your poor!'

And Monsieur Jeufroy, blushing, stuffed the gold piece into his cassock.

Give back the basin, the sacrificial basin! Never! They even wanted to learn Hebrew, mother tongue of Celtic – unless it is derived from it! They were planning to tour Brittany, starting with Rennes, where they had a rendezvous with Larsonneur, to study the urn mentioned in the memoirs of the Celtic Academy and which seems to have contained the ashes of Queen Artémise, when the mayor came in, hat on head, unceremoniously, like the coarse man he was.

'That's not the end of it, my lads! You've got to give it back!'

'But what?'

'Funny joke! I know you are hiding *it*.'

They had been betrayed.

They replied that they were keeping it with the curé's permission.

'We'll see about that.'

And Foureau went off.

He came back an hour later.

'The curé says it is not so! Come and explain yourselves.'

They stood their ground.

First the holy water stoup was not needed, and was not a holy water stoup anyway. They would prove it by a mass of scientific arguments. Then they offered to acknowledge in their will that it belonged to the commune.

They even proposed buying it.

'And anyhow it is my property!' Pécuchet repeated. The twenty francs accepted by Monsieur Jeufroy was evidence of the contract and if they had to go before the magistrate, well, that was too bad, he would swear a false oath!

During these debates he had seen the soup tureen again several times, and in his heart had grown the desire, the thirst, the itch for this piece of china. If it were agreed he should have it, he would return the basin. Otherwise not.

Weary or afraid of scandal Monsieur Jeufroy gave up the tureen.

It was put in their collection, near the Cauchois bonnet. The basin decorated the church porch, and they consoled themselves for not having it any more with the thought that the people of Chavignolles did not know its value.

But the tureen gave them a taste for china: fresh subject of study and country expeditions.

It was the time when distinguished people were looking for old Rouen dishes. The lawyer had one or two, and thereby acquired some kind of artistic reputation, injurious for his profession but redeemed by his serious features.

When he learned that Bouvard and Pécuchet had acquired the tureen he came to propose an exchange.

Pécuchet refused.

'Let's say no more about it,' and Marescot examined their ceramics.

All the pieces hung along the walls were blue on a dirty white background, and some displayed their cornucopia in green and reddish tones, shaving dishes, plates and saucers, objects long sought and brought back, close to the heart, in the folds of the frock-coat.

Marescot praised them, talked about other china, Hispano-Arab, Dutch, English, Italian, and when he had dazzled them with his erudition: 'Could I see your tureen again?'

He made it ring with a flick of his finger, then contemplated the two S's painted under the lid.

'The Rouen mark!' said Pécuchet.

'Oh, oh! Strictly speaking Rouen never had a mark. When Moutiers was unknown all French china came from Nevers. The same with Rouen today! Besides, it is imitated to perfection at Elbeuf.'

'It's not possible!'

'Majolica is certainly imitated! Your piece is worthless and I was going to make a real fool of myself!'

When the lawyer had disappeared Pécuchet collapsed prostrate in his chair!

'We should never have given back the basin,' said Bouvard, 'but you get so worked up! You always get carried away!'

'Yes, I do get carried away,' and Pécuchet seized the tureen and threw it as far as he could, against the sarcophagus.

Bouvard, with more calm, picked up the bits, one by one; and a little later it occurred to him:

'Marescot might have played a trick on us out of jealousy!'

'How?'

'I am by no means sure that the tureen is not genuine! Maybe the other pieces he pretended to admire are false instead?'

They spent the last of the day in uncertainty and regrets.

This was no reason for giving up the trip to Brittany. They were even intending to take Gorju along to help with their digging.

For some time he had been sleeping in the house so as to finish mending the chest more quickly. The prospect of moving displeased him, and as they talked of the menhirs and tumuli they expected to see, he said: 'I know something better. In Algeria, in the South, near the springs of Bou-Mursoug, you find lots of them.' He even described a tomb, which by chance had been opened in front of him, containing a skeleton, squatting like a monkey, with both arms round its legs.

Larsonneur, whom they apprised of the fact, did not want to believe a word of it.

Bouvard went into the matter, and started him off again.

How is it that the Gaulish monuments are shapeless, while these same Gauls were civilized at the time of Julius Caesar? No doubt they originate from an older people.

Such a hypothesis, according to Larsonneur, was unpatriotic.

What does that matter? There is nothing to say that these monuments are the Gauls' work. 'Show us a text!'

The academician was annoyed, and did not answer any more, which made them very glad, for they had become very bored with the Druids.

If they did not know where they stood with ceramics and Celticism it was because they were ignorant of history, especially the history of France.

Anquetil's work was in their library, but the series of rois fainéants, inactive kings, was of very little interest to them. The wickedness of the mayors of the Palace did not make them indignant and they gave up Anquetil, put off by the ineptitude of his reflections.

Then they asked Dumouchel 'What is the best history of France?'

Dumouchel took out a subscription in their name to a circulating library and sent them Augustin Thierry's *Letters*, with two volumes of Monsieur de Genoude.

According to that writer, royalty, religion and national assemblies are the 'principles' of the French nation, going back to the Merovingians. The Carolingians revoked them. The Capetians, in agreement with the people, strove to maintain them. Under Louis XIII absolute power was established to conquer Protestantism, the last effort of feudalism, and 1789 marks a return to the constitution of our forefathers.

Pécuchet admired these ideas.

Bouvard found them pitiful, having read Augustin Thierry first:

'What are you going on about, with your French nation? Since there was no France and no national assemblies! And the Carolingians did not usurp anything at all! And the kings did not give the communes their freedom! Read for yourself!'

Pécuchet yielded before the weight of evidence, and soon overtook him in scientific rigour! He even made it a point of honour to avoid saying Charlemagne, instead of Karl the Great, Clovis instead of Clodowig.

Nevertheless he was won over by Genoude, and thought it was

clever to get the two ends of French history to join up so that the middle is just padding, and to clear their minds about it they took up the Buchez and Roux collection.

But the emotionalism of the prefaces, this amalgam of socialism and catholicism sickened them; the details were too numerous to allow them to see the whole.

They had recourse to Monsieur Thiers.

It was during the summer of 1845, in the garden, under the arbour, Pécuchet, with his feet up on a small seat, was reading aloud in his booming voice, tirelessly, only stopping to dip his fingers into his snuff-box. Bouvard was listening to him, pipe in mouth, legs apart, the top of his trousers undone.

Old men had talked to them of 1793, and memories which were almost personal enlivened the prosaic descriptions of the author. At that time the main roads were covered with soldiers singing the Marseillaise. Women sat by their doors sewing canvas for tents. Sometimes a stream of men in red bonnets arrived, brandishing at the end of a pike some discoloured head with trailing hair. The high platform of the Convention rose above a cloud of dust, amidst which angry faces clamoured for the death penalty. When at mid-day one passed by the pond in the Tuileries the thudding of the guillotine sounded like a piston.

The breeze stirred the vines in the arbour, the ripe barley swayed at intervals, a blackbird whistled. As they looked around them they savoured the peace and quiet.

What a pity that people had not been able to agree from the start! For if the royalists had thought like the patriots, if the court had been more open and its opponents less violent, many misfortunes would never have occurred!

As they chatted on about all this they became excited. Bouvard, liberal and sensitive, was for the Constitution, the Gironde, Thermidor. Pécuchet, bilious and inclined to authoritarianism, declared himself a *sans-culotte* and even for Robespierre.

He approved the condemnation of the king, the most violent decrees, the cult of the Supreme Being. Bouvard preferred that of Nature. He would have been happy to salute the image of an ample woman, with breasts pouring forth for her admirers not water but Chambertin.

Wanting more facts to support their arguments they procured other works. Montgaillard, Prudhomme, Gallois, Lacretelle, etc.; and the contradictions in these books did not worry them a bit. Each took from them whatever might defend his cause.

Thus Bouvard did not doubt that Danton had accepted 100,000 francs to propose motions which would destroy the Republic, and, according to Pécuchet, Vergniaud had asked for 6,000 francs a month.

'Not on your life! Explain to me instead why Robespierre's sister drew a pension from Louis XVIII?'

'Not at all! It was from Bonaparte, and if you are going to take that line, who is the person who had a secret conference with Philippe Egalité shortly before he died? I should like to see them reprint the paragraphs suppressed in Madame Campan's memoirs! The Dauphin's death looks fishy to me. The Grenelle powder magazine killed two thousand people when it blew up! Unknown cause, they said, what nonsense!' For Pécuchet all but knew the cause, and attributed all crimes to the machinations of the aristocrats and foreign gold.

To Bouvard's mind, 'Ascend to Heaven, son of St Louis', the virgins of Verdun and the breeches made of human skin were beyond dispute. He accepted Prudhomme's lists, exactly one million victims.

But the Loire, red with blood from Saumur to Nantes, a distance of forty-five miles, made him think twice. Pécuchet also began to have doubts and they lost faith in historians.

The Revolution is for some a satanic event. Others proclaim that it was a sublime exception. The defeated ones on each side are, of course, martyrs.

In connection with the barbarians Thierry demonstrates how foolish it is to enquire whether a prince was good or bad. Why not follow that method in examining some recent periods? But history must avenge morality; we are grateful to Tacitus for having torn Tiberius to shreds. After all, whether or not the queen had lovers, whether Dumouriez planned treachery from the time of Valmy, whether in Prairial it was the Mountain or the Gironde who began, and in Thermidor the Jacobins or the Plain, what does it matter for the development of the Revolution, whose origins go deep and whose results are incalculable?

Therefore it had to take place, be what it was, but suppose that the king's flight had not been impeded, that Robespierre had escaped or Bonaparte been assassinated – chances dependent on a less unscrupulous innkeeper, an open door, or a sleeping sentry – and the way of the world would have changed.

As regards the men and events of the period, they no longer had a single solid idea.

To judge impartially they would have had to read all the histories, all the memoirs, all the journals, and all the manuscript documents, for the slightest omission may cause an error which will lead to others ad infinitum. They gave up.

But they had acquired a taste for history, a need for truth in itself.

Perhaps the truth can be more easily discovered in ancient periods? The authors, being remote from events, must talk of them dispassionately. They began the worthy Rollin.

'What a load of rubbish!' cried Bouvard at the very first chapter.

'Wait a bit,' said Pécuchet, rummaging at the bottom of their library, where lay piles of books from the last owner, an old lawyer, eccentric and cultivated; after shifting a lot of novels and plays, as well as a Montesquieu and some translations of Horace, he found what he was looking for: Beaufort's work on Roman history.

Livy credits Romulus with the foundation of Rome, Sallust attributes it to Aeneas's Trojans. Coriolanus died in exile according to Fabius Pictor, through the wiles of Attius Tullius if we are to believe Dionysius; Seneca asserts that Horatius Cocles went home victorious, Dion that he was wounded in the leg. And La Mothe le Vayer expresses similar doubts concerning other peoples.

There is no agreement on the antiquity of the Chaldaeans, the century of Homer, the existence of Zoroaster, the two Assyrian empires. Quintus Curtius invented stories. Plutarch contradicts Herodotus. We should have a different idea of Caesar if Vercingetorix had written his commentaries.

Ancient history is obscure for lack of documents, which abound in modern history. Bouvard and Pécuchet returned to France, started on Sismondi.

The succession of so many men made them want to know them better, to become involved with them. They wanted to look through the originals, Gregory of Tours, Monstrelet, Commines, all those with odd or attractive names.

But they became muddled about events because they did not know the dates.

Fortunately they possessed Dumouchel's memory training system, a bound volume in duodecimo, with this epigraph: 'Instruction through entertainment'.

It combined the three systems of Allevy, Pâris and Fenaigle.

Allevy turns numbers into figures, number 1 being expressed by a tower, 2 by a bird, 3 by a camel and so on. Pâris catches the imagination with rebus; a chair adorned with screw-in studs gives *Clou*[1], *vis*[2] – Clovis; and as frying makes a noise that sounds like 'ric, ric', whitings in a frying-pan will recall Chilperic. Fenaigle divides the universe into houses containing rooms, each having four walls with nine panels, each panel bearing an emblem. Thus the first king of the first dynasty will occupy the first panel in the first room. A lighthouse[3] on a mountain[4] will tell you his name, Phar-a-mond, in the Pâris system, and according to Allevy's recommendations, if you put above this a mirror signifying 4, a bird 2, and a hoop 0, you will get 420, date of that prince's accession.

To make things clearer they took as the mnemotechnic base their own house, attaching to each of its parts one distinct fact, and the yard, the garden, the surroundings, the whole region no longer had any other sense than to aid memory. Boundary stones in the countryside delimited certain periods, the apple-trees were genealogical trees, bushes were battles, the whole world became a symbol. They looked on the walls for a lot of things that were not there, ended up by seeing them but no longer knew the dates they represented.

Besides, dates are not always authentic. They learned in a school manual that Christ's birth should be brought back five years earlier than is generally reckoned, that the Greeks had three ways of counting Olympiads, and the Latins eight ways of beginning the year. These were all so many occasions for error, apart from those resulting from different zodiacs, eras and calendars.

From carelessness about dates they passed on to contempt for facts.

What matters is the philosophy of history!

1. stud. 2. screw. 3. *phare*. 4. *mont*.

Bouvard was not able to finish Bossuet's famous discourse.

'The Eagle of Meaux must be joking! He forgets China, India and America, but he is careful to tell us that Theodosius was "the joy of the universe", that Abraham "treated kings like an equal" and that Greek philosophy comes down from the Hebrews! His preoccupation with the Hebrews gets on my nerves.'

Pécuchet shared this opinion and tried to make him read Vico.

'How can you admit,' Bouvard objected, 'that fables are truer than the truths of historians?'

Pécuchet tried to explain myths, and lost himself in the *Scienzia Nuova*.

'Are you going to deny the plan of Providence?'

'I don't know it,' said Bouvard.

And they decided to seek Dumouchel's advice.

The professor confessed that he had now lost his bearings when it came to history.

'It is changing every day. The kings of Rome and the journeys of Pythagoras are disputed. There are attacks against Belisarius, William Tell and even the Cid, who thanks to the latest discoveries has become a mere bandit. Let us hope there will be no more discoveries, and the Institute even ought to draw up some sort of canon to prescribe what is to be believed!'

As a postscript he sent some critical rules taken from Daunou's course.

'Quoting the testimony of the masses as evidence is bad evidence; they are not there to answer.

'Reject impossible things. They showed Pausanias the stone swallowed by Saturn.

'Architecture can lie, for example: the arch of the Forum on which Titus is called first conqueror of Jerusalem, which Pompey had conquered before him.

'Medals are sometimes deceptive. Under Charles IX, Henri II coins were minted.

'Take into account the skill of forgers and the personal interests of apologists and calumniators!'

Few historians have worked according to these rules, but all with a view to some special cause, religion, nation, party, system, or to scold kings, counsel the people, offer moral examples.

Others who claim simply to narrate are no better; because one cannot say everything, there must be some choice. But in choosing documents a certain spirit will prevail, and as it varies according to the writer's conditions, history will never be fixed.

'How sad,' they thought.

However, one could take a subject, exhaust the sources, analyse it carefully, then condense it in a narrative, which would be a kind of resumé of events, reflecting the whole truth. Such a work seemed feasible to Pécuchet.

'How would you like it if we tried to compose a history?'

'I would like nothing better. But which?'

'Indeed, which?'

Bouvard had sat down, Pécuchet was walking up and down in the museum, when the butter-jar caught his eye and he suddenly stopped:

'Supposing we wrote the life of the Duc d'Angoulême?'

'But he was an idiot!' replied Bouvard.

'What does that matter! Secondary characters sometimes have enormous influence, and perhaps he was at the hub of affairs!'

Books would give them information, and Monsieur de Faverges no doubt had some of his own, or through some old aristocratic friends of his.

They meditated about this project, debated it, and finally resolved to spend two weeks at the municipal library in Caen pursuing their researches.

The librarian put at their disposal some general works of history and some pamphlets, and a coloured lithograph representing a three-quarter portrait of His Grace the Duc d'Angoulême.

The blue cloth of his uniform jacket could hardly be seen for the epaulettes, stars and great red sash of the Legion of Honour. An extremely high collar encased his long neck. His pear-shaped head was framed by his wavy hair and thin side-whiskers, and heavy eyelids, very large nose and thick lips gave his face an expression of kindly insignificance.

When they had taken notes they drew up a programme:

Uninteresting birth and childhood. One of his tutors was Abbé Guénée, Voltaire's enemy. At Turin he is said to have cast a cannon, and he studied Charles VIII's campaigns. So he is appointed, despite his youth, colonel of a regiment of noble guards.

1797 His marriage.

1814 The English seize Bordeaux. He runs up behind them and shows himself to the inhabitants. Description of the prince's appearance.

1815 Bonaparte surprises him. At once he calls in the King of Spain and Toulon, without Masséna, was given up to England.

Operations in the South – he is beaten, but released on his promise to give back the crown diamonds, which the king, his uncle, had made off with at top speed.

After the Hundred Days he returns with his parents and lives quietly. Several years go by.

Spanish War – Once he has crossed the Pyrenees victory follows the grandson of Henri IV everywhere. He takes the Trocadéro, reaches the pillars of Hercules, crushes sedition, embraces Ferdinand and goes home.

Triumphal arches, girls presenting flowers, dinners in prefectures, Te Deums in cathedrals. The Parisians are completely intoxicated. The city gives a banquet for him. Allusions to the hero are sung on stage.

Enthusiasm dies down. Because in 1827, at Cherbourg, a subscription ball is a failure.

As he is Grand-Admiral of France, he inspects the fleet about to leave for Algiers.

July 1830. Marmont tells him the state of affairs. Then he flies into such a rage that he hurts his hand on the general's sword.

The king entrusts him with command of all the forces.

In the Bois de Boulogne he meets detachments of the line and does not find a single word to say to them.

From Saint-Cloud he hastens to the Pont de Sèvres. Coldness of the troops. He is unshaken. The royal family leaves Trianon. He sits down at the foot of an oak, unfolds a map, meditates, mounts his horse again, passes in front of Saint-Cyr and sends the pupils words of hope.

At Rambouillet the bodyguards bid their farewells.

He takes ship, and is ill the whole way across. End of his career.

The importance of bridges in his career must be brought out. First he exposes himself unnecessarily on the bridge over the Inn, he captures the Pont Saint-Esprit and the bridge of Lauriol; at Lyon, the two bridges are disastrous for him, and his fortune gives out before the Pont de Sèvres.

Picture of his virtues. Unnecessary to extol his courage, to which he added great political sense. For he offered sixty francs to each soldier to abandon the emperor, and in Spain he tried to bribe the constitutionals with money.

He was so deeply reserved that he consented to the marriage mooted between his father and the Queen of Etruria, to the formation of a new cabinet after the ordinances, to abdication in favour of Chambord, to anything that was wanted.

He did not however lack firmness. At Angers he dismissed the infantry of the Garde Nationale, who, being jealous of the cavalry, had managed by a manoeuvre to escort him, with the result that His Highness was so caught up with the foot soldiers that he had his knees squashed. But he blamed the cavalry, who had caused the disorder, and forgave the infantry, a true judgement of Solomon.

His piety was distinguished by numerous acts of devotion, and his clemency by securing a pardon for General Debelle, who had borne arms against him.

Intimate details, aspects of the prince:

At the Château de Beauregard, in his childhood, he enjoyed digging with his brother a pond which can still be seen. Once he visited the Chasseurs' barracks, asked for a glass of wine and drank to the king's health.

When he was out walking he would keep step by repeating to himself: 'One, two, one, two, one, two!'

Some of his apt remarks have been preserved.

To a deputation from Bordeaux: 'What consoles me for not being at Bordeaux is to be among you!'

To the Protestants of Nîmes: 'I am a good Catholic, but I shall never forget that my most illustrious ancestor was a Protestant.'

To the pupils of Saint-Cyr, when all was lost: 'Good, my friends! The news is good! It is going well, very well!'

After Charles X's abdication: 'Since they don't want me, let them make their own arrangements!'

And in 1814, in any context, in the smallest village: 'No more war, no more conscription, no more indirect taxes!'

His style was as good as his oratory. His proclamations surpass all.

The first of the Comte d'Artois began thus: 'Frenchmen, your king's brother has come!'

That of the prince: 'I am coming. I am the son of your kings! You are French.'

Order of the day dated from Bayonne: 'Soldiers, I am coming!'

Another, when defection was at its height: 'Continue to wage the struggle you have begun with the vigour of a French soldier. France expects it of you!'

His last, at Rambouillet: 'The king has begun negotiations for an agreement with the government set up in Paris, and there is every reason to believe that this agreement is on the point of being concluded.' The 'every reason to believe' was sublime.

'One thing worries me,' said Bouvard, 'no one mentions his love affairs?'

And they made a note in the margin: 'Look into the prince's amours!'

When they were just about to go the librarian remembered something, and showed them another portrait of the Duc d'Angoulême.

In this one he appeared as a colonel of cuirassiers, in profile, eyes smaller than ever, open mouthed, with straight hair, prancing.

How were these two portraits to be reconciled? Was his hair straight or curly, unless he was vain enough to have it waved?

A serious question, according to Pécuchet, because hair style gives temperament, temperament the individual.

Bouvard thought that one can know nothing of a man so long as one does not know about his passions; and to clear up these two points they presented themselves at the Château de Faverges. The count was not there, which delayed their work. They went home in annoyance.

The house door was wide open; there was no one in the kitchen. They climbed the stairs, and what did they see in the middle of Bouvard's room? Madame Bordin, looking right and left.

'Excuse me,' she said, trying to laugh. 'I have been looking for your cook for an hour, I need her for my jam.'

They found her in the woodshed, on a chair, fast asleep. They shook her. She opened her eyes.

'What is it this time? You are always badgering me with your questions!'

It was clear that in their absence Madame Bordin had been questioning her.

Germaine came out of her torpor and complained of indigestion.

'I'll stay to look after you,' said the widow.

Then in the yard they caught sight of a large bonnet, with nodding plumes. It was Madame Castillon, the farmer's wife. She cried: 'Gorju! Gorju!'

And from the loft their little servant's voice answered loudly:

'He is not here!'

She came down after five minutes, cheeks flushed, upset. Bouvard and Pécuchet scolded her for being so slow. She undid their gaiters without a murmur.

Then they went to see the chest.

Its shattered pieces lay strewn about the bakehouse, the carvings were damaged, the doors broken.

At this sight, this fresh disappointment, Bouvard held back his tears and Pécuchet had a fit of trembling.

Gorju, appearing almost at once, explained the situation: he had just put the chest out to varnish it when a stray cow had knocked it over.

'Whose cow?' said Pécuchet.

'I don't know.'

'Well, you had left the door open as it was a moment ago! It's your fault!'

They gave up in any case; he had been putting them off for too long and they wanted nothing more to do with him or his work.

The gentlemen were wrong. The damage was not so great. It would be finished in less than three weeks, and Gorju accompanied them int .e kitchen as Germaine dragged herself in to prepare dinner.

They noticed on the table a bottle of Calvados, three-quarters empty.

'I suppose you did that?' Pécuchet said to Gorju.

'Me? Never!'

Bouvard objected:

'You were the only man in the house.'

'Well, what about the women?' replied the workman, with a sidelong glance.

Germaine caught him at it:

'Why don't you say it's me?'

'Certainly it's you!'

'And I suppose I'm the one who smashed up the cupboard?'

Gorju did a pirouette:

'Can't you see then that she is drunk?'

Then they had a violent row, he pale, she purple-faced, tearing out tufts of grey hair from under her cotton bonnet. Madame Bordin spoke up for Germaine, Mélie for Gorju.

The old woman exploded.

'Of all the abominable things! You spend all day together in the copse, not to speak of the nights! Miserable Parisian womanizer! Coming here to our masters to take them in with your tricks!'

Bouvard's eyes opened wide.

'What tricks?'

'I say that you are being fooled!'

'Nobody fools me!' cried Pécuchet, and indignant at her insolence, angered at the commotion, dismissed her; she had to clear out. Bouvard did not oppose this decision, and they withdrew, leaving Germaine sobbing over her misfortune, while Madame Bordin tried to comfort her.

In the evening, when they were calm, they went over these events again, wondered who had drunk the Calvados, how the chest had been broken, what Madame Castillon wanted when she called Gorju, and whether he had dishonoured Mélie.

'We don't know,' said Bouvard, 'what is happening in our own household, and we presume to discover the sort of hair and love-life that the Duc d'Angoulême had!'

Pécuchet added:

'How many questions there are of a quite different importance, and how much more difficult!'

From which they concluded that external facts are not everything. They must be completed by psychology. Without imagination history is defective – 'Let's send for some historical novels!'

5

FIRST they read Walter Scott.

They were as surprised as if they had found a new world.

The men of the past who had been mere names or phantoms for them became living beings, kings, princes, sorcerers, servants, gamekeepers, monks, gypsies, merchants and soldiers, deliberating, fighting, travelling, trading, eating and drinking, singing and praying, in castle guardrooms, on the blackened benches of taverns, along the winding streets of towns, beneath the awnings of market stalls, in monastery cloisters. Artistically composed landscapes surround the scenes like stage sets. One's eyes follow a rider galloping along the shore. Amid the broom one breathes in the cool breeze, on moonlit lakes a boat glides by, the sun gleams on breastplates, rain falls on leafy huts. Without knowing the models they found these depictions lifelike, the illusion was complete. So the winter passed by.

After lunch they installed themselves in the small living-room, at either side of the fireplace; facing each other, with book in hand, they would read silently. When dusk began to fall they would go for a walk along the highway, then dine in haste and continue their reading into the night. As a protection against the glare of the lamp Bouvard wore blue eye-shades, Pécuchet kept the peak of his cap pulled down over his forehead.

Germaine had not gone, and Gorju came from time to time to dig in the garden, because they had given in out of indifference, oblivious to material things.

After Walter Scott, Alexandre Dumas entertained them to a kind of magic lantern show. His characters, artful as monkeys, strong as oxen, gay as larks, enter and speak abruptly, leap from rooftop to cobblestones, receive fearful wounds from which they recover, are given up for dead and reappear. There are trap-doors under the floor, antidotes, disguises, and everything is a confused rush, which finally sorts itself out, without a moment for reflection. Love preserves the decencies, fanaticism is cheerful, massacres bring a smile.

These two masters made them hard to please, so that they could not stand the rubbish of *Belisarius*, the silliness of *Numa Pompilius*, Marchangy or Arlincourt.

Frédéric Soulié struck them as insufficiently colourful (like the bibliophile Jacob), and Monsieur Villemain scandalized them by showing, on page eighty-five of his *Lascaris*, a Spanish woman smoking a pipe, 'a long Arab pipe', in the middle of the fifteenth century.

Pécuchet consulted the *Biographie Universelle*, and undertook to revise Dumas from a scientific point of view.

The author, in *The Two Dianas*, gets the dates wrong. The marriage of the Dauphin François took place on 14th October 1548, and not 20th March 1549. How does he know (see *The Duke of Savoy's Page*) that Catherine de Médicis, after her husband's death, wanted to start the war again? It is very unlikely that the Duc d'Anjou was crowned at night, in a church, an episode that graces the *Lady of Montsoreau*. *Queen Margot* especially abounds in errors. The Duc de Nevers was not absent. He gave his opinion at the council before St Bartholomew, and Henri de Navarre did not follow the procession four days later. Besides, there were so many old stories! The miracle of the hawthorn, Charles IX's balcony, Jeanne d'Albret's poisoned gloves; Pécuchet lost faith in Dumas.

He even lost all respect for Walter Scott, because of the blunders in his *Quentin Durward*. The Bishop of Liège's murder is brought forward fifteen years. Robert de Lamarck's wife was Jeanne d'Arschel and not Hameline de Croy. Far from being killed by a soldier, he was put to death by Maximilian, and Charles the Bold's face, when his body was found, bore no expression of menace, because it had been half eaten by wolves.

This did not stop Bouvard from going on with Walter Scott, but eventually he was bored by repetition of the same effects. The heroine usually lives in the country with her father, and the lover, a stolen child, is reinstated in all his rights and triumphs over his rivals. There is always a philosophical beggar, a gruff lord of the manor, pure young maidens, witty servants and interminable dialogues, stupid prudery, total lack of depth.

Bouvard, coming to detest bric-à-brac, took up George Sand.

He was filled with enthusiasm for beautiful adulterers and noble lovers, would have liked to be Jacques, Simon, Benedict, Lélio and live in Venice! He sighed and sighed, did not know what was wrong with him, found he had changed.

Pécuchet, working on historical literature, was studying plays.

He swallowed two Pharamonds, three Clovises, four Charlemagnes, several Philip Augustusses, a crowd of Joan of Arcs, and numerous Marquises de Pompadour and Cellamare conspiracies.

Almost all of them seemed to him even sillier than the novels, because there exists a conventional history for the theatre which nothing can destroy. Louis XI will never fail to kneel down before the images fixed to his hat; Henri IV will be consistently jovial, Mary Stuart tearful, Richelieu cruel, in short all the characters are displayed in a single block, from love of simple ideas and respect for ignorance, so that the playwright, far from raising the level, lowers it; instead of instructing, he dulls.

As Bouvard had sung the praises of George Sand, Pécuchet began to read *Consuelo*, *Horace*, *Mauprat*, was charmed by the defence of the oppressed, the social and republican side, the theses.

According to Bouvard they spoilt the fiction and he asked for love stories from the lending library.

Reading aloud, one after the other, they ran through *La Nouvelle Héloise*, *Delphine*, *Adolphe*, *Ourika*, but the one who was listening yawned so much that it affected his companion, from whose hands the book soon fell to the ground.

What they objected to in all these books was that they said nothing about the background, the period, the costume of the characters. Only their heart is dealt with; always sentiment, as if there was nothing else in the world!

Then they tried humorous novels, such as *Journey round my Room* by Xavier de Maistre, *Under the Lime Trees* by Alphonse Karr. In this type of book the narrator must break off to talk about his dog, his slippers or his mistress. Such a free and easy approach delighted them at first, then appeared stupid, because the author effaces his work by using it to exhibit his person.

Needing some drama they plunged into adventure stories; the more involved, extraordinary and impossible the plot was, the more it interested them. They tried hard to guess the outcome, became very good at it, and wearied of such a frivolous pastime, unworthy of serious minds.

Balzac's work filled them with wonder, being at once like a teeming Babylon and specks of dust under the microscope. The most ordinary things revealed new aspects. They had not suspected that modern life had such depths.

'What an observer!' cried Bouvard.

'Personally I find him fanciful,' Pécuchet finally said. 'He believes in occult sciences, the monarchy, the nobility, is dazzled by scoundrels, shoves millions around like centimes, and his bourgeois are not bourgeois but supermen. Why inflate something that is flat and describe so many idiotic things! He writes one novel about chemistry, another about banking, another on printing machines. Just as a certain Ricard did "the cabby", "the water-carrier", "the coconut vendor". We'll have one on every trade and every province, then on every town and every floor of every house, and every individual, and it will not be literature, but statistics or ethnography.'

The process was of small importance to Bouvard. He wanted to learn, deepen his knowledge of human ways. He re-read Paul de Kock, thumbed through the old *Hermit of the Chaussée d'Antin*.

'How can anyone waste time on such drivel!' said Pécuchet.

'But it will turn out to have curiosity value as documents.'

'Go to blazes with your documents! I want something to cheer me up, take me away from all the wretchedness of life!'

And Pécuchet, attracted to the ideal, imperceptibly turned Bouvard towards tragedy.

The remoteness of its action, the interests discussed and the status of its characters impressed them with a certain feeling of grandeur.

One day Bouvard took *Athalie* and recited the dream so well that Pécuchet wanted to try it in his turn. From the first phrase his voice degenerated into a kind of booming. It was monotonous, and though powerful, indistinct.

The experienced Bouvard advised him to make it more supple by exercising it from the highest to the lowest note, and then going in the other direction, by uttering two scales, one rising, the other falling; and he gave himself up to this exercise in the morning, in bed, lying on his back, according to the precepts of the Greeks. Meanwhile Pécuchet worked in the same way; they had their doors closed, and brayed away separately.

What pleased them in tragedy was the bombast, political discourses, perverse maxims.

They learned off by heart the most famous dialogues of Racine and Voltaire, and declaimed them in the corridor. Bouvard, as at the Comédie Française, walked with his hand on Pécuchet's shoulder, stopping at intervals, rolling his eyes, throwing out his arms, cursing the fates. He produced fine crises of grief in La Harpe's *Philoctète*, a beautiful hiccough in *Gabrielle de Vergy*, and when he did Dionysius, tyrant of Syracuse, he had a way of looking at his son and calling him 'Monster worthy of me!' that was really terrible. It made Pécuchet forget his part. What he lacked was talent, not goodwill.

Once in Marmontel's *Cléopâtre* he had the idea of reproducing the asp's hiss, as the automaton specially invented by Vaucanson must have done. The effect did not come off but kept them laughing until the evening. Tragedy fell in their esteem.

Bouvard was the first to tire of it, and being quite frank about it, showed how artificial and stiff-jointed it is, how foolish its methods are, the absurdity of confidants.

They approached comedy, which is the school of nuances. One must split sentences, emphasize words, weigh syllables. Pécuchet could not manage it and failed completely as Célimène.

Besides, he found the lovers very cold, the spokesman for reason boring, the servants intolerable; Clitandre and Sganarelle as false as Egisthe and Agamemnon.

There remained serious comedy or bourgeois tragedy, in which one sees fathers afflicted, servants saving their masters, rich men offering their fortune, innocent dressmakers and infamous corrupters, a genre extending from Diderot to Pixérécourt. All these plays preaching virtue shocked them as vulgar.

The 'drama' of 1830 delighted them with its movement, its colour, its youthfulness.

They hardly distinguished between Victor Hugo, Dumas or Bouchardy, and diction no longer had to be pompous or subtle, but lyrical, disordered.

One day when Bouvard was trying to make Pécuchet understand how Frédérick Lemaître acted, Madame Bordin suddenly appeared with her green shawl, and a volume of Pigault-Lebrun which she was returning, as the gentlemen were sometimes kind enough to lend her novels.

'But do go on!' For she had been there a minute or two and enjoyed listening to them.

They made excuses. She insisted.

'Good Lord!' said Bouvard, 'there's nothing to stop us!'

Pécuchet objected from false modesty that they could not improvise their act without costume.

'Indeed! We would need to disguise ourselves!'

Bouvard looked for some object or other, but only found the Greek bonnet, which he took.

As the corridor was not wide enough, they went down to the drawing-room.

Spiders ran along the walls and the geological specimens cluttering up the floor had covered the velvet chairs with white dust. They spread a duster over the least filthy so that Madame Bordin could sit down.

They had to find something good to offer her. Bouvard favoured the *Tour de Nesle*, but Pécuchet was afraid of parts which demand too much action.

'She would prefer something classical! *Phèdre*, for instance?'

'All right.'

Bouvard told the story – 'There is a queen whose husband has a son by another wife. She has become crazy about the young man. Is that clear? Off we go!'

> Yes, prince, I languish, I burn for Theseus,
> I love him!

Speaking to Pécuchet's profile, he admired his bearing, his face, 'this charming look', regretted not having met him in the Greek fleet, wished he could have been lost with him in the labyrinth.

The tassel on the red bonnet bent over lovingly, and his trembling voice and kind face implored the cruel man to take pity on his passion. Pécuchet, turning away, panted to indicate emotion.

Madame Bordin sat motionless and wide-eyed, as if looking at conjuring tricks; Mélie was listening behind the door; Gorju, in shirt sleeves, watched them through the window.

Bouvard went into the second tirade. His acting expressed delirium, remorse, despair, and he threw himself on Pécuchet's imaginary sword so violently that he stumbled over the stones and almost fell.

'Take no notice! Then Theseus arrives and she takes poison.'

'Poor woman!' said Madame Bordin.

Then they invited her to pick a piece for them.

The choice embarrassed her. She had only seen three plays: *Robert the Devil* in the capital, *The Young Husband* in Rouen, and another at Falaise, which was very funny and was called *The Vinegar-man's Barrow*.

Finally Bouvard proposed the big scene in *Tartuffe*, in the third act.

Pécuchet thought some explanation necessary:

'You should know that Tartuffe ...'

Madame Bordin interrupted him. 'We all know what a Tartuffe is!'

Bouvard would have liked a dress for a certain passage.

'All I can think of is the monk's habit,' said Pécuchet.

'It doesn't matter! Put it on!'

He reappeared with it, and a Molière.

The beginning was mediocre, but when Tartuffe started to fondle Elmire's knees, Pécuchet took on a policeman's tones:

'What is your hand doing there?'

Bouvard very quickly answered in a syrupy voice:

'I am feeling your dress, the material is so soft.' And he darted his eyes, pursed his lips, sniffed, looked extremely lubricious, and even ended by addressing Madame Bordin.

She was upset by this man looking at her, and when he stopped, humble and palpitating, she was almost trying to find an answer.

Pécuchet had recourse to the book: 'the declaration is most gallant.'

'Oh yes!' she cried. 'He is a masterly charmer!'

'He is, isn't he?' Bouvard proudly replied. 'But here is another declaration, more fashionable and up to date.' He undid his coat, squatted on a bit of stone, and with head thrown back declaimed:

Flood my lids with flames from your eyes,
Sing me a song, as once, at eventide,
You used to sing, with tears in your dark eyes.

'That is like me,' she thought.

Let us be happy! Drink, for the cup is full.
This hour belongs to us, all else is folly.

'How funny you are!'
And she gave a little throaty laugh, revealing her teeth.

Is it not sweet to love,
And to know that your lover kneels to you!

He knelt down.
'Well, finish, then!'

Oh, let me sleep and dream upon your breast,
Doña Sol, my beauty, and my love!

'Here bells are heard, a mountaineer disturbs them.'

'Fortunately, because otherwise ...' And Madame Bordin smiled, instead of finishing her sentence. Dusk was falling. She stood up.

It had just been raining, and the path through the beeches was not easy. It was better to go back through the fields. Bouvard accompanied her into the garden to open the gate for her.

First they walked along by the fruit trees, without speaking. He was still moved by his declamation, and in her heart she felt a kind of surprise, a delight caused by literature. On certain occasions art can shake very ordinary spirits, and whole worlds can be revealed by its clumsiest interpreters.

The sun had come out again, making the leaves glisten, casting bright patches on the thickets, here and there. Three sparrows hopped chirping onto the trunk of an old fallen lime-tree. A thorn-bush in blossom spread out its pink sheaf, lilacs bent over with their weight.

'Oh, that does one good!' said Bouvard, breathing in great lungfuls of air.

'And you put so much into it!'

'It is not that I have any talent, but what I do have is enthusiasm.'

'Anyone can see,' she went on, spacing out the words, 'that you were . . . in love . . . once.'

'Once, just once, you think?'

She stopped.

'I just don't know!'

'What does she mean?' Bouvard found his heart beating.

A puddle in the middle of the sand made them go round under the arbour.

Then they talked about the performance.

'What was your last piece called?'

'It's taken from the drama *Hernani*.'

'Oh!' Then slowly, talking to herself: 'It must be very nice to have a gentleman saying such things to you – and really meaning it.'

'I am at your orders,' answered Bouvard.

'You?'

'Yes, me.'

'You're joking!'

'Not a bit of it!'

And giving a quick look round, he took her by the waist, from behind, and passionately kissed the back of her neck.

She went very pale as though she were going to faint, and leaned with one hand against a tree, then she opened her eyes and shook her head.

'It's over.'

He looked at her in amazement.

He opened the gate and she stepped on to the threshold of the little entrance. There was a stream of water flowing on the other side. She gathered up the folds of her skirt, and stood hesitating on the edge:

'Would you like me to help?'

'There is no need.'

'Why?'

'Oh, you are too dangerous!'

And as she made her jump she showed white stockings.

Bouvard blamed himself for missing the opportunity. Bah! She would be there another time, and, then, all women are not the same. Some you must treat brusquely, boldness is disastrous with others. All in all he was pleased with himself, and if he did not confide his hopes to Pécuchet, it was for fear of comment, not at all out of delicacy.

From that day on they often declaimed before Mélie and Gorju, only regretting that they did not have a dramatic society.

The little maid found it enjoyable without understanding it, amazed at the language, fascinated by the sonority of the lines. Gorju applauded the philosophical tirades in the tragedies and every popular sentiment in the melodramas, to such an extent that, delighted with his taste, they thought of giving him lessons, so that he could go on to become an actor. The prospect dazzled the workman.

Rumour of their labours had spread. Vaucorbeil spoke to them about it slightingly. Generally they were despised.

This gave them a still better opinion of themselves. They became dedicated artists. Pécuchet wore moustaches, and Bouvard, with his round face and bald head, could find nothing better than to imitate Béranger's appearance.

Finally they resolved to write a play.

The difficult thing was the subject.

They tried to find one over lunch, and drank coffee, a liquid indispensable for the brain, then two or three glasses of spirits. Then they lay down to sleep on their beds, after which they went down into the orchard, walked about there, only to go out again in search of inspiration, then they marched side by side, and came home exhausted.

Or they would lock and bolt the door. Bouvard cleared the table, put paper before him, dipped his pen and stayed staring up at the ceiling, while Pécuchet, in the armchair, meditated, with legs straight out and head drooping.

Sometimes they felt a shiver and, as it were, the breath of an idea; as soon as they made to seize it, it had disappeared.

But there are methods for hitting on subjects. You take a title at random and a fact emerges from it; you develop a proverb, or combine several adventures into one. None of these gave any result. They ran in vain through collections of anecdotes, several volumes of *Causes célèbres*, a lot of histories.

They dreamed of being put on at the Odéon, thought about shows, missed Paris.

'I was meant to be an author, not bury myself in the country!' said Bouvard.

'Me too,' replied Pécuchet.

Light suddenly dawned on him; if they were having so much trouble it was because they did not know the rules.

They studied them, in d'Aubignac's *Theatrical Practice*, and in several less obsolete works.

These works discuss important questions; whether comedy can be written in verse; whether tragedy does not exceed its limits by taking its story from recent history; whether heroes should be virtuous; what kind of villains it involves; how far horrors are permissible; that the details should combine in a single aim, that interest should mount, that the end should correspond to the beginning, no doubt!

> Invent a plot to hold me fast,

says Boileau.

How is one to invent plots?

> See that in all you write the passion roused
> Goes for the heart to excite and stir it.

How is one to stir the heart?

So rules are not enough, one needs genius as well.

And genius is not enough. According to the French Academy Corneille did not understand anything about the theatre. Geoffroy denigrated Voltaire, Subligny scoffed at Racine. The name of Shakespeare made La Harpe roar.

Disgusted with the old criticism, they wanted to know about the new, and sent for newspaper reviews of plays.

What assurance! What obstinacy! What dishonesty! Outrageous treatment of masterpieces, deference for the platitudes and idiocies of those who pass for learned, and the stupidity of others hailed as witty!

Perhaps one should rely on the public?

But works which met with applause sometimes displeased them, and in those that were hissed they found something they liked.

So the opinion of men of taste is misleading and mass judgement is inconceivable.

Bouvard put the dilemma to Barberou. Pécuchet for his part wrote to Dumouchel.

The former travelling salesman was amazed at the way provincial life had softened him up; his old Bouvard was growing flabby, in short 'was no longer up to it at all'.

The theatre is a consumer article like any other. It comes under the heading of fancy goods. You go to a show for entertainment. The good ones are those that amuse.

'But you idiot,' cried Pécuchet, 'what amuses you does not amuse me, and other people, and you yourself will get tired of it later. If plays are written absolutely for performance, how is it that the best ones are always read?' He waited for Dumouchel's reply.

According to the professor a play's immediate fate proves nothing. *Misanthrope* and *Athalie* were failures. *Zaïre* is not understood any more. Who talks to-day of Ducange and Picard? And he recalled all the great contemporary successes, from *Fanchon la Vielleuse* to *Gaspardo le Pêcheur*, deploring the decadence of our stage. The reason for it is contempt for literature, or rather style.

Then they asked themselves exactly what constitutes style, and thanks to authors indicated by Dumouchel they learned the secret of all its genres.

How to obtain the majestic, the temperate, the simple, the expressions which are noble, the words which are base. 'Dogs' is enhanced by 'devouring'. 'Vomit' is only used figuratively. 'Fever' applies to the passions. 'Valour' is fine in poetry.

'Suppose we wrote love poetry?' said Pécuchet.

'Later! Let's deal with prose first.'

It is formally recommended that one should choose a classic to mould one's style on, but they all have their dangers, and have sinned in style as well as in language.

Such an assertion disconcerted Bouvard and Pécuchet and they began to study grammar.

Does French have definite and indefinite articles like Latin? Some think it does, others not. They did not dare to decide.

The subject always agrees with the verb, except on those occasions when the subject does not agree.

There used to be no distinction between the verbal adjective and the present participle; but the Academy makes one which it is very hard to grasp.

They were glad to learn that the pronoun *leur*[1] is used for persons, but also for things, while *où* and *en* are used for things and sometimes for persons.

Should the adjective in 'this woman has a kind face' agree with the woman or the face? – 'a log of dry wood' or 'a dry log of wood' – with *ne laisser de*[2] use *que* or not – 'a band of robbers arrives' or 'arrive'?

Other difficulties: 'round and around',[3] in which Racine and Boileau saw no difference; *imposer* or *en imposer*,[4] synonyms in Massillon and Voltaire; *croasser* and *coasser*,[5] confused by La Fontaine, who knew how to tell a crow from a frog none the less.

The grammarians, it is true, do not agree, some seeing beauty where others see error. They admit principles whose consequences they reject, proclaim consequences whose principles they refuse, rely on tradition, reject the masters, and have odd refinements. Ménage, instead of *lentilles* and *cassonade*, proposes *nentilles* and *castonade*, Bouhours *jérarchie* and not *hiérarchie*, and Monsieur Chapsal *oeils de la soupe*.

Pécuchet was particularly astonished by Génin. What? It is better to ignore the 'h' in *hannetons*[6] and *haricots*, and elide it, while under Louis XIV *Rome* was pronounced *Room* and Monsieur de *Lionne*, Monsieur de *Lioune*!

Littré finished them off by affirming that there has never been positive orthography, nor ever could be.

Whence they concluded that syntax is a fantasy and grammar an illusion.

At that time in any case a new rhetoric was proclaiming that one should write as one speaks and then all will be well, so long as one has felt and observed.

As they had felt, and thought they had observed, they judged themselves capable of writing: the narrowness of the framework makes a play awkward, but the novel has greater freedom. They searched their memories in an attempt to compose one.

Pécuchet recalled one of his office superiors, a very nasty gentle-

1. their. 2. not fail to. 3. *autour, à l'entour*. 4. impose upon. 5. caw, croak. 6. cockchafers.

man, and conceived the ambition of avenging himself through a book.

Bouvard had known, in a local bar, a drunken, wretched old writing master. Nothing could be funnier than this character.

At the end of the week they had the idea of fusing these two subjects into one, but went no further, and passed on to the next: a woman responsible for a family's misfortunes, – a woman, her husband, and her lover, – a woman being virtuous because she was misshapen, an ambitious man, a bad priest.

They tried to connect these vague conceptions into items furnished by their memory, cut some things, added others.

Pécuchet was all for feelings and ideas, Bouvard for pictures and colour, and they began to fall out, each surprised to find the other so narrow-minded.

The science called aesthetics would perhaps resolve their differences. A friend of Dumouchel, a professor of philosophy, sent them a list of works on the subject. They worked separately and shared their reflections.

First of all, what is the Beautiful?

For Schelling it is the infinite expressing itself in the finite; for Reid, an occult quality; for Jouffroy an indestructible fact; for de Maistre what is agreeable to virtue; for Père André what conforms to reason.

And there are several kinds of Beautiful; a beautiful in the sciences, geometry is beautiful; a beautiful in ethics, Socrates' death is undeniably beautiful. A beautiful in the animal kingdom. A dog's beauty consists in its sense of smell. A pig could not be beautiful, given its filthy habits, nor a serpent, for it evokes ideas of baseness.

Flowers, butterflies, birds can be beautiful. In short the primary condition of the Beautiful is unity in variety, that is the principle.

'Yet,' said Bouvard, 'two squinting eyes are more varied than two straight ones and have a less good effect – usually.'

They tackled the question of the sublime.

Certain objects are sublime in themselves, the thunder of a torrent, deep darkness, a tree struck by a storm. A character is beautiful when it triumphs, and sublime when it struggles.

'I understand,' said Bouvard, 'the Beautiful is the Beautiful, and the Sublime the very Beautiful.' How can they be distinguished?

'By intuition,' answered Pécuchet.

'And where does that come from?'

'From taste!'

'What is taste?'

It is defined as special discernment, rapid judgement, the ability to distinguish certain relationships.

'What it comes to is that taste is taste, and none of that tells you how you get it.'

Conventions must be observed, but they vary, and however perfect a work may be it will not always be above reproach. Yet there is an indestructible Beautiful, whose laws we do not know, because its origin is mysterious.

Since an idea cannot be translated by every form, we must recognize limits between the arts and, in each of the arts, several genres; but combinations arise in which the style of one will enter into another, or else miss the target, fail to be true.

The Truth too slavishly applied impairs Beauty, and preoccupation with Beauty impedes Truth; however, without an ideal there is no truth; which is why the reality of types is more continuous than that of portraits. Besides, art only deals with verisimilitude, but that depends on the observer, is something relative, transitory.

So they lost themselves in lines of reasoning. Bouvard was coming to believe less and less in aesthetics.

'Either it is all a joke or its rigour can be demonstrated by examples. Now listen!'

And he read out a note which had cost him a lot of research.

'Bouhours accuses Tacitus of lacking the simplicity required by history.'

'A professor, a Monsieur Droz, criticizes Shakespeare for his mixture of serious and farcical, Nisard, another professor, considers André Chénier as a poet to be beneath those of the seventeenth century. The Englishman Blair deplores Virgil's picture of the Harpies. Marmontel groans over the licence taken by Homer. Lamotte does not admit the immorality of his heroes. Vida is indignant about his similes. In fact all these people who compose books of rhetoric, poetics and aesthetics seem complete idiots to me!'

'You're going too far!' said Pécuchet.

He was disturbed by doubts, for if, as Longinus observes,

mediocre spirits are incapable of faults, faults belong to masters, and they ought perhaps to be admired? That is too much! Yet masters are masters! He wanted to reconcile doctrines with works, critics with poets, grasp the essence of the Beautiful; and these questions exercised him so much that his liver was upset. As a result he got jaundice.

It was at its peak when Marianne, Madame Bordin's cook, came to Bouvard to ask for an appointment on behalf of her mistress. The widow had not reappeared since the drama session. Was this an advance? But why use Marianne as an intermediary? Throughout the night Bouvard's imagination ran wild.

Next day, at about two o'clock, he was walking about in the corridor, looking out of the window from time to time; a bell rang. It was the lawyer.

He crossed the yard, went up the stairs, sat down in the armchair, and after an initial exchange of compliments said that, tired of waiting for Madame Bordin, he had gone ahead. She wanted to buy Les Écalles.

Bouvard felt a chill run over him and went into Pécuchet's room.

Pécuchet did not know what to answer. He was worried, as Monsieur Vaucorbeil was due to arrive any minute.

At last she came. Her delay was explained by the care she had taken over dressing: a cashmere shawl, a hat, glacé kid gloves, a suitable outfit for serious occasions.

After a lot of preliminaries she asked if a thousand francs would not be enough.

'An acre! A thousand francs? Never!'

She fluttered her eyelids: 'Oh! For me!'

All three stayed silent. Monsieur de Faverges came in.

Under his arm he held a morocco briefcase, like a solicitor, which he put on the table:

'Here are some pamphlets! They deal with Reform, a burning question; but here is something which doubtless belongs to you!' And he handed Bouvard the second volume of *The Devil's Memoirs*.

Mélie had just been reading it in the kitchen; and as one must keep an eye on how people like that behave, he thought it would be a good thing to confiscate the book.

Bouvard had lent it to his servant. They talked about novels.

Madame Bordin liked them when they were not gloomy.

'Writers,' said Monsieur de Faverges, 'paint life for us in flattering colours!'

'Painting is necessary!' objected Bouvard.

'Then, all you have to do is follow the example!...'

'It's not a question of example!'

'You will at least agree that they may fall into the hands of some young girl. I have one myself.'

'Charming!' said the lawyer, putting on the expression he wore on the days when marriage contracts were signed.

'Well, for her sake, or rather for the sake of the people around her, I forbid them in my house, for the people, my dear sir!...'

'What about the people?' said Vaucorbeil, suddenly appearing at the door.

Pécuchet, who had recognized his voice, came to join the company.

'I maintain,' the count went on, 'that certain reading matter must be kept out of their way...'

Vaucorbeil replied:

'So you are not in favour of education?'

'Oh yes I am! Excuse me!'

'When every day,' said Marescot, 'there are attacks on the government!'

'What harm in that?'

And the aristocrat and the doctor began to denigrate Louis-Philippe, recalling the Pritchard affair, the September laws against the freedom of the press.

'And freedom of the theatre!' added Pécuchet.

Marescot could stand no more. 'It goes too far, that theatre of yours!'

'That I grant you!' said the count, 'plays exalting suicide!'

'Suicide is beautiful! Look at Cato,' objected Pécuchet.

Without replying to the argument Monsieur de Faverges stigmatized those works in which the most sacred things are mocked, like the family, property, marriage!

'And what about Molière?' said Bouvard.

Marescot, the man of taste, retorted that Molière would not be accepted any more, and anyhow was a bit overrated.

'When all is said and done,' said the count, 'Victor Hugo showed no pity, absolutely no pity, for Marie-Antoinette when he pilloried the very type of the queen in the person of Mary Tudor!'

'What!' cried Bouvard. 'As an author I am not entitled...'

'No, sir, you are not entitled to show us the crime without reserving a corrective, without offering us a lesson.'

Vaucorbeil also thought that art should have a purpose: the improvement of the masses! 'Sing to us of science, our discoveries, patriotism,' and he admired Casimir Delavigne.

Madame Bordin vaunted the Marquis de Foudras. The lawyer replied: 'But his language, can you have thought of that?'

'Language? What do you mean?'

'They are talking about style!' cried Pécuchet. 'Do you find his works well written?'

'Certainly, very interesting!'

He shrugged his shoulders, and she flushed at the impertinence.

Several times Madame Bordin had tried to return to her affair. It was too late to conclude it. She went out on Marescot's arm.

The count distributed his pamphlets, which he urged them to spread around.

Vaucorbeil was going to leave when Pécuchet stopped him.

'You are forgetting me, doctor.'

His yellow face was pitiful, with his moustaches and black hair hanging down under a badly fastened neckerchief.

'Take a purge,' said the doctor, and giving him a couple of slaps as if he were a child: 'Too full of nerves, too artistic!'

This familiarity pleased him. He was reassured, and once they were alone: 'You don't think it is serious?'

'No! Of course not!'

They resumed what they had just heard. The morality of art consists, for everyone, in the side that flatters his own interests. People do not like literature.

Then they flicked through the count's pamphlets. They all demanded universal suffrage.

'It seems to me,' said Pécuchet, 'that we are soon going to have some trouble.' For he saw the gloomy side of everything, perhaps because of his jaundice.

6

In the morning of 25th February 1848 the news reached Chavignolles, through someone coming from Falaise, that Paris was covered with barricades, and next day the proclamation of the Republic was posted up at the Town Hall.

This great event stupefied the citizens.

But when it became known that the Supreme Court, the Court of Appeal, the Audit Office, the Commercial Court, the Law Society, the Bar, the Council of State, the University and Monsieur de la Rochejaquelein himself were rallying to the Provisional Government, everyone heaved a sigh of relief; and as they were planting freedom trees in Paris, the municipal council decided that there must be one at Chavignolles.

Bouvard presented one, patriotically overjoyed at the triumph of the people; as for Pécuchet, the fall of the monarchy fulfilled his prophecies too well for him not to feel happy.

Gorju, eagerly obeying them, dug up one of the poplars lining the meadow below the Mound and carted it to the 'Pas de la Vaque' at the entrance to the village, the place appointed.

Before the time for the ceremony they were all three waiting for the procession.

A drum beat, a silver cross came in sight; then appeared two torches held by choristers, and the curé in stole, surplice and biretta. Four servers escorted him, a fifth carried the holy water bucket, and the sacristan followed.

He climbed up on to the edge of the hole in which stood the poplar, decked with tricolour ribbons. Facing him could be seen the mayor and his two deputies, Beljambe and Marescot, then the notables, Monsieur de Faverges, Vaucorbeil, Coulon, the justice of the peace, a sleepy-faced character; Heurtaux was wearing a policeman's cap, and Alexandre Petit, the new schoolmaster, had put on his frock-coat, a shabby green thing, his Sunday best. The firemen, commanded by Girbal, clutching his sabre, stood in one rank; on the other side shone the white plaques on some old shakoes from

La Fayette's time, five or six, no more – for the National Guard had fallen into disuse at Chavignolles. Peasants and their wives, workmen from neighbouring factories, children piled up behind. Placquevent, the rural constable, from the height of his five-foot-eight, controlled them with a look, as he walked up and down with folded arms.

The curé's address was like that of other priests in similar circumstances. After fulminating against kings, he extolled the republic. Do we not speak of the republic of letters, the Christian commonwealth? Could anything be more innocent than the one, more beautiful than the other? Christ formulated our sublime device: the tree of the people was the tree of the cross. For religion to yield its fruits it needs charity, and in the name of charity the ecclesiastic adjured his brethren to commit no disorder and peacefully to return home.

Then he sprinkled the sapling with holy water, calling on God's blessing: 'May it grow and remind us of liberation from all bondage and of a brotherhood that does more good than the shadow of its branches! Amen!'

Voices repeated 'Amen!' and after a roll on the drum the church party, chanting a Te Deum, made their way back to the church.

Their intervention had produced an excellent effect. Simple folk saw in it a promise of good fortune, patriots an act of deference, of homage paid to their principles.

Bouvard and Pécuchet thought that someone should have thanked them for their gift, or at least alluded to it; and they confided in Faverges and the doctor.

What did such complaints matter? Vaucorbeil was delighted with the Revolution, the count too. He execrated the house of Orléans. They would not be seen again; good riddance! All for the people from now on! And followed by Hurel, his factotum, he went to join the curé.

Foureau walked with head bent between the lawyer and the innkeeper, annoyed by the ceremony, afraid of commotion; and he instinctively turned back towards the rural constable who was deploring, with the captain, Girbal's inadequacy and the poor bearing of his men.

Workmen passed by on the road, singing the Marseillaise. Gorju, in the midst of them, brandished a stick; Petit escorted them, eyes flashing.

'I don't like that,' said Marescot, 'all this shouting and excitement!'

'Good Heavens!' replied Coulon. 'The young must have their fun!'

Foureau sighed: 'Funny sort of fun! And then the guillotine at the end!' He had visions of the scaffold, and expected horrible things.

Chavignolles felt the repercussions of the agitation in Paris. The townspeople took out subscriptions to newspapers. In the morning the post office was packed, and the postmistress would never have managed without the captain, who sometimes helped out. Then people would stay talking in the main square.

The first violent discussion concerned Poland.

Heurtaux and Bouvard demanded her liberation.

Monsieur de Faverges thought otherwise.

'By what right would we go there? It would be unleashing Europe against us. No follies!' And with everyone approving him, the two pro-Poles kept quiet.

Another time Vaucorbeil defended Ledru-Rollin's circulars

Foureau retorted with the forty-five centimes tax.

But, said Pécuchet, the government had suppressed slavery.

'What do I care about slavery?'

'All right, and the abolition of the death penalty for political offences?'

'Damn it!' replied Foureau. 'They'd like to abolish everything. Yet, who knows? The tenants are already making such demands!'

'All the better!' The landlords, according to Pécuchet, had the advantage. 'Anyone who owns a building...'

Foureau and Marescot interrupted him, crying that he was a communist.

'Me! Communist!'

Everyone was talking at once when Pécuchet proposed founding a political club! Foureau had the audacity to answer that such a thing would never be seen at Chavignolles.

Then Gorju demanded guns for the National Guard, since public opinion had appointed him instructor.

The only guns there were belonged to the firemen. Girbal insisted on it. Foureau did not care about handing them over.

Gorju looked at him: 'Yet I am considered able to use one.'

For he included poaching among his other activities and the mayor and innkeeper often bought a hare or rabbit off him.

'My word! Take them!' said Foureau.

That very evening the drill began.

It was on the grass in front of the church. Gorju, with a blue smock, a tie round his waist, carried out the movements automatically. His voice, when he gave orders, was brutal. 'Keep your bellies in!' Straight away Bouvard, holding his breath, hollowed his stomach, stretched out his rear. 'No one told you to make an arch, damn it!'

Pécuchet mixed up files and ranks, right-about and left-about turn; but the most pathetic was the schoolmaster; sickly and skinny, with a fringe of blonde beard, he staggered under the weight of his gun, and his bayonet made his neighbours uneasy.

They wore trousers of all colours, filthy crossbelts, old uniform jackets that were too short, and exposed their shirts at each side; everyone claimed 'not to have the means to act differently'. A subscription was opened to find clothes for the most needy. Foureau was stingy, while some women distinguished themselves. Madame Bordin gave five francs, despite her hatred of the republic. Monsieur de Faverges equipped twelve men and never missed the parades. Then he would install himself at the grocer's and pay for drinks for anyone who turned up.

The men in power at that time flattered the lower classes. Everyone came after the workers. People sought the privilege of being one of them. They became aristocrats.

Most of those in the district were weavers; others worked in cotton factories, or at a newly established paper-mill.

Gorju fascinated them with his glib talk, taught them savate fighting, took his cronies to drink at Madame Castillon's.

But the peasants were more numerous and on market days, as Monsieur de Faverges walked round the square, he inquired about their needs, and tried to convert them to his ideas. They listened without answering, like old Gouy, ready to accept any government so long as taxes were reduced.

By talking so much Gorju made a name for himself. Perhaps he would win election to the Assembly.

Monsieur de Faverges thought about that too, while striving not to compromise himself. The conservatives hesitated between Foureau and Marescot, but as the lawyer wanted to keep his practice, Foureau was chosen: a boor, an idiot. The doctor was furious about it.

Withered fruit of the examination system, he missed Paris, and awareness of his failure in life made him look morose. A wider career was going to open up; what a turning of tables! He drew up a profession of faith and came to read it to Bouvard and Pécuchet.

They congratulated him on it; their doctrines were the same. However, they wrote better, knew history, could cut as good a figure as he in the Chamber of Deputies. Why not? But which of them should stand? A contest of delicacy began. Pécuchet preferred his friend to himself. 'No, it is yours by right! You have more presence!'

'Maybe,' answered Bouvard, 'but you have more nerve!' Without solving the difficulty they drew up a plan of action.

The heady ambition to be elected deputy had seized others too. The captain dreamed about it under his policeman's cap, while he smoked his pipe, so did the schoolmaster, in his school, and the curé as well, in between prayers, so much so that he sometimes caught himself gazing up to heaven and saying: 'Oh Lord, grant that I may be a deputy!'

The doctor, after receiving some encouragement, called on Heurtaux and represented the chances he had.

The captain was very blunt about it. Vaucorbeil was admittedly well-known, but unpopular with his colleagues, especially chemists. They would all run him down; the people did not want a gentleman; his best patients would leave him; and after weighing these arguments the doctor regretted his weakness.

As soon as he had gone Heurtaux went to see Placquevent. Old soldiers try to oblige one another! But the rural constable, quite devoted to Foureau, flatly refused to help him.

The curé explained to Monsieur de Faverges that the hour had not yet come. They must give the republic time to wear out.

Bouvard and Pécuchet represented to Gorju that he would never be strong enough to beat the coalition of peasants and middle classes, filled him with uncertainty, sapped all his confidence.

Petit, out of pride, had made his desire apparent. Beljambe warned him that if he failed he was certain to lose his job.

Finally His Lordship the bishop ordered the curé to keep quiet.

So there only remained Foureau.

Bouvard and Pécuchet campaigned against him, recalling how unhelpful he had been about the guns, his opposition to the club, his reactionary ideas, his avarice, and even persuaded Gouy that he wanted to bring back the old regime.

Vague as such a thing was for the peasant, he execrated it with a hatred built up for ten centuries in the hearts of his forbears, and he turned against Foureau all his family, and that of his wife, brothers-in-law, cousins, great-nephews, a whole horde.

Gorju, Vaucorbeil and Petit continued demolishing the mayor, and with the ground thus cleared, Bouvard and Pécuchet, without anyone suspecting, might be able to succeed.

They drew lots to find who should stand. The lots were inconclusive, and they went to consult the doctor about it.

He gave them some news. Flacardoux, editor of *Calvados*, had declared himself a candidate. The two friends were greatly disappointed; each felt the disappointment of the other, as well as his own. But politics excited them. On the day of the elections they watched the poll. Flacardoux carried the day.

Monsieur le Comte had fallen back on the National Guard, without winning a commander's epaulette. The people of Chavignolles had the idea of appointing Beljambe.

Such strange and unforeseen public favour threw Heurtaux into consternation. He had neglected his duties, confining himself to an occasional inspection of exercises, with some comments. No matter! He thought it monstrous that an innkeeper should be preferred to a former captain of the Empire, and said, after the invasion of the Chamber on 15th May: 'If that is how they award military ranks in the capital I am not surprised any more at what goes on!'

Reaction was beginning.

People believed in Louis Blanc's pineapple purées, Flocon's golden bed, Ledru-Rollin's royal orgies, and as the provinces claim to know all that goes on in Paris, the citizens of Chavignolles did not doubt these inventions and accepted the most absurd rumours.

One evening Monsieur de Faverges came to look for the curé to inform him of the arrival in Normandy of the Comte de Chambord.

Joinville, according to Foureau, was preparing with his sailors to wipe out the socialists. Heurtaux asserted that Louis Bonaparte would soon be consul.

The factories were idle. The poor were roaming about the countryside in large groups.

One Sunday (it was at the beginning of June) a gendarme suddenly went off towards Falaise. The workers of Acqueville, Liffard, Pierre-Pont and Saint-Rémy were marching on Chavignolles.

Shutters were closed; the municipal council met, and resolved, in order to forestall trouble, that no resistance would be offered. The gendarmes were even confined to barracks, under orders not to show themselves.

Soon there was a noise like the rumbling of thunder. Then the Girondins' song shook the windows; and men with linked arms debouched from the Caen road, dusty, sweaty and ragged. They filled the square. A great hubbub rose up.

Gorju and two of his companions came into the room. One was thin and weasel-faced, wearing a knitted waistcoat with rosettes hanging down. The other, black with coal, no doubt an engineer, had cropped hair, thick eyebrows and list slippers. Gorju wore his jacket slung over his shoulder like a hussar.

All three remained standing, and the councillors seated round the table, covered with a blue cloth, looked at them, pale with anxiety.

'Citizens,' said Gorju, 'we need work!'

The mayor trembled; he had lost his voice.

Marescot answered for him that the council would give it immediate consideration; and when the companions had gone out, several ideas were discussed.

The first was to collect stones.

To make use of the stones Girbal proposed a road from Angleville to Tournebu.

The Bayeux road served exactly the same purpose.

They could clean out the pond! That was not a big enough job! Or dig a second pond! But where?

Langlois wanted to make an embankment along Les Mortins, in case there were floods; it would be better, according to Beljambe, to clear up the heathland. It was impossible to come to any conclusion! . . . To calm the crowd Coulon went down onto the peristyle and announced that they were setting up charity workshops.

'Charity? Thank you!' cried Gorju. 'Down with the nobs! We want the right to work!'

It was the question of the moment, he used it as a means of winning prestige, and was applauded.

Turning round he bumped into Bouvard, whom Pécuchet had brought along, and they entered into conversation. There was no hurry; the Town Hall was surrounded; the council would not escape.

'Where is the money to be found?' said Bouvard.

'From the rich! Besides, the government will order jobs of work.'

'And if no jobs are needed?'

'They will be done in advance!'

'But wages will go down,' retorted Pécuchet. 'When there is a shortage of work, it is because too much is being produced! And you are demanding that it should go up!'

Gorju bit his moustache. 'All the same . . . if work is organized . . .'

'Then the government will be boss!'

Some people around them murmured: 'No! No! No more bosses!'

Gorju became annoyed. 'No matter! The workers must be given some capital, or credits must be set up!'

'How?'

'Oh, I don't know! But credits must be set up!'

'That'll do,' said the engineer, 'they are being a nuisance, those jokers.'

And he went up the steps, declaring that he would break the door down.

Placquevent received him, right leg bent, fists clenched: 'Just come on a bit!'

The engineer retreated.

Catcalls from the crowd reached them inside; they all stood up and wanted to run away. The help from Falaise was not coming! Monsieur le Comte's absence was deplored. Marescot was twiddling a pen about. Old Coulon was groaning. Heurtaux was raging that the gendarmes should be brought in.

'Give the command!' said Foureau.

'I have no orders!'

Meanwhile the noise was increasing. The square was full of people, and everyone was watching the first floor of the Town Hall when at the middle window, under the clock, who should appear but Pécuchet.

He had smartly taken the service stairs, and, trying to imitate Lamartine, began to harangue the people.

'Citizens!'

But his cap, his nose, his coat, his whole person lacked prestige.

The man in the waistcoat called out to him:

'Are you a worker?'

'No.'

'A boss, then?'

'No, not that either.'

'All right, go away!'

'Why?' replied Pécuchet proudly.

And forthwith he disappeared into the embrasure, seized by the engineer. Gorju came to his help.

'Let him be! He is a good chap!' They struggled.

The door opened and Marescot, in the doorway, proclaimed the municipal decision. Hurel had suggested it.

The Tournebu road would have a branch going off to Angleville, which would lead to the Château of Faverges.

The commune was imposing this sacrifice on itself in the interest of the workers.

They dispersed.

As they went home Bouvard and Pécuchet's ears were assailed by women's voices. The servants and Madame Bordin were loudly exclaiming, the widow crying the loudest, and as she saw them:

'Oh! A fine thing! I've been waiting three hours for you! My poor garden, not a single tulip left! Filth everywhere on the lawn! Can't get him to move!'

'But who?'

'Old Gouy!'

He had come with a cartload of manure, and had thrown it just anywhere in the middle of the grass. 'Now he is digging it in! Hurry up so that he will finish!'

'I'll come with you!' said Bouvard.

Outside at the bottom of the steps a horse in the shafts of a wagon was chewing a tuft of oleander. The wheels scraping along the flowerbeds had crushed the box-hedge, snapped off a rhododendron, flattened the dahlias, and heaps of black manure, like molehills, studded the lawn. Gouy was enthusiastically digging.

One day Madame Bordin had casually said that she wanted to turn it over. He had set to work, and despite her order to stop, was going on. This was how he understood the right to work, since Gorju's speeches had quite turned his head.

He only left when Bouvard's threats became violent. In compensation Madame Bordin did not pay for his labour and kept the manure. She was judicious; the doctor's wife and even the lawyer's, although of higher social rank, looked up to her.

The charity workshops lasted a week. No trouble occurred. Gorju had left the district.

However, the National Guard was still called up: a parade on Sundays, periodic military marches and nightly patrols. They worried the village.

They rang people's doorbells for a joke; they went into rooms where married couples snored on the same bolster; then they made bawdy remarks, and the husband would get up and give them a tot of something. Then they went back to the guardroom to play a hundred of dominoes, to drink cider, to eat cheese, and the sentry who stood bored at the door kept opening it all the time. Indiscipline reigned, thanks to Beljambe's slackness.

When the June Days broke out everyone agreed on 'flying to the aid of Paris', but Foureau would not leave the Town Hall, Marescot his office, the doctor his patients, Girbal his firemen. Monsieur de Faverges was at Cherbourg. Beljambe took to his bed. The captain grumbled: 'Nobody wanted me, too bad!' and Bouvard was sensible enough to restrain Pécuchet.

The patrols through the countryside were extended widely.

There were outbreaks of panic, caused by the shadow of a hayrick, or the shape of some branches; once all the National Guardsmen took to their heels. In the moonlight they had noticed, in an apple-tree, a man with a gun trained on them.

Another time, one dark night, the patrol, halting under the beeches, heard someone in front of them.

'Who goes there?'

No answer.

The person was allowed to continue on his way, but they followed at a distance, for he might have a pistol or a club; but when they came to the village, within reach of help, the twelve men in the platoon, altogether, rushed on him, shouting: 'Your papers!' He was jostled, insulted left and right. The men in the guardroom had come out. They dragged him in, and by the light of the candle burning on the stove they finally recognized Gorju.

A wretched lasting coat was tearing at the shoulders. His toes came through the holes in his boots. Scratches and bruises made his face bleed. He had become terribly thin and rolled his eyes like a wolf.

Foureau, who had quickly run up, asked him how he came to be under the beeches, what had brought him back to Chavignolles, how he had spent his time for the past six weeks.

That was no business of theirs. He was a free man.

Placquevent searched him for cartridges. They were going to lock him up provisionally.

Bouvard intervened.

'No good!' replied the mayor. 'Your opinions are known.'

'All the same...'

'Oh! Be careful, I warn you! Be careful!'

Bouvard did not insist.

Then Gorju turned to Pécuchet: 'And you, sir, aren't you going to say something?'

Pécuchet bent his head, as if doubting his innocence.

The poor devil smiled bitterly.

'I defended you, though!'

At daybreak two gendarmes took him to Falaise.

He was not brought before a court-martial, but condemned in the police court to three months in prison for words likely to cause sedition.

From Falaise he wrote asking his former masters to send without delay a certificate of good conduct and character, and as their signatures had to be legally attested by the mayor or his deputy, they preferred to ask Marescot for this small service.

They were shown into a dining-room, decorated with old china plates, with a Boule clock on the narrowest panel. On the mahogany table, without a cloth, were two napkins, a teapot, bowls. Madame Marescot crossed the room in a blue houserobe. She was a Parisian and bored by the country. Then the lawyer came in, legal hat in one hand, newspaper in the other; and at once, very cordially, he affixed his seal, though their protégé was a dangerous man.

'Really,' said Bouvard, 'for a few words...'

'But, my dear sir, when words lead to crimes, if you will allow me!'

'However,' replied Pécuchet, 'how are you going to distinguish between innocent and guilty phrases? Something that is forbidden now may come to be applauded!' And he criticized the savage treatment meted out to the insurgents.

Marescot naturally brought up the defence of society, public safety, supreme law.

'I'm sorry!' said Pécuchet. 'One man's rights deserve as much respect as those of all, and the only objection you can offer is that of force if he turns the axiom against you.'

Marescot, instead of answering, scornfully raised his eyebrows. As long as he went on drawing up his deeds, living among his plates, in his cosy little interior, all kinds of injustice could occur without moving him. Business called him. He excused himself.

His doctrine of public safety had made them angry. The conservatives were now talking like Robespierre.

Another cause for amazement: Cavaignac was losing ground. The Mobile Guard became suspect. Ledru-Rollin had destroyed himself, even in Vaucorbeil's opinion. The debates on the Constitution interested nobody, and on 10th December the people of Chavignolles voted for Bonaparte.

The six million votes cooled Pécuchet's ardour for the people, and Bouvard and he studied the question of universal suffrage.

Since it is common to all, it cannot have any intelligence. An ambitious man will always lead the way, the others will obey like sheep, since the electors do not even have to be literate: that is why, according to Pécuchet, there were so many frauds in the presidential election.

'No intelligence at all,' Bouvard went on, 'I believe instead in the stupidity of the people. Think of all those who buy products like la Revalescière, Dupuytren pommade, the Châtelaines' water, etc. These ninnies make up the electoral mass and we are subject to their will. Why can't you make three thousand francs a year out of rabbits? Because excessive overcrowding makes them die. In the same way the mere fact of having a crowd means that the germs of stupidity it contains develop, with incalculable results.'

'Your scepticism appals me!' said Pécuchet.

Later, in the spring, they met Monsieur de Faverges, who told them of the expedition to Rome. There would be no attack on the Italians, but we needed guarantees. Otherwise our influence would be ruined. Nothing could be more legitimate than this intervention.

Bouvard's eyes opened wide. 'Over Poland you argued just the opposite?'

'It is not the same any more!' Now the Pope was involved.

And Monsieur de Faverges, saying 'We wish for good, we shall do good, we count for good,' represented a group.

Bouvard and Pécuchet were as disgusted by the minority as by the majority. The common people, in fact, were as good as the nobility.

The right to intervene seemed to them suspect. They looked for the principles in Calvo, Martens, Vattel, and Bouvard concluded:

'You can intervene to put a prince back on his throne, to liberate a people, or as a precaution, faced with some danger. In both cases it is an assault on the rights of others, an abuse of force, hypocritical violence!'

'However,' said Pécuchet, 'there is solidarity between peoples as between men.'

'Maybe!' And Bouvard began to dream.

Soon began the internal expedition to Rome.

In their hatred of subversive ideas the élite among the bourgeois of Paris sacked two printing works. The great party of law and order was formed.

Its leaders in the district were the count, Foureau, Marescot and the curé. Every day at about four o'clock they would walk from one end of the square to the other discussing events. The main business was the distribution of pamphlets. The titles did not lack savour: *It will be God's Will*; *The Share-out*; *Let's Get Out of the Mess*; *Where are We Going?* The best of it were the dialogues in rustic style, with oaths and bad French, to raise the peasants' morale. A new law put the prefects in charge of peddling pamphlets and Proudhon had just been clapped into Sainte-Pélagie: an immense victory.

The freedom trees were generally cut down. Chavignolles obeyed the order. With his own eyes Bouvard saw the pieces of his poplar on a wheelbarrow. They were used to warm up the gendarmes and the stump was given to Monsieur le Curé, who had blessed it! What derision!

The schoolmaster did not conceal what he thought.

Bouvard and Pécuchet congratulated him one day when they were passing by his door.

Next day he came to their house. At the end of the week they returned his visit.

Dusk was falling, the children had just gone, and the schoolmaster in shirt sleeves was sweeping the yard. His wife, with a bandanna on her head, was feeding a child. A little girl hid behind her skirts; a hideous infant was playing on the ground at her feet; the soapsuds from her washing in the kitchen were running over the lower part of the house.

'You see,' said the teacher, 'how the government treats us.' And he launched at once into an attack on the infamy of capital. It must be made democratic, the stuff must be freed!

'I should like nothing better!' said Pécuchet.

At least the right to assistance should be recognized.

'One more right!' said Bouvard.

No matter! The Provisional Government had been soft in not decreeing fraternity.

'Try to set it up then!'

As there was no more light, Petit brutally ordered his wife to bring up a torch into his study.

On the plaster walls were pinned lithographed portraits of left-wing orators. A rack full of books rose above a pinewood desk.

All there was to sit on was a hard chair, a stool and an old soap-box; he affected to laugh at it. But poverty stamped his cheeks, and his narrow temples indicated the obstinacy of a mule, intractable pride. He would never yield.

'That's what keeps me going!'

That was a pile of newspapers, on a plank, and in feverish words he expounded the articles of his faith: disarm the troops, abolish the magistrature, equalize wages, have an average level, then you would get a golden age, in the form of a republic, with a dictator at its head, a fine fellow who would get things going with a swing!

Then he found a bottle of anisette and three glasses to drink the toast of the hero, the immortal victim, the great Maximilien![1]

At the door appeared the curé's black robe.

Briskly saluting the company, he approached the teacher and said almost in a whisper:

'How do we stand with our Saint Joseph affair?'

'They didn't give anything,' answered the schoolmaster.

'That's your fault!'

'I did what I could!'

'Oh, really?'

Bouvard and Pécuchet stood up out of discretion. Petit made them sit down again, and addressed the curé.

'Is that all?'

Abbé Jeufroy hesitated, then with a smile to temper his rebuke:

'It is thought that you rather neglect Bible history.'

'Oh, Bible history!' said Bouvard.

'What have you got against it, sir?'

'Me, nothing. Only perhaps there are more useful things than the Jonah anecdote and the kings of Israel.'

'That's up to you,' the priest drily replied.

And heedless of the strangers, or because of them:

'The catechism hour is too short!'

Petit shrugged his shoulders.

'Look out, you will lose your boarders.'

The ten francs a month for these pupils was the best part of his job. But the cassock annoyed him:

1. Robespierre.

'Too bad, have your revenge.'

'A man of my character does not take revenge,' said the priest unmoved. 'Only I would remind you that the law of 15th March puts us in charge of primary education.'

'Oh, I know!' cried the teacher. 'It even falls under colonels of gendarmerie! Why not the rural constable? That would make it complete!'

And he collapsed on the stool, biting his fist, holding back his rage, choked by the feeling of his own impotence.

The ecclesiastic touched him lightly on the shoulder.

'I didn't intend to distress you, my friend! Calm yourself! Be a bit reasonable! It will soon be Easter: I hope you will set an example by taking communion with the others.'

'Oh! That's too much! Me, me! Subject myself to idiocies like that!'

The curé paled at such blasphemy. His eyes flashed. His jaw trembled.

'Be quiet, you wretch, be quiet! And it is his wife who looks after the church linen!'

'Well, what about it? What has she done?'

'She is never at mass! Like you, in fact!'

'Oh, you don't sack a schoolmaster for that!'

'He can be moved!'

The priest said no more. He was at the back of the room, in the shadows. Petit, head sunk on chest, reflected.

They would arrive at the other end of France, having spent their last penny on the journey, and there he would find, under different names, the same curé, the same director of education, the same prefect; all of them, up to the minister, were like the links in the chain that was crushing him! He had already had one warning, others would follow. Then? In a sort of hallucination he saw himself walking along the highway, a sack on his back, his loved ones beside him, hand stretched out to a post-chaise!

At that moment his wife, in the kitchen, was seized with a fit of coughing: the newborn baby began to wail and the infant cried.

'Poor children!' said the priest in a gentle voice.

Then the father burst out into sobs:

'Yes! Yes! Whatever you like!'

'I'll rely on it,' replied the curé.

And, making his bow:

'A very good evening to you, gentlemen!'

The schoolmaster stayed with his face in his hands. He pushed Bouvard away.

'No, let me be! I want to die! I am a wretch!'

The two friends went home, congratulating themselves on their independence. The power of the clergy frightened them.

It was being applied now to strengthen the social order. The republic was soon going to disappear.

Three million electors found themselves excluded from the universal suffrage. The security required for newspapers was raised, censorship re-established. The serial novels were not approved of. Classical philosophy was reputed to be dangerous. The middle class preached the dogma of material interests and the people seemed content.

In the country the people went back to their former masters.

Monsieur de Faverges, who had property in the Eure, was elected to the Legislative Assembly, and his re-election to the General Council of Calvados was a foregone conclusion.

He thought it would be a good thing to give a luncheon to the local notables.

The vestibule, where three servants waited to take their coats, the billiard-room and the two connecting drawing-rooms, the plants in Chinese vases, bronzes on the mantelpieces, gold fillets on the panelling, thick curtains, ample armchairs, all this luxury at once flattered them as if it were a courtesy being paid to them; and going into the dining-room, the sight of a table covered with victuals on silver dishes, with glasses ranged in front of each plate, *hors d'œuvre* here and there, and a salmon in the middle, made every face beam.

They numbered seventeen, including two stout farmers, the sub-prefect from Bayeux and an individual from Cherbourg. Monsieur de Faverges asked his guests to excuse the countess, prevented by a migraine from attending; and after compliments had been paid on the pears and grapes which filled baskets in the four corners, the great news was discussed: the plan for a landing in England by Changarnier.

Heurtaux wanted it as a soldier, the curé because he hated Protestants, Foureau in the interests of trade.

'You are expressing medieval sentiments!' said Pécuchet.

'There were some good things about the Middle Ages!' replied Marescot. 'Our cathedrals, for instance!...'

'However, sir, the abuses!...'

'No matter, the Revolution would not have come!...'

'Oh, the Revolution, that is the trouble!' said the ecclesiastic with a sigh.

'But everyone contributed to it! And (excuse me, Monsieur le Comte) the nobles did so themselves through their alliance with the philosophers.'

'What do you expect? Louis XVIII legalized spoliation! Since then the parliamentary regime has been undermining the foundations!'

A joint of roast beef appeared, and for a few minutes all that could be heard was the noise of forks and jaws, with the steps of the servants moving over the parquet floor and repetition of the two words: 'Madeira! Sauterne!'

Conversation was resumed by the gentleman from Cherbourg. How was one to stop on the slope of the abyss?

'In the case of the Athenians,' said Marescot, 'in the case of the Athenians, with whom we have some affinities, Solon checked the democrats by raising the qualifying sum for electors.'

'It would be better,' said Hurel, 'to suppress the Chamber; all the disorders come from Paris.'

'Decentralize!' said the lawyer.

'Widely!' added the count.

According to Foureau the commune ought to be absolute master, going so far as to ban its roads to travellers if it saw fit.

And as one dish followed another, chicken in gravy, crayfish, mushrooms, vegetable salad, roast larks, many subjects were treated: the best tax system, the advantages of large-scale farming, the abolition of the death penalty; the sub-prefect did not forget to quote the delightful remark of a witty man: 'You may begin your murdering, gentlemen!'

Bouvard was surprised by the contrast between the things around him and what people said, for it always seems as though words should correspond to surroundings, and that high ceilings are made for lofty thoughts. Nevertheless he was flushed when it came to the dessert, and dimly saw the fruit dishes as through a haze.

They had drunk claret, Burgundy and Malaga wines. Monsieur de Faverges, who knew worldly ways, had some champagne opened. The guests drank a toast to the success of the election, and it was past three o'clock when they moved into the smoking-room for coffee.

A caricature from *Charivari* lay on a console table, among numbers of the *Univers*; it depicted a citizen whose coat-tails parted to show a tail with an eye on the end. Marescot explained it. There was loud laughter.

They absorbed liqueurs, and cigar ash dropped into the upholstery of the furniture. The abbé, trying to convince Girbal, attacked Voltaire. Coulon fell asleep. Monsieur de Faverges declared his devotion for Chambord. 'The bees prove the monarchy.'

'But the ant-hills prove the republic.' Besides, the doctor had had enough.

'You are right!' said the sub-prefect. 'The form of government matters very little!'

'Granted freedom!' objected Pécuchet.

'An honest man doesn't need it,' replied Foureau. 'I don't make speeches! I am not a journalist! And I maintain that France wants to be governed by an iron hand!'

Everyone demanded a saviour.

As they left, Bouvard and Pécuchet heard Monsieur de Faverges saying to Abbé Jeufroy:

'Obedience must be re-established. Authority dies if it is open to discussion! Divine right, it is the only thing!'

'Absolutely, Monsieur le Comte!'

The pale rays of the October sunshine were lengthening behind the woods, a damp wind blew; and as they walked over the dead leaves they breathed like men set free.

All that they had been unable to say came out in exclamations:

'What idiots! What mean spirits! How is such obstinacy conceivable! First of all, what does divine right mean?'

Dumouchel's friend, the professor who had enlightened them about aesthetics, answered their question in a learned letter.

The theory of divine right was formulated under Charles II by the Englishman Filmer.

It says:

The creator gave the first man sovereignty over the world. It was transmitted to his descendants, and the king's power emanates from God: 'He is in God's image,' writes Bossuet. Paternal rule accustoms people to domination by a single person. Kings were made on the model of fathers.

But, according to Locke, paternal power is to be distinguished from monarchical, for each subject has the same power over his children as the monarch has over his. Royalty only exists by popular choice, and election was even recalled in the coronation ceremony, when two bishops presented the king and asked the nobles and commoners if they accepted him as such. Thus power comes from the people. They have the right 'to do anything they wish', says Helvétius, 'to change their constitution', says Vattel, to revolt against injustice, claim Glafey, Hotman, Mabley, etc.! St Thomas Aquinas authorizes them to deliver themselves from a tyrant. They are even, says Jurieu, dispensed from being right.

Amazed at this axiom they took up Rousseau's *Social Contract.*

Pécuchet read right to the end of it; then, closing his eyes and throwing back his head, he gave an analysis of it.

'A convention is assumed whereby the individual alienated his freedom.

'The people at the same time undertook to defend him against natural inequalities, and made him owner of the things he held.

'Where is the proof of the contract?

'Nowhere! And the community offers no guarantee. The citizens will henceforth concern themselves exclusively with politics. But as trades are necessary, Rousseau advises slavery. Sciences have been the ruin of the human race. The theatre is corrupting, money deadly, and the State must impose some religion on pain of death.'

What! they said to themselves, so that is the pontiff of democracy!

All reformers have copied him, and they procured the *Examination of Socialism* by Morant.

The first chapter expounded the doctrine of Saint-Simon.

At the top is the Father, both pope and emperor. Abolition of inheritance, all property, movable and immovable, making up a social fund, which will be hierarchically exploited. Industrialists will govern public wealth. But there is no cause for alarm: the leader will be 'the one who loves most'.

One thing is missing, woman. The salvation of the world depends on the advent of woman.

'I don't understand.'

'Neither do I!'

And they tried Fourierism.

All troubles come from constraint. Once attraction is free, harmony will be established.

Our soul contains twelve main passions: five selfish, four spiritual, three distributive. The first tend to the individual, the next to groups, the last to groups of groups, or series, which together make up the phalanx, a society of 1,800 persons, living in a palace. Every morning vehicles take the workers into the country, and bring them back in the evening. Banners are carried, feasts are held, cakes eaten. Every woman, if she wishes, possesses three men: husband, lover, progenitor. For the unmarried, dancing girls are provided.

'That just suits me!' said Bouvard, and he lost himself in dreams of the harmonious world.

With the restoration of climates the world will become a better place; by crossing races, human life will become longer. Clouds will be directed as thunder is now, at night rain will fall on towns to clean them. Ships will cross the polar seas, thawed out under the Northern Lights. For everything results from the conjunction of two fluids, male and female, spurting from the poles, and the Northern Lights are a symptom of planetary rutting, a prolific emission.

'That's beyond me,' said Pécuchet.

After Saint-Simon and Fourier the problem reduces itself to the question of wages.

Louis Blanc, in the workers' interest, wants external trade abolished; Lafarelle, a tax on machines; another wants drink to be tax-free, or the old guild courts to be restored, or the setting up of soup kitchens. Proudhon imagines a uniform tariff, and demands a state monopoly of sugar.

'Your socialists,' said Bouvard, 'always demand tyranny.'

'No!'

'Yes, they do!'

'You are absurd!'

'And you revolt me!'

They sent for books of which they only knew summaries. Bouvard noted several passages, and showed them:

'Read for yourself! They suggest the examples of the Essenes, the Moravian Brotherhood, the Jesuits in Paraguay, even the regime in prisons.

'With the Icarians lunch takes twenty minutes, women give birth in hospital; as for books, it is forbidden to print any without authorization of the republic.'

'But Cabet is an idiot!

'Now here is some Saint-Simon: publicists will submit their work to a committee of industrialists.

'And Pierre Leroux: the law will force citizens to hear an orator.

'And Auguste Comte: priests will educate the young, will direct all intellectual work, and will pledge the Government to control procreation.'

These documents distressed Pécuchet. That evening, at dinner, he replied.

'I agree that there are absurdities in the Utopists; yet they deserve our love. The hideousness of the world saddened them, and in order to make it more beautiful they endured every suffering. Remember Thomas More beheaded, Campanella put to the torture seven times, Buonarotti with a chain round his neck, Saint-Simon dying of poverty, many others. They could have led a quiet life; but no! They trod their path, head held high, like heroes.'

'Do you think,' went on Bouvard, 'that the world will change thanks to some gentleman's theories?'

'What does it matter?' said Pécuchet. 'It is time to stop rotting away in selfishness! Let us look for the best system!'

'So you reckon on finding it?'

'Certainly!'

'You?'

And Bouvard was shaken by a laugh which made his shoulders and belly jump in unison. Redder than the jam on the table, napkin under his armpit, he repeated: 'Ha! Ha! Ha!' in a most irritating way.

Pécuchet left the room, slamming the door.

Germaine went all over the house calling him, and they tracked him down to his room, sitting in an armchair, with neither fire nor candle and with his cap pulled over his eyes. He was not ill, but was giving himself up to his reflections.

When the quarrel was over they recognized that their studies lacked a basis: political economy.

They went into supply and demand, capital and rent, imports, prohibition.

One night Pécuchet was woken up by the crunch of a boot in the corridor. In the evening, as usual, he had drawn all the bolts himself, and he called Bouvard, who was sleeping soundly.

They stayed motionless under the bedclothes. The noise did not start again.

But as they walked round their garden, they noticed in the middle of the flowerbeds, near the fence, the mark of a bootsole, and two sticks of the trellis had been broken. Someone had obviously climbed it.

The rural constable had to be warned.

As he was not at the Town Hall, Pécuchet went to the grocer's.

Whom should he see at the back of the shop, beside Placquevent, amongst the drinkers? Gorju! Gorju got up like a respectable citizen, treating the company.

This meeting had no significance.

Soon they came to the question of progress.

Bouvard did not doubt it in the scientific field. But in literature it is not so clear; and if prosperity is increasing, life is no longer so splendid.

To convince him Pécuchet took a piece of paper:

'I trace a wavy line at an angle. Anyone who followed it would lose sight of the horizon every time the line dips. However, it rises up again, and in spite of its detours they will reach the top. That is the image of progress.'

Madame Bordin came in.

It was 3rd December 1851. She brought the newspaper.

They read rapidly and side by side the appeal to the people, the dissolution of the Chamber, the imprisonment of the deputies.

Pécuchet went white. Bouvard looked at the widow.

'What! Have you nothing to say?'

'What do you expect me to do about it?' They forgot to offer her a seat. 'I came here, thinking you would be pleased! Oh, you are not very nice today!' And she went out, shocked at their discourtesy.

Surprise had rendered them speechless. Then they went into the village to air their indignation.

Marescot, who received them amid his contracts, thought differently. All the talking in the Chamber was over, thank heaven. From now on they would have a policy of action.

Beljambe knew nothing of the events, and in any case did not care.

In the covered market they stopped Vaucorbeil.

The doctor had got over all that: 'You are very wrong to torment yourselves!'

Foureau passed near them, saying scornfully: 'That's done for the democrats!' And the captain, on Girbal's arm, cried from a distance: 'Long live the emperor!'

But Petit was bound to understand them, and when Bouvard tapped at the window, the schoolmaster left his class.

He thought it extremely funny that Thiers was in prison. That would avenge the people.

'Now, honourable members, it's your turn!'

The shooting on the boulevards won the approval of Chavignolles. No mercy for the defeated, no pity for the victims! As soon as anyone rebels he is a scoundrel.

'Let us thank Providence,' said the curé, 'and then Louis Bonaparte! He surrounds himself with men of the greatest distinction! The Comte de Faverges will become a senator.'

Next day they had a visit from Placquevent.

The two gentlemen had talked a lot. He urged them to hold their tongues.

'Do you want to know my opinion?' said Pécuchet.

'Since the bourgeois are savage, the workers jealous, the priests servile, and the people will accept any tyrant, so long as he leaves their snouts in the trough, Napoleon has done well! Let him gag them, trample them, exterminate them! Nothing will ever be too much for their hatred of the law, their cowardice, their ineptitude, their blindness!'

Bouvard thought: 'Ah, progress, what a farce!' He added: 'And politics, what a filthy mess!'

'It's not a science,' replied Pécuchet. 'The art of war is better, you can anticipate what is happening; should we try it?'

'Oh, thank you!' replied Bouvard. 'Everything makes me sick. Let us rather sell up our place and "damn well go where the savages are".'

'As you like!'

Mélie was drawing water in the yard.

The wooden pump had a long lever. To bring it down she bent at the waist so that one could see her blue stockings right up to her calves. Then, with a rapid gesture, she lifted her right arm, turning her head a little, and as he looked at her Pécuchet felt something quite new, a charm, an infinite pleasure.

7

GLOOMY days began.

They stopped their studies for fear of disappointment, the inhabitants of Chavignolles kept away from them, the newspapers that were tolerated told them nothing, their solitude was profound, their inactivity complete.

Sometimes they opened a book and closed it again; what was the point? On other days they had the idea of tidying up the garden, but after a quarter of an hour they felt tired; or of looking at their farm, but they came back sick at heart; or doing household jobs, but Germaine cried out in protest; they gave up.

Bouvard wanted to catalogue the museum, and declared that all the objects were stupid. Pécuchet borrowed Langlois's fowling-piece to shoot larks; the weapon, bursting at the first shot, nearly killed him.

So they lived in that rural boredom which weighs so heavily when a pale sky crushes beneath its monotony a heart bereft of hope. You listen to the footsteps of someone in clogs going along the wall, or the raindrops falling from the roof on to the ground. From time to time a dead leaf brushes against the window, spins round, disappears. Vague sounds of tolling bells are borne on the wind. Down in the shed a cow moos.

They yawned in front of each other, consulted the calendar, looked at the clock, waited for meals; and the horizon was always the same: fields facing them, the church on the right, a screen of poplars on the left, tops swaying in the mist, perpetually, mournfully.

Habits which they had tolerated now upset them. Pécuchet became a nuisance with his mania for putting his handkerchief on the tablecloth, Bouvard's pipe was always in his mouth, and he swayed about as he talked. Arguments blew up, about particular dishes, or the quality of the butter. When they were together they thought about different things.

A certain event had staggered Pécuchet.

Two days after the riot at Chavignolles, as he was walking off his political disappointment, he came to a lane covered by bushy elms, and heard a voice behind him cry: 'Stop!'

It was Madame Castillon. She was running on the other side, without noticing him. A man walking in front of her turned round. It was Gorju, and they met each other a few feet from Pécuchet, separated from him by the line of trees.

'Is it true?' she said. 'You're going to fight?'

Pécuchet slipped into the ditch to hear them.

'Oh yes!' replied Gorju. 'I'm going to fight! What difference does it make to you?'

'He asks me that!' she cried, wringing her hands. 'But if you are killed, my love? Oh, do stay!' Her blue eyes, even more than her words, besought him.

'Leave me alone! I must be off!'

She sneered angrily: 'The other one let you, eh?' 'Don't talk about it!' He raised his clenched fist.

'No, my friend, no! I'll shut up, I won't say anything.' Big tears rolled down her cheeks into the pleats of her collar.

It was midday. The sun shone on the countryside, covered with yellow corn. Far off the hood of a cart slowly slid by. Torpor filled the still air, no bird sang, no insect buzzed. Gorju had cut himself a switch and was scraping the bark off. Madame Castillon did not raise her head.

She was thinking, poor woman, how vain her sacrifices had been: the debts she had paid off, her future commitments, her lost reputation. Instead of complaining she reminded him of the early days of their love, when she went every night to meet him in the barn, so that once her husband, thinking there was a thief about, had fired a pistol out of the window. The bullet was still in the wall. 'From the moment I knew you, you looked as handsome as a prince. I love your eyes, your voice, your walk, your smell!' She added, in a lower voice: 'I am quite crazy about you!'

He smiled, his pride flattered.

She clasped both hands on his body, with head thrown back as if in worship.

'Dear heart! Dear love! My soul! My life! Come on, speak, what do you want? Is it money? We'll find some. I have been wrong!

I got on your nerves! Forgive me! Order yourself clothes from the tailor, drink champagne, lead a gay life, I'll let you do anything, anything!' She made a supreme effort and murmured: 'Even her... so long as you come back to me!'

He bent down over her mouth, an arm round her waist to prevent her from falling, and she stammered: 'Dear heart! Dear love! How handsome you are! Goodness, how handsome!'

Pécuchet stood motionless, the earth in the ditch up to his chin, looking at them, breathing heavily.

'No weakness!' said Gorju. 'I would only have to miss the coach! They are getting up a really big job, and I'm part of it! Give me ten sous so that I can buy the driver a drink.'

She took five francs out of her purse. 'You will soon pay me back. Have a bit of patience! All the time he has been paralysed! Just think! And if you wanted to, we could go to the chapel at La Croix-Janval and there, my love, I would swear before the Blessed Virgin to marry you as soon as he is dead!'

'Oh, he'll never die, that husband of yours!'

Gorju had turned on his heels, she caught him up, and clinging to his shoulders:

'Let me go away with you! I'll be your servant! You need someone. But don't go! Don't leave me! I'd rather die! Kill me!'

She dragged herself at his knees, trying to grasp his hands to kiss them; her bonnet fell off, followed by her comb, and her short hair fell loose. It had gone white under her ears, and as she looked up at him, convulsed with sobs, with reddened eyelids and swollen lips, he was suddenly annoyed and pushed her away.

'Get back, old woman! Good night!'

When she was on her feet again, she snatched off the gold cross hanging round her neck and threw it at him:

'Take it! You scum!'

Gorju went off, hitting the leaves of the trees with his switch.

Madame Castillon did not cry. With mouth open and eyes lifeless she stood motionless, petrified in her despair; she was no longer a human being, but a ruined thing.

What he had just come upon was, for Pécuchet, like the discovery of another world, a whole world, with dazzling lights, a riot of wild blooms, oceans, tempests, treasures and abysses of infinite depth;

it struck terror into the heart, but what did that matter? He dreamed of love, longed to feel it like her, inspire it like him.

Yet he execrated Gorju and in the guardroom had found it hard not to betray him.

Madame Castillon's lover humiliated him by his slim build, his even row of kiss curls, his fleecy beard, his conquering air, while his own hair . . . stuck to his skull like a wet wig; his torso in his overcoat looked like a bolster, two front teeth were missing and his features were severe. He thought heaven unjust, felt as though he were disinherited, and his friend no longer loved him.

Bouvard abandoned him every evening. After the death of his wife there would have been nothing to stop him taking another – who would now be cossetting him, looking after his house. He was too old to think of it.

But Bouvard looked at himself in the mirror. His cheeks still had their colour, his hair curled as it used to, not a tooth had gone, and at the idea that he might still be attractive, his youth returned. Madame Bordin rose up in his memory. She had made advances to him, the first time, when the ricks caught fire, the second at their dinner, then in the museum, during the declamation, and recently she had come without ill-feeling three Sundays running. So he went to see her, and went again, promising himself he would seduce her.

Ever since the day that Pécuchet had watched the young servant drawing water he spoke to her more often; and whether she was sweeping the corridor, hanging out the washing, turning the saucepans, he could not have enough of the pleasure of seeing her, surprising himself with his emotions, as during adolescence. He had the same fevers and languors, and was persecuted by the memory of Madame Castillon embracing Gorju.

He questioned Bouvard on the way libertines set about getting themselves women.

'You give them presents, take them out to restaurants.'

'Very good! But then?'

'Some pretend to faint, so that you carry them onto a sofa, others drop their handkerchief, the best ones openly give you a rendezvous.' Bouvard spread himself in descriptions, which inflamed

Pécuchet's imagination like obscene engravings. 'The first rule is not to believe what they say. I have known women who were real Messalinas beneath a saintly exterior! Above all you must be bold!'

But boldness does not come to order. Every day Pécuchet postponed his decision, and was in any case intimidated by Germaine's presence.

Hoping she would ask for her notice, he demanded more and more work, noted how many times she was drunk, commented aloud on her dirtiness, her laziness, and finally secured her dismissal.

Then Pécuchet was free!

How impatiently he waited for Bouvard to go out! How his heart beat as soon as the door closed!

Mélie was working at a small table, near the window, by candlelight; from time to time she snapped off the thread in her teeth, then blinked her eyes to get it through the needle.

First he wanted to know what sort of men she liked. Was it for example Bouvard's type? Not at all; she preferred thin men. He dared to ask her if she had ever had lovers.

'Never!'

Then, coming closer, he studied her delicate nose, her narrow mouth, the curve of her features. He complimented her and exhorted her to be good.

As he leaned over he saw in her corsage white shapes, which gave off a warm smell that made his cheeks burn. One evening he touched his lips to the wisps of hair at her neck and felt stirred to the marrow of his bones. Another time he kissed her on the chin, and had to prevent himself from actually biting her flesh, it tasted so sweet. She returned his kiss. The room spun round. He could no longer see clearly.

He gave her a present of a pair of boots, and often treated her to a glass of anisette.

To save her trouble, he rose early, broke up sticks, lit the fire, went so far in his attentiveness as to clean Bouvard's shoes.

Mélie did not faint, or drop her handkerchief, and Pécuchet did not know what to resolve, his desire increased by his fear of satisfying it.

Bouvard went on assiduously paying court to Madame Bordin.

She received him, a little constricted in her dress of dove-grey silk, which creaked like a horse's harness, toying the while, for appearance's sake, with her gold chain.

Their conversation turned on the people of Chavignolles or 'her late husband', who had been a court official at Livarot.

Then she enquired about Bouvard's past, curious to know 'the pranks of his youth', and incidentally the state of his fortune, the interests linking him to Pécuchet.

He admired the way she kept her house and, when he dined with her, the spotless service, the excellent table. A succession of very appetizing dishes, regularly punctuated by an aged Pommard, brought them to the dessert, when they spent a very long time over their coffee; and Madame Bordin, dilating her nostrils, drank from the saucer with her full lips, lightly shadowed with downy, dark hairs.

One day she appeared in décolleté. Her shoulders fascinated Bouvard. As he was sitting on a small chair in front of her, he began to stroke her arms with both hands. The widow became annoyed. He did not start again, but pictured to himself marvellously ample and solid curves.

One evening when Mélie's cooking had disgusted him, he felt a sudden joy as he went into Madame Bordin's drawing-room. That is where he should have lived!

The lamp-globe, covered with a pink paper shade, shed a gentle light. She sat beside the fire; and her foot showed beyond the edge of her dress. From the first words conversation died out.

However, she looked at him through half-closed lashes, languorously, insistently.

Bouvard could take no more! Kneeling on the parquet floor he stammered: 'I love you! Let's get married!'

Madame Bordin breathed hard, then, looking ingenuous, said he must be joking; people would surely laugh, it was not reasonable, this declaration bemused her.

Bouvard objected that they needed no one's consent. 'What is stopping you? Is it the trousseau? Our linen has the same mark, *B*! We'll unite our two capitals!'

The argument pleased her. But a major affair prevented her from deciding before the end of the month. Bouvard groaned.

She had the delicacy to see him home, accompanied by Marianne, carrying a lantern.

The two friends had hidden their passion from each other.

Pécuchet intended to go on concealing his intrigue with the maid. If Bouvard was against it, he would take her somewhere else, even Algeria, where life is not too dear! But he rarely worked out such hypotheses, full of his love, without thinking of the consequences.

Bouvard planned to turn the museum into the conjugal bedroom, unless Pécuchet were to refuse; then he would live in his future wife's home.

One afternoon in the following week, it was at her home, in the garden, the buds were beginning to open, and between the clouds there were big patches of blue; she bent down to pick some violets and said, as she presented them:

'Greet Madame Bouvard!'

'What! Is it true?'

'Perfectly true.'

He wanted to seize her in his arms; she repulsed him.

'What a man!' Then, becoming serious, she warned him that she would soon be asking him a favour.

'I grant it!'

They fixed the signing of their contract for the following Thursday.

Up to the last moment no one was to know anything about it.

'Agreed!'

And he went out, eyes turned heavenward, spry as a kid.

Pécuchet, on the morning of the same day, had promised himself that he would die if he did not win the favours of his maid, and he had accompanied her into the cellar, hoping that the darkness would make him bold.

Several times she had tried to go; but he kept her back to count the bottles, choose laths, or look at the bottom of the barrels. All that had been going on for some time.

She stood facing him, under the light from the ventilator, quite straight, with lowered eyelids and the corner of her mouth slightly turned up.

'Do you love me?' Pécuchet abruptly said.

'Yes! I love you.'

'All right then, prove it!'

Putting his left arm round her he began with his other hand to unfasten her bodice.

'Are you going to hurt me?'

'No! My little angel! Don't be afraid!'

'If Monsieur Bouvard...'

'I won't tell him anything! Don't worry!'

A pile of logs lay behind. She fell back onto them, breasts clear of her chemise, head back, then hid her face under one arm, and anyone else would have understood that she was not without experience.

Bouvard soon arrived for dinner.

The meal passed in silence, each fearing to give himself away. Mélie served them, expressionless as usual; Pécuchet averted his eyes to avoid hers, while Bouvard, looking at the walls, thought of improvements.

Eight days later, on the Thursday, he came home furious.

'The bloody bitch!'

'But who?'

'Madame Bordin.'

And he recounted how he had been insane enough to want to make her his wife; but it was all over, finished a quarter of an hour ago, in Marescot's office.

She had claimed Les Écalles as a dowry, but he could not dispose of it since he had paid for it, like the farm, partly with someone else's money.

'Indeed!' said Pécuchet.

'And I had been stupid enough to promise her any favour she chose! This was it! I was obstinate about it; if she loved me she would have given in!' The widow, on the contrary, had got carried away with insults, had denigrated his physique, his paunch. 'My paunch! I ask you!'

Pécuchet meanwhile had gone out several times, walking with his legs wide apart.

'Are you unwell?' said Bouvard.

'Oh, yes, I am unwell!'

And, when he had shut the door, Pécuchet after much hesitation confessed that he had just discovered that he had caught an intimate disease.

'You?'

'Me!'

'Oh, my poor chap! Who gave it to you?'

He went redder still, and said in a still lower voice:

'It can only be Mélie!'

Bouvard stayed dumbfounded.

The first thing was to dismiss the young person.

She protested with candour.

Pécuchet's case was serious, however; but ashamed of his turpitude he did not dare see the doctor.

Bouvard thought of turning to Barberou.

They sent him the details of the sickness, so that he could show them to a doctor who would treat it by correspondence.

Barberou went about it zealously, convinced that it concerned Bouvard, and called him a gay old dog, while congratulating him at the same time.

'At my age!' said Pécuchet. 'Isn't it dismal! But why did she do that to me?'

'She liked you.'

'She should have warned me.'

'Is passion reasonable?' And Bouvard complained of Madame Bordin.

He had often come upon her stopping in front of Les Écalles, in Marescot's company, conferring with Germaine – so many machinations for a bit of land!

'She is avaricious! That's the explanation!'

So they ruminated over their misfortune, in the little room by the fireside, Pécuchet swallowing his medicine, Bouvard smoking his pipe, and they discoursed about women.

'Strange need, is it a need? They drive men to crime, heroism, madness. Hell beneath a skirt, paradise in a kiss, turtle dove's plumage, serpent's coils, cat's claws, treacherous as the sea, changeable as the moon.' They repeated all the commonplaces that women have inspired far and wide.

It was the desire to have one that had suspended their friendship. They were seized with remorse. No more women, right? And they embraced each other tenderly.

Some reaction was necessary; and Bouvard, after Pécuchet's cure, opined that hydrotherapy would do them good.

Germaine, who had returned once the other had gone, carted the bathtub into the corridor every morning.

The two fellows, naked as savages, hurled full buckets of water at each other, then ran back to their rooms. They could be seen from the fence, and some people were scandalized.

8

SATISFIED with their regime, they tried to improve their condition with gymnastics.

They took Amoros's manual, and went through the plates.

All these lads squatting, upside down, standing, bending their knees, stretching their arms, waving their fists, weight-lifting, straddling beams, climbing up ladders, swinging about on trapezes, such a display of strength and agility aroused their envy.

However, they were depressed at the splendours of the gymnasium described in the preface. For they could not acquire a hall for the equipment, a racetrack for running, a swimming pool or 'a mountain of glory', an artificial hill a hundred feet high.

A wooden vaulting-horse with padding would have been expensive, and they gave it up; the fallen lime-tree in the garden served as a horizontal bar; and when they had become skilled at going along it from one end to the other, in order to have a vertical bar they replanted one of the buttresses of the espaliers. Pécuchet climbed up to the top. Bouvard kept slipping and falling off, and finally gave up.

He liked the 'orthosomatic sticks' rather better, that is two broom staves connected by two cords, the first passing under the armpits, the second over the wrists; and for hours he kept this apparatus on, with chin up, chest out, elbows in.

As a substitute for dumb-bells the wheelwright turned four pieces of ashwood for them, looking like sugarloaves ending in bottle necks. You are supposed to swing these clubs right, left, front and rear; but being too heavy they slipped from their fingers, and risked crushing their legs. That did not matter, and they worked hard at the 'Indian clubs' and even, fearing every evening that they might split, rubbed them with wax and a piece of cloth.

Then they looked for ditches. When they had found one that suited them, they pushed a long pole into the middle, took off with the left foot, reached the other side, then began all over again. The countryside was flat, so that they could be seen from far off;

and the villagers wondered what these two extraordinary creatures were, leaping about on the horizon.

With the coming of autumn, they started on indoor gymnastics; it bored them. Why did they not have the shaker, or post-chair, invented under Louis XIV by the Abbé de Saint-Pierre? How was it made, where could they find out? Dumouchel did not even deign to answer.

Then they fixed up an arm-operated see-saw in the bakehouse. Through two pulleys screwed to the ceiling passed a cord, holding a crossbar at each end. As soon as they had taken hold of it, one of them pushed the ground with his toes, the other lowered his arms to floor level; the first, by his weight, pulled up the other, who loosing the cord a little, rose up in his turn; in less than five minutes their limbs were dripping with sweat.

In an attempt to follow the prescriptions in the manual they tried to become ambidextrous, to the point of doing without their right hands temporarily. They went further: Amoros indicates the passages of verse to sing during the exercises, and Bouvard and Pécuchet repeated hymn number nine: 'A king, a just king, is a blessing on earth.' When they beat their breasts: 'Friends, the crown and glory, etc.' As they ran at the double:

> The timid beast is ours!
> Let us catch the rapid stag!
> Aye! We shall overcome!
> Run! Run! Run!

And panting more than dogs they became excited at the sound of their own voices.

One aspect of gymnastics made them enthusiastic; its use in rescues.

But they needed children so that they could learn how to carry them in sacks, and they asked the schoolmaster to provide one or two. Petit objected that the families would be annoyed. They fell back on first aid for the injured. One of them pretended to faint and the other pushed him along in a wheelbarrow, with all kinds of precautions.

As for military escalades, the author recommends Bois-Rosé's ladder, so called after the captain who once surprised Fécamp by climbing up the cliff.

Following the engravings in the book, they fitted rungs onto a rope, and fastened it under the shed.

As soon as you have straddled the first rung, and grasped the third, you throw your legs outwards so that the second rung, which a moment ago was against your chest, comes just below the thighs. You straighten up, seize the fourth, and go on up. Despite prodigious wriggling of their hips they found it impossible to reach the second rung.

Perhaps it would not be so hard to cling to stones with their hands as Bonaparte's soldiers did at the attack on Fort-Chambray? To enable you to perform such a feat Amoros has a tower in his establishment.

The ruined wall might take its place. They attempted to assault it.

But Bouvard withdrew his foot too quickly from a hole, took fright and had an attack of dizziness.

Pécuchet blamed their methods; they had neglected the part concerning the knuckles, and must go back to the principles.

His exhortations were in vain; and in his pride he tried stilts.

Nature seemed to have destined him for that, because he at once used the large size, with footrests four feet above the ground, and balancing on them he strode up and down the garden, like some gigantic stork out for a walk.

Bouvard, at the window, saw him stagger, and then collapse in a mass on the runner beans, whose branches, as they broke, deadened his fall. They picked him up, covered with dirt, nose bleeding, face ashen, and he thought he had strained himself.

Gymnastics were definitely not suitable for men of their age; they gave it up, did not dare move for fear of accidents, and sat all day long in the museum dreaming of other occupations.

This change of habit affected Bouvard's health. He became very heavy, puffed like a grampus after meals, tried to lose weight, ate less, grew weaker.

Pécuchet too felt 'run down', his skin itched and he had spots in his throat. 'There's something wrong,' they said, 'something wrong.'

Bouvard had the idea of going to the inn to choose a few bottles of Spanish wine to get the wheels turning again.

As he came out, Marescot's clerk and three other men were

carrying in to Beljambe a big walnut table; 'Monsieur' thanked them profusely. It had behaved perfectly.

Bouvard thus learned of the new fashion for table-turning. He joked about it to the clerk.

However, throughout Europe, America, Australia and India millions of mortals spent their lives making tables turn, and people were discovering how to make canaries prophesy, give concerts without instruments, correspond by means of snails. The press, offering such humbug to the public in all seriousness, only reinforced its credulity.

Rapping spirits had turned up at the Château of Faverges, and thence had spread to the village. The lawyer in particular asked them questions.

Shocked by Bouvard's scepticism he invited the two friends to a table-turning evening.

Was it a trap? Madame Bordin would be there. Pécuchet went, alone.

Those present were the mayor, the tax-collector, the captain, other citizens and their wives, Madame Vaucorbeil, Madame Bordin indeed; in addition, a former assistant mistress of Madame Marescot, Mademoiselle Laverrière, a slightly dubious person with grey hair falling in ringlets to her shoulders, in the fashion of 1830. In an armchair sat a cousin from Paris, wearing a blue suit and an impertinent look.

The two bronze lamps, the whatnot full of curiosities, the illustrated ballads on the piano, and tiny watercolours in huge frames were always a source of amazement at Chavignolles, but that evening all eyes were drawn to the mahogany table. They would shortly be putting it to the test, and it took on the importance of anything that contains a mystery.

Twelve guests sat down round the table, hands outstretched, little fingers touching. All that could be heard was the ticking of the clock. Their faces registered the deepest attention.

After ten minutes several of them complained of pins and needles in their arms. Pécuchet was uncomfortable.

'You are pushing!' the captain said to Foureau.

'Not at all!'

'Yes, you are!'

'Oh, sir!'

The lawyer calmed them.

By listening hard they thought they could hear wood creaking – an illusion! Nothing was moving.

The other day, when the Aubert and Lormeau families had come over from Lisieux, and Beljambe's table had been borrowed specially, everything had gone so well! But the one today was so obstinate... why?

The carpet probably hindered it, so they went into the dining-room.

The chosen piece of furniture was a large console-table at which Pécuchet, Girbal, Madame Marescot and her cousin, Monsieur Alfred, installed themselves.

The table, which was on castors, slid towards the right; the operators, without undoing their fingers, followed its movement; and of its own accord it made two more turns. Everyone was stupefied.

Then Monsieur Alfred said loud and clear:

'Spirit, how do you find my cousin?'

The table, slowly oscillating, rapped nine times.

According to a placard, on which the number of strokes was translated into letters, that meant 'charming'. Applause broke out.

Then Marescot, teasing Madame Bordin, called on the spirit to declare her exact age.

The foot of the table fell five times.

'What! Five years old?' cried Girbal.

'The decades don't count,' replied Foureau.

The widow smiled, inwardly vexed.

The answers to the other questions were unsuccessful, because the alphabet was so complicated. The planchette board was better, and an expeditious method which Mademoiselle Laverrière had even used to note down in an album direct communications from Louis XII, Clémence Isaure, Franklin, Jean-Jacques Rousseau, etc. These instruments were on sale in the Rue d'Aumale; Monsieur Alfred promised one, then, addressing the assistant mistress:

'But for the quarter hour break, a little piano music, don't you think? A mazurka!'

Two thumping chords vibrated. He took his cousin round the

waist, disappeared with her, came back. Her dress made a cool draught, and brushed against the doors as she went by. She threw back her head, he crooked his arm. The company admired her grace and his dashing appearance; and without waiting for the petit-fours, Pécuchet withdrew, astonished by the evening.

It was no good his repeating: 'I saw it! I saw it!' Bouvard denied the facts but nevertheless agreed to experiment himself.

For weeks they spent their afternoons facing each other, their hands on a table, then on a hat, a basket, plates. All these objects remained motionless.

The phenomenon of turning tables is none the less certain for that. Popular opinion attributes it to spirits, Faraday to the prolongation of nervous action, Chevreul to unconscious efforts, or perhaps, as Ségouin admits, an assembly of individuals gives off an impulse, a magnetic current?

This hypothesis sent Pécuchet into a reverie. He took from his library Montacabère's *Magnetizer's Guide*, re-read it carefully and initiated Bouvard into the theory.

All animate bodies receive and communicate the influence of the stars, a property analogous to the power of the magnet. By directing this force one can heal the sick, such is the principle. Science, since Mesmer, has developed, but it is still important to pour out the fluid and make the passes which must first induce sleep.

'All right, put me to sleep!' said Bouvard.

'Impossible,' replied Pécuchet, 'for someone to experience the magnetic action and transmit it faith is indispensable.'

Then, considering Bouvard:

'Oh, what a pity!'

'What?'

'Yes, if you were willing, with a bit of practice, there wouldn't be another magnetizer like you!'

For he had everything required: prepossessing manner, robust constitution and solid morale.

This faculty which he had just been found to possess flattered Bouvard. He plunged stealthily into Montacabère.

Then, as Germaine had buzzings in her ears which made her deaf, he said one evening in a casual way:

'Supposing we tried magnetism?'

She did not refuse. He sat down in front of her, took her two thumbs in his hands and stared at her as if he had never done anything else all his life.

The good woman, with a foot-warmer under her heels, began by bending her neck; her eyes closed and quite gently she began to snore. After they had looked at her for an hour, Pécuchet said in a low voice: 'What do you feel?'

She woke up.

Later, no doubt, lucidity would come.

This success encouraged them, and confidently resuming their practice of medicine, they treated Chamberlan, the beadle, for pains between the ribs, Migraine, the mason, affected by nervous indigestion, old mother Varin, whose swelling under the collarbone required feeding with meat poultices, old Lemoine, who had gout and hung around wineshops, a consumptive, a hemiplegic, and many others. They also treated colds and chilblains.

After investigating the ailment, they looked at each other questioningly to know what passes to use, whether they should be large or small currents, ascending or descending, longitudinal, transversal, with two, three or even five fingers. When one had had too much the other took over. Then, once they were home, they noted down their observations in the treatment records.

Their unctuous manners won people's hearts. However, Bouvard was the favourite, and his reputation spread as far as Falaise, when he cured Barbée, daughter of old Barbey, a former ocean-going skipper.

She felt a stabbing pain in the head, spoke in a hoarse voice, often went several days without eating, then devoured plaster or coal. Her nervous attacks began with sobs and ended with a flood of tears, and every remedy had been applied, from tisanes to moxas, so that from sheer weariness she accepted Bouvard's offers.

When he had dismissed the servant and shot the bolts, he began to rub her abdomen, pressing on the site of the ovaries. A feeling of well-being was manifested by sighs and yawns. He placed a finger between her eyebrows at the top of her nose; suddenly she became inert. When her arms were raised they fell back: her head stayed in whatever position he chose, and her half-closed lids, vibrating spasmodically, revealed the eyeballs, rolling slowly; they stayed fixed in the corners, convulsed.

Bouvard asked her if she was in pain; she answered that she was not; what did she feel now? She could make out the inside of her body.

'What can you see there?'

'A worm.'

'What is the way to kill it?'

Her forehead creased:

'I am trying... I can't, I can't.'

At the second session she prescribed herself a broth of nettles; at the third, catmint. The attacks diminished, disappeared. It was really like a miracle.

Digital contact on the nose did not work with the others, and to induce somnambulism they planned to construct a mesmeric tub. Pécuchet had already collected filings and cleaned a score of bottles when a scruple stopped him. Among the patients would come members of the fair sex.

'And what shall we do if they are seized with attacks of erotic frenzy?'

That would not have stopped Bouvard; but because of gossip and perhaps blackmail it was better to abstain. They contented themselves with a harmonica and carried it with them into people's houses, to the delight of the children.

One day when Migraine was worse they resorted to it. The crystalline notes exasperated him; but Deleuze tells you not to be frightened by complaints. The music continued.

'Enough, enough!' he cried.

'A little patience,' replied Bouvard.

Pécuchet was tapping still faster on the strips of glass, the instrument was vibrating, and the poor man howling, when the doctor appeared, attracted by the noise.

'What, you again!' he cried, furious at finding them again with his patients.

They explained their magnetic method. Then he fulminated against magnetism, a lot of conjuring tricks, whose effects derive from the imagination.

However, animals can be magnetized. Montacabère says so, and Monsieur Lafontaine once managed to magnetize a lioness. They did not have a lioness. Chance provided them with another animal.

Because next day at six o'clock a ploughboy came to tell them that they were wanted at the farm, for a cow in a desperate state.

They ran.

The apple-trees were in blossom and the grass in the yard steamed under the rising sun. At the edge of the pond, half covered with a cloth, a cow was lowing, shivering with the pails of water that had been thrown over it, and so immeasurably swollen that it looked like a hippopotamus.

No doubt it had eaten some 'poison' as it grazed in the clover. Old Gouy and his wife were distraught, for the vet would not come, and a wheelwright who knew words to use against swelling did not want to be bothered; but our two gentlemen, with their famous library, must have some secret knowledge.

They rolled up their sleeves and placed themselves one at the horns, the other at the tail, and with great inward efforts and frantic gesticulation they spread out their fingers to pour out streams of fluid over the animal, while the farmer and his wife, their lad and some neighbours looked on almost in terror.

The rumblings that could be heard in the cow's belly made their own insides bubble. It broke wind. Then Pécuchet said:

'That opens the door to hope, there is a way out, perhaps.'

The way out worked, hope gushed out in a tub full of yellow matter exploding like a bomb. Hearts were eased. The cow's swelling went down. An hour later, nothing showed.

It was not the effect of imagination, that was certain. So the fluid does contain some peculiar property. It can be enclosed in objects where it can later be collected, without any loss of strength. Such a method saves moving around. They adopted it, and sent their patients magnetized discs, magnetized handkerchiefs, magnetized water, magnetized bread.

Then, continuing their studies, they gave up mesmeric passes for Puységur's system, which replaces the magnetizer by an old tree, with a cord rolled round its trunk.

A pear-tree in their yard seemed just made for it. They prepared it by hugging it tightly several times. A bench was set up underneath. Their clients sat there in line and they obtained such marvellous results that, to confound Vaucorbeil, they invited him to a session, with the local notables.

Not one failed to attend.

Germaine received them in the small parlour, begging their pardon, her masters were coming.

From time to time they heard a bell ring. It was the patients, whom she was admitting elsewhere. The guests pointed out with a nudge the dusty windows, the stains on the panels, the peeling paint; and the garden was lamentable. Dead wood everywhere! Two sticks, in front of the gap in the wall, barred off the orchard.

Pécuchet presented himself: 'At your orders, gentlemen!' And in the background, under the Édouin pear-tree, they saw several people sitting.

Chamberlan, beardless, like a priest, and in a short cassock of lasting with a leather skull-cap, was shuddering helplessly at the pain in his ribs; Migraine, whose stomach still hurt, was grimacing beside him. Old mother Varin, to hide her swelling, wore a shawl wrapped round her several times. Old Lemoine, bare feet stuck into his slippers, had his crutches under his calves, and Barbée, in Sunday best, was extraordinarily pale.

On the other side of the tree were some other people; a woman with the face of an albino was mopping the glands suppurating in her neck. The features of a little girl were half hidden beneath blue spectacles. An old man, whose spine was deformed by a contraction, kept bumping involuntarily against Marcel, a sort of idiot dressed in a ragged blouse and patched trousers. His badly stitched hare-lip showed his incisors, and bandages swathed his cheek, swollen by an enormous abscess.

They all held a string coming down from the tree, and birds were singing; the scent of the warm grass wafted through the air. The sun came down through the branches. Moss lay underfoot.

However, the subjects, instead of sleeping, had their eyes wide open.

'So far it is not much fun,' said Foureau. 'You begin. I am just going off for a minute.'

He came back, smoking an Abd-el-Kader, last vestige of the pipe doorway.

Pécuchet remembered an excellent method of magnetization. He put the noses of all the patients into his mouth, and inhaled their breath to draw electricity to him, while at the same time Bouvard embraced the tree, with the aim of increasing the fluid.

The mason interrupted his hiccoughs, the beadle went quieter, the man with the contractions stopped jerking. It was now possible to approach them, put them through all the tests.

The doctor, with his lancet, pricked Chamberlan under the ear, and he started slightly. The sensitivity of the others was obvious; the man with gout cried out. As for Barbée, she smiled as though in a dream, and a streak of blood ran under her jaw. Foureau tried to seize the lancet to test her himself, and when the doctor refused he pinched the patient hard. The captain tickled her nostrils with a feather, the tax-collector was going to stick a pin into her skin.

'Leave her alone, will you,' said Vaucorbeil, 'there's nothing surprising after all! A hysteric! You can't expect any sense out of that!'

'That one', said Pécuchet, pointing out Victoire, the woman with scrofula, 'is a doctor! She recognizes ailments and prescribes remedies.'

Langlois longed to consult her about his catarrh: he did not dare; but Coulon, more venturesome, asked for something for his rheumatism.

Pécuchet put Coulon's right hand in Victoire's left, and, with eyes still closed, cheeks a little flushed, lips trembling, the somnambulist, after some wandering, prescribed *valum becum*.

She had once worked for a chemist at Bayeux. Vaucorbeil inferred that she meant *album graecum*, a word half-glimpsed, perhaps, in the pharmacy.

Then he approached old Lemoine, who, according to Bouvard, could see distant objects through opaque bodies.

He was a former schoolmaster, fallen into squalor. White hair straggled round his face, and with his back to the tree and hands spread open, he lay asleep in the sunshine, a majestic figure.

The doctor bound a double cravat over his eyes and Bouvard, presenting him with a newspaper, said imperiously:

'Read!'

He bent his head, moved his facial muscles, then threw back his head and finally spelled out:

'Cons-ti-tution-al.'

But with a little skill any bandage can be slipped!

These denials from the doctor revolted Pécuchet. He was bold enough to claim that Barbée could describe what was going on in his own house at that moment.

'All right,' answered the doctor. Then, drawing out his watch: 'What is my wife doing?'

Barbée hesitated a long time, then with a sulky look: 'Let's see. Oh, I've got it! She is sewing ribbons on a straw hat!'

Vaucorbeil tore a page out of his notebook and wrote a note, which Marescot's clerk hastened to deliver.

The session was over. The patients dispersed.

Bouvard and Pécuchet, all in all, had not succeeded. Was this due to the temperature, or the smell of tobacco, or Abbé Jeufroy's umbrella, which had copper trimmings, a metal inimical to the emission of the fluid?

Vaucorbeil shrugged his shoulders.

However, he could not dispute the good faith of Messieurs Deleuze, Bertrand, Morin, Jules Cloquet. Now these masters affirm that somnambulists have predicted events, and endured, without feeling pain, cruel operations.

The priest related still more astonishing stories. A missionary once saw Brahmins walking across a vault head downwards, the Grand Lama of Tibet strains his bowels open to give oracles.

'Are you joking?' said the doctor.

'Not at all!'

'Come on now, that's a tall story!'

And as they went off the question everyone produced anecdotes.

'I once had a dog,' said the grocer, 'who was always sick when the month began with a Friday.'

'There were fourteen of us,' went on the Justice of the Peace. 'I was born on the fourteenth, married on the fourteenth, and my name day is the fourteenth! Just explain that!'

Beljambe had often dreamed the number of travellers whom he would have at his inn next day, and Petit told the story of Cazotte's supper.

Then the priest reflected:

'Why not see in all this quite simply...'

'Devils, you mean?' said Vaucorbeil.

The cleric, instead of answering, nodded his head.

Marescot spoke of the Delphic Pythia.

'Quite indubitably miasmas!'

'Oh, now it's miasmas!'

'Personally I admit a fluid,' replied Bouvard.

'Neuro-sidereal,' added Pécuchet.

'But prove it! Show it, that fluid of yours! Besides, fluids are out of date; listen to me.'

Vaucorbeil went further off into the shade. The worthies followed him.

'If you say to a child: "I am a wolf. I am going to eat you," he imagines you are a wolf and he is afraid; so that is a dream controlled by words. In the same way a somnambulist will accept any fantasy you like. He remembers and does not imagine, only has feelings when he believes he is thinking. This is how crimes are suggested and virtuous people may see themselves as wild beasts and become cannibals.'

They looked at Bouvard and Pécuchet. Their science could be dangerous for society.

Marescot's clerk reappeared in the garden, brandishing a letter from Madame Vaucorbeil.

The doctor unsealed it, went pale and finally read out these words:

'I am sewing ribbons on a straw hat.'

People were too stupefied to laugh.

'A coincidence upon my word! That proves nothing.' And as the two magnetizers were looking triumphant he turned back in the doorway to say:

'Don't go on! These are dangerous amusements!'

The priest, leading away his beadle, scolded him roundly:

'Are you mad? Without my permission! Goings-on forbidden by the Church!'

Everyone had just gone; Bouvard and Pécuchet were chatting on the knoll with the schoolmaster when Marcel shot out of the orchard, his chinstrap undone, stammering:

'Cured! Cured! Kind sirs!'

'Good! That's enough! Leave us alone!'

'Oh kind sirs, I love you! At your service!'

Petit, the progressive, had found the doctor's explanation prosaic, bourgeois. Science is a monopoly in the hands of the rich. It excludes the people: it is time for the old analysis of the Middle Ages to be succeeded by a wide and spontaneous synthesis! Truth must be obtained through the heart, and, declaring himself to be a spiritist, he indicated several works, no doubt defective, but which were the signs of a new dawn.

They sent for them.

Spiritism asserts as dogma that our species must inevitably improve. Earth will one day become heaven, and that is why this doctrine delighted the teacher. Without being Catholic it calls in St Augustine and St Louis. Allan-Kardec has even published fragments dictated by them which are at the level of contemporary opinions. It is practical, beneficent and reveals, like the telescope, higher worlds.

Spirits are transported to the higher worlds after death, and in ecstasy. But sometimes they come down onto our globe, where they make furniture creak, join in our entertainments, taste the beauties of nature and the pleasures of art.

However, several of us possess an aromal proboscis, that is a long tube behind the skull which rises from our hair up to the planets and enables us to converse with the spirits of Saturn; intangible things are no less real, and from the earth to the stars, from the stars to the earth, there is a coming and going, a transmission, a continual interchange.

Then Pécuchet's heart swelled with uncontrolled aspirations, and when night had fallen Bouvard came upon him at the window contemplating these luminous spaces populated by spirits.

Swedenborg travelled about there extensively, for in less than a year he explored Venus, Mars, Saturn, and, twenty-three times, Jupiter. Moreover, in London he saw Christ, he saw St Paul, he saw St John, he saw Moses, and, in 1736, he even saw the Last Judgement.

Thus he gives us descriptions of heaven.

There are flowers there, palaces, markets and churches, exactly as we have them.

The angels, who used to be men, put down their thoughts on

sheets of paper, talk about household things or spiritual matters, and ecclesiastical employment goes to those who in their earthly life cultivated Holy Writ.

As for hell, it is full of a sickening stench, with squalid hovels, heaps of filth, people in rags.

Pécuchet racked his brains trying to understand what beauty there can be about such revelations. To Bouvard they seemed like an idiot's raving. All that goes beyond the bounds of nature! Who knows them though? They indulged in the following reflections:

Jugglers can delude a crowd; a man stirred by violent passions can move others; but how could the will alone act on inert matter? A Bavarian is said to make grapes ripen; Monsieur Gervais revived a heliotrope; someone even more powerful, at Toulouse, dispels clouds.

Must we admit some intermediate substance between the world and ourselves? The od, a new imponderable, a sort of electricity, is perhaps just that? Its emissions would explain the glow which magnetized people think they see, wandering lights in cemeteries, the shape of ghosts.

So these images would not be illusory, and the extraordinary gifts of the possessed, like those of somnambulists, could have a physical cause?

Whatever their origin, there is an essence, a secret, universal agent. If we could hold on to it, there would be no need for the power of time. What takes centuries could be developed in a moment, any miracle would be practicable and the universe would be at our disposal.

Magic derived from this eternal desire of the human spirit. Its value has no doubt been exaggerated, but it is no lie. Orientals who know it perform prodigies. All travellers say so, and at the Palais-Royal Monsieur Dupotet can disturb a magnetized needle with his finger.

How does one become a magician? Such an idea seemed foolish to them at first, but it returned, tormented them, and they gave in, while affecting to laugh at it.

A preparatory regime is indispensable.

In order to reach exaltation more easily, they lived by night, fasted, and in an attempt to make Germaine into a more sensitive medium, rationed her food. She made up for it with drink, and drank so much spirits that she ended up an alcoholic. They woke her up by prowling in the corridor. She confused the sound of their footsteps with the buzzing in her ears and the imaginary voices she heard coming out of the walls. One day when, in the morning, she had put a plaice in the cellar, she took fright when she saw it all covered with fire, felt worse from then on and ended by believing they had cast a spell on her.

Hoping to have visions they squeezed one another's necks, made themselves belladonna sachets, finally adopted the magic box: a little box with a nail-studded button rising out of it, kept over the heart by a ribbon worn round the chest. It all failed; but they were able to use Dupotet's circle.

Pécuchet drew with charcoal a rough black circle on the ground to keep in the animal spirits which were to help the ambient spirits, and, happy to dominate Bouvard, said to him in a pontifical manner: 'I defy you to cross it!'

Bouvard considered this round space. Soon his heart thudded, his eyes clouded. 'Oh, let's be done with it!' And he jumped over it to get away from an inexpressible feeling of unease.

Pécuchet, who was becoming more and more excited, wanted to make a dead man appear.

Under the Directory a man in the Rue de l'Échiquier used to show the victims of the Terror. There are countless examples of ghosts. Even if they are only apparitions, what does it matter? The thing is to produce them.

The closer the deceased is to us, the more easily he responds to our call; but he had no relic of his family, no ring, no miniature, not a hair, while Bouvard was in a position to call up his father; and as he showed signs of repugnance, Pécuchet asked him:

'What are you afraid of?'

'Me? Nothing at all! Do what you like!'

They bribed Chamberlan, who secretly provided them with an old skull. A tailor made them two long black coats, with hoods, as on a monk's habit. The Falaise coach brought them a long roll in an envelope. Then they set to work, one of them curious to carry it out, the other afraid to believe in it.

The museum was draped like a catafalque. Three torches burned on the edge of the table, which had been pushed up against the wall, under the portrait of Bouvard's father, with the skull above it. They had even stuck a candle inside the skull, and its rays shone out through the two eye sockets.

In the middle, on a foot-warmer, incense smoked. Bouvard stood behind; and Pécuchet, with his back to him, threw handfuls of sulphur into the hearth.

Before calling up the dead one must have the demons' consent. Now, this particular day being a Friday, a day belonging to Bechet, they had first to concern themselves with Bechet. Bouvard, bowing to right and left, bent his chin and raised his arms, and began:

'By Enathiel, Amazin, Ischyros...'

He had forgotten the rest.

Pécuchet hurriedly prompted him with words noted on a card:

'Ischyros, Athanatos, Adonai, Sadai, Eloy, Messias' – it was a long litany – 'I conjure you, I obsecrate you, oh Bechet!' Then, lowering his voice: 'Where are you, Bechet? Bechet! Bechet! Bechet!'

Bouvard collapsed into the armchair, and was very glad not to see Bechet, for some instinct condemned his attempt as sacrilege. Where was his father's soul? Could it hear him? Supposing it were suddenly to come?

The curtains slowly stirred in the breeze coming in through a cracked pane, and the candles threw wavering shadows on the death's-head and the portrait. A drab colour made them both look the same shade of brown. The cheeks were eaten up with mildew, the eyes were lustreless, but a flame shone above them from the holes of the empty head, which sometimes seemed to take the place of the other one, and set itself on the coat collar, put on the side whiskers; and the canvas, half adrift from its nails, rippled and shook.

Gradually they felt a light touch as of someone breathing, an impalpable being coming near. Drops of sweat dampened Pécuchet's brow, and then Bouvard's teeth began to chatter, he felt cramp in the pit of his stomach; the floor flowed away beneath his heels, like water; the sulphur burning in the fireplace swirled down in great clouds; at the same time bats wheeled about; a cry rose; what was it?

Under their hoods their faces were so distraught that their terror increased, and they did not dare make a gesture or even speak; then, behind the door, they heard groans as if from a soul in torment.

Finally they ventured forth.

It was their old servant who, spying on them through a crack in the partition, thought she had seen the devil, and was kneeling in the corridor repeatedly making the sign of the cross.

Any discussion was pointless. She left them that very evening, unwilling to serve such people any longer.

Germaine gossiped. Chamberlan lost his job, and a secret coalition was formed against them under the auspices of Abbé Jeufroy, Madame Bordin and Foureau.

Their way of life, which was not that of other people, gave offence. They became suspect and even inspired a vague terror.

What ruined them above all in public esteem was their choice of a servant. Failing anyone else they had taken on Marcel.

His hare-lip, his hideousness and his incoherent speech put people off. Abandoned as a child, he had grown up in the fields as best he could, and his long years of want had left him with an insatiable hunger. Animals who had died of disease, rotting bacon, a run-over dog, anything would do for him, so long as the piece was big, and he was gentle as a lamb but completely stupid.

Gratitude had impelled him to offer himself as servant to Messieurs Bouvard and Pécuchet; and then, believing them to be sorcerers, he hoped for extraordinary rewards.

In the first few days he confided a secret to them. On the heath at Poligny a man had once found a gold ingot. The historians of Falaise relate the anecdote, but do not know the sequel: twelve brothers, before leaving on a journey, had hidden twelve similar ingots, all along the road from Chavignolles to Bretteville, and Marcel begged his masters to start searching. These ingots, they told themselves, might perhaps have been buried at the time of emigration.

It was a case for using the diviner's wand. Its properties are doubtful. However, they studied the question, and learned that a certain Pierre Garnier gives scientific ground for defending these properties: springs and metals supposedly emit corpuscles with some affinity for the wood.

That was not very likely, but who knows? Let us try!

They cut a forked twig of hazelwood, and one morning set off on a treasure hunt.

'We'll have to give it back,' said Bouvard.

'Oh no! Goodness me!'

After walking for three hours a thought stopped them: 'The road from Chavignolles to Bretteville? Was it the old or the new road? It must be the old one!'

They retraced their footsteps, and went over the surrounding area at random, because the line of the old road was not easily recognizable.

Marcel ran to right and left, like a spaniel out hunting. Every five minutes Bouvard was obliged to call him back; Pécuchet went forward, step by step, holding the wand by its two arms, point upwards. It often seemed as though some force, a sort of hook, pulled it down towards the ground, and Marcel quickly made a notch on the trees nearby to enable them to find the place later.

Pécuchet however was slowing down. His mouth fell open, his eyeballs became convulsed. Bouvard spoke to him, shook him by the shoulders: he did not stir and remained inert, exactly like Barbée.

Then he described how he had felt a kind of tearing sensation round his heart, a peculiar state, no doubt caused by the wand; and he did not want to touch it again.

Next day they returned to where the trees had been marked. With a spade Marcel dug holes, but their search never revealed anything, and each time they were extremely crestfallen. Pécuchet sat down beside a ditch; and as he dreamed, with his head held high, trying to hear the spirit voices through his aromal proboscis, wondering if he even had one, he fixed his gaze on the peak of his cap; he fell into the same trance as the day before. It lasted a long time, became frightening.

Above the oats, in a lane, a felt hat appeared; it was Monsieur Vaucorbeil trotting along on his mare. Bouvard and Marcel hailed him.

The crisis was about to finish when the doctor arrived. He pushed up Pécuchet's cap to examine him better, and observing a forehead covered with coppery spots:

'Ah, ah! The fruits of war! These are syphilitic sores, old chap! You must have that seen to! Devil take it! Love is not a joking matter!'

Pécuchet, shamefaced, put his cap on again; it was a sort of beret, puffed out over a semi-circular peak, on a pattern he had taken from the Amoros drawings.

The doctor's words stunned him. He was thinking about them, looking upwards, when he suddenly had another seizure.

Vaucorbeil watched him, then with a flick of his fingers knocked the cap off.

Pécuchet recovered his faculties.

'I thought as much,' said the doctor. 'That shiny peak hypnotized you like a mirror, and the phenomenon is by no means rare with people who look too closely at some bright object!'

He indicated how to conduct the experiment on hens, mounted his nag, and slowly disappeared.

A mile or two further on they noticed a pyramidal object rising on the horizon, in a farmyard. It looked like a monstrous bunch of black grapes, dotted here and there with red spots. Following the Norman usage it was a long mast with crossbars on which perched turkeys preening themselves in the sun.

'Let's go in.' And Pécuchet approached the farmer, who acceded to their request.

They drew a line with whiting in the middle of the cider press, tied the feet of a turkey, then laid it face downwards, with its beak on the line. The animal closed its eyes and soon seemed to be dead. It was the same with the others. Bouvard briskly handed them over to Pécuchet, who lined them up on one side as soon as they were comatose. The farm people showed some anxiety, the farmer's wife cried, a little girl wept.

Bouvard untied all the birds. They gradually came back to life, but no one knew what the consequences would be. When Pécuchet objected somewhat harshly, the farmer seized his pitchfork.

'Off with you, by God! Or I'll have your guts out!'

They decamped.

No matter! The problem was solved; ecstasy depends on a material cause.

What then is matter? What is spirit? How does one influence the other, and vice versa?

For a better understanding they researched in Voltaire, Bossuet, Fénelon, and even took out a new subscription to a lending library.

The old masters were inaccessible because their works were so long and their language so difficult, but Jouffroy and Damion initiated them into modern philosophy, and they had authors dealing with that of the previous century.

Bouvard drew his arguments from La Mettrie, Locke, Helvétius; Pécuchet from Monsieur Cousin, Thomas Reid and Gérando. The former gave his allegiance to experience, the ideal was everything for the latter. There was something of Aristotle in the one, of Plato in the other, and they had discussions.

'The soul is immaterial!' said one.

'Not at all!' said the other. 'Madness, chloroform, bleeding completely upset it, and since it does not always think, it is not solely a thinking substance.'

'However,' Pécuchet observed, 'I have within me something superior to my body, which sometimes contradicts it.'

'A being within being? *Homo duplex!* Come now! Different tendencies reveal opposing motives, that's all.'

'But this something, this soul, remains identical beneath external changes. Therefore it is simple, indivisible, and thus spiritual!'

'If the soul were simple,' replied Bouvard, 'the newborn child would remember and imagine like the adult. On the contrary, thought follows brain development. As for being indivisible, the scent of a rose or the appetite of a wolf can no more be cut in half than a volition or affirmation.'

'That's nothing to do with it!' said Pécuchet. 'The soul is free from the qualities of matter!'

'Do you admit gravity?' replied Bouvard. 'Now if matter can fall, it can similarly think. If our soul has a beginning it must have an end and, being dependent on organs, disappear with them.'

'Well, I claim it is immortal! God cannot want...'

'But if God does not exist?'

'What?' And Pécuchet came out with the three Cartesian proofs:

'First, God is included in the idea we have of him; second, existence is possible for him; third, as a finite being, how could I have an idea of the infinite? And since we have such an idea, it comes to us from God, therefore God exists!'

He went on to the evidence of conscience, popular traditions, the need for a creator.

'When I see a clock ...'

'Yes! Yes! We know all about that! But where is the clock-maker's father?'

'There must be a cause, though!'

Bouvard was doubtful about causes. 'From the fact that one phenomenon succeeds another, you conclude that it derives from it. Prove it!'

'But the sight of a universe indicates an intention, a plan!'

'Why? Evil is organized just as perfectly as good. The worm which grows in a sheep's head and makes it die is equivalent, anatomically, to the sheep itself. Monstrosities go beyond normal functions. The human body could be better constructed. Three quarters of the globe are sterile. The moon, that luminary, is not always visible! Do you think the ocean was destined for ships, and the wood from trees for heating our houses?'

Pécuchet answered:

'Yet the stomach is made for digesting, the legs for walking, the eyes for seeing, although dyspepsia, fractures and cataract can occur! No arrangement without a purpose! Effects happen now or later. Everything depends on laws. Therefore final causes exist.'

Bouvard thought that Spinoza might provide him with arguments, and he wrote to Dumouchel to get Saisset's translation.

Dumouchel sent him a copy, belonging to his friend, Professor Varelot, exiled on the 2nd December.

The ethics frightened him with their axioms, their corollaries. They read only the passages marked in pencil, and understood as follows:

Substance is what is of itself, by itself, without cause and without origin. That substance is God.

He alone is extension, and extension has no limits: what could limit it?

But although it is infinite, it is not absolute infinity, for it contains only one kind of perfection, and the absolute contains them all.

They often stopped for time to reflect. Pécuchet absorbed pinches of snuff and Bouvard was flushed with concentration.

'Do you find this interesting?'

'Yes, certainly! Do go on!'

God develops himself in an infinity of attributes, which express, each in its way, the infinity of his being. We know only two of them: extension and thought.

From thought and extension flow countless modes, which in their turn contain others.

Anyone who embraced at the same time all thought and all extension would see nothing contingent, nothing accidental, but a geometrical succession of terms, bound together by necessary laws.

'Ah! That would be splendid!' said Pécuchet.

So there is no liberty in man, or in God.

'Do you hear that?' cried Bouvard.

If God had a will, a purpose, if he acted for some cause, then he would have a need, he would lack some perfection. He would not be God.

Thus our world is only a point in the totality of things, and the universe is impenetrable to our knowledge, one portion of an infinity of universes giving out infinite modifications beside ours. Extension envelops our universe, but is enveloped by God, who contains in his thought all possible universes, and his thought itself is enveloped in his substance.

They felt as though they were in a balloon, at night, in icy cold, borne away in endless flight to a bottomless abyss, with nothing around them but the incomprehensible, the immobile, the eternal. It was too much for them. They gave up.

Wanting something less harsh, they bought the *Philosophy Course*, for use in schools, by Monsieur Guesnier.

The author wonders which will be the right method, the ontological or the psychological?

The first suited societies in their infancy, when man's attention was directed to the outside world. But now that he turns it in on himself 'we think that the second method is the more scientific' and Bouvard and Pécuchet decided on it.

The aim of psychology is to study the facts taking place 'in the heart of the self'. They are discovered by observation.

'Let us observe!' And for two weeks, usually after lunch, they searched their consciousness, at random, hoping to make great discoveries, and made none, which greatly astonished them.

A phenomenon occupies the self, that is the idea. What is its nature? It has been supposed that objects are reflected in the brain and the brain sends these images to our mind, from which comes our knowledge of them.

But if ideas are spiritual, how is matter to be represented? Thence, scepticism about external perceptions. If it is material, would spiritual objects not be represented? Thence scepticism about internal notions.

'Besides, be careful! That hypothesis could lead to atheism!'

For as an image is a finite thing it is impossible for it to represent the infinite.

'However,' objected Bouvard, 'when I think of a forest, a person, a dog, I see that forest, person, dog. So ideas do represent them.'

They tackled the origin of ideas.

According to Locke, there are two, sensation and reflection – Condillac reduces everything to sensation.

But then there will be no basis for reflection. It needs a subject, a sentient being; and it is incapable of providing us with the great fundamental truths: God, merit and demerit, the just, beautiful, etc., so-called innate notions, that is, anterior to the facts, and universal.

'If they were universal we should have them from birth.'

'That word implies some dispositions for having them, and Descartes...'

'Your Descartes is all at sea! For he maintains that the foetus possesses them and elsewhere he confesses that it does so implicitly.'

Pécuchet was astonished.

'Where did you find that?'

'In Gérando,' and Bouvard tapped him lightly on the stomach.

'Stop that now!' said Pécuchet. Then coming to Condillac: 'Our thoughts are not metamorphoses of sensation! It occasions them, sets them off. To set them off there must be a mover. For matter by itself cannot produce movement, and that I found in your Voltaire,' added Pécuchet, bowing low before him.

So they worked over the same arguments, each despising the other's opinions, without convincing him of his own.

But philosophy enhanced their self esteem. They recalled with pity their preoccupations with agriculture, literature, politics.

The museum now filled them with distaste. They would have liked nothing better than to sell off its bits and pieces, and they went on to the second chapter: the faculties of the soul.

These number three, no more! Those of feeling, knowing, willing.

Within the faculty of feeling let us distinguish physical sensibility from moral sensibility.

Physical sensations fall naturally into five classes, being conveyed by the sense organs.

The facts of moral sensibility, on the other hand, owe nothing to the body: 'What is there in common between Archimedes' pleasure at discovering the laws of gravity and Apicius' filthy delight at devouring a boar's head!'

This moral sensibility has four types, and the second type, 'moral desires', can be divided into five kinds, while the phenomena of the fourth type, 'affections', are subdivided into two other kinds, among which is self-love, 'a legitimate tendency, no doubt, but which, when exaggerated, is called egoism'.

Within the faculty of knowing comes rational perception, in which are found the principal movements and four degrees.

Abstraction can provide stumbling blocks for people of strange intelligence.

Memory links us with the past as foresight does with the future.

Imagination is rather a peculiar faculty, *sui generis*.

So many complications to demonstrate platitudes, the author's pedantic tone, the monotony of his phrases: 'We are ready to recognize – Far from us the thought – Let us interrogate our conscience,' the sempiternal eulogy of Dugald-Stewart, in fact all this verbiage sickened them so much that, skipping the faculty of will, they embarked on logic.

This taught them what analysis is, as well as synthesis, induction, deduction, and the main causes of our errors.

They almost all come from using words wrongly.

'The sun sets, the weather is overcast, winter approaches', incorrect expressions which might make one think of personal entities when it is only a question of very simple events! 'I remember such and such an object, axiom, truth', an illusion! These are ideas, not things at all, which remain in the self, and linguistic rigour demands: 'I remember such and such an act of my mind by which I perceived this object, deduced this axiom, admitted this truth.'

As the term designating an accident does not embrace it in all its modes, they tried only to employ abstract words, so that instead of saying: 'Let us take a stroll – It is time for dinner – I have colic,' they came out with these phrases: 'A walk would be salutary – Now is the time to absorb nourishment – I feel a need for relief.'

Once they had mastered logic, they reviewed the different criteria, starting with that of common sense.

If one individual cannot know anything, why should all individuals be able to know more? An error, even 100,000 years old, by the mere fact of being old does not constitute truth! The crowd invariably follows routine. On the other hand it is the minority which leads the way in progress.

Is it better to trust the evidence of the senses? They sometimes deceive, and their information never goes beyond appearances. The basic content escapes them.

Reason offers more guarantees, since it is immutable and impersonal, but to be made manifest it must be incarnate. Then reason becomes my reason, a rule has little weight if it is false. There is nothing to prove this one right.

We are recommended to check reason by the senses; but they can make the darkness still denser. A confused sensation leads us to induce a definitive law which will later prevent a clear view of things.

There remains ethics. This is bringing God down to the level of the useful, as if our needs were the measure of the absolute!

As for evidence, denied by some, affirmed by others, it is its own criterion. Monsieur Cousin demonstrated that.

'I can see nothing left but Revelation,' said Bouvard. 'But in order to believe in it one must admit two antecedent types of knowledge: that of the body which felt, of the intelligence which perceived; one must admit sense and reason, which are human evidence, and consequently suspect.'

Pécuchet reflected and crossed his arms: 'But we are going to fall into the awful abyss of scepticism.'

According to Bouvard, it was awful only for those of feeble intellect.

'Thanks for the compliment,' replied Pécuchet. 'However, there are some incontrovertible facts. One can reach the truth within certain limits.'

'What limits? Do two and two always make four? Is the content, in some way, smaller than the container? What is the meaning of an approximate truth, a fraction of God, part of something indivisible?'

'Oh! You are just a sophist!' And Pécuchet was so vexed he sulked for three days.

They spent the time running through the table of contents of several volumes. Bouvard smiled from time to time, and took up the conversation again:

'The fact is that it is hard to doubt. So the proofs of Descartes, Kant and Leibniz concerning God are not the same, and mutually cancel each other out. The creation of the world by atoms, or by a spirit, remains inconceivable.'

'I feel myself to be both matter and thought, while I do not know what either of them is.'

'Impenetrability, solitude, gravity seem to me as much of a mystery as my soul, and *a fortiori* the union of soul and body.'

'In order to explain it Leibniz invents his harmony, Malebranche "pre-motion", Cudworth a mediator, and Bossuet sees a perpetual miracle, which is silly; a perpetual miracle would not be a miracle.'

'Quite so!' said Pécuchet.

They both confessed that they were tired of philosophers. So many systems only confuse you. Metaphysics is useless. One can live without it.

Besides, their financial embarrassment was becoming worse. They owed Beljambe for three casks of wine, Langlois for twelve kilos of sugar, 120 francs to the tailor, sixty to the cobbler. Expenditure continued and farmer Gouy was not paying.

They went to Marescot to see if he could find them some money, either by selling Les Écalles, or by mortgaging their farm, or transferring their house, which would be paid for by life annuities and of which they would keep the usufruct. The method was not practicable, said Marescot, but a better scheme was being arranged and they would be advised.

Then they thought of their poor garden. Bouvard undertook to prune the arbour, Pécuchet to trim the espalier, Marcel was to dig up the beds.

After a quarter of an hour they stopped, one closed his pruning knife, the other put down his shears, and they began slowly to walk up and down: Bouvard in the shade of the lime-trees, with no waistcoat, chest thrust forward, arms bare; Pécuchet along the wall, head bent, hands behind his back, the peak of his cap turned round over his neck for safety's sake; and thus they walked on parallel courses, without even seeing Marcel, who was resting at the side of the hut, eating a hunk of bread.

Their meditation had given rise to thoughts; they approached each other, afraid to lose them; and metaphysics returned.

They returned in connection with the rain or the sun, a piece of gravel in their shoe, a flower on the lawn, in connection with everything.

As they watched the candle burn they wondered if the light is in the object or in our eye. Since some stars may have disappeared by the time their light reaches us, perhaps we admire things that do not exist.

Discovering a Raspail cigarette in the bottom of a waistcoat pocket, they shredded it over water and the camphor turned.

So there is movement in matter! A higher degree of movement would produce life.

But if matter in movement were enough to create beings, they would not be so varied. For originally there did not exist land, or water, or men, or plants. What then is this primordial matter, which no one has ever seen, which is none of the things in the world and has produced them all?

Sometimes they needed a book. Dumouchel, tired of helping them, did not reply any more, and they really worked at the question, especially Pécuchet.

His need for truth became a raging thirst.

Moved by Bouvard's arguments he gave up spiritualism, soon resumed it, only to abandon it again, and cried out, head in hands: 'Oh! Doubt! Doubt! I should rather have nothing at all!'

Bouvard realized the inadequacy of materialism, and tried to hang on to it, incidentally declaring that it was driving him mad.

They began to reason on some solid basis; it collapsed; and suddenly the idea had gone, like a fly escaping when you try to clutch it.

During the winter evenings they chatted in the museum, at the fireside, looking at the glowing embers. The wind whistling through the corridor shook the window panes, the dark bulk of the trees swayed to and fro, and the melancholy of the night added to the solemnity of their thoughts.

Bouvard, from time to time, went to the end of the room, then came back. The torches and basins against the walls cast oblique shadows on the ground, and the statue of St Peter, seen in profile, displayed on the ceiling the silhouette of its nose like some monstrous hunting-horn.

It was not easy to move around among the objects, and often Bouvard inadvertently banged against the statue. With its wide eyes, drooping lip and drunken look, it also troubled Pécuchet. For a long time they had been wanting to get rid of it, but their indifference made them put it off from day to day.

One evening, in the middle of a dispute about the monad, Bouvard stubbed his toe on St Peter's thumb, and, venting his annoyance against him:

'He gets on my nerves, that clown; let's sling him out!'

This was difficult to do by the stairs. They opened the window and leaned him gently over the edge. Pécuchet, on his knees, tried to raise the statue's heels, while Bouvard pushed down on the shoulders. The stone effigy did not budge; they had to resort to the halberd as a lever, and finally managed to lay him out full length. Then, after tipping up and down, he dived into the void, tiara first, a dull thud resounded, and next day they found him. broken into a dozen pieces, in the old compost pit.

An hour later the lawyer came in, bringing them good news. A certain person in the neighbourhood would advance them a thousand francs in return for a mortgage on their farm; and as they rejoiced: 'Excuse me! There is a proviso: you must sell this person

Les Écalles for 1,500 francs. The loan will be paid over this very day. I have the money in my office.'

They both wanted to give in. Bouvard finally answered 'Good Heavens! . . . All right!'

'Agreed!' said Marescot, and he told them the name of the person, who was Madame Bordin.

'I thought as much!' cried Pécuchet.

Bouvard kept quiet in his humiliation.

She or another, what matter! The main thing was to get out of their embarrassing situation.

Once they had the money (that for Les Écalles would come later) they at once paid all their bills, and were on their way home when, as they went round by the market, old Gouy stopped them.

He was coming to see them to report a disaster. The wind, the night before, had blown down twenty apple-trees in the farmyards, knocked down the distillery, taken the roof off the barn. They spent the rest of the afternoon reckoning up the damage, and next day too, with the carpenter, the mason and the roofer. The repairs would add up to 1,800 francs at least.

Then in the evening Gouy presented himself. Marianne herself had just told him about the sale of Les Écalles. A magnificently productive piece of property, which just suited him, hardly needed cultivating, the best bit of the entire farm! And he asked for a reduction in rent.

Our two gentlemen refused this. The case was submitted to the Justice of the Peace, and he found for the farmer. The loss of Les Écalles, the deed reckoned at 2,000 francs meant annual damages to him of seventy, and in the courts he would certainly win.

Their fortune was diminished. What was to be done? And, soon, how were they going to live?

They both sat down to table full of discouragement. Marcel had absolutely no idea how to cook; this time his dinner surpassed all the others. The soup was like dish water, the rabbit smelt bad, the beans were uncooked, the plates filthy, and at the dessert Bouvard exploded, threatening to smash everything over his head.

'Let's be philosophical,' said Pécuchet, 'a little less money, a woman's intrigues, a servant's awkwardness, what does all that amount to? You are too absorbed by material things!'

'But when they bother me,' said Bouvard.

'I just don't admit them!' replied Pécuchet.

He had recently read an analysis of Berkeley, and added: 'I deny extension, time, space, even substance! Because true substance is the mind perceiving qualities.'

'Fine!' said Bouvard, 'but once you do away with the world, there won't be any proofs for the existence of God.'

Pécuchet protested at length, although he had a cold in the head caused by iodide of potassium and a permanent fever contributed to his excitement. Bouvard, becoming alarmed, sent for the doctor.

Vaucorbeil prescribed orange syrup with iodide, and later bathing with sulphate of mercury.

'What's the good?' asked Pécuchet. 'Sooner or later the form will disappear. The essence does not perish!'

'Certainly,' said the doctor, 'matter is indestructible. Yet...'

'But no! No! It is being that is indestructible. This body which is there in front of me, yours, doctor, prevents me from knowing your person, it is only a garment, so to speak, or rather, a mask.'

Vaucorbeil thought he was mad. 'Good evening! Take care of your mask!'

Pécuchet was undeterred. He obtained an introduction to Hegelian philosophy, and tried to explain it to Bouvard.

'Everything that is rational is real. In fact there is nothing real but ideas. The laws of the mind are the laws of the universe, man's reason is identical with God's.'

Bouvard pretended to understand him.

'Therefore the absolute is at once subject and object, the unity in which all differences come together. Shade makes light possible, cold mixed with heat produces temperature, the organism only remains in being through the destruction of the organism; throughout there is a dividing principle, a linking principle.'

They were on the knoll, and the curé went by along the fence, breviary in hand.

Pécuchet asked him in, to complete the exposition of Hegel in front of him and see what he would say about it.

The man in the cassock sat down beside them, and Pécuchet started on Christianity.

'No religion has so firmly established the truth: "Nature is only a moment of the idea!"'

'A moment of the idea!' murmured the priest, stupefied.

'Yes! By assuming a visible envelope, God has shown his consubstantial union with Nature.'

'With Nature? Oh, oh!'

'By dying he bore witness to the essence of death: so death was in him, formed, still forms, part of God.'

The ecclesiastic took offence.

'No blasphemy! It was to save the human race that he endured sufferings.'

'Quite wrong! We consider death in the individual, where it certainly is an evil, but relative to things it is different. Do not separate mind and matter.'

'Yet, sir, before creation ...'

'There was no creation. It always existed. Otherwise it would be a new being added to the divine thought, which is absurd.'

The priest rose, business called him elsewhere.

'I flatter myself, I put him in his place!' said Pécuchet. 'One word more! Since the existence of the world is only a continual passage from life to death, and from death to life, far from everything being, nothing is. But everything is becoming, do you understand?'

'Yes, I understand, or rather no!' In the end idealism annoyed Bouvard. 'I don't want any more of it: the famous *cogito* is a bore. The ideas of things are taken for the things themselves. What we barely understand is explained by means of words that we do not understand at all! Substance, extension, force, matter and soul, are all so many abstractions, figments of the imagination. As for God, it is impossible to know how he is, or even if he is! Once he was the cause of wind, thunder, revolutions. Now he is getting smaller. Besides, I don't see what use he is.'

'And where do morals come into all that?'

'Oh, that's too bad!'

'They lack a basis, to be sure,' said Pécuchet to himself.

He stayed silent, pushed into an impasse, following from the premises which he had laid down himself. It was a surprise, a crushing blow.

Bouvard no longer even believed in matter.

The certainty that nothing exists, deplorable as it may be, is still a certainty. Few people are capable of feeling it. This transcendence filled them with pride, and they would have liked to display it; an opportunity offered.

One morning, going to buy tobacco, they saw a collection of people in front of Langlois's door. They were surrounding the Falaise coach, and there was some talk of Touache, a former convict from the galleys who was roaming the countryside. The driver had met him at La Croix-Verte between two gendarmes and the people of Chavignolles breathed a sigh of deliverance.

Girbal and the captain stayed in the square; then the Justice of the Peace arrived, curious for information, and Monsieur Marescot in a velvet cap and sheepskin slippers.

Langlois invited them to honour his shop with their presence. They would be more comfortable there, and in spite of the customers and the noise of the bell, the gentlemen went on discussing Touache's misdeeds.

'My goodness!' said Bouvard. 'He had the wrong instincts, that's all!'

'One can triumph over them through virtue,' replied the lawyer.

'But if one does not have virtue?' And Bouvard positively denied free will.

'Yet,' said the captain, 'I can do what I want! I am free for example to move my leg.'

'No, sir, for you have a reason for moving it!'

The captain tried to find an answer, and failed. But Girbal shot off this quip:

'A republican who speaks against liberty! That's funny!'

'It makes you laugh!' said Langlois.

Bouvard addressed him:

'What stops you giving away your fortune to the poor?'

The grocer, with an envious look, surveyed his shop.

'Well! Not bad! I'll keep it for myself!'

'If you were St Vincent de Paul you would act differently, since you would have his character. You obey your own. So you are not free!'

'That's quibbling!' the assembly replied in chorus.

Bouvard did not waver, and pointing to the scales on the counter:

'It will remain still as long as one of its scales is empty. The will is the same; and the scales oscillating between two apparently equal weights represents our mind working as it weighs up different reasons, up to the moment when the stronger one wins and determines it.'

'None of that', said Girbal, 'helps Touache or stops him from being a rather nasty piece of work.'

Pécuchet took up the discussion:

'Vices are properties of nature like floods and storms.'

The lawyer stopped him, and rising on tiptoe at each word:

'I consider your system to be completely immoral. It gives free rein to every excess, excuses crimes, exonerates the guilty.'

'Quite so,' said Bouvard. 'The wretch who follows his appetites has a right to do so, as much as the decent man who listens to reason.'

'Don't defend monsters!'

'Why monsters? When a blind man, an idiot, a murderer is born, it looks to us like a breach of order, as if order were something known to us, as if nature acted for a purpose!'

'So you question providence?'

'Yes, I do question it!'

'Look at history instead,' cried Pécuchet. 'Remember the kings assassinated, the peoples massacred, the families torn with dissension, individuals grieving.'

'And at the same time,' added Bouvard, for they were exciting each other, 'this providence looks after little birds and makes the claws of crayfish grow again. Ah! If by providence you mean a law which rules everything, then I will agree, more than agree!'

'However, sir,' said the lawyer, 'there are such things as principles!'

'What is the tale you are telling me? According to Condillac, a science is all the better for having no principles! They only sum up knowledge acquired and send us back to precisely those notions that are debatable.'

'Have you, like us,' went on Pécuchet, 'scrutinized, searched through the arcane mysteries of metaphysics?'

'True, gentlemen, true!'

And the gathering dispersed.

But Coulon, drawing them aside, told them paternally that he was certainly no lover of religion, and even loathed the Jesuits. However, he would not go as far as they! Oh no, to be sure! And on the corner of the square they passed the captain, who was relighting his pipe, grumbling to himself:

'All the same, I do what I like, damn it!'

Bouvard and Pécuchet put forward their abominable paradoxes on other occasions. They cast doubt on the honesty of men, the chastity of women, the intelligence of the government, the good sense of the people, in a word undermined the basic principles.

Foureau became excited about it and threatened them with prison if they continued holding forth like that.

Their obvious superiority caused offence. As they maintained immoral theses, they must be immoral: calumnies were invented.

Then a lamentable faculty developed in their minds, that of noticing stupidity and finding it intolerable.

Insignificant things depressed them: newspaper advertisements, the profile of some worthy citizen, a silly remark overheard by chance.

Thinking about the things people said in their village, thinking that even as far as the Antipodes there were other Coulons, other Marescots, other Foureaus, they felt as if the heaviness of the entire earth were weighing down on them.

They stopped going out, had no one in.

One afternoon a dialogue arose in the yard between Marcel and a gentleman with a hard-brimmed hat and dark glasses. It was the academician Larsonneur. He did not fail to observe a curtain half open, doors closing. His visit was an attempt at reconciliation, and he went away in a fury, asking the servant to inform his masters that he regarded them as boors.

Bouvard and Pécuchet did not care. The world was becoming less and less important; they observed it as though in a cloud, falling from their brains onto their eyes.

Is it not, in any case, an illusion, a bad dream? Perhaps in the end good and bad fortune balance out? But the good of the species is no consolation for the individual. 'And what do other people matter to me?' Pécuchet would say.

His despair distressed Bouvard. It was he who had pushed him that far, and the dilapidated state of their home kept their gloom alive with daily irritations.

To cheer themselves up they debated together, prescribed tasks to do, and soon fell back into more intense lethargy, profound discouragement.

After meals they stayed, their elbows on the table, moaning lugubriously. Marcel stared at them, then went back to his kitchen, where he gorged all alone.

In the middle of the summer they received a formal announcement of the marriage of Dumouchel to Madame Olympe-Zulma Poulet, widow.

'God bless him!' And they recalled the time when they were happy.

Why did they no longer follow the reapers? Where were the days when they used to go into farms, looking everywhere for antiques? Nothing now could bring about those delightful hours filled with distilling or literature. A gulf kept them away. Something irrevocable had happened.

They tried to go, as they used to, for a walk in the country, went a very long way, got lost. Little fleecy clouds sailed through the sky, the wind made the ripe oats sway, a stream murmured beside a meadow, when suddenly a putrid smell halted them, and they saw, lying on stones amongst brambles, a dog's corpse.

The four legs were all dried up. The jaws grinned to reveal ivory fangs beneath bluish lips; in place of the belly was a muddy coloured mass, so swarming with vermin that it seemed to palpitate. It shook, struck by the sun, under the buzzing flies, in this intolerable stench, a savage and almost devouring stench.

Meanwhile Bouvard's brow became furrowed and his eyes swam with tears.

Pécuchet said stoically: 'One day we shall be like that!'

The idea of death had gripped them. They talked about it on their way back.

After all, there is no such thing. You go off into the dew, the breeze, the stars. You become some part of the sap in the trees, the brilliance of precious stones, the plumage of birds. You give back to nature what she has lent you, and the void that lies before us has no more terrors than that which lies behind.

They tried to imagine it in the form of intense darkness, a bottomless pit, a continual swoon, anything was better than this monotonous, absurd, hopeless existence.

They recapitulated their unsatisfied needs. Bouvard had always wanted horses, carriages, the finest Burgundies, and lovely, willing women in a splendid residence. Pécuchet's ambition was philosophical knowledge. Now the greatest problem of all, the one that contains the others, can be solved in a moment. When would that moment come?

'Might as well have done with it at once.'

'As you like,' said Bouvard.

And they examined the question of suicide.

What is wrong with throwing off a crushing burden and committing an act that does nobody any harm? If it offended God, should we have such a power? It is not an act of cowardice, whatever people may say, and it is a fine piece of insolence to flout, even to one's own detriment, what men esteem most.

They deliberated on the kind of death.

Poison causes pain. Cutting one's throat takes too much courage. Asphyxia often does not work.

In the end Pécuchet set up in the loft two of their gymnastic ropes. Then, tying them to the same crossbeam in the roof, he let a running knot hang down and put two chairs underneath to reach the ropes.

This was the method agreed upon.

They wondered what impression it would create in the neighbourhood; where their books, papers, collections would go afterwards. The thought of death softened their hearts, but they did not abandon their plan, and through talking about it became used to the idea.

On the eve of 25th December, between ten and eleven o'clock, they were meditating in the museum, dressed differently. Bouvard had a smock on over his knitted waistcoat, and for three months Pécuchet had not changed his monk's habit for reasons of economy.

As they were very hungry (for Marcel, who had gone out at

dawn, had not reappeared), Bouvard thought it would be healthy to drink a flask of spirits, and Pécuchet to have some tea.

As he picked up the kettle he spilled some water over the parquet floor.

'Clumsy!' cried Bouvard.

Then, finding the infusion too weak, he wanted to make it stronger by putting in two more spoonfuls.

'It will be disgusting,' said Pécuchet.

'Not at all!'

Each of them pulled the box towards him, the tray fell, one of the cups was broken, the last of the best china service.

Bouvard went pale. 'Go on! Break the place up! Don't stand on ceremony!'

'A great disaster indeed!'

'Yes, a disaster! I inherited it from my father!'

'Natural father,' added Pécuchet, with a sneer.

'Ah! You're insulting me!'

'No, but I make you tired! Admit it!'

And Pécuchet was overcome by anger, or rather rage. Bouvard too; they both shouted together, one irritated by hunger, the other by alcohol. All that came out of Pécuchet's throat was a kind of death-rattle.

'A life like this is hellish: I'd rather die! Farewell!'

He took the torch, turned on his heels, slammed the door.

Bouvard, left in the dark, had trouble opening it, ran after him, came to the loft.

The candle was on the ground; Pécuchet stood on one of the chairs with the rope in his hand.

Bouvard was carried away with a spirit of imitation: 'Wait for me!' And he was climbing onto the other chair, when, suddenly stopping:

'But... we haven't made our wills!'

'Well, well! That's right!'

Their chests heaved with sobs. They stood at the window to get some air.

The air was cold, and numerous stars shone in the inky-black sky.

The whiteness of the snow covering the ground faded away into the misty horizon.

They noticed little lights at ground level, then, getting bigger, coming closer, they all went towards the church.

Curiosity drove them there.

It was the midnight mass. The lights came from the shepherds' lanterns. Some of them, in the porch, were shaking their cloaks.

The serpent was booming, incense smoking. Glasses, hung the length of the nave, formed three garlands of many-coloured lights, and at the end of the perspective, on each side of the tabernacle, gigantic candles sent up scarlet flames. Above the heads of the crowd and the hoods of the women, beyond the choir, the priest could be seen in his golden chasuble: his shrill voice was answered by the loud voices of the men who filled the rood loft, and the wooden vault shook on its stone arches. Pictures representing the Stations of the Cross decorated the walls. In the middle of the choir, in front of the altar, lay a lamb, its feet drawn up under its belly, its ears erect.

The warmth of the temperature filled them with a singular sense of well-being, and their thoughts, which had recently been so tumultuous, became gentle, like waves subsiding.

They listened to the Gospel and the Creed, observed the priest's movements. Meanwhile old and young, poor women in rags, farmers' wives in tall bonnets, sturdy lads with fair whiskers, everyone was praying, absorbed in the same profound joy, and saw on the straw of a cowshed the body of the infant God, radiant as the sun. Such faith on the part of others touched Bouvard despite his reason, and Pécuchet despite the hardness of his heart.

There was a silence; every back was bowed, and, as a bell rang out, the little lamb bleated.

The priest held up the host for all to see, raising his arms as high as possible. Then a song of gladness burst out, summoning the world to the feet of the King of Angels. Bouvard and Pécuchet involuntarily joined in, and they felt as if a new dawn had broken in their souls.

9

MARCEL reappeared next day at three o'clock, looking green, red-eyed, with a bump on his forehead, torn trousers, stinking of spirits, filthy dirty.

According to his annual habit he had been to a place some fifteen miles away, near Iqueuville, to spend Christmas Eve with a friend; and stammering worse than ever, weeping, trying to beat himself, he begged forgiveness as if he had committed a crime. His masters granted it. A strange calm made them feel indulgent.

The snow had suddenly melted, and they were strolling in their garden, breathing in the warm air, happy to be alive.

Was it just chance that had diverted them from death? Bouvard felt moved, Pécuchet recalled his first communion; and full of gratitude for the Force, the Cause on which they depended, they conceived the idea of reading some works of piety.

The Gospel made their souls expand, dazzled them like sunshine. They saw Jesus, standing on the mountain, with one arm raised, and the crowd listening below; or on the edge of the lake, amid the Apostles drawing their nets; then on the donkey, amid the clamour of alleluias, hair windswept from the waving palms; finally up on the cross, with head inclined, shedding dew eternally upon the world. What won them over, delighted them, was his tenderness for the humble, his defence of the poor, his exaltation of the oppressed. In this book in which heaven unfolds, there is nothing theological among so many precepts; not one dogma, no requirement other than a pure heart.

As for the miracles, their reason was not taken by surprise; they had known of them since childhood. The sublimity of St John delighted Pécuchet and made him want to understand the *Imitation* better

Here there were no more parables, flowers or birds, but laments, a closing in of the soul on itself. Bouvard was saddened as he turned over these pages, seemingly written in foggy weather, deep in some cloister, between a steeple and a tomb. Our mortal life appears so lamentable that we must forget it and turn back to God, and our two worthy men, after all their disappointments, felt the need to be simple, to love something, to find peace of mind.

They tried Ecclesiastes, Isaiah, Jeremiah.

But the Bible frightened them with its prophets roaring like lions, the thunder crashing in the clouds, all the weeping in Gehenna, and its God scattering empires as the wind scatters clouds.

They would read it on Sundays, at the hour of Vespers, while the bell was ringing.

One day they went to mass, then went again. It was something to do at the weekend. The Comte and Comtesse de Faverges greeted them from a distance, which was duly noted. The Justice of the Peace said to them, with a wink: 'Splendid! I approve.' All the local ladies now sent them blessed bread.

Abbé Jeuffroy paid them a visit, which they returned; they saw each other quite often, and the priest did not talk about religion.

They were amazed at this reserve, to such an extent that Pécuchet, casually, asked how to set about acquiring faith.

'Practise it first.'

They began to practise, the one hopefully, the other defiantly, Bouvard being convinced that he would never be a religious person. For a whole month he regularly followed all the services, but, unlike Pécuchet, was not willing to submit to fasting.

Was it a health measure? We all know what that is worth! A matter of convention? Down with convention! A sign of submission to the Church? He cared equally little! In short he declared this rule absurd, pharisaical, and contrary to the spirit of the Gospel.

On other Good Fridays they had eaten what Germaine served them.

But this time Bouvard had ordered a steak for himself. He sat down, cut up the meat, and Marcel looked at him scandalized while Pécuchet gravely dissected his slice of cod.

Bouvard stayed with his fork in one hand, knife in the other. At last he made up his mind and lifted a mouthful to his lips. Suddenly his hands trembled, his fat face went pale, his head fell back.

'Do you feel ill?'

'No! But ...' and he made a confession. As a result of his upbringing, it was just too much for him, he could not eat meat on that day for fear of dying.

Without abusing his victory Pécuchet took advantage of it to live as he chose.

One evening he came home, his face marked by profound joy, and let slip that he had just been to confession.

Then they discussed the importance of confession.

Bouvard admitted confession as practised by the early Christians in public: the modern way is too easy. However he did not deny that such self-examination was an element of progress, a moral leavening.

Pécuchet, in his desire for perfection, sought out his vices; it was a long time since he had had a burst of pride. His liking for work exempted him from idleness; as for gluttony, no one could be more temperate. Sometimes he was carried away by anger.

He swore that this would not happen again.

Next one must acquire virtues, first of all humility, that is, one must believe oneself incapable of any merit, unworthy of the slightest reward, sacrifice one's spirit, abase oneself so that others tread on you like the mud on the road. He was still far from having such dispositions.

He was lacking in another virtue: chastity. Because, inwardly, he missed Mélie, and the pastel of the lady in the Louis XV dress disturbed him with its décolleté.

He shut it up in a cupboard, took modesty so far as to be afraid of looking at himself, went to bed in his drawers.

So much concern about lust developed it. Especially in the morning he had to endure great struggles, as did St Paul, St Benedict and St Jerome, up to an advanced age; they at once resorted to savage penances. Pain is an expiation, a remedy and a means, a homage to Christ. All love demands sacrifices, and what could be more painful than that of our bodies!

In order to mortify himself, Pécuchet stopped his glass of spirits after meals, cut himself down to four pinches of snuff a day, left off his cap in the coldest weather.

One day Bouvard, who was tying up the vine, set a ladder against the wall of the terrace near the house, and unintentionally found himself looking into Pécuchet's room.

His friend, stripped to the waist, was gently beating his shoulders with the clothes-beater, then, warming to his task, took off his breeches, lashed his backside, and fell into a chair, out of breath.

Bouvard was disturbed as one is at discovering any mystery which is not meant to be detected.

For some time he had noticed that the windows were cleaner, the napkins had fewer holes in them, the food was better; changes due to the intervention of Reine, the curé's servant.

Mixing ecclesiastical and kitchen matters, strong as a ploughman, and loyal, though disrespectful, she introduced herself into households, gave advice, became the real mistress. Pécuchet relied absolutely on her experience.

On one occasion she had brought him a plump individual, with little slanting eyes and a nose like a vulture's beak. It was Monsieur Goutman, a dealer in pious objects; he unpacked some of them from their boxes in the shed: crosses, medals, and rosaries of every size, candelabras for oratories, portable altars, artificial jewellery bouquets, sacred hearts in blue cardboard, red-bearded St Josephs, china calvaries. Pécuchet coveted them. Only the price deterred him.

Goutman did not care for money. He preferred exchanges, and going up into the museum he offered a stock of his merchandise in return for the old ironwork and all the lead.

Bouvard found the things hideous, but Pécuchet's look, Reine's insistence and the dealer's flow of words finally convinced him. When Goutman saw him so pliable, he wanted the halberd as well; Bouvard, tired of demonstrating how to wield it, gave it up. When the total estimate was complete the gentlemen still owed 100 francs. An arrangement was concluded, involving four promissory notes at three months' delay, and they congratulated themselves on the bargain.

Their acquisitions were distributed all round the rooms. A crib full of hay and a cork cathedral decorated the museum. On Pécuchet's mantelpiece stood a wax St John the Baptist; along the corridor were portraits of leading lights of the episcopate, and at the foot of the stairs, beneath a lamp suspended on chains, a Blessed Virgin in azure mantle, crowned with stars. Marcel cleaned these wonders, and could not imagine anything more beautiful in Paradise.

What a pity that the St Peter was smashed, and how well he would have looked in the vestibule! Pécuchet sometimes stopped in front of the old compost pit, where one could recognize the tiara, a sandal, a bit of ear, and heaved a sigh or two, then went on gardening, for he now combined manual labour with religious exercises and dug the ground, dressed in his monk's habit, comparing himself to St Bruno. Dressing up like this might be sacrilege; he gave it up.

But he began to adopt the ecclesiastical manner, no doubt from associating with the curé. He had his smile, his voice, and, as though he were feeling cold, like him would slip both hands into his sleeves, up to the wrists. The day came when the cock crowing irked him, roses disgusted him; he did not go out any more or else looked round the countryside with hostile eyes.

Bouvard allowed himself to be taken along to the Marian month. The children singing hymns, the sprays of lilac and garlands of greenery had given him the feeling of imperishable youth, as it were. God was revealed to his heart through the shape of the nests, the clear water of springs, the beneficial sunshine, and his friend's piety seemed to him excessive and tedious.

'Why do you groan during meals?'

'We must groan as we eat,' answered Pécuchet, 'for this is the way man lost his innocence,' a phrase he had read in the *Seminarists' Manual*, two duodecimo volumes borrowed from Monsieur Jeufroy. He drank water from La Salette, indulged behind closed doors in jaculatory prayers, hoped to join the confraternity of St Francis.

To obtain the gift of perseverance he resolved to make a pilgrimage to the Virgin.

The choice of locality embarrassed him. Should it be to Our Lady of Fourvière, Chartres, Embrun, Marseille or Auray? Our Lady of Deliverance, which was nearer, was just as suitable.

'You will come with me!'

'I would look a proper idiot!' said Bouvard.

After all, he might come back a believer; he did not refuse to be one, and yielded so as not to be awkward.

Pilgrimages should be accomplished on foot. But forty-three kilometres would be hard, and as coaches are not conducive to meditation, they hired an old cabriolet, which after a twelve-hour journey set them down before the inn.

They had a room with two beds, with two washstands bearing two water-jugs in little oval basins, and the innkeeper told them that under the Terror it had been the 'Capuchins' room'.

The statue of Our Lady of Deliverance had been so carefully hidden there that the good fathers said mass there in secret.

That pleased Pécuchet, and he read aloud some notes on the chapel, found down in the kitchen.

It was founded at the beginning of the second century by St Regnobert, first bishop of Lisieux, or by St Ragnobert, who lived in the seventh century, or by Robert the Magnificent in the middle of the eleventh.

The Danes, Normans and above all Protestants burned and sacked it at different times.

About 1112 the original statue was discovered by a sheep, which indicated the place where it lay by striking its hoof in a meadow, and on this site Count Baudouin built a sanctuary.

Her miracles are innumerable. A Bayeux merchant, captive of the Saracens, invokes her: his chains fall off and he escapes. A miser discovers a horde of rats in his loft, calls on her and the rats go away. An old materialist of Versailles is brought to repentance on his deathbed by contact with a medal which had fleetingly touched her effigy. She restored the power of speech to Monsieur Adeline, who had lost it through his blasphemies; and through her protection Monsieur and Madame de Bacqueville had the strength to live chastely though married.

Among others cured of hopeless illnesses by her are mentioned Mademoiselle de Palfresne, Anne Lorieux, Marie Duchemin, François Dufai and Madame de Jumillac, née d'Osseville.

Notable personages have visited her: Louis XI, Louis XIII, two daughters of Gaston d'Orléans, Cardinal Wiseman, Patriarch Samirrhi of Antioch, Monseigneur Véroles, Apostolic Vicar of Manchuria; and Archbishop de Quélen came to thank her for the conversion of the Prince de Talleyrand.

'She may manage to convert you too!' said Pécuchet.

Bouvard, already in bed, gave a sort of grunt, and fell fast asleep.

Next morning at six o'clock they went into the chapel.

Another one was being built; tiles and planks cluttered up the nave, and the monument, in rococo style, did not appeal to Bouvard, especially the red marble altar with Corinthian pilasters.

The miraculous statue, in a niche to the left of the choir, is wrapped in a sequin robe; the verger arrived, with a candle for each of them. He stuck it onto a sort of grand candelabra, overlooking the balustrade, asked for three francs, bowed and disappeared.

Next they looked at the ex-votos.

There are inscriptions on plaques expressing the gratitude of the faithful. Things to be admired include two crossed swords presented by a former pupil of the École Polytechnique, bridal bouquets, military medals, silver hearts, and, in the corner, at floor level, a forest of crutches.

From the sacristy a priest emerged bearing the ciborium.

When he had spent a few moments at the foot of the altar he ascended the three steps, said the *Oremus*, *Introit* and *Kyrie*, which the kneeling server recited all in one breath.

The congregation was sparse, twelve or fifteen old women. One could hear the rattling of their rosaries, and the sound of a hammer hitting stones. Pécuchet, bent over his prie-dieu, answered the Amens. During the elevation he begged Our Lady to send him a constant and indestructible faith.

Bouvard, in a chair at his side, took his Eucology from him and stopped at the litanies of the Virgin.

'Most pure, most chaste, venerable, amiable, powerful, merciful, ivory tower, golden mansion, morning gate.' These words of adoration, these hyperboles carried him off to her who is celebrated with so many tributes.

He dreamed of her as she appears in pictures in church, on a pile of clouds, cherubim at her feet, the God-Child at her breast, mother of the tenderness demanded by all earthly afflictions, ideal of womanhood transported to Heaven; for, fruit of her womb, man exalts her love and his only aspiration is to rest on her heart.

When mass was over, they passed along the booths set against the wall at the side of the main square. There are to be seen images, holy-water stoups, urns decorated in gold thread, Christs in coconut shell, ivory rosaries; and the sun, shining on the glass of the frames, was dazzling, brought out the crudity of the paintings, the hideousness of the designs. Bouvard, who at home found such things abominable, was indulgent about them. He bought a little blue plaster Virgin. Pécuchet contented himself with a rosary as a souvenir.

The dealers were crying: 'Come on! Come on! For five francs, for three francs, for sixty centimes, for ten centimes, don't refuse Our Lady!'

The two pilgrims strolled round without choosing anything. Disobliging comments could be heard.

'What are they after, those chaps?'

'Perhaps they are Turks?'

'More likely Protestants!'

A tall girl pulled at Pécuchet's coat; an old man in spectacles put a hand on his shoulder; they were all braying at once; then, leaving their booths, they came up to surround them, renewing their solicitations and insults.

Bouvard could stand no more: 'Leave us alone, for God's sake!' The mob broke up.

But a stout woman followed them for a while across the square and cried out that they would be sorry.

Back at the inn they found Goutman in the café. His business called him to these parts, and he was chatting with an individual who was examining accounts on a table in front of them.

This individual had on a leather cap and very wide trousers; his complexion was ruddy and figure slender despite his white hair; he looked a cross between a retired officer and an old actor.

From time to time he let out an oath, then at a quieter word from Goutman calmed down at once and went on to another paper.

Bouvard, who was watching him, after a quarter of an hour went up to him.

'Barberou, I believe?'

'Bouvard!' cried the man with the cap, and they embraced.

For the past twenty years Barberou had endured the most varied of fortunes.

Manager of a newspaper, insurance agent, director of an oyster farm. 'I'll tell you the story.' Finally, reverting to his original trade, he was travelling for a Bordeaux firm, and Goutman, 'who did the diocese', secured orders for his wines from the clergy.

'But excuse me; I'll be with you in a moment.'

He had gone back to his accounts, when, leaping from his seat:

'What, two thousand?'

'That's right!'

'Ah, that's a bit much, that one!'

'I beg your pardon?'

'I saw Hérambert myself,' Barberou answered angrily. 'It says 4,000 on the invoice; no joking.'

The dealer was quite unperturbed.

'Very well; that leaves you free! What then?'

Barberou stood up, and seeing his face go first quite pale and then purple, Bouvard and Pécuchet thought that he was going to strangle Goutman.

He sat down again, crossed his arms.

'You are a rotten twister, you must admit!'

'No insults, Monsieur Barberou; there are witnesses; be careful!'

'I'll take you to court!'

'Well, well!' Then, fastening his briefcase, Goutman tipped the edge of his hat: 'My compliments!' and left.

Barberou explained the facts: in return for a credit of 1,000 francs, which had doubled as a result of various operations, he had delivered 3,000 francs worth of wine to Goutman, which would pay off his debt with a profit of 1,000 francs, but on the contrary he now owed 3,000. His employers would dismiss him, he would be prosecuted! 'Rogue! Robber! Dirty Jew! And that thing goes to dine in presbyteries! Anyhow, anything to do with priests . . .!' He fulminated against the clergy, and banged on the table so violently that the statuette almost fell off.

'Easy!' said Bouvard.

'Well now, what's that?' and Barberou unwrapped the little Virgin. 'A pilgrimage knick-knack! Is it yours?'

Instead of answering Bouvard smiled ambiguously.

'It's mine!' said Pécuchet.

'You grieve me,' replied Barberou, 'but I will educate you on that score, never fear!' And since one must be philosophical and it does no good to be gloomy, he invited them to lunch.

All three sat down to table.

Barberou was friendly, recalled old times, put his arm round the servant's waist, wanted to measure Bouvard's stomach. He would soon be going to their place and would bring a book to make them laugh.

The idea of his visit caused them modified rapture. They talked about it in the cabriolet, for an hour, as the horse trotted along. Then Pécuchet closed his eyes. Bouvard too went quiet. Inwardly he was inclining towards religion.

Monsieur Marescot had come the day before with an important message for them. Marcel did not know any more about it.

The lawyer could not receive them until three days later, and at once explained the matter. In return for an income of 7,500 francs, Madame Bordin was proposing to Monsieur Bouvard that she should buy their farm.

She had had her eye on it since her youth, knew all its ins and outs, good and bad points; and this desire was eating away at her like a cancer. For the good lady, like any true Norman, cherished above all *property*, not so much for the sake of capital security as for the pleasure of treading on ground actually belonging to oneself. In the hope of getting this land she had made enquiries, watched it every day, saved up for a long time, and was now impatiently waiting for Bouvard's answer.

He was embarrassed, because he did not want Pécuchet to find himself one day without means; but this was an opportunity to be grasped, and the effect of the pilgrimage: providence was for a second time manifesting itself in their favour.

They offered the following conditions: the income, not of 7,500 but of 6,000, would devolve on the one to survive; Marescot pointed out that one of them had poor health. The other was disposed by temperament to apoplexy, and Madame Bordin signed the contract, carried away by passion.

Bouvard remained melancholy. Someone wanted him to die and this reflection inspired solemn thoughts, ideas about God and eternity.

Three days later Monsieur Jeufroy invited them to the formal meal which he gave once a year for colleagues.

Dinner began about two in the afternoon and finished at eleven in the evening.

They drank perry, made puns. Abbé Pruneau made up an acrostic just like that. Monsieur Bougon did card tricks, and Cerpet, a young curate, sang a little ballad that was almost daring. Such company entertained Bouvard. He was less gloomy next day.

The curé frequently came to see him. He painted religion in glowing colours. What is one risking, after all? And Bouvard soon agreed to go up to the altar. Pécuchet would join in the sacrament at the same time as he.

The great day arrived.

Because of the first communions the church was crowded. The well-to-do citizens and their wives were crammed into their pews, and humbler folk stood at the back, or in the gallery above the door.

What was about to begin was inexplicable, thought Bouvard, but reason does not suffice for understanding certain things. The greatest men have admitted this one. One might as well do like them, and in a sort of daze he gazed at the altar, the thurible, the torches, a little light-headed because he had not eaten anything, and felt oddly weak.

Meditating on Christ's Passion, Pécuchet worked himself up into a fervour of love. He would have liked to offer Christ his soul, others' souls, the ecstasies, transports, illuminations of the saints, every creature, the whole universe. Although he prayed with fervour, the different parts of the mass seemed rather long to him.

At last the small boys knelt on the first of the altar steps, their dark suits merging into a solid black band, with fair or dark hair topping it unevenly. They were replaced by the little girls, with veils falling from beneath their headbands; from a distance it looked like a row of white clouds at the back of the choir.

Then it was the turn of the adults.

The first on the Gospel side was Pécuchet, but no doubt under too great emotional stress he let his head sway from right to left. The curé had difficulty in putting the host into his mouth, and he received it with rolling eyes.

Bouvard, on the other hand, opened his jaws so wide that his tongue hung out over his lip like a flag. As he stood up he bumped into Madame Bordin. Their eyes met. She smiled; without knowing why he went red.

After Madame Bordin came Mademoiselle de Faverges, the countess, their companion and a gentleman, a stranger to Chavignolles, who all communicated together.

The last two were Placquevent and Petit, the teacher, when suddenly Gorju appeared.

He no longer wore a beard, and he went back to his place with his arms crossed over his chest, in a most edifying manner.

The curé harangued the small boys. They must be careful later on not to be like Judas who betrayed his God, and they must always keep their vesture of innocence. Pécuchet regretted losing his, but the chairs were being moved; mothers were impatient to embrace their children.

As they came out the parishioners exchanged congratulations. Some were weeping. Madame de Faverges, as she waited for her carriage, turned to Bouvard and Pécuchet and introduced her future son-in-law: 'Monsieur le Baron de Mahurot, engineer.' The count was sorry not to have seen them. He would be back next week. 'Make a note of it, please!' The carriage had come; the ladies from the château went off, and the crowd dispersed.

In their yard they found a packet in the middle of the grass. The postman, finding the house closed, had thrown it over the wall. It was the book Barberou had promised: *Examination of Christianity*, by Louis Hervieu, sometime pupil of the École Normale. Pécuchet pushed it away. Bouvard did not want to know about it.

He had been told repeatedly that the sacrament would transform him; for several days he watched out for some new blossoming in his conscience. He was still the same, and felt painfully surprised.

What! God's body mingles with ours and has no effect on it! The thought that rules worlds does not enlighten our spirit! The supreme power abandons us to impotence!

Monsieur Jeufroy tried to reassure him and ordered Abbé Gaume's *Catechism*.

On the other hand Pécuchet's piety had developed. He would like to have communicated in both kinds, he sang psalms as he walked about the corridor, stopped local people to have discussions and try to convert them. Vaucorbeil openly laughed at him. Girbal shrugged his shoulders and the captain called him Tartuffe. People now thought they were going too far.

It is an excellent habit to look at things as so many symbols. If thunder rumbles, picture to yourself the Last Judgement; faced with a cloudless sky, think of the sojourn of the blessed; say to yourself when you are out walking that every step brings you nearer death. Pécuchet observed this method. When he put on his clothes he thought of the fleshly covering with which the second person of the Trinity clothed himself, the ticking of the clock reminded him of his heart beating, a pinprick of the nails of the Cross; but it was in vain that he stayed kneeling for hours, fasted more often than ever, made efforts of imagination; self-detachment did not come about; perfect contemplation was unattainable.

He had recourse to mystic authors: St Teresa, John of the Cross, Luis of Granada, Scupoli, and more modern ones, like Monseigneur Chaillot. Instead of the sublimity he expected, he encountered only platitudes, a very careless style, cold images and numerous comparisons drawn from the lapidaries' shop.

He learned however that there is an active and a passive purgation, an interior and exterior vision, four kinds of prayer, nine sorts of excellence in love, six degrees in humility, and that a wound in the soul is not very different from spiritual flight.

Some points worried him.

'Since the flesh is accursed, how is it that we must thank God for the blessing of existence? What proportion should be kept between the fear indispensable to salvation and the hope which is no less so? Where is the sign of grace, etc.?'

Monsieur Jeufroy's answers were simple.

'Don't torment yourself. Anyone who tries to get to the bottom of everything is sliding down a dangerous slope.'

The *Catechism of Perseverance* by Gaume had so put Bouvard off that he took Louis Hervieu's volume. It was a summary of modern exegesis forbidden by the government. Barberou, as a republican, had bought it.

It aroused doubts in Bouvard's mind, first about original sin. 'If God created man sinful, he should not have punished him, and evil is previous to the Fall because there were already volcanoes, wild beasts. In a word, this dogma upsets my idea of justice.'

'What do you expect?' said the curé. 'It is one of those truths that everyone agrees about without being able to advance any proofs; and we ourselves visit the children with the sins of their fathers. So custom and law justify this decree of providence, which reappears in nature.'

Bouvard nodded his head. He also had doubts about Hell.

'Because every punishment should aim at improving the guilty person, which becomes impossible with an eternal penalty; and how many have to endure it! Just think, all the Ancients, Jews, Moslems, idolaters, heretics and unbaptized infants, these children created by God, and to what end? In order to punish them for a fault they did not commit!'

'That is St Augustine's opinion,' added the curé, 'and St Fulgentius includes even foetuses in damnation. It is true, the Church has come to no decision in that respect. One remark though; it is not God, but the sinner, who damns himself, and since the offence is infinite, God being infinite, the punishment must be infinite too. Is that all, sir?'

'Explain the Trinity to me,' said Bouvard.

'With pleasure. Let us take a comparison: the three sides of a triangle, or rather our soul, which contains being, knowing, willing; what in man is called a faculty is in God a person. That is the mystery.'

'But each of the three sides of the triangle is not the triangle; these three faculties of the soul do not make three souls, and your persons of the Trinity are three Gods.'

'Blasphemy!'

'Then there is only one person, one God, one substance affected in three ways!'

'Let us worship without understanding,' said the curé.

'Very well,' said Bouvard.

He was afraid of being taken for irreligious, and being disapproved of at the château.

They now went there three times a week, at about five o'clock in winter, and the cup of tea warmed them up. Monsieur le Comte by his manners 'recalled the elegance of the former court'; the comtesse, placid and plump, showed great discernment about everything. Mademoiselle Yolande, their daughter, was 'the very model of a young person', the angel of the lockets, and Madame de Noaris, their companion, looked like Pécuchet, with the same pointed nose.

The first time they went into the drawing-room she was defending someone.

'I assure you he has changed! His gift proves it.'

This someone was Gorju. He had just given the bridal couple a Gothic prie-dieu. It was brought in. The arms of the two houses were displayed in coloured reliefs. Monsieur de Mahurot seemed pleased with it, and Madame de Noaris said to him:

'You will remember my protegé!'

Then she led in two children, a lad of about twelve and his sister, who might have been about ten. Through the holes in their ragged clothes could be seen their limbs, red with cold. One had on a pair of old slippers, the other just one clog. Their hair covered their foreheads, and they looked around them with smouldering eyes like frightened young wolves.

Madame de Noaris explained that she had met them that morning on the highway. Placquevent was unable to provide any details.

They were asked their names.

'Victor, Victorine.' – 'Where was their father?'

'In prison.' – 'And what did he do before that?'

'Nothing.' – 'Where did they come from?' – 'Saint-Pierre.'

'But which Saint-Pierre?'

The two children only answered, amid sniffs:

'Don't know, don't know.'

Their mother was dead and they were begging.

Madame de Noaris talked about the dangers of abandoning them; she touched the heart of the countess and the honour of the count, and, supported by Mademoiselle, persisted and won the day. The gamekeeper's wife would look after them. They would be found work later, and, as they could not read or write, Madame de Noaris would give them lessons herself, to prepare them for catechism.

Whenever Monsieur Jeufroy came to the château the two children were sent for; he questioned them, then gave a lecture, somewhat pretentious because of his audience.

Once, when he had discoursed about the patriarchs, Bouvard, going home with him and Pécuchet, criticized them strongly.

Jacob distinguished himself by his cheating, David by murders, Solomon by debauches.

The priest answered that one must see beyond that. Abraham's sacrifice is a figure of the Passion; Jacob is another figure of the Messiah; like Joseph, the brazen serpent, Moses.

'Do you believe,' said Bouvard, 'that he composed the *Pentateuch*?'

'Yes, certainly!'

'Yet his death is described there; the same goes for *Joshua*, and as for *Judges*, the author tells us that in the period whose history he is recounting Israel did not yet have kings. So the book was written under the kings. The prophets amaze me too.'

'He is going to deny the prophets now!'

'Not at all! But their excited spirits saw Jehovah in different forms, as a fire, as a bush, an old man, a dove, and they were not certain of Revelation since they were always asking for a sign.'

'Ah! And where did you discover these fine things?'

'In Spinoza.'

The name made the curé jump.

'Have you read him?'

'God forbid!'

'Yet, sir, science ...'

'Sir, one cannot be learned unless one is Christian.'

Science inspired him to sarcasm:

'Will your science make an ear of corn grow? What do we know?' he said.

But he knew the world was created for us; he knew that archangels are above angels; he knew that the human body will rise again in the state it was at about the age of thirty.

His sacerdotal assurance annoyed Bouvard, who, from distrust of Louis Hervieu, wrote to Varlot, and Pécuchet, better informed, asked Monsieur Jeufroy for explanations regarding Scripture.

The six days of *Genesis* mean six great ages. The Jews' theft of the precious vessels from the Egyptians must be interpreted as intellectual riches, the arts whose secret they had stolen. Isaiah did not strip completely, *nudus* in Latin meaning naked to the waist: thus Virgil advises one to strip for ploughing, and that author would never have issued a precept contrary to modesty! There is nothing extraordinary about Ezekiel devouring a book: do we not say 'devour' a pamphlet, a newspaper?

But if one sees metaphors everywhere, what will become of the facts? The abbé maintained, however, that they were real.

Such a way of taking them seemed dishonest to Pécuchet. He carried his researches further and brought along a note on the contradictions in the Bible.

We learn from *Exodus* that for forty years they made sacrifices in the desert; according to Amos and Jeremiah there were none. *Chronicles* and *Esdras* do not agree about the numbering of the people. In *Deuteronomy* Moses sees the Lord face to face; according to *Exodus* he was never able to see him. Where then is the inspiration?

'One more reason for admitting it,' replied Monsieur Jeufroy with a smile. 'Imposters need connivance, genuine people are not concerned about it. In case of doubt let us refer to the Church. She is always infallible.'

What is the basis of infallibility?

The councils of Basle and Constance attribute it to the councils. But councils often differ, witness what happened with Athanasius and Arius; those of Florence and the Lateran ascribe it to the Pope. But Adrian VI asserts that the Pope, like anyone else, may be mistaken.

Quibbles! None of that affects the permanence of dogma.

Louis Hervieu's book indicates the variations: baptism was formerly reserved for adults. Extreme unction only became a sacrament in the ninth century, the Real Presence was decreed in the eighth, Purgatory recognized in the fifteenth, the Immaculate Conception only yesterday.

Pécuchet came to the point when he no longer knew what to think about Jesus. Three Gospels make him out to be a man. In a passage of St John he appears to make himself equal to God, in another, also in St John, to acknowledge himself to be inferior.

The abbé retorted with King Abgar's letter, the Acts of Pilate and the evidence of the Sibyls, 'basically true'. He found the Virgin among the Gauls, the announcement of a redeemer in China, the Trinity everywhere, the cross on the Grand Lama's hat, in Egypt in the gods' hands; and he even showed an engraving, representing a nilometer, which, according to Pécuchet, was a phallus.

Monsieur Jeufroy secretly consulted his friend Pruneau, who

looked out proofs for him in the authors. A contest of erudition ensued; and stung by *amour-propre* Pécuchet became transcendent, a mythologist.

He compared the Virgin to Isis, the Eucharist to the Homa of the Persians, Bacchus to Moses, Noah's Ark to Xithuros' vessel, and these similarities demonstrated for him the identity of religions.

But there cannot be several religions, since there is only one God, and when he had run out of arguments the clerical gentleman cried: 'It is a mystery!'

What does the word mean? Lack of knowledge; very well. But if it designates something of which the mere statement implies contradiction, it is an absurdity, and Pécuchet never left Monsieur Jeufroy alone. He caught him in the garden, waited for him in the confessional, hunted him down in the sacristy.

The priest thought up ruses for escaping him.

One day when he had gone to Sassetot to administer someone, Pécuchet stood in front of him in the road, so as to make conversation inevitable.

It was evening, towards the end of August. The crimson sky grew darker, and a big cloud formed, with a regular base and scrolls at the top.

Pécuchet at first talked of indifferent things, then, letting slip the word 'martyr':

'How many do you think there have been?'

'Twenty millions or so, at least.'

'The numbers are not so great, says Origen.'

'Origen, you know, is rather suspect.'

There was a sudden gust of wind, bending the grass in the ditches and the two lines of elms stretching out to the far horizon.

Pécuchet went on: 'Included among the martyrs are many Gaulish bishops killed resisting the Barbarians, but that is no longer the question.'

'Are you going to defend the emperors?'

According to Pécuchet they had been the victims of calumny: 'The story of the Theban legion is a fable. I also question Symphorosus and his seven sons, Felicity and her seven daughters, and the seven virgins of Ancyra, condemned to be raped, although they were seventy, and the 11,000 virgins of St Ursula, who had a companion called Undecemilla, a name mistaken for a number; even more the martyrs of Alexandria!'

'All the same! . . . All the same they are to be found in reliable authors.'

Drops of rain fell. The curé opened his umbrella, and Pécuchet, when he was underneath, dared to claim that the Catholics had martyred more Jews, Moslems, Protestants and free-thinkers than all the Romans in the past.

The ecclesiastic protested: 'But there were as many as ten persecutions from Nero to Galera Caesar!'

'All right! And the Albigensian massacres? And St Bartholomew? And the Revocation of the Edict of Nantes?'

'Deplorable excesses, certainly, but you are surely not going to compare those people with St Stephen, St Laurence, Cyprian, Polycarp, a crowd of missionaries?'

'Excuse me! Let me just remind you of Hypathia, Jerome of Prague, John Huss, Bruno, Vanini, Anne Dubourg!'

The rain fell more heavily, and spattered so violently that the jets of water bounced off the ground like little white rockets. Pécuchet and Monsieur Jeufroy walked slowly, pressing close together, and the curé said:

'After abominable tortures they were thrown into cauldrons!'

'The Inquisition used torture too, and made a good job of burning you!'

'Noble ladies were exposed in brothels!'

'Do you think Louis XIV's dragoons behaved decently?'

'And note that the Christians had not done anything against the state!'

'Nor had the Huguenots!'

The wind drove the rain, swept it into the air. It beat on the leaves, streamed along the edge of the path, and the muddy sky merged into the fields, stripped bare after the harvest. Not a roof to be seen, only afar off a shepherd's hut.

Pécuchet's skimpy coat was soaked through and through. The water ran along his spine, into his boots, his ears, his eyes, despite the peak of his Amoros cap; the curé picked up the skirts of his cassock with one arm, baring his legs, and the points of his tricorn hat gushed water over his shoulders like gargoyles in a cathedral.

They had to stop, and turning their backs to the storm, they stood face to face, belly to belly, holding in their four hands the swaying umbrella.

Monsieur Jeufroy had not interrupted his defence of the Catholics.

'Did they crucify your Protestants like St Simeon or have men devoured by two tigers, as happened to St Ignatius?'

'But do you count so many wives separated from their husbands, children torn from their mothers, as meaning anything? And the poor driven into exile, through the snow, with precipices all round! They were crammed into prisons; and they were hardly dead before they were being dragged along on hurdles.'

The abbé scoffed: 'You will allow me not to believe a word of it! And our martyrs are less dubious. St Blandine was delivered in a net to an enraged cow. St Julitte was beaten to death. St Tarachus, St Probus, and St Andronicus had their teeth broken with a hammer, their sides lacerated with iron combs, their hands pierced with red-hot nails, and then they were scalped.'

'You exaggerate,' said Pécuchet. 'The death of martyrs in those days was an amplification of rhetoric!'

'What do you mean, rhetoric?'

'Oh yes! Whereas I, sir, am quoting history. The Catholics in Ireland ripped open pregnant women to take their children!'

'Never!'

'And give them to the swine!'

'Come now!'

'In Belgium they buried them alive!'

'What humbug!'

'Their names are known!'

'And even so,' objected the priest, shaking his umbrella furiously, 'you can't call them martyrs. There are none outside the Church.'

'Just a word. If the martyr's value depends on doctrine, how can he be used to demonstrate the excellence of doctrine?'

The rain calmed down. They reached the village without further talk.

But on the threshold of the presbytery the abbé said:

'I pity you! I really pity you!'

Pécuchet at once described his altercation to Bouvard. It had filled him with ill-will against religion, and an hour later, sitting before a fire of vine branches, he was reading the curé Meslier. Such ponderous denials shocked him; then, reproaching himself for having perhaps failed to recognize heroes, he ran through, in the *Biography*, the story of the most illustrious martyrs.

How the people clamoured when the martyrs entered the arena! And if the lions and jaguars were too gentle, they spurred them on with gestures and shouts. The martyrs stood there, all covered in blood, smiling, looking up at heaven; St Perpetua tied up her hair so as not to look distressed. Pécuchet began to reflect. The window was open, the night still, many stars were out. Something must have taken place in their souls of which we no longer have any idea, a joy, a divine convulsion! As a result of dreaming about it Pécuchet said that he understood and would have done like them.

'You?'

'Certainly.'

'No joking! Do you believe, or don't you?'

'I don't know.'

He lit a candle, then, as his eyes fell on the crucifix in the alcove:

'How many wretches have turned to him!' And after a silence: 'He has been misrepresented! It is Rome's fault; Vatican policy!'

But Bouvard admired the Church for its magnificence and would like to have been a cardinal in the Middle Ages.

'I would have looked well in the purple, you must agree!'

Pécuchet had put his cap by the fire but it was still not dry. As he stretched it he felt something in the lining and a St Joseph medal fell out. They were disturbed, seeing no way to explain the fact.

Madame de Noaris wanted to know if Pécuchet had not felt some kind of change, or happiness, and gave herself away by her questions. Once, while he was playing billiards, she had sewn the medal into his cap.

Obviously she loved him; they could have married; she was a widow and he did not suspect this love, which might perhaps have brought happiness into his life.

Although he showed himself to be more religious than Monsieur

Bouvard, she had dedicated him to St Joseph, whose help is excellent for conversions.

No one knew as well as she did all the rosaries and the indulgences they secure, the effect of relics, the privileges of holy waters. Her watch hung on a chain which had touched St Peter's chains.

Among the trinkets she wore shone a golden pearl, in imitation of the one in the church at Allouagne containing one of Our Lord's tears; a ring on her little finger enclosed some hairs of the curé d'Ars, and as she picked herbal remedies for the sick her room resembled a sacristy and chemist's laboratory.

She spent her time writing letters, visiting the poor, breaking up couples living in sin, distributing photographs of the Sacred Heart. A gentleman was supposed to be sending her some 'martyrs' paste', a mixture of wax from the paschal candle and human dust taken from the catacombs, to be used in desperate cases as pills or patches. She promised some to Pécuchet.

He appeared shocked by such materialism.

In the evening one of the servants from the château brought him a pile of pamphlets, relating pious words uttered by the great Napoleon, clerical witticisms in inns, terrifying deaths of impious persons. Madame de Noaris knew it all by heart, as well as an infinite number of miracles.

She told of stupid, pointless miracles, as if God had effected them to astound people. Her own grandmother had put away in a cupboard some prunes covered with a cloth, and when the cupboard was opened a year later, thirteen of them lay on the cloth in the form of a cross. 'Explain that to me.' That was what she always said after her stories, which she maintained with mulish obstinacy, though she was a good woman and of cheerful disposition.

Once however 'she acted out of character'. Bouvard challenged the miracle of Pezilla: a dish in which hosts had been hidden during the Revolution turned gold all by itself.

'Perhaps there was a little golden colour at the bottom caused by humidity?'

'No! No! I repeat! The cause of the gilding was contact with the Eucharist.'

And as evidence she gave the bishops' attestation.

'They say it is like a shield, a . . . a palladium over the diocese of Perpignan. Ask Monsieur Jeufroy instead!'

Bouvard could stand no more, and, going over his Louis Hervieu, took Pécuchet along.

The ecclesiastic was just finishing dinner. Reine offered them a seat, and at a sign from him went for two small glasses, which she filled with rosolio.

After which Bouvard explained what brought him.

The abbé did not reply frankly. 'Anything is possible for God and miracles are a proof of religion.'

'There are laws however!'

'That makes no difference. He upsets them to instruct, to correct.'

'How do you know he upsets them?' retorted Bouvard. 'As long as nature follows her routine, we do not think about it; but in any extraordinary phenomenon we see the hand of God.'

'Which may well be there,' said the ecclesiastic, 'and when an event is certified by witnesses?'

'Witnesses swallow anything, because there are false miracles.'

The priest went red:

'Yes, indeed . . . sometimes.'

'How can you distinguish them from true ones? And if the true ones which are given as proof themselves need proofs, why work them?'

Reine intervened, and, preaching like her master, said that one must obey.

'Life is transitory, but death is eternal.'

'In short,' added Bouvard, drinking up the rosolio, 'the miracles of the past are no better demonstrated than the miracles of today; similar reasons support those of Christians and pagans.'

The curé threw his fork on the table.

'Pagan miracles were false, I tell you again! No miracles outside the Church!'

'Well now,' Pécuchet said to himself, 'the same argument as for the martyrs; doctrine depends on facts and facts on doctrine.'

Monsieur Jeufroy drank a glass of water and went on:

'Though you deny them, you believe in them. The world converted by twelve fishermen; that seems a fine miracle to me!'

'Not at all!'

Pécuchet accounted for it differently.

'Monotheism comes from the Hebrews, the Trinity from the Indians, the Logos belongs to Plato, the Virgin mother to Asia.'

No matter! Monsieur Jeufroy insisted on the supernatural, would not admit that humanly speaking Christianity could have the slightest reason for existing, although he saw prodromes or deformations of it in all peoples. The mocking impiety of the eighteenth century he would have tolerated, but modern criticism, with its politeness, exasperated him.

'I prefer the blaspheming atheist to the argumentative sceptic!'

Then he looked at them with an air of bravado as if to dismiss them.

Pécuchet went home in melancholy mood. He had hoped for the conciliation of faith and reason.

Bouvard made him read this passage of Louis Hervieu:

'If you wish to know the gulf that separates them contrast their axioms:

'Reason tells you: the whole includes the part, and faith answers with substantiation; Jesus communicating with his apostles had his body in his hand and his head in his mouth.

'Reason tells you: three is three, and faith declares: three is one.'

They paid no more visits to the abbé.

It was the time of the war in Italy.

Decent people trembled for the Pope. There were violent attacks against Victor Emmanuel. Madame de Noaris went as far as wishing him dead.

Bouvard and Pécuchet made only timid protests. When the drawing-room door turned before them and they looked at their reflections as they passed the tall mirrors, while through the windows could be seen the avenues on which a servant's red waistcoat stood out against the greenery, they felt some pleasure; and the luxury of the surroundings made them indulgent to the words that were uttered there.

The count lent them all the works of Monsieur de Maistre. He developed their principles to a circle of intimates: Hurel, the curé, the Justice of the Peace, the lawyer and the baron, his future son-in-law, who came from time to time to spend twenty-four hours at the château.

'What is abominable,' said the count, 'is the spirit of 1789! First they challenge God; next they debate about government; then comes liberty. Liberty of insult, revolt, enjoyment, or rather pillage, so that Church and State have to proscribe independents and heretics. There will no doubt be an outcry against persecution, as though executioners persecuted criminals. To sum up: no State without God! Since the law can only command respect if it comes from above, and at the moment it is not a question of the Italians, but of knowing who will win, the Revolution or the Pope, Satan or Christ.'

Monsieur Jeufroy approved monosyllabically, Hurel with a smile, the Justice of the Peace wagging his head. Bouvard and Pécuchet looked at the ceiling; Madame de Noaris, the countess and Yolande were working for the poor, and Monsieur de Mahurot, near his fiancée, was glancing through the papers.

Then there were silences, when everyone seemed absorbed in working out some problem. Napoleon III was no longer a saviour, and even gave a deplorable example by allowing the masons at the Tuileries to work on a Sunday.

'It should never be allowed,' was Monsieur le Comte's usual phrase. Social economy, fine arts, literature, history, scientific doctrines, he decided everything, in his capacity as Christian and paterfamilias, and would to God that the government in this respect showed the same rigour as he exercised in his house! Government alone may judge the dangers of science; if it is too widespread it fills the people with disastrous ambitions. They were happier, these poor people, when the lords and bishops tempered royal absolutism. Now they are exploited by industrialists. They are about to become slaves.

They all sighed for the *ancien régime*: Hurel because he was vulgar, Coulon because he was ignorant, Marescot because he was an artist.

Once he was home Bouvard soaked himself in La Mettrie, d'Holbach etc.; and Pécuchet felt estranged from a religion which had become a means of government. Monsieur de Mahurot had taken communion as a means of winning over 'these ladies' more easily, and if he practised it was because of the servants.

Mathematician and dilettante, he played waltzes on the piano and admired Töpffer, and was characterized by a well-bred scepticism. Stories of feudal abuses, of the Inquisition or the Jesuits were just prejudices, and he extolled progress, although he despised anyone who was not of noble birth or a product of the École Polytechnique.

Monsieur Jeufroy similarly displeased them. He believed in spells, made jokes about idols, asserted that all idioms derive from Hebrew; his rhetoric lacked all surprise; inevitably it was the stag at bay, the honey and the gall, gold and lead, perfumes, urns, and the Christian soul compared to the soldier who must say when confronted with sin: 'You shall not pass!'

To avoid his talks they arrived at the château as late as possible.

One day, however, they found him there.

He had been waiting for his two pupils for an hour. Suddenly Madame de Noaris came in.

'The girl has disappeared. I'm bringing Victor. Ah! The poor wretch!'

She had seized from his pocket a silver thimble which had been missing for three days, then choking with sobs: 'That is not all! That is not all! While I was scolding him he showed me his backside!' And before the count and countess had said anything: 'Besides, it is my fault; forgive me!'

She had concealed from them the fact that the two orphans were the children of Touache, now in prison.

What was to be done?

If the count sent them away, they would be lost, and his act of charity would be taken for a caprice.

Monsieur Jeufroy was not surprised. As man was naturally corrupt he must be punished if he is to improve.

Bouvard protested. Gentleness was better.

But the count once more dwelt on the iron hand as being essential for children as for peoples. These two were thoroughly vicious: the little girl was a liar, the boy brutal. This theft could, after all, be excused, but insolence never, since education should instil respect.

So, Sorel, the gamekeeper, would immediately administer a sound thrashing to the lad.

Monsieur de Mahurot, who had something to see him about, took the errand on himself. He took a gun from the antechamber and called Victor, who had stayed in the middle of the yard, with downcast head.

'Follow me!' said the baron.

As the road to the gamekeeper's house was not much out of the way for Chavignolles, Monsieur Jeufroy, Bouvard and Pécuchet accompanied him.

A hundred yards from the château he asked them to stop talking while he went along the wood.

The ground sloped down to the edge of the river, where great lumps of rock stood. Patches of gold showed where it reflected the setting sun. The green hills opposite were becoming lost in shadow. A keen breeze was blowing.

Rabbits came out of their burrows and cropped the turf.

A shot rang out, then a second, and a third, and the rabbits leaped up, ran out of cover. Victor flung himself down to seize them and was soon panting and soaked in sweat.

'You are making a fine mess of your clothes!' said the baron. His ragged blouse was bloodstained.

The sight of the blood revolted Bouvard. He did not accept that blood should be shed.

Monsieur Jeufroy answered: 'Circumstances sometimes require it. If it is not the guilty giving his own, it has to be that of another, a truth which Redemption teaches us.'

According to Bouvard it had not been of much use, since almost all men were damned in spite of Our Lord's sacrifice.

'But he renews it daily in the Eucharist.'

'And the miracle is done with words,' said Bouvard, 'however unworthy the priest.'

'That is the mystery, sir.'

Meanwhile Victor's eyes were glued to the gun, and he even tried to touch it.

'Take your paws off!' Monsieur de Mahurot took a path through the undergrowth.

The ecclesiastic had Pécuchet on one side, Bouvard on the other, and said to him: 'Be careful, you know: *Debetur pueris . . .*'

Bouvard assured him that he humbled himself before the Creator, but was indignant that people should make him human. They fear his vengeance, work for his glory, he has all the virtues, an arm, an eye, a policy, a dwelling place. 'Our Father who art in Heaven, what does that mean?'

And Pécuchet added:

'The world has expanded, the earth is not the centre any more. It turns among the infinite multitude of worlds like it. Many exceed it in size, and this shrinking of our globe brings about a more sublime ideal of God.'

So, religion had to change. Paradise is something childish with its blessed ones always rapt in contemplation, always singing and looking down on the tortures of the damned. When you think that the basis of Christianity is an apple!

The curé became annoyed.

'Deny Revelation, that would be simpler.'

'How do you claim that God spoke?' said Bouvard.

'Prove that he did not speak!' said Jeufroy.

'Once again, who says so?'

'The Church!'

'Fine evidence!'

This discussion bored Monsieur de Mahurot, and as they walked along he said:

'Why don't you listen to the curé? He knows more about it than you!'

Bouvard and Pécuchet made signs to each other to take another path, then at the Croix-Verte:

'A very good evening to you!'

'Your servant!' said the baron.

This would all be related to Monsieur de Faverges, and perhaps a breach would result. Too bad. They felt that these nobles despised them. They were never invited to dinner, and they were tired of Madame de Noaris, with her continual remonstrating.

They could not however keep the de Maistre, and a fortnight later they returned to the château, thinking they would not be received.

They were.

The whole family was in the boudoir, including Hurel, and, quite unusually, Foureau.

The correction had not corrected Victor. He refused to learn his catechism, and Victorine used foul language. In short the boy would go to a reformatory, the girl to a convent. Foureau had taken the arrangements on himself, and he was going off when the countess called him.

They were waiting for Monsieur Jeufroy to fix the wedding date together; it would take place at the Town Hall well before the church ceremony, to show that they condemned civil marriage.

Foureau tried to defend it. The count and Hurel attacked it. What was a municipal function compared to priesthood! And the baron would not have considered himself married if it took place only before a tricolour sash.

'Bravo!' said Monsieur Jeufroy, coming in. 'Marriage being established by Jesus...'

Pécuchet stopped him: 'In which gospel? In apostolic times marriage was so little thought of that Tertullian compares it to adultery!'

'Ah! Fancy that!'

'Oh yes! And it is not a sacrament! A sacrament needs a sign. Show me the sign in marriage!' It was no good the curé answering that it was a figure of Christ's union with the Church. 'You no longer understand Christianity! And the Law!'

'Law bears the stamp of Christianity,' said Monsieur de Faverges, 'but for that it would authorize polygamy!'

A voice replied: 'What would be wrong about that?'

It was Bouvard, half hidden by a curtain.

'A man can have several wives, like the patriarchs, Mormons, Moslems, and still be honest!'

'Never!' cried the priest. 'Honesty consists in paying what is due. We owe homage to God. Now anyone who is not Christian is not honest!'

'As much as anyone else,' said Bouvard.

The count, thinking he saw in this repartee an attack on religion, praised it highly. It had freed the slaves.

Bouvard quoted passages to prove the opposite.

'St Paul recommends them to obey their masters as they would Jesus. St Ambrose calls slavery a gift of God. *Leviticus*, *Exodus* and the councils have sanctioned it. Bossuet classifies it under the law of nations. And Monseigneur Bouvier approves of it.'

The count objected that Christianity, no less, had developed civilization.

'And idleness by making a virtue out of poverty.'

'However, sir, what about the morality of the Gospels?'

'Eh, eh! Not so moral! The workers of the last hour are paid as much as those of the first. To him that hath shall be given, and from him that hath not shall be taken away even that which he hath. As for the precept of turning the other cheek and letting oneself be robbed, it encourages audacity, cowardice and knavery.'

The scandal increased when Pécuchet declared that he liked Buddhism just as much.

The priest burst out laughing: 'Ha, ha! Buddhism!'

Madame de Noaris threw up her arms: 'Buddhism!'

'What . . . Buddhism!' the count repeated.

'Do you know about it?' Pécuchet said to Monsieur Jeufroy, who was confused. 'Very well, listen to this! Buddhism recognized the vanity of earthly things better and earlier than Christianity. Its practices are austere, its faithful are more numerous than all Christians put together, and as for the Incarnation, Vishnu did not have one but nine! So, judge from that!'

'Travellers' lies,' said Madame de Noaris.

'Supported by Freemasons,' added the curé.

And everyone speaking at once: 'Come along – Go on – Very fine – Personally I find it funny – Impossible!' To such an extent that Pécuchet, in annoyance, declared that he was going to become a Buddhist!

'You are insulting Christian women!' said the baron. Madame de Noaris collapsed into a chair. The countess and Yolande were silent. The count rolled his eyes; Hurel waited for orders. The abbé, to contain himself, read his breviary.

This sight pacified Monsieur de Faverges, and considering the two men:

'Before criticizing the Gospel, and when there are blemishes in one's life, there are certain reparations . . .'

'Reparations?'

'Blemishes?'

'That's enough, gentlemen! You must understand me!'

Then addressing Foureau:

'Sorel has been told! Go ahead!'

And Bouvard and Pécuchet withdrew without taking leave.

At the end of the avenue they all three voiced their resentment. 'They treat me like a servant,' Foureau grumbled, with the others approving; despite the memory of the haemorrhoids he had a certain sympathy for them.

Roadmen were working in the countryside. Their foreman came up; it was Gorju. They began to chat. He was in charge of laying stones on the road voted in 1848, and owed this job to Monsieur de Mahurot, the engineer.

'The one who is to marry Mademoiselle de Faverges! You have just come from there, I suppose?'

'For the last time,' said Pécuchet brutally.

Gorju looked innocent: 'A quarrel? Well, well!'

And if they could have seen his face when their backs were turned they would have understood that he suspected the cause.

A little further on they stopped before a trellised fence enclosing dog-kennels, and a red-tiled cottage.

Victorine was at the door. There was loud barking. The gamekeeper's wife appeared.

Knowing why the mayor had come, she called for Victor.

Everything was ready, and their bundles were in two handkerchiefs fastened by pins.

'Pleasant journey!' she said, glad to be rid of such vermin.

Was it their fault if they were the children of a convict father? On the contrary they seemed very mild, and were not even worried about the place to which they were being taken.

Bouvard and Pécuchet looked at them walking ahead.

Victorine was singing some indistinct words, her handkerchief over her arm like a dressmaker carrying a box. She turned round from time to time, and Pécuchet, seeing her fair curls and pleasant appearance, was sorry not to have a child like that. If she were brought up in different conditions she would be charming later. What a delight to see her grow, to hear her chirping like a bird every day, to kiss her when he liked, and a feeling of tenderness, rising from his heart to his lips, made his eyes moist, and slightly oppressed him.

Victor had put his baggage on his back like a soldier. He whistled, threw stones at the crows in the furrows, went in under the trees to cut switches. Foureau called him back; and Bouvard, holding him by the hand, enjoyed feeling in his fingers these robust and youthful ones. The poor little devil only asked to develop freely, like a flower in the open air! He would rot away behind walls, with lessons, punishments, a lot of nonsense! Bouvard was overcome by revolt and pity, indignation against fate, one of those rages when one wants to pull down the government.

'Run off!' he said. 'Have a good time! Enjoy what you have left!'

The lad escaped.

He and his sister would sleep at the inn, and at daybreak the Falaise messenger would take Victor and drop him at the Beaubourg penitentiary, while a nun from the orphanage at Grand-Camp would take Victorine.

When Foureau had given them these details he relapsed into his thoughts. But Bouvard wanted to know how much the maintenance of the two brats might cost.

'Bah! ... perhaps as much as 300 francs! The count gave me twenty-five for the first expenses! What a miser!'

Keeping in his heart the contempt shown for his sash, Foureau hurried on in silence.

Bouvard murmured: 'I am sorry for them. I would be glad to take them on!'

'So would I,' said Pécuchet, as they had both had the same idea.

No doubt there were obstacles?

'None!' replied Foureau. Besides, he had the right, as mayor, to entrust abandoned children to whoever he chose. And after a long hesitation: 'All right, yes! Take them! That will make him angry!'

Bouvard and Pécuchet took them along.

When they reached home they found Marcel at the foot of the stairs, beneath the madonna, on his knees, praying fervently. With his head thrown back, his eyes half-closed, his hare-lip swollen, he looked like a fakir in ecstasy.

'What a brute!' said Bouvard.

'Why? Perhaps he is taking part in things which you would envy if you could see them. Are there not two quite distinct worlds? The object of an argument is less important than the manner of arguing. What does the belief matter? The main thing is to believe.'

Such were Pécuchet's objections to Bouvard's remark.

10

THEY obtained a number of books about education and decided on their system. All metaphysical ideas must be banished, and according to the experimental method they must follow natural development. There was no hurry, the two pupils must just forget what they had learned.

Although they had sturdy constitutions, Pécuchet, like a Spartan, wanted to harden them still more, accustom them to hunger, thirst and bad weather, and even wanted them to wear shoes with holes in to keep colds away. Bouvard was against it.

The dark room at the end of the corridor became their bedroom. It was furnished with two camp-beds, two basins, a jug; the skylight opened above their heads, spiders ran along the plaster.

They often remembered the inside of a hut where people were quarrelling. Their father had come home one night with blood on his hands. Some time later the gendarmes had come. Then they had lived in a wood. Men who made clogs would kiss their mother. She died, a cart had taken them away. They had often been beaten, they had got lost. Then they saw the rural constable, Madame de Noaris, Sorel and, without asking why they were in this new home, they were happy there. So it was a painful surprise for them when after eight months lessons began again.

Bouvard took charge of the girl, Pécuchet the boy.

Victor could distinguish letters, but could not manage to form syllables. He mumbled, then suddenly stopped and looked stupid. Victorine asked questions. Why does *ch* sound like a *k* in 'orchestra' and differently in 'orchard'? Sometimes two vowels must be joined together, at other times separated. All that is unfair. She became indignant.

Their masters gave lessons at the same time, in their respective rooms, and as the partition was thin their four voices, one shrill, one deep, and two sharp, made an abominable cacophony. To put an end to it and encourage the children through emulation, they thought of making them work together in the museum, and started on writing.

The two pupils at each end of the table copied from an example, but their posture was wrong. They had to sit up. Their pages fell down, the pens split, the wooden inkwell was upset.

On some days Victorine got on all right for three minutes, then started scribbling, and overcome by discouragement remained staring at the ceiling. Victor soon went to sleep, sprawling in the middle of the desk.

Perhaps they were not well? Too much strain can harm young brains. 'Let's stop,' said Bouvard.

Nothing is so stupid as to make people learn things by heart: however, if the memory is not used it will atrophy, and they repeated La Fontaine's first fables to them. The children approved of the ant storing up its treasure, the wolf eating the lamb, the lion taking everyone's share.

Becoming bolder they wrecked the garden. But how were they to be entertained?

Jean-Jacques in *Émile* advises the tutor to get the pupil to make his own toys, helping him a little without his realizing. Bouvard could not succeed in making a hoop, nor Pécuchet in sewing up a ball.

They went on to instructional games like cutting out, and a burning glass. Pécuchet showed them his microscope, and by candlelight Bouvard drew with his fingers on the wall shadow pictures of a hare or a pig. The public found it boring.

Some authors extol the pleasures of picnics, or boating trips; was this really practicable? Fénelon recommends 'an occasional innocent conversation'. None was imaginable!

They went back to lessons, and balls with different facets, stripes, printing sets, everything had failed when they thought of a stratagem.

As Victor was inclined to be greedy, they presented him with the name of some dish; he was soon able to read the *French Cookery Book* fluently. Victorine was rather a coquette, so she would be given a dress if she wrote to the dressmaker for it. In less than three weeks she accomplished this feat. It was indulging their faults, a pernicious method, but it worked.

Now that they could read and write, what should they be taught? Another problem. Girls do not need to be such good scholars as boys. Never mind, they are usually brought up as complete idiots, their whole intellectual baggage being confined to mystic nonsense.

Was it right to teach them languages? 'Spanish and Italian', claims the Swan of Cambrai,[1] 'are of hardly any use except for reading dangerous books.' It seemed foolish to do it for that reason. Yet Victorine would have no use for those languages, while English is in much wider use. Pécuchet studied its rules; he demonstrated, quite seriously, the way to pronounce *th*, 'like this, you see, *the, the, the!*' But before teaching a child one must know its aptitudes. These can be divined by phrenology. They immersed themselves in this study; then they tried to check its assertions on themselves. Bouvard showed the bump of benevolence, imagination, worship and amorous energy, commonly called eroticism.

On Pécuchet's temples could be detected philosophy, and enthusiasm combined with guile.

Such were their characters.

They were more surprised to recognize in each other an inclination towards friendship, and delighted with the discovery they embraced tenderly.

They then proceeded to examine Marcel.

His greatest fault, of which they were well aware, was his enormous appetite. Nevertheless Bouvard and Pécuchet were appalled to find above the ear, level with the eye, the organ of alimentivity. With age their servant might become like the woman at the Salpétrière Hospital who ate eight pounds of bread every day, once swallowed twelve plates of soup and another time sixty bowls of coffee. They would never be able to satisfy him.

There was nothing curious about their pupils' heads; they probably went about it the wrong way. A very simple method developed their experience.

On market days they slipped among the peasants in the main square, between the sacks of oats, the baskets of cheese, the calves and horses, heedless of jostling; and when they found a young lad with his father, they would ask to feel his skull for scientific purposes.

1. Fénelon.

The majority did not even answer; others, thinking it was about some pomade against ringworm, refused angrily; a few, not caring, let themselves be led under the church porch, where it was quiet.

One morning when Bouvard and Pécuchet were beginning their operations the curé suddenly appeared and, seeing what they were doing, accused phrenology of leading to materialism and fatalism. The thief, murderer or adulterer henceforth had only to put the blame for his crimes onto his bumps.

Bouvard objected that the organ predisposes one to action, but does not force one into it. The fact that a man has the seeds of a vice in no way proves that he will be vicious. 'Besides, I have to admire the orthodox; they support innate ideas and reject inclinations. What inconsistency!'

But phrenology, according to Monsieur Jeufroy, denied divine omnipotence, and it was unseemly to practise it in the shadow of the sanctuary, actually before the altar.

They installed themselves in Ganot's barber's shop. To overcome all hesitation Bouvard and Pécuchet went so far as to treat the parents to a shave or wave.

One afternoon the doctor came for a haircut. As he sat down in the chair he saw, reflected in the mirror, the two phrenologists running their fingers over childish heads.

'You've come to that sort of nonsense, have you?' he said.

'Why nonsense?'

Vaucorbeil smiled contemptuously, then asserted that the brain does not contain a number of organs.

So, one man can digest food that another man cannot? Must we suppose the stomach contains as many stomachs as there are tastes?

However, one kind of work takes away the fatigue caused by another, an intellectual effort does not stretch all the faculties at once, so each one has a distinct seat.

'The anatomists have never found it,' said Vaucorbeil.

'That is because they did their dissecting wrongly,' replied Pécuchet.

'What?'

'But yes! They cut slices, disregarding the connection between the parts,' a sentence he recalled from some book.

'There's a stupid mistake,' cried the doctor. 'The skull is not moulded round the brain, the outside round the inside. Gall is wrong, and I challenge you to justify his doctrine by taking any three persons in this shop.'

The first was a peasant woman with big blue eyes.

Pécuchet said, as he observed her:

'She has a very good memory.'

Her husband confirmed the fact and offered himself for investigation.

'Oh, as for you, my lad, you are not easily led.'

According to the others there was no one to touch him for obstinacy.

The third test was on a small boy escorted by his grandmother.

Pécuchet declared that he must be fond of music.

'I should think so,' said the good woman, 'show these gentlemen what you have got.'

He took a jew's harp out of his pocket and began blowing it.

There was a crash, as the doctor went out, violently slamming the door.

They had no further doubts about themselves, and recalling their two pupils began once more analysing their skulls.

Victorine's was generally smooth, a sign of thoughtfulness, but her brother had a deplorable cranium; a pronounced projection in the mastoidal corner of the parietal bones indicated the organ of destruction and murder; lower down a swelling signified covetousness and theft. Bouvard and Pécuchet were depressed for a week.

However, what is called fighting spirit implies contempt for death. If it causes homicide it can equally well inspire rescues. Acquisitiveness embraces a pickpocket's skill and a businessman's zeal. Irreverence is parallel to critical sense, guile to circumspection. Instincts can always be divided into two parts: one good, one bad. The second can be destroyed by cultivating the first, and by this method a daring lad, far from being a bandit, will become a general. The coward will be left only with prudence, the miser with thrift, the spendthrift with generosity.

A magnificent dream preoccupied them; if they made a success of educating their pupils, they would found an establishment aimed at correcting intelligence, taming character, ennobling the heart. They were already talking about subscriptions and building.

Their triumph at Ganot's had made them famous and people came to consult them, to be told their fortunes.

There was a procession of all kinds of skull; round, piriform, like a sugarloaf, square, lofty, compact, flattened, with bovine jaws, birdlike faces, pig eyes; such a flow of people interfered with the barber's work. Their elbows rubbed against the glass-fronted cupboard of perfumes; combs were disturbed, the washbowl broken, when he flung out all the enthusiasts and asked Bouvard and Pécuchet to follow them, which ultimatum they accepted without a murmur, being rather tired of looking at crania.

Next day, passing the captain's bit of garden, they saw him in conversation with Girbal, Coulon, the rural constable and his younger son Zéphyrin, in choirboy's costume. His robe was quite new; he was parading about in it before putting it back in the sacristy, and was receiving compliments.

Placquevent asked the gentlemen to feel his young man's head, curious to know what they would think of it.

The skin on the forehead looked as though it had been stretched; a thin nose, very bony at the tip, fell crookedly onto pinched lips; his chin was pointed, his eyes shifty, his right shoulder too high.

'Take off your skull-cap,' his father told him.

Bouvard ran his hands into the straw-coloured hair; then it was Pécuchet's turn, and in a low voice they exchanged observations: Obvious biophilia! Ah ha! Absence of approbation, and conscientiousness! No sign of affection!

'Well?' said the constable.

Pécuchet opened his snuff-box and took a pinch.

'Nothing good, eh?'

'My word,' said Bouvard, 'it is not exactly wonderful.'

Placquevent went red with humiliation: 'All the same, he will do what I tell him!'

'Oh! Oh!'

'But I am his father, blast it! And I surely have the right...'

'Up to a point,' replied Pécuchet.

Girbal joined in:

'Paternal authority is indisputable.'

'But if the father is an idiot?'

'It doesn't matter,' said the captain, 'it does not make his power any less absolute.'

'In the interest of the children,' added Coulon.

According to Pécuchet they owed nothing to the authors of their days, while the parents, on the other hand, owe them food, education, care, in fact everything.

The good citizens protested against such an immoral opinion. Placquevent was as hurt as if he had been insulted.

'Come to that, they are a fine lot, the ones you pick up on the highway; they will go far. Look out!'

'Look out for what?' said Pécuchet sharply.

'Oh, I'm not afraid of you!'

'Nor am I!'

Coulon intervened, calmed down the constable and made him go away.

For a few minutes there was silence, then they started talking about the captain's dahlias, and he would not let his visitors go until he had exhibited the flowers one by one.

Bouvard and Pécuchet were on the way home when, a hundred yards ahead, they recognized Placquevent, and Zéphyrin beside him was holding up his elbow like a shield to protect himself from blows.

What they had just heard expressed, in a different form, the count's idea; but the example of their pupils would show how far freedom is superior to constraint. A little discipline was however necessary.

Pécuchet nailed up in the museum a board for demonstrations; they would keep a journal from which the child's actions, noted each evening, would be read again next day. Everything would be done at the stroke of a bell. Like Dupont de Nemours they would first use paternal, then military injunctions, and the familiar form of address was forbidden.

Bouvard tried to teach Victorine arithmetic. Sometimes he went wrong, they both laughed, then she would kiss him on the neck, in the place where there was no beard, and ask to run off; he let her go.

At lesson-time it was no good Pécuchet ringing the bell and

crying military injunctions out of the window: the boy did not come. His socks were always hanging round his ankles; even at table he stuffed his fingers up his nose and broke wind. On that subject Broussais forbids reprimands 'because one must obey the solicitations of an instinct for self-preservation'.

Victorine and he spoke dreadfully, saying '*mé-itou*' for '*moi aussi*',[1] '*bère*' for '*boire*',[2] '*al*' for '*elle*', '*deventiau, iau*';[3] but as grammar is unintelligible to children, who will learn it if they hear people speaking correctly, our two good men were so careful of their own speech that it became a nuisance to them.

Their opinions differed about geography. Bouvard thought it more logical to begin with the commune, Pécuchet with the whole world.

With a watering-can and some sand he tried to demonstrate what a river, an island, a gulf were, and even sacrificed three flowerbeds for the three continents; but Victor could not get the cardinal points into his head.

One January night Pécuchet took him out into open country. As he walked he extolled astronomy; sailors use it in their voyages; without it Christopher Columbus would not have made his discovery. We should be grateful to Copernicus, Galileo and Newton.

It was freezing hard, and a vast number of lights were twinkling against the dark blue of the sky. Pécuchet looked up. What, no Great Bear? Last time he had seen it it was turned to another side; finally he recognized it, then showed the Pole Star, always in the north, and the one from which one takes bearings.

Next day he put a chair in the middle of the drawing-room and began dancing round it.

'Imagine that this chair is the sun, and that I am the earth; this is how it moves.'

Victor looked at him, full of amazement.

Then he took an orange, put a stick through it to signify the poles, then drew a circle round it with charcoal to mark the equator. After that he moved the orange round a candle, pointing out that all the points on its surface were not lit up simultaneously, which is the cause of climatic differences, and to show the difference be-

1. me too. 2. drink. 3. apron, water (in dialect).

tween seasons he put it at an angle, because the earth is tilted, and this causes equinoxes and solstices.

Victor did not understand any of it. He thought that the earth pivots on a long needle and that the equator is a ring going round its circumference.

Pécuchet explained Europe to him with an atlas, but bewildered by so many lines and colours he could not find the names. Basins and mountains did not fit in with kingdoms, the political order became confused with the physical. Perhaps that would all be cleared up by studying history.

It would have been more practical to begin with the village, then the arrondissement, the department, the province, but as Chavignolles had no records, there was nothing for it but to stick to universal history.

He found so much material an embarrassment, obliging him to pick out only the gems.

In Greek history there is: 'We will fight in the shade'; the envious man who banished Aristides, Alexander's confidence in his doctor. In Roman history the Capitoline geese, Scaevola's tripod, Regulus' barrel. For America, Guatamozin's bed of roses is worthy of note. As for France, there is the Soissons vase, St Louis's oak, the death of Joan of Arc, Henri of Béarn's chicken in the pot; there is too much to choose from. Not to speak of 'To me, the Auvergnes!' and the wreck of the *Vengeur*.

Victor mixed up men, centuries and countries.

However Pécuchet was not going to throw him into subtle considerations, and the mass of facts is a real maze.

He fell back on the names of the kings of France. Victor forgot them, because he did not know their dates. But if Dumouchel's memory training system had not worked with them, what would it do for him! Conclusion: history can only be learned through much reading. This they would do.

Drawing is useful in a great number of circumstances; now Pécuchet was bold enough to teach it himself, from nature, starting right away on landscape.

A bookshop in Bayeux sent him paper, india rubber, two millboards, pencils and fixative for their work, which, put behind glass and framed, would adorn the museum.

Up at dawn, they set off with a bit of bread in their pockets, and wasted a lot of time looking for a site. Pécuchet wanted at one and the same time to reproduce what lay at his feet, the far horizon and the clouds, but the distant features always dominated the foreground; the river spilled down from the sky, the shepherd walked on top of his flock, a sleeping dog looked as if it were running. For his part he gave up.

Remembering that he had read the definition: 'Drawing consists of three things: line, stippling, fine stippling, and in addition the master stroke – but this can only be provided by the master,' he rectified the line, helped with the stippling, supervised the fine stippling, and waited for a chance to provide the master stroke. The chance never came, so incomprehensible was his pupil's landscape.

His sister, as lazy as he was, yawned in front of Pythagoras' table. Mademoiselle Reine showed her how to sew, and when she was marking linen she raised her fingers so daintily that Bouvard subsequently had no heart for tormenting her with his arithmetic lesson. One of these days they would try it again. No doubt arithmetic and sewing are necessary in a household, but it is cruel, Pécuchet objected, to bring up girls exclusively with a view to their future husband. They are not all destined for marriage, and if they are expected later to get on without men, they must be taught a lot of things.

One can teach science with reference to the most ordinary objects; say, for instance, what wine consists of; and once the explanation had been provided, Victor and Victorine had to repeat it. It was the same with spices, furniture, lighting; but light for them was the lamp, and it had nothing in common with the spark from a stone, a candle flame or moonlight.

One day Victorine asked what makes wood burn. Her masters looked at each other in embarrassment, the theory of combustion being beyond them.

Another time, Bouvard, from the soup to the cheese, talked about the nutritive elements and stunned the children with fibrine, caseine, fat and gluten.

Then Pécuchet tried to explain to them how our blood is renewed, and he floundered about over the circulation.

The dilemma is a troublesome one. If you start from facts, the simplest fact requires reasons which are far too complicated, and if you first lay down principles, you begin with the absolute, faith.

What should they decide to do? To combine the two forms of teaching, rational and empirical; but a double means to a single end is the opposite of method. Well, too bad!

To initiate them into natural history they attempted some scientific walks.

'You see,' said Pécuchet, pointing to a donkey, 'a horse, an ox, animals with four feet, are quadrupeds. Birds generally have feathers, reptiles scales, and butterflies belong to the insect family.' They had a net to catch them in, and Pécuchet, handling the creature carefully, pointed out the four wings, six feet, two antennae and the bony proboscis that sucks up nectar from flowers.

He picked herbs on the edge of ditches, gave their names, and invented some to keep his prestige. Besides, nomenclature is the least important part of botany.

He wrote this axiom on the board: 'Every plant has leaves, a calix and a corolla, enclosing an ovary or pericarp containing the seed.'

Then he ordered his pupils to collect plants at random in the country, picking the first they saw.

Victor brought back some buttercups (a sort of ranunculus with a yellow flower), Victorine a tuft of gramens; he looked at it vainly for a pericarp.

Bouvard, who distrusted his own knowledge, searched all through the library, and discovered, in the *Ladies' Redouté*, a drawing of a rose; the ovary was not situated in the corolla, but below the petals.

'That is an exception,' said Pécuchet.

They found a rubiacea which had no calix. Thus the principle set out by Pécuchet is wrong.

There were tuberoses in their garden, all without calix.

'What a blunder! Most of the liliaceae don't have one!'

But by chance they saw a Sherardia which does have a calix.

'Well now! If the exceptions themselves are not true, who is to be trusted?'

One day, during one of these walks, they heard a peacock's cry, looked over the wall and, at first sight, did not recognize their farm. The barn had a slate roof, the fences were new, the paths gravelled. Farmer Gouy appeared: 'It's not possible! Is it you?' So much had happened in the past three years, his wife's death among other things. As for him, he was still stout as an oak. 'Just come in for a moment.'

It was early April, and the apple-trees stood in blossom in the three yards with their pink and white tufts neatly aligned; there was not a cloud in the blue satin sky; tablecloths, sheets and towels hung straight down, held by wooden pegs onto tight clothes-lines. Farmer Gouy lifted up the washing to go by, when they suddenly met Madame Bordin, bareheaded in a smock, with Marianne handing her great bundles of washing.

'Your servant, gentlemen! Make yourselves at home! I am going to sit down. I am exhausted.'

The farmer offered everyone a drink.

'Not now,' she said, 'I am too hot.'

Pécuchet accepted and disappeared in the direction of the cellar with Farmer Gouy, Marianne and Victor.

Bouvard sat on the ground beside Madame Bordin. He received his income punctually, had no grounds for complaint, and no hard feelings towards her.

The bright light lit up her profile; one of her black plaits had fallen down too far, and the curls at the nape of her neck were sticking to her golden skin, damp with sweat. Each time she breathed her breasts rose and fell. The scent of the grass mingled with the honest smell of her solid flesh, and Bouvard felt a new surge of emotion which filled him with joy. Then he paid her compliments about her property.

She was delighted with it and spoke of her plans. To enlarge the yards she was going to knock down the bank.

At that moment Victorine was climbing up the slope, picking primroses, hyacinths and violets, quite unafraid of an old horse cropping the grass at the bottom.

'She is nice, isn't she?' said Bouvard.

'Yes, a little girl is always nice.'

And the widow heaved a sigh which seemed to express the long suffering of a whole life.

'You could have had one.'

She lowered her head.

'It depended only on you.'

'What do you mean?'

He looked at her in such a way that she flushed deeply, as if at the touch of a brutal embrace; but straight away, fanning herself with her handkerchief:

'You have missed the boat, my dear.'

'I don't understand,' and without getting up he came closer.

She looked him up and down for a long time, then with a smile and moist eyes: 'It is your fault.'

The sheets all round them enclosed them like curtains round a bed.

He leaned on his elbow, brushing his face against her knees.

'Why? Eh, why?' And as she remained silent and he was in a state where promises cost nothing, he tried to justify himself, accused himself of folly, pride: 'Forgive me! It will be as it used to be! Will you?' And he took her hand, which she left in his.

A sudden gust of wind blew up the sheets, and they saw two peacocks, male and female. The hen was standing still, legs bent, rump in the air. The cock strutted round her, spreading out his tail, preening himself, gurgling, then jumped on her, dragging his feathers round her like an arbour, and the two great birds shook with a single shudder.

Bouvard felt it in Madame Bordin's palm. She loosed herself quickly. In front of them stood Victor, gaping and almost petrified as he watched; a little further away Victorine, stretched on her back in the sunshine, was sniffing at the flowers she had picked.

The old horse, frightened by the peacocks, broke one of the lines as he reared up, got his legs tangled in it, and galloped through the three yards, pulling the washing behind him.

At Madame Bordin's furious shouts Marianne ran up. Farmer Gouy was swearing at his horse: 'Lousy old bag of bones! Thieving nag!' kicking him in the belly, hitting him on the ears with the handle of his whip.

Bouvard was indignant at seeing an animal beaten.

The peasant answered: 'It's my right! He belongs to me!'

This was not a reason.

And Pécuchet added, as he came up, that animals had their rights too, because they had a soul, like ours, always supposing that ours exists!

'You are an enemy of religion!' cried Madame Bordin.

Three things annoyed her: the washing that had to be done again, her beliefs which were being outraged and the fear of having been seen a moment before in a compromising position.

'I thought that you were tougher than that!' said Bouvard.

She replied haughtily: 'I do not like lewdness!'

Gouy attacked them for ruining his horse, whose nose was bleeding. He grumbled in a very low voice:

'Damned Jonahs! I was going to tether him when they arrived.'

The two men withdrew, shrugging their shoulders.

Victor asked them why they were angry with Gouy.

'He misuses his strength, and that is bad.'

'Why is it bad?'

Could it be that children have no idea of justice? Maybe.

That evening Pécuchet, with Bouvard on his right, and some notes handy, put the two pupils in front of him and began a course of ethics.

This science teaches us how to direct our actions.

They can have two motives; pleasure, self-interest, or a third, more imperious one, duty.

Duties can be divided into two classes: first, duties towards ourselves, which consist in looking after our bodies, protecting ourselves from injury. They understood that perfectly; second, duties towards others, that is to be always sincere, gentle and even fraternal, since the human race is a single family. Something often suits us which harms our fellows; self-interest differs from good, because good is in itself irreducible. The children did not understand. He put off until next time the sanctioning of duties.

In all this, according to Bouvard, he had not defined the good.

'How do you expect it to be defined? One feels it.'

So moral lessons were only suitable for moral persons, and Pécuchet's course came to a halt.

They made their pupils read little stories tending to inspire love of virtue. They thoroughly bored Victor.

To catch his imagination Pécuchet hung on the walls of his room pictures showing the life of the good and bad character. The first, Adolphe, kissed his mother, studied German, helped a blind man, was admitted to the École Polytechnique.

The bad one, Eugène, began by disobeying his father, had a quarrel in a café, beat his wife, fell down dead drunk, smashing a cupboard, and a final picture showed him in prison, where a gentleman, accompanied by a small boy, pointed him out, saying: 'You see, my son, the dangers of misconduct.'

But for children the future does not exist. It was no good saturating them with the maxim: 'Work is honourable and the rich are sometimes unhappy.' They had known workmen who had not been honoured at all and remembered the château where life seemed good. The pangs of remorse were depicted to them with so much exaggeration that they sensed humbug and were suspicious of the rest.

They tried guiding them with the sense of honour, the idea of public opinion and desire for fame, by extolling great men, especially useful men, like Belzunce, Franklin, Jacquard! Victor showed not the slightest desire to resemble them.

One day when he had done an addition sum without mistakes Bouvard sewed a ribbon on his jacket representing the plus sign. He preened himself with it; but when he forgot Henri IV's death, Pécuchet stuck a dunce's cap on his head. Victor began braying so loudly and long that his cardboard ass's ears had to be removed.

His sister like him showed herself proud of praise and indifferent to blame.

To make them more sensitive they were given a black cat which they had to look after, and allowed two or three sous so that they could give alms. They thought the claim unjust, the money belonged to them.

In conformity with the wishes of some pedagogues they called Bouvard 'uncle' and Pécuchet 'friend', but used the familiar form of address, and half of the lessons were usually spent in quarrelling.

Victorine treated Marcel badly, jumped on his back, pulled his hair, mocked at his hare-lip by talking through her nose like him, and the poor man loved the little girl so much that he did not dare to complain. One evening his raucous voice rose to an extraordinary degree. Bouvard and Pécuchet went down to the kitchen.

Their two pupils were watching the fireplace, and Marcel, clasping his hands together, was crying: 'Take it out! This is too much! This is too much!'

The saucepan's lid sprang up like a shell bursting. A greyish mass leapt up to the ceiling, then spun round and round in a frenzy, letting out abominable cries.

They recognized the cat, emaciated, hairless, tail like a cord, huge eyes starting out of its head, milky white, drained, but still staring.

The hideous beast went on screaming, flung itself into the hearth, disappeared, then fell back among the ashes, inert.

It was Victor who had committed this atrocity, and the two men recoiled, pale with stupefaction and horror. When they reproached him, he answered as the constable had done about his son and the farmer about his horse: 'Well! It's mine, isn't it?' – quite unperturbed, naïvely, placidly, now that his instinct was satisfied.

Boiling water from the saucepan lay all over the floor, pots, tongs, torches were strewn over the flags.

It took Marcel some time to clean up the kitchen, and his masters buried the poor cat in the garden, under the pagoda.

Then Bouvard and Pécuchet had a long talk about Victor. Paternal blood was coming out. What was to be done? Giving him back to Monsieur de Faverges or entrusting him to others would be an admission of failure. He might improve a little.

No matter! It was a doubtful hope, there was no more affection there. What a delight to have at your side an adolescent eager for your ideas, whose progress you can observe, who later becomes like a brother; but Victor was lacking in intelligence, and even more so in heart! And Pécuchet sighed, clasping his hands round his knee.

'His sister is no better,' said Bouvard.

He imagined a girl of about fifteen, a delicate, sensitive, lively soul, adorning the house with her youthful elegance; and as if he had been her father and she had just died, the good fellow wept.

Then, trying to excuse Victor, he quoted Rousseau's opinion: A child has no responsibility, cannot be moral or immoral.

These two, according to Pécuchet, had reached the age of discretion, and they studied ways to correct them.

For a punishment to be right, says Bentham, it must be proportionate to the fault, be its material consequence. A child breaks a window pane, which is not replaced; let it be cold; if when it is no longer hungry it asks for another helping, give in; indigestion will soon bring remorse. If he is lazy, let him stay idle; boredom will be enough to bring him back to work.

But Victor would not feel the cold, his constitution could endure excesses and idleness would suit him very well.

They adopted the opposite system, medicinal punishment, so he was given impositions, and became lazier; he was deprived of jam, his greed increased. Perhaps irony might be more successful? Once when he came to lunch with dirty hands, Bouvard mocked him, calling him a pretty lad, a dandy, really smart. Victor listened to him with downcast mien, suddenly went pale and threw his plate at Bouvard's head, then, furious at missing, flung himself on him. It took all the strength of the three men to master him. He rolled on the floor, trying to bite. Pécuchet sprinkled water over him from a distance; he calmed down at once, but was hoarse for three days. It was not the right method.

They adopted another. At the slightest symptom of anger, treating him as if he were ill, they put him to bed; Victor enjoyed that, and sang songs. One day he unearthed an old coconut shell from the library and was beginning to split it, when Pécuchet came up:

'My coconut!'

It was a souvenir of Dumouchel! He had brought it from Paris to Chavignolles; he threw up his arms in indignation. Victor began to laugh. 'Good friend' could not contain himself any longer, and with a massive clout sent him spinning to the end of the room, then, trembling with emotion, went to complain to Bouvard.

Bouvard rebuked him: 'How stupidly you go on about your coconut! Hitting people brutalizes them! Terror debilitates! You are degrading yourself!'

Pécuchet objected that corporal punishment is sometimes indispensable. Pestalozzi used it, and the celebrated Melanchthon admits that he would have learned nothing without it.

But cruel punishments have driven children to suicide; examples are recorded.

Victor had barricaded himself in his room. Bouvard parleyed

outside the door and, to make him open it, promised him a plum tart. From then on he got worse.

There remained the method recommended by Dupanloup: 'the stern look'. They tried to set their faces in a frightening expression and had no effect.

'The only thing left is to try religion,' said Bouvard.

Pécuchet objected. They had banished it from their programme.

But reasoning does not satisfy every need. The heart and imagination want something else. For many souls the supernatural is indispensable, and they resolved to send the children to catechism.

Reine suggested taking them. She was coming to the house again and knew how to win affection by ingratiating ways.

Victorine changed at once, became more reserved, honey-tongued, would kneel before the Madonna, admired the sacrifice of Abraham, sneered at the mere name of Protestant.

She declared that she had been ordered to fast. They made enquiries, it was not true. On Corpus Christi some rockets disappeared from a flowerbed to decorate the altar of repose; she brazenly denied having cut them. Another time she took a franc from Bouvard which she put in the collection plate at Vespers.

From this they concluded that morality is distinct from religion; when it has no other basis, its importance is secondary.

One evening, during dinner, Monsieur Marescot came in. Victor fled immediately.

The lawyer refused a seat and explained what had brought him; young Touache had beaten his son almost to death.

As Victor's origins were known, and as he was unpleasant, the other boys called him convict, and a little while before he had given Monsieur Arnold Marescot an insolent thrashing. Dear Arnold bore the marks of it on his body.

'His mother is in despair, his suit is torn to shreds, his health impaired! What are we coming to?'

The lawyer demanded rigorous punishment, and that Victor should stop going to catechism to prevent further collisions.

Bouvard and Pécuchet, although hurt by his arrogant tone, promised everything he wanted, gave in.

Had Victor obeyed the sense of honour or revenge? In any case he was not a coward.

But his brutality frightened them. Since music softens behaviour, Pécuchet had the idea of teaching him sol-fa.

Victor found it very hard to read notes fluently and distinguish the terms *adagio*, *presto*, *forzando*. His master strove hard to explain the scale, perfect harmony, diatonic, chromatic and the two kinds of interval, called major and minor. He made him stand quite upright, chest out, mouth wide open, and in order to teach him by example sang notes in a voice which was off-key; Victor contracted his larynx so much that his voice emerged with great difficulty; when the bar began with a breath, he started at once, or else too late.

Pécuchet nevertheless made a start on two-part melody. He took a stick as a substitute for a bow and waved his arm about as imperiously as though he had had an orchestra behind him; but with two tasks to occupy him, he lost the beat, his mistake caused his pupil to make others, and frowning, straining their neck muscles, they went on at random to the bottom of the page.

At last Pécuchet told Victor: 'You are not likely to shine in a choral society.' And he gave up his music lessons.

'Besides, Locke may be right: music brings you into such dissolute company that it is better to occupy yourself with something else.'

Without wishing to make a writer of him, Victor would find it convenient if he knew how to compose a letter. One consideration deterred them: epistolary style cannot be learned, because it is an exclusively feminine talent.

Then they thought of filling his memory with some pieces of literature, and with too much to choose from they consulted Madame Campan's work.

She recommends the scene with Eliacim, the choruses in *Esther*, the whole of Jean-Baptiste Rousseau. That was a little old. As for novels, she prohibits them for depicting the world in too favourable a light.

However, she permits *Clarissa Harlowe* and Miss Opy's *Paterfamilias*. Who is this Miss Opy?

They could not discover her name in Michaud's *Biography*. There remained fairy-tales. 'They will hope for diamond palaces,' said Pécuchet. Literature develops the mind but exalts the passions.

Victorine was sent home from catechism because of her passions. She had been caught kissing the lawyer's son, and Reine was not joking; her face was serious under her frilly bonnet. After such a scandal, how could they keep so corrupt a young girl?

Bouvard and Pécuchet called the curé a silly old woman. His housekeeper defended him. They retorted, and she went off rolling her eyes furiously, muttering: 'We know you! We know you!'

Victorine had indeed conceived an affection for Arnold, whom she found so nice with his embroidered collar, his velvet jacket, his sweet-smelling hair, and she brought him posies until she was denounced by Zéphyrin.

What absolute nonsense this adventure was! The two children were perfectly innocent!

Should they be taught the facts of life?

'I don't see any harm in it,' said Bouvard. The philosopher Basedow told his pupils about it, though explaining in detail only pregnancy and childbirth.

Pécuchet thought differently. Victor was beginning to worry him.

He suspected him of a certain bad habit. Why not? Grave men retain it all their lives, and the Duc d'Angoulême is supposed to have indulged in it. He interrogated his disciple in such a way as to give him ideas and a little later he had no doubts.

Then he called him a criminal, and, as a treatment, wanted to make him read Tissot. This masterpiece, according to Bouvard, was more pernicious than useful.

It would be better to inspire some poetic feeling in him. Aimé Martin reports that a mother in a similar case lent her son *La Nouvelle Héloïse*, 'and to make himself worthy of love the young man rushed on to the path of virtue'.

But Victor was incapable of dreaming up an angel.

'Supposing we took him instead to a brothel?'

Pécuchet expressed his horror of prostitutes.

Bouvard considered it idiotic and even talked of making a special journey to Le Havre.

'What are you thinking of? We should be seen going in!'

'All right! Buy him an appliance!'

'But the truss-maker might think it is for me,' said Pécuchet.

He really needed some exciting sport like hunting; it would involve the expense of a gun, a dog; they preferred to tire him out with exercise, and arranged cross-country races.

The boy escaped from them. Although they relayed each other, they could not go on and in the evening did not have the strength to hold the paper.

While they were waiting for Victor they chatted to people passing by, and feeling a pedagogic urge tried to teach them hygiene, deplored the waste of water and of manure.

They went so far as to inspect children's nurses and waxed indignant at the diet of their infants; some women give them gruel to drink, which makes them waste away; others stuff them with meat before they are six months old and they die of indigestion; several clean them up with their own spittle, all handle them brutally.

When on one door they saw an owl crucified they went into the farm and said:

'You are wrong, those animals live on rats and field mice; an owl's stomach has been found to contain as many as fifty caterpillar larvae.'

The villagers knew them because they had seen them, first as doctors, then hunting out antique furniture, then looking for stones, and they replied:

'Off with you and your jokes! Don't try and teach us!'

Their conviction was shaken, since sparrows keep kitchen-gardens clean but eat up cherries. Owls devour insects, but also bats, which are useful, and if moles do eat slugs, they throw up the earth as well. One thing they were sure of was that one had to destroy all game harmful to crops.

One evening when they were going through the Faverges wood they came to the gamekeeper's house. At the roadside Sorel was gesticulating to three individuals with him.

The first was a certain Dauphin, a cobbler, a little thin, sly looking man. The second, old Aubain, a commissionaire in the villages, wore an old yellow coat with blue drill trousers.

The third, Eugène, one of Monsieur Marescot's servants, was distinguished by his beard, which was trimmed in judicial style.

Sorel showed them a loop of copper wire attached to a silk thread held by a brick, commonly called a snare, which he had caught the cobbler setting.

'You are witnesses, aren't you?'

Eugène nodded approval, and old Aubain answered: 'If you say so.'

What infuriated Sorel was the brazen cheek of setting a trap so near his house, for the rascal had reckoned that no one would think of suspecting one in such a place.

Dauphin put on a doleful expression.

'I walked over it, I even tried to break it.' People were always accusing him, they had it in for him, he did not have any luck.

Sorel, without replying, had taken out of his pocket a notebook, pen and ink to write down a report.

'Oh no!' said Pécuchet.

Bouvard added: 'Let him go, he is a good chap!'

'Him, a poacher!'

'Well, supposing he were?' And they began to defend poaching; it is known for a start that rabbits nibble young shoots, hares damage cereals, except woodcock, perhaps...

'Leave me alone, will you.' And the gamekeeper wrote, clenching his teeth.

'What obstinacy!' murmured Bouvard.

'One more word and I'll send for the gendarmes!'

'You are a very rude person!' said Pécuchet.

'And you are not up to much,' retorted Sorel.

Bouvard forgot himself so much as to call him a boor, a bully! And Eugène repeated: 'Calm down! calm down!' while old Aubain groaned a few feet away on a pile of stones.

Disturbed by the voices all the dogs in the pack came out of their kennels; through the grill one could see their blazing eyes and black muzzles as they ran up and down barking fearsomely.

'Don't bother me any more,' cried their master, 'or I'll set them at your breeches!'

The two friends went off, pleased to have supported progress, civilization.

Already next day they received a summons to attend the police court, for insulting behaviour towards the keeper, and to hear themselves condemned to 100 francs damages 'unless the public prosecutor lodges an appeal in view of the offences committed by them: cost six francs, seventy-five centimes. Tiercelin, usher'.

Why the public prosecutor? It made their heads swim, then they calmed down and prepared their defence.

On the day appointed Bouvard and Pécuchet arrived at the Town Hall an hour early. No one was there, upright chairs and three with arms surrounded an oval baize-covered table, a recess was scooped out of the wall to take a stove, and the Emperor's bust, on a small pedestal, dominated everything.

They strolled up to the loft, where there was a fire pump, several flags, and, in a corner on the ground, several other plaster busts; the great Napoleon without a diadem, Louis XVIII with epauletted frock-coat, Charles X, recognizable by his drooping lip, Louis-Philippe, with arched eyebrows and hair done in a pyramid; the pitch of the roof brought it close to his neck, and the busts were all filthy, fly-blown and dusty. The sight demoralized Bouvard and Pécuchet. They felt sorry for governments when they came back to the main room.

There they found Sorel and the constable, one with his plaque on his arm, the other with his kepi. A dozen or so people were chatting, charged with failing to sweep properly, stray dogs, not having a light on their carriage, or keeping a wineshop open during mass.

At last Coulon presented himself garbed in a robe of black serge and a round hat with velvet at the bottom. His clerk sat on his left, the mayor in his sash on his right, and the first case to be called was that of Sorel against Bouvard and Pécuchet.

Louis, Martial, Eugène Lenepveur, manservant of Chavignolles (Calvados) took advantage of his position as witness to air all he knew on a mass of matters extraneous to the debate.

Nicolas-Juste Aubain, labourer, was afraid of displeasing Sorel and doing the gentlemen harm; he had heard strong language, but was doubtful about it, stating that he was hard of hearing.

The Justice of the Peace made him sit down again and then addressed the keeper: 'Do you persist in your statements?'

'Certainly!'

Coulon then asked the two accused what they had to say.

Bouvard maintained that he had not insulted Sorel; but in speaking on Dauphin's behalf had defended rural interests; he recalled feudal abuses, the ruinous way great lords hunted.

'No matter! The offence...'

'Stop, please!' cried Pécuchet. 'The words offence, crime and misdemeanour are meaningless. If you take the penalty as a basis for classifying punishable acts then you are taking an arbitrary basis. You might as well tell citizens: "Do not worry about the moral value of your actions, that is determined solely by the State's punishment." Besides, the penal code seems to me to be an irrational piece of work, devoid of principles.'

'That may be so!' answered Coulon, and he was about to pronounce his judgement. 'Whereas...' But Foureau, who was public prosecutor, stood up. The keeper had been insulted in the course of his duties. If the proprieties are not respected, all is lost. In short, would the judge please apply the maximum penalty.

This amounted to ten francs, as damages to Sorel.

'Very well!' murmured Bouvard.

Coulon had not finished: 'And they are moreover condemned to a fine of five francs for being guilty of the offence noted by the public prosecutor.'

Pécuchet turned towards the audience: 'A fine is a trifle for the rich, but a disaster for the poor. It means nothing to me!' And he gave the impression of mocking the court.

'Gentlemen,' said Coulon, 'I am amazed that people of intelligence...'

'The law dispenses you from having any!' retorted Pécuchet. 'The Justice of the Peace sits for an indefinite period, while the judge of the supreme court is deemed capable up to the age of seventy-five, and the judge of first instance only up to seventy.'

But at a sign from Foureau, Placquevent came forward. They protested.

'Oh! If you were appointed in a competition!'

'Or by the local council.'

'Or a committee of magistrates.'

'From a serious list!'

Placquevent pushed them, and they went out, booed by the other accused, who thought to curry favour by such despicable behaviour.

That evening they went to Beljambe's to give vent to their anger.

His café was empty, as the local worthies usually left at about ten o'clock. The light had been turned down; the walls and bar appeared somewhat hazily.

A woman arrived.

It was Mélie.

She did not look disturbed, and poured them two beers with a smile. Pécuchet, feeling uncomfortable, soon left the establishment.

Bouvard returned alone, entertained some of the locals with sarcastic comments about the mayor, and from then on regularly visited the café.

Six weeks later Dauphin was acquitted for lack of evidence. How shameful! Suspicion fell on the same witnesses whose evidence had been believed against them.

Their anger became uncontrollable when the Registry Office notified them that the fine was due. Bouvard attacked the Registry as being harmful to property.

'You are mistaken!' said the tax collector.

'Come now! Property bears a third of the charge on the public! I should like tax procedure to be less vexatious, a better land survey, changes in the mortgage system and the suppression of the Bank of France, which is privileged to practise usury.'

Girbal was not up to it, fell from public esteem and did not appear again.

However, the innkeeper liked Bouvard; he drew people in and while he waited for the regulars chatted familiarly with the servant.

He expressed some funny ideas about primary education. On leaving school people should be able to look after the sick, understand scientific discoveries, take an interest in the arts! The demands of his programme made him fall out with Petit; and he offended the captain by claiming that soldiers, instead of wasting time drilling, would do better growing vegetables.

When the question of free exchange came up he brought Pécuchet along; and throughout the winter the café was full of furious looks, scornful attitudes, insults, shouts and fists banging on the table so that the mugs jumped.

Langlois and the other tradesmen defended national trade; Voisin, owner of a spinning mill, Oudot, manager of a rolling mill, and Mathieu, a goldsmith, defended national industry; the landowners and farmers, national agriculture, each of them demanding privileges for himself to the detriment of the majority. They were alarmed by what Bouvard and Pécuchet had to say.

As they were accused of failing to recognize practice, of favouring levelling down and immorality, they developed these three conceptions: replace surnames by a registration number; arrange the French in a hierarchy where you must periodically take an examination to keep your rank; no more punishments, no more rewards, but every village would keep an individual chronicle which would be handed down to posterity.

Their system was derided.

They wrote an article on it for the Bayeux journal, a note to the prefect, a petition to the Assembly, a memorandum to the Emperor.

The journal did not publish their article. The prefect did not deign to reply. Parliament was dumb, and they waited a long time for a word from the Palace. What did the Emperor spend his time on? Courtesans, no doubt!

Foureau advised them on behalf of the sub-prefect to be more discreet.

They cared nothing for the sub-prefect, the prefect, and the prefectoral councils, indeed the Council of State. Administrative justice was a monstrosity, because the administration, through favours and threats, rules its officials with impunity.

In fact they became a nuisance, and the local worthies instructed Beljambe to stop admitting these two individuals.

Then Bouvard and Pécuchet wanted to distinguish themselves by some work which would oblige their fellow citizens to respect them, while astonishing and dazzling them, and all they could think of were plans for embellishing Chavignolles.

Three quarters of the houses would be pulled down, a monumental square would be built in the town centre, a hospice on the Falaise side, abattoirs on the Caen road, and at the Pas de la Vaque a polychrome Romanesque church.

Pécuchet drew up a sketch in Indian ink, not forgetting to colour woods yellow, fields green, buildings red. Pictures of an ideal Chavignolles pursued him in his dreams; he tossed and turned on his mattress.

One night this woke up Bouvard.

'Are you ill?'

Pécuchet muttered: 'Haussmann is keeping me awake.'

About this time he received a letter from Dumouchel asking the price of sea-bathing on the Norman coast.

'He can go to the devil with his bathing! As if we had time to write!'

When they had acquired a surveyor's chain, a graphometer, a water-level and a compass, other studies began.

They invaded people's homes, and the townsfolk were often surprised to see two men sticking markers in the yard.

Bouvard and Pécuchet calmly announced what the outcome would be.

The inhabitants became anxious; perhaps the authorities would follow their opinion?

Sometimes they were roughly dismissed. Victor would climb up walls and onto the roof to fix a signal, showing himself willing and even enthusiastic.

They were more pleased with Victorine.

When she did the ironing she would sing softly as she ran the iron over the board, she took an interest in housekeeping, made a skull-cap for Bouvard and won praise from Romiche for her quilting.

He was one of those tailors who go round the farms repairing clothes. He stayed two weeks with them.

Hunchbacked, with bloodshot eyes, he made up for his bodily defects by clownish humour. While the masters were out he amused Marcel and Victorine with funny stories, put out his tongue as far as his chin, imitated the cuckoo, did ventriloquism, and in the evening, to save the cost of the inn, went to bed in the bakehouse.

Now one morning, very early, Bouvard felt cold and went to get some chips to light his fire.

He was petrified by what he saw.

Behind the debris of the chest, on a straw mattress, Romiche and Victorine were sleeping together.

He had his arm round her waist, and his other hand, as long as a monkey's paw, held one of her knees, his eyes were half closed, his face still convulsed with a spasm of pleasure. She lay on her back, smiling. Her unfastened bodice revealed her childish bosom, red in patches from the hunchback's caress; her fair hair fell loose, and the first light of dawn cast a pale radiance over the two of them.

Bouvard had felt at first as though he had been hit in the chest. Then a certain modesty prevented him from making a single gesture; he was assailed by painful reflections.

'So young! Lost! Lost!'

Then he went to wake up Pécuchet, and told him everything in a word.

'Oh! The wretch!'

'There is nothing we can do! Calm yourself!'

And they spent a long time sighing as they faced each other, Bouvard coatless and arms crossed, Pécuchet on the edge of his bed, with feet bare and a nightcap.

Romiche was due to leave that day, having finished his work; they paid him haughtily, in silence.

But providence held it against them.

Marcel stealthily took them into Victor's room and showed them a twenty franc piece at the bottom of the chest of drawers. The lad had asked him to change it for him.

Where did it come from? Stolen, to be sure, and while they were doing their rounds as engineers. If anyone claimed it they would look like accomplices.

At last they called Victor and ordered him to open his drawer. The coin was no longer there.

However, they had handled it only a short time ago, and Marcel was incapable of lying.

This business had thrown him into such a turmoil that since that morning he had kept in his pocket a letter for Bouvard.

'Sir – Fearing that Monsieur Pécuchet may be ill, I address myself to your kindness...'

Whose was the signature then?

'Olympe Dumouchel, née Charpeau.'

She and her husband wanted to know in which bathing resort, Courseulles, Langrune, Ouistreham or Luc, was the best and most respectable company to be found; what transport there was, the price of laundry, etc.

Such importunity made them furious with Dumouchel; then fatigue plunged them into deeper despondency.

They recapitulated all the trouble they had taken, so many lessons, precautions, worries!

'And to think,' they said, 'that we once wanted to make an assistant mistress of her! And finally a Works Department foreman of him!'

'If she is vicious it is not the fault of her reading.'

'I tried to make him honest by teaching him the biography of Cartouche.'

'Perhaps they missed a family, a mother's care?'

'I was one!' objected Bouvard.

'Alas!' replied Pécuchet. 'But there are some natures devoid of moral sense, and education can do nothing about it!'

'Oh yes! Education is a fine thing!'

They would look for two places in service for them, as orphans without a trade, and then, God willing, they would have no more to do with them. Henceforth 'uncle' and 'good friend' made them eat in the kitchen.

But they soon became bored, their minds needed some task, their existence some aim.

Besides, what does one failure prove? What had failed with children might be less difficult with men. And they thought of setting up a course for adults.

They would need a lecture to explain their ideas. The main room in the inn would suit perfectly.

Beljambe, as deputy mayor, was afraid of compromising himself, first refused, then changed his mind, and sent a message by his servant. Bouvard, overcome with joy, kissed her on both cheeks.

The mayor was away, his other deputy, Monsieur Marescot, fully occupied with legal business; so the lecture would take place, and the town crier announced it for three o'clock the following Sunday.

Only the evening before did they think of what to wear.

Pécuchet fortunately had kept an old formal coat with a velvet collar, two white ties and black gloves. Bouvard put on his blue coat, a nankeen waistcoat, beaver shoes; and they felt very moved as they went through the village.

[This is the end of Flaubert's manuscript, but he left a draft plan showing how the book was to have ended.]

PLAN

LECTURE

The inn. Two lateral wooden galleries on the first floor with a projecting balcony – main building at the back – café on the ground floor – dining-room, billiard-room, doors and windows are open.
Crowd: notables, ordinary people.
Bouvard: 'We must first prove the value of our plan, our studies give us the right to speak.'

Pécuchet's speech – pedantic.

Stupidity of government and administration.
Too many taxes, two savings to be effected: suppress the army budget and the Church budget.
He is accused of impiety.
On the contrary, but a religious revival is necessary.
Foureau arrives and tries to disperse the meeting.
Bouvard gets a laugh at the mayor's expense with his idiotic prizes for owls. – Objection! 'If animals which harm plants must be destroyed, then so must the cattle which eat the grass.'

Foureau withdraws.

Bouvard's speech – familiar.

Prejudices: clerical celibacy, futility of adultery – female emancipation: Woman's earrings are the sign of her former bondage – Stud farm for men.
They are criticized for the bad behaviour of their pupils – And why adopt a convict's children?
Theory of rehabilitation. They would dine with Touache.
Foureau comes back, and to avenge himself on Bouvard reads out a petition he sent to the town council asking that a brothel should be set up in Chavignolles. – (Reasons from Robin).
The meeting is suspended amid great commotion.

On their way home they see Foureau's servant galloping along the Falaise road as fast as he can go.
They go to bed exhausted, without suspecting all the hatred being worked up against them – reasons for resentment of the curé, doctor, mayor, Marescot, people, everyone.
Next day at lunch they talk again about the lecture.
Pécuchet takes a gloomy view of the future of mankind.
Modern man had been diminished and has become a machine.
Final anarchy of the human race (Buchner, I, 11).
Impossibility of peace (id.).
Barbarity caused by excessive individualism and ravings of science.
Three hypotheses: 1. Pantheistic radicalism will break every link with the past, and inhuman despotism will result; 2. if theistic absolutism triumphs, the liberalism which has pervaded mankind since the Reformation will collapse, everything is overturned; 3. if the convulsions existing since the Revolution of 1789 continue endlessly between two outcomes, these oscillations will carry us away with their own strength.
There will be no more ideal, religion, morality.
America will have conquered the world.
Future of literature.
Universal vulgarity. There will be nothing left but a vast working-class spree.
End of the world because heat runs out.

Bouvard takes rosy view of future of mankind. Modern man is progressing.
Europe will be regenerated by Asia. The law of history being that civilization goes from East to West – role of China – two branches of mankind will finally be merged.
Future inventions; means of travel. Balloon. Submarine boat with windows; always in calm waters, as the sea is only disturbed on the surface – It will be possible to see fish go by and landscapes at the bottom of the ocean. – Animals tamed – All kinds of cultivation.
Future of literature (other side of industrial literature).
Future sciences – Control magnetic pull.
Paris a winter-garden – fruit espaliers on the boulevards.
The Seine filtered and warm – abundance of artificial precious

stones – lavish gilding – house lighting – light will be stored, because certain bodies have this property, like sugar, the flesh of certain molluscs and Bologna phosphorus. House façades will be compulsorily painted with the phosphorescent substance and their radiation will light up the streets.

Evil will disappear as want disappears. Philosophy will be a religion.

Communion of all peoples. Public holidays.

There will be travel to the stars – and when the earth is used up mankind will move over to the stars.

He has hardly finished when the gendarmes come in.

The children are terrified at seeing them, moved by vague memories.

Marcel's grief.

Bouvard and Pécuchet's distress – Have they come to arrest Victor?

The gendarmes produce a warrant of arrest.

The lecture is the reason. They are accused of offences against religion, public order, incitement to revolt, etc.

Sudden arrival of Monsieur and Madame Dumouchel, with their luggage; they are coming to have a holiday by the sea. Dumouchel has not changed. Madame wears glasses and makes up stories – their amazement.

The mayor, knowing that the gendarmes are at Bouvard and Pécuchet's house, arrives, encouraged by their presence.

Gorju, seeing that authority and public opinion are against them, has tried to take advantage of it and escorts Foureau. Supposing Bouvard to be the richer of the two, he accuses him of having once seduced Mélie. 'I, never!' And Pécuchet trembles. 'And even giving her venereal disease.' Bouvard protests. He should at least give her an allowance for the child about to be born, as she is pregnant. This second accusation is based on Bouvard's intimacy in the café.

The public gradually invades their house.

Barberou, in the region on business, has just heard at the inn what is going on and turns up.

He believes Bouvard to be guilty, takes him aside, and persuades him to give in, to provide an allowance.

Arrival of the doctor, the count, Reine, Madame Bordin, Madame Marescot, with her sunshade. Other dignitaries. The village lads, outside the gate, throw stones into the garden. (It is now well kept and the population is jealous.)
Foureau wants to drag Bouvard and Pécuchet off to jail.
Barberou intervenes, and like him Marescot, the doctor and the count intervene with insulting pity.
Explain the warrant. The sub-prefect, on receiving Foureau's letter, has sent them a warrant to frighten them, with a letter to Marescot and Faverges, saying they should be left alone if they show signs of regret.

*

Everything calms down. Bouvard will give Mélie an allowance. But they cannot be allowed to go on looking after the children – They object; but they have not legally adopted the orphans, the mayor takes them back.
They show disgusting indifference.
Bouvard and Pécuchet weep.
Monsieur and Madame Dumouchel go off.
So everything has come to pieces in their hands.
They have no interest left in life.
Each of them secretly harbours a bright idea. They hide it from each other – From time to time they smile when it occurs to them – then simultaneously they tell each other; become copyists.
Construction of a double-sided desk – (For this they apply to a carpenter. Gorju, who has heard of their invention, offers to make it for them – Recall the chest).
Purchase of registers and instruments, eraser, sandarach, etc.
They go to work.

FLAUBERT'S DICTIONARY OF RECEIVED IDEAS

As mentioned in the Introduction, Flaubert had intended to fill much of the second volume of *Bouvard* with various collections of what he considered to be idiocies. One of these has been reconstructed from papers he left, and follows here. It will be seen that it consists largely of clichés, social noises to be uttered in bourgeois society by anyone wishing to conform. The response, even when it amounts to a blank profession of ignorance, is meant to be unthinking and automatic. A number of factual errors occur, and also certain ritual pieces of word-play, offered as instant humour in society, but which defy translation. It is not possible to give full annotation, but where this has been practical and seemed useful some indication of the original is supplied.

The version which is presented here was completed by Robert Baldick, former joint editor of Penguin Classics, shortly before his tragic death. I have made a few minor alterations and added the few notes, but it is otherwise as he left it. It is a pleasure and a privilege to pay this tribute to an outstanding translator, who was also a valued friend and colleague.

A.J.K.

THE DICTIONARY
OF
RECEIVED IDEAS

A

ABELARD No need to have any idea of his philosophy, nor even to know the titles of his works. Refer discreetly to the mutilation inflicted on him by Fulbert. The grave of Abelard and Héloïse: if someone proves to you that it is apocryphal, exclaim: 'You are robbing me of my illusions!'

ABSALOM If he had worn a wig, Joab could not have murdered him. Facetious name for a bald friend.

ABSINTHE Extra violent poison: one glass and you're a dead man. Newspapermen drink it while writing their copy. Has killed more soldiers than the Bedouins.

ACADEMY, FRENCH Run it down but try to belong to it if you can.

ACCIDENT Always 'regrettable' or 'unfortunate' (as if a mishap could ever be a cause for rejoicing).

ACHILLES Add 'fleet-footed': people will think you've read Homer.

ACTRESSES The ruin of young men of good family. Are terribly lascivious, engage in orgies, run through fortunes, and end up in the workhouse. 'I beg to differ: some make excellent mothers!'

ADMIRAL Always brave. Their sole expletive: 'Shiver my timbers!'

ADVERTISING A source of wealth.

AGRICULTURE One of the two breasts of the state (the state is masculine but never mind). Should be encouraged. Short of manpower.

AIR Always beware of fresh air. The air is always at variance with the temperature. If the temperature is warm, the air is cold, and vice versa.

ALABASTER Used to describe the most beautiful parts of a woman's body.

ALBION Always 'white', 'perfidious' or 'positivist'. Napoleon only just failed to conquer it. Praise it: 'freedom-loving England.'

ALCIBIADES Famous for his dog's tail. The typical debauchee. Consorted with Aspasis.

ALCOHOLISM Cause of all modern diseases. (See ABSINTHE and TOBACCO.)

AMBITION Always 'insane' unless it is 'noble'.

AMBITIOUS In the provinces, anyone who gets himself talked about. 'I'm not ambitious' means selfish or incompetent.

AMERICA Fine example of injustice: Columbus discovered it and it is named after Amerigo Vespucci. If it weren't for the discovery of America, we shouldn't have syphilis and Phylloxera. Praise it all the same, especially if you've never been there. Expatiate on self-government.

ANDROCLES Mention his lion if anyone speaks of animal tamers.

ANGEL Creates a good effect in love and literature.

ANGER Stirs the blood: it is healthy to be angry now and then.

ANIMALS 'If only animals could speak! There are some which are more intelligent than men.'

ANT Model to hold up to a spendthrift. Suggested the idea of savings banks.

ANTICHRIST Voltaire, Renan...

ANTIQUES Are always modern fakes.

ANTIQUITY (AND EVERYTHING CONNECTED WITH IT) Dull and boring.

APLOMB Always 'perfect' or 'diabolical'.

APRICOTS 'We shan't have any again this year.'

ARCHIMEDES On hearing his name, say: 'Eureka!' Or else: 'Give me a fulcrum and I will lift the world.' There is also Archimedes' screw, but you aren't expected to know what it is.

ARCHITECTS All idiots; they always forget to put staircases in houses.

ARCHITECTURE There are only four types of architecture. Leaving aside, of course, the Egyptian, Cyclopean, Assyrian, Indian, Chinese, Gothic, Romanesque, etc.

ARISTOCRACY Despise and envy it.

ARMY The bulwark of society.

ARSENIC Is to be found in everything (mention Madame Lafarge). And yet certain peoples eat it.

ART Leads to the workhouse. What use is it since machines can make things better and quicker?

ARTISTS All charlatans. Praise their disinterestedness (*old-fashioned*). Express surprise that they dress like everyone else (*old-fashioned*). They earn huge sums, but squander them. Often asked to dine out. A woman artist must be a whore. What artists do can't be called work.

ASP Animal known through Cleopatra's basket of figs.

ASTRONOMY An admirable science. Useful only to sailors. In speaking of it, poke fun at astrology.

ATHEISTS A nation of atheists cannot survive.

AUTHORS One should 'know a few authors': no need to know their names.

DICTIONARY OF RECEIVED IDEAS

B

BACCALAUREATE Thunder against it.

BACHELORS All selfish and immoral. Should be taxed. Doomed to a lonely old age.

BACK A slap on the back can give you tuberculosis.

BAGNOLET Town famous for its blind people.

BALDNESS Always 'premature'. Caused by youthful excesses, or the hatching of great thoughts.

BALLOONS Thanks to them, man will one day reach the moon. But it will be a long time before they can be steered.

BANDITS Always 'ferocious'.

BANKERS All rich. Sharks and swindlers.

BANQUET Always 'a festive occasion'. Nobody will ever forget it, and the guests never leave without promising to meet again at the one next year. Some joker must refer to 'the banquet of life'.

BARBER Call him a 'tonsorial artist' or a 'Figaro'. Louis XI's barber. Barbers used to bleed you.

BASES (OF SOCIETY). *Id est* property, the family, religion, respect for authority. Show anger if these are attacked.

BASILICA Grandiose synonym for church. Always 'imposing'.

BASQUES The people who are best at running.

BATTLE Always 'bloody'. There are always two sets of victors: those who won and those who lost.

BEAR Generally called Bruin. Tell the story of the disabled soldier who, seeing a watch which had fallen into a bear-pit, went down and was eaten alive.

BEARD Sign of strength. Too much beard causes baldness. Helps to protect cravats.

BEDROOM In an old chateau, Henry IV is sure to have slept there.

BEER Don't drink beer. It makes you liable to colds.

BEETHOVEN Don't pronounce *Beatoven*. Be sure to swoon when one of his works is being played.

BELLOWS Never use them.

BELLY Say 'abdomen' when there are ladies present.

BIBLE The oldest book in the world.

BILL Always too high.

BILLIARDS A noble game. Indispensable in the country.

BIRD Wish you were one, saying with a sigh: 'Oh, for a pair of wings!' This shows a poetic soul.

BLACK Always followed by 'as ebony' or preceded by 'jet'.

BLONDES Hotter than brunettes. (See BRUNETTES.)

BLOOD-CLEANSER Is taken in secret.

BLOOD-LETTING Have yourself bled in the spring.

BLUESTOCKING Term of contempt applied to women with intellectual interests. Quote Molière in support: 'When her intelligence she over-reaches . . .'

BOARDING-SCHOOL Say this in English when it's a girls' school.

BODY If we knew how the human body is made, we wouldn't dare to move a muscle.

BOILED BEEF Healthy food. Inseparable from carrots.

BOILS See PIMPLES.

BOOK Always too long, whatever the subject.

BOOTS In very hot weather, always refer to policemen's boots or postmen's shoes (permissible only in the country, in the open). Boots are the best footwear.

BOY 'My boy, it's all off.' [The French is *gendre*, son-in-law.]

BREAD Nobody knows what filth goes into it.

BREATH To have a strong breath is a sign of distinction. Avoid references to flies and say that it comes from your stomach.

BRETONS All good souls, but pig-headed.

BRONZE Metal of antiquity.

BRUNETTES Hotter than blondes. (See BLONDES.)

BUDDHISM 'False religion of India.' (Definition in Bouillet's Dictionary, first edition.)

BUDGET Never balanced.

BUFFON Used to put on lace cuffs before writing.

BULL Father of the calf! The ox is only the uncle.

BURIAL Too often premature. Tell stories of corpses which had eaten an arm off to appease their hunger.

BUSINESS [Fr. *affaires*] Come first. A woman must avoid talking about hers. The most important thing in life. The be-all and end-all of existence.

BUTCHERS Awe-inspiring in times of revolution.

BUYING and SELLING The goal of life.

C

CABINET-MAKER Craftsman who rarely makes a cabinet.

CAMEL Has two humps and the dromedary only one; or else the camel has one and the dromedary two – nobody can ever remember which.

CANDOUR Always 'disarming'. One is either full of it or completely devoid of it.

CANNONADE Affects the weather.

CANNONBALL The rush of air it creates causes blindness.

CARBUNCLE See PIMPLES.

CARRIAGE It's better to hire than to own one; like that, you don't have to bother about grooms and horses, which are always falling sick.

CARTHUSIANS Spend their time making Chartreuse, digging their own graves and saying to one another: 'Brother, you too must die.'

CASTLE Has always withstood a siege under Philip Augustus.

CATHOLICISM Has had a very good influence on art.

CATS Are treacherous. Call them 'drawing-room tigers'. Cut off their tails to prevent vertigo.

CATS AND DOGS When you see a dark cloud, don't fail to say: 'It's going to rain cats and dogs.'

CAUCUS Wax indignant on hearing this word.

CAVALRY Nobler than the infantry.

CAVES Usual residence of robbers. Always full of snakes.

CEDAR The one at the Botanical Garden was brought over in a man's hat.

CELEBRITIES Find out the smallest details of their private lives, so that you can run them down.

CENSORSHIP A good thing, whatever people may say.

CERUMEN 'Human wax.' Shouldn't be removed, as it keeps insects from entering the ears.

CHAMBERMAIDS Prettier than their mistresses. Know all their secrets and betray them. Always undone by the son of the house.

CHAMPAGNE The sign of a grand dinner. Pretend to despise it, saying: 'It isn't really a wine.' Arouses the enthusiasm of the lower orders. Russia drinks more of it than France. The medium through which French ideas have been spread throughout Europe. During the Regency people did nothing but drink champagne. But one doesn't drink champagne: one 'sips' it.

CHATEAUBRIAND Best known through the type of steak which bears his name.

CHEATING Cheating the Customs isn't dishonest; rather a proof of cleverness and political independence.

CHEESE Quote Brillat-Savarin's maxim: 'Dessert without cheese is like a beauty with only one eye.'

CHESS Symbol of military tactics. All great generals were good at it. Too serious to be a game, too trivial to be a science.

CHESTNUT Female of the horse-chestnut [*châtaigne/marron* in French].

CHIAROSCURO Nobody knows what this means.

CHILBLAINS Sign of good health. Come from warming oneself up after being cold.

CHILDREN Display a lyrical fondness for them when there are people present.

CHIMNEY Always smokes. Subject of discussion about heating systems.

CHIMNEY-SWEEP Winter's swallow.

CHOLERA You catch it by eating melons. You cure it by drinking a lot of tea with rum in it.

CHRISTIANITY Freed the slaves.

CHRISTMAS Wouldn't be Christmas without the pudding.

CIDER Spoils the teeth.

CIGARS Those sold under government monopoly are always abominable. The only good ones are smuggled in.

CIRCUS TRAINERS Use obscene practices.

CITY FATHERS Thunder against them apropos of the paving of streets: 'What can our city fathers be thinking of!'

CLARINET Playing it causes blindness: all blind men play the clarinet.

CLASSICS You are supposed to know them all.

CLOAK Always the colour of stone walls, for amorous adventures.

CLOGS All self-made men were wearing clogs when they first arrived in Paris.

CLOTH All comes from Elbeuf.

CLOWN His body was put out of joint in infancy.

CLUB One should always belong to a club. Political clubs arouse the anger of conservatives. Doubt and argument about the correct pronunciation of the word.

COBBLER *Ne sutor ultra crepidem* ('The cobbler should stick to his last').

COCKS A thin man must always say that fighting cocks are never fat.

COFFEE Induces wit. No good unless it comes through Le Havre. After a big dinner party, should be drunk standing up. Drinking it without sugar is very smart: it gives the impression that you have lived in the East.

COGNAC Very harmful. Excellent for several ailments. A glass of cognac never did anybody any harm. Taken before breakfast, kills intestinal worms.

COITUS, COPULATION Words to avoid. Say: 'Intimacy occurred...'

COLD Healthier than heat.

COLLEGE Sounds better than 'boarding-school'.

COLONIES (OUR) Show sadness when speaking of them.

COMB (LARGE-TOOTHED) Makes the hair fall out.

COMEDY In verse, no longer suited to our times. However, high comedy deserves respect. *Castigat ridendo mores.*

COMETS Make fun of our ancestors who feared them.

COMFORT Important modern discovery.

COMMUNION One's first communion: the greatest day of one's life.

COMPETITION The soul of trade.

COMPOSITION At school, skill at composition shows application, whereas skill at translation shows intelligence. But out in the world, scoff at those who were good at composition.

COMPROMISE Always advocate it, even when the alternatives are irreconcilable.

CONCERT Respectable way of killing time.

CONCESSIONS Never make any. They were the ruin of Louis XVI.

CONCUPISCENCE Ecclesiastic term for carnal desire.

CONFECTIONERS All the inhabitants of Rouen are confectioners.

CONFINEMENT Avoid the word: replace by 'happy event': 'When is the happy event expected?'

CONGRATULATIONS Always 'hearty', 'sincere', etc.

CONSERVATIVE Politician with a pot-belly. 'You are a narrow-minded conservative!!' – 'I admit it, my good sir. Better a narrow mind than a thick head.'

CONSERVATOIRE It is absolutely essential to subscribe to its concerts.

CONSPIRATORS Always have a mania for drawing up lists of their names.

CONSTIPATION All literary men are constipated. Affects political convictions.

CONSTITUTIONAL RULES Are killing us. Under them, no government is possible.

CONTRALTO Nobody knows what this means.

CONVERSATION Politics and religion must be kept out of it.

CONVICTS Always look it. All clever with their hands. Our prisons contain many a man of genius.

COOKING In restaurants, always bad for the blood; at home, always wholesome; in the South, too oily or spicy.

COPAIBA BALSAM Pretend not to know what it is for [venereal disease].

CORNS Indicate changes in the weather, better than a barometer. Very dangerous when badly cut: cite examples of fatal consequences.

CORSET Prevents childbearing.

COSSACKS Eat tallow candles.

COTTON-WOOL Chiefly useful for putting in one's ears.

COUNTENANCE A pleasing countenance is the best of passports.

COUNTRY People in the country better than those in towns. Envy their lot. In the country, anything goes – casual clothes, practical jokes, etc.

COUNTY (FAMILIES) Show contempt for them.

COUSIN Advise husbands to beware of young male cousins.

CRAYFISH Female of the lobster [*langouste/homard* in French]. Walks backward. Always call reactionaries 'crayfish'.

CREOLE Lives in a hammock.

CRIMINAL Always 'vile'.

CRIMSON Nobler word than red.

CRITIC Always 'eminent'. Supposed to know everything, to have read everything, to have seen everything. When you dislike him, call him a Zoilus, a eunuch.

CROCODILE Imitates the cry of a child to lure people.

CROOK Always in high society. (See SPY.)

CROSSBOW A good excuse for bringing up the story of William Tell.

CRUCIFIX Looks well above a bed – or on the scaffold.

CRUSADES Benefited Venetian trade.

CUCKOLD Every woman is expected to make her husband a cuckold.

CURAÇAO The best comes from Holland, because it is made in Curaçao in the West Indies.

CUSTOMS DUTIES Rebel against them, and try to cheat them. (See TOLLS.)

CUT-PRICE Excellent for a shop-sign; inspires confidence.

CYPRESS Grows only in cemeteries.

CZAR Pronounce Tsar, and now and then Autocrat.

D

DAGUERREOTYPE Will take the place of painting. (See PHOTOGRAPHY.)

DAMASCUS The only place where people know how to make swords. Every good blade comes from Damascus.

DANCING People don't dance any more, they walk about.

DANTON 'Let us dare, and dare again, and go on daring.'

DARWIN The fellow who says we're descended from monkeys.

DAYS The master has days: for trimming the beard taking a purge, etc. And Madame has days too, which she calls 'critical', at certain times of the month.

DEBAUCHERY Cause of all the diseases from which bachelors suffer.

DEFEAT Is sustained, and is so complete that no one is left to carry news of it.

DEICIDE Wax indignant over it, even though the crime is somewhat infrequent.

DEMOSTHENES Never made a speech without a pebble in his mouth.

DENTISTS All liars. Use 'steel medicine'. Are generally believed to be chiropodists too. Call themselves surgeons, just as opticians call themselves engineers.

DENTURES Third set of teeth. Take care not to swallow them while asleep.

DEPUTY To be elected is the height of glory. Thunder against the Chamber of Deputies. Too many talkers there. They do nothing.

DERBY Racing term: very smart.

DESCARTES *Cogito, ergo sum.*

DESERT Produces dates.

DESSERT Deplore the fact that people no longer sing at dessert. Virtuous persons despise it: 'Pastry! Heavens, no! I never touch it.'

DEVICE Obscene term.

DEVOTION Complain how little other people show. 'We are inferior to the dog in this respect.'

DIAMONDS The time will come when man will manufacture them! To think that they're nothing but coal; if we came across one in its natural state, we wouldn't bother to pick it up!

DIANA Goddess of the chaste (chased).

DICTIONARY Say of it: 'It's only for ignoramuses!' A rhyming dictionary? – 'I'd rather die than use one!'

DIDEROT Always accompanied by d'Alembert.

DILETTANTE Wealthy man who is a regular opera-goer.

DIMPLES Always tell a pretty girl that little loves are hiding in her dimples.

DINNER In the old days people dined at noon. Now they dine at impossible hours. The dinner of our fathers' time is our lunch, and our lunch is their dinner. A meal as late as our dinner shouldn't be called dinner, but supper.

DINNER JACKET In the provinces, the acme of ceremony and inconvenience.

DIOGENES 'I am looking for a man.' 'Get out of my light.'

DIPLOMA Emblem of knowledge. Proves nothing.

DIPLOMACY A fine career, but beset with difficulties and full of mystery. Suitable only for aristocrats. A profession of vague importance, though superior to trade. Diplomats are always subtle and shrewd.

DIRECTORY A scandalous period. In those days honour had taken refuge in the army. Women in Paris went about naked.

DISGUSTING Must be said of any work of art or literature which the *Figaro* will not let you admire.

DISSECTION An insult to the majesty of death.

DISTINCTION Always preceded by 'rare'.

DIVA All women singers must be called divas.

DIVIDERS Perfect eyesight has them built in.

DIVORCE If Napoleon had not divorced Josephine, he would still be on the throne.

DJINN The name of an oriental dance.

DOCTOR Always preceded by 'the good'. Is a marvel while he enjoys your confidence, a fool as soon as you've fallen out. Are all materialists: 'You can't find the soul with a scalpel.'

DOCTRINAIRES Despise them. Why? Nobody can say.

DOCUMENT Invariably 'of the highest importance'.

DOG Specially created to save its master's life. Man's best friend.

DOGE Wedded the sea. Only one is known – Marino Faliero.

DOLMEN Something to do with the ancient Gauls. Stone used for the Druids' sacrifices. Found only in Brittany. (Nothing else is known about them.)

DOLPHIN Carries children on its back.

DOME Tower with an architectural shape. Express surprise that it stays up. Cite two examples: the Dome of the Invalides and that of St Peter's in Rome.

DOMESTICITY Never fail to speak of it with respect.

DOMINOES One can play them all the better for being tight.

DORMITORIES Always 'spacious and airy'. Preferable to single rooms for the pupils' morals.

DOUBT Worse than negation.

DRAWING (ART OF) 'Consists of three things: line, stippling and fine stippling. There is also the masterstroke; but the masterstroke can only be given by the master' (Christophe).

DREADFUL 'Absolutely dreadful' – when alluding to erotic expressions: one may commit the act, but not speak of it. 'It was in the darkness of a dreadful night.'

DREAMS Any lofty ideas one doesn't understand.

DRESSES (LADIES') Disturb the imagination.

DUCKS Always come from Rouen.

DUEL Thunder against it. It is no proof of a man's courage. Prestige of the man who has fought a duel.

DUNGEON Always horrible. The straw in it is always damp. Nobody has ever come across a delightful one.

DUPE It is better to be a knave than a dupe.

DUPUYTREN Famous for his ointment and his museum.

DUTIES Insist on others 'fulfilling them', but dispense yourself from them. Others have duties towards us, not we towards them.

DWARF Tell the story of General Tom Thumb, and if by any chance you shook his hand, boast of the fact.

E

EARLY RISING A sign of morality. If one goes to bed at four in the morning and rises at eight, one is lazy; but if one goes to bed at nine in the evening and gets up the next day at five, one is an active type.

EARTH Refer to the four corners of the earth, since it is round.

ECHO Mention the one in the Panthéon and the one under the bridge at Neuilly.

ECLECTICISM Thunder against it as being an immoral philosophy.

EDUCATION Create the impression that you have had a good education. The common people need no education to earn their living.

EGG Starting point for a philosophic lecture on the origin of life.

ELEPHANTS Noted for their memories, and worship the sun.

EMBONPOINT Sign of wealth and idleness.

EMBRACE 'Kiss' is more decent. If not 'stolen' a kiss is bestowed on a damsel's brow, a mother's cheek, a pretty woman's hand, a child's neck, and a mistress's lips.

ÉMIGRÉS Earned their livelihood by giving guitar lessons and mixing salads.

EMIR Used only for Abd-el-Kadr.

EMPIRE 'The Empire means Peace' (Napoleon III).

EMPRESSES All beautiful.

ENAMEL The secret of this art is lost.

ENCYCLOPÉDIE Laugh at it pityingly for being quaint and old-fashioned, or else thunder against it.

ENGINEERING The finest career for a young man. An engineer knows all the sciences.

ENGLISHMEN Are all rich.

ENGLISHWOMEN Express surprise that they can have pretty children.

ENTHUSIASM Caused exclusively by the return of Napoleon's ashes. Always 'indescribable', and the newspaper takes two columns to describe it.

EPICURUS Despise him.

EPISTOLARY STYLE Reserved exclusively for women.

ERECTION Said only of monuments.

EROSTRATUS Mention him in any conversation about the fires of the Commune.

ESPLANADE Found only near the Invalides.

ETRUSCAN All antique vases are Etruscan.

ETYMOLOGY The easiest thing in the world with the help of Latin and a little ingenuity.

EUNUCH Never has children . . . Fulminate against the castrati singers of the Sistine Chapel.

EVACUATION Often copious and always alarming.

EVIDENCE Is crystal-clear when it doesn't leap to the eye.

EXASPERATION Always at its height.

EXCEPTION Say that it proves the rule. Don't venture to explain how.

EXECUTIONER Office handed down from father to son.

EXECUTIONS Pity the women who go to see them.

EXERCISE Prevents all illnesses. Recommend it at all times.

EXHIBITION Cause of delirious excitement in the nineteenth century.

EXPIRE Verb applied exclusively to newspaper subscriptions.

EXTIRPATE Verb applied only to heresies and corns.

F

FAÇADE Great men look well on it.

FACE The mirror of the soul. So some people must have very ugly souls.

FACTORY Dangerous neighbourhood.

FAITHFUL Inseparable from 'dog' and 'friend'. Never miss a chance to quote: 'Faithful are the wounds of a friend' and 'So faithful in love, so dauntless in war.'

FAME Vanity of vanities.

FANFARE Always 'loud'.

FAREWELL Choke back a sob when referring to Napoleon's farewell at Fontainebleau.

FARM When visiting a farm, one must eat nothing but wholemeal bread and drink nothing but milk. If eggs are added, exclaim:

'Heavens, how fresh they are! Not a hope of finding any like these in town!'

FARMER Always address him as 'Squire' So-and-so. All well-off.

FARM-WORKERS What would we do without them?

FAT Fat people don't need to learn to swim. Are the despair of executioners owing to the difficulty of beheading them: e.g. Madame Dubarry.

FATAL An exclusively Romantic word. Applied to a man means that he has the evil eye.

FAVOUR It is doing children a favour to cuff them; animals, to beat them; servants, to sack them; criminals, to punish them.

FEAR Lends wings.

FELICITY Always 'perfect'. If your cook is named Felicity, then she is perfect.

FEMALE Use only in speaking of animals. Unlike the human race, the females of animals are less beautiful than the males, e.g. the pheasant, the cock, the lion, etc.

FENCING Fencing masters know secret thrusts.

FEUDALISM No need to have any clear idea what it was, but thunder against it.

FEVER A sign of strong blood. Caused by plums, melons, the April sun, etc.

FIGARO (MARRIAGE OF) Another of the causes of the Revolution!

FIGLEAF Emblem of virility in the art of sculpture.

FINGER God's finger is in every pie.

FINGERBOWLS Sign of wealth in a house.

FIRE Purifies everything. On hearing the cry of 'Fire!' begin by losing your head. A sight worth seeing.

FIRING SQUAD Nobler than the guillotine. Delight of the man who is granted the favour of facing one.

FIST To govern France, an iron fist is needed.

FLAG The sight of it makes the heart beat faster.

FLAGRANTE DELICTO Applied only to cases of adultery.

FLAMINGO Bird so called because it comes from Flanders [*flamant* (the bird) sounds exactly like *flamand* (Flemish)].

FLAT (BACHELOR) Always in a mess, with feminine garments lying here and there. Smell of cigarettes. If you hunted around, you would find the most extraordinary things.

FLATTERERS Never miss the chance to quote: 'I can stand anything but flattery' and 'Flattery's the food of fools.'

FLIES *Puer abige muscas* ('Boy, drive away those flies').

FLOOD VICTIMS Always along the Loire.

FOETUS Any anatomical specimen preserved in spirits of wine.

FOOD In boarding-schools, always 'wholesome and plentiful'.

FOOT-ODOUR A sign of good health.

FOREHEAD High and bald, a sign of genius or of composure.

FOREIGN Enthusiasm for everything foreign is a sign of a liberal mind. Contempt for everything that isn't French is a sign of patriotism.

FORGERS Always work in cellars.

FORK Should always be of silver, which is less dangerous. Use it in the left hand: this is easier and more distinguished.

FORNARINA She was a beautiful woman. No need to know anything more about her.

FORTUNE *Audaces fortuna juvate* ('Fortune favours the bold'). The rich are happy, because they have a fortune. When told of any large fortune, never fail to say: 'Yes, but is it safe?'

FOSSIL A proof of the Flood. A joke in good taste when alluding to members of the Academy.

FOUNDATION All news is without it.

FRANC-TIREUR More to be feared than the enemy.

FREEMASONRY Yet another cause of the Revolution. The initiation is a terrible ordeal. Cause of dissension among married couples. Distrusted by the clergy. What can its secret be?

FREE TRADE Cause of all business troubles.

FRENCH The greatest people in the world. 'There is simply one more Frenchman,' said the Comte d'Artois. 'How proud one is to be French when one looks at the Colonne Vendôme.'

FRENCH DASH Always call it *furia francese*.

FRESCOES Nobody paints them any more.

FRICASEE Only good in the country.

FROG Female of the toad [*grenouille*/*crapaud* in French].

FUCK Use this word only as a swear-word, if at all.

FUGUE Nobody knows what it is, but you must assert that it is extremely difficult and extremely dull.

FULMINATE Nice verb.

FUNCTIONARY Inspires respect, whatever his function may be.

FUNERAL About the deceased: 'To think that I had dinner with him only a week ago.' Called obsequies in the case of a general, inhumation in the case of a philosopher.

FUNNY Should be used on all occasions: 'That's funny!'

FUR Sign of wealth.

FURNITURE Always fear the worst for your furniture.

FUSION Keep hoping for the fusion of the two branches of the royal family.

G

GAIETY Always preceded by 'frantic'.

GALANT HOMME According to circumstances, pronounce '*galantuomo*' or 'gentleman'.

GALLOPHOBE Use this term in speaking of German journalists.

GAMBLING Wax indignant at this fatal passion.

GAME Good only when high.

GAMIN Always of Paris. Never let your wife say: 'When I feel gay, I love to act like a *gamin*.'

GARDENS (ENGLISH) More natural than French ones.

GARLIC Kills intestinal worms and encourages amorous combat. Henry IV's lips were rubbed with it at birth.

GARRET At twenty, one can be very happy in a garret.

GARTER Must always be worn above the knee by society women, below it by women of the people. A woman must never neglect this point of dress: there are so many ill-bred men in this world.

GENERAL Always 'brave'. Generally does something unconnected with his job, such as being an ambassador, a town councillor or the head of a government.

GENERATION (SPONTANEOUS) A socialistic idea.

GENIUS No use admiring it: it's a neurosis.

GENOVEFAN Nobody knows what it is.

GENTLEMEN There aren't any left.

GEOMETRICIAN 'Let no one who is not a geometrician enter.'

GERMANS Always preceded by 'blond', 'dreamy'. But what an efficient army they have! A people of dreamers (*old-fashioned*). 'No wonder they beat us, we weren't ready!'

GIAOUR Fierce expression of unknown meaning, though it is known to be connected with the Orient.

GIBBERISH Foreigners' way of talking. Always make fun of the foreigner who speaks your language badly.

GIFT It isn't the value that gives it a price, or the price that gives it value. The gift is nothing, it's the thought behind it that matters.

GIRAFFE Polite word to avoid calling a woman an old cow.

GIRONDISTS More sinned against than sinning.

GLOBE Genteel way of referring to a woman's breasts: 'Let me kiss your adorable globes.'

GLORIA [Spirits with coffee.] Never without its *consolation.*

GLOVES Confer an air of respectability.

GOBELINS A gobelins tapestry is an amazing piece of work which takes fifty years to make. On seeing it, exclaim: 'It's more beautiful than a painting!' The workman doesn't know what he's doing.

GOD Voltaire himself said: 'If God did not exist, it would be necessary to invent him.'

'GODDAM' The basis of the English language, as Beaumarchais said. Snigger in a superior way.

GODFATHER Always the godchild's real father.

'GOD SAVE THE KING' Pronounced in Béranger's verses: 'God savé té King'; it rhymes with *sauvé, préservé,* etc...

GOG Always goes with Magog.

GOLDEN NUMBER, DOMINICAL LETTER, ETC. On all calendars but nobody knows what it means.

GORDIAN KNOT Has something to do with antiquity. (The way the ancients tied their neckties.)

GOSPELS Divine, sublime, and so forth, works.

GOTHIC Architectural style which inspires religious feeling more than any other.

GRAMMAR Teach it to children, however young, as something clear and easy.

GRAMMARIANS All pedants.

GRAPESHOT The only way to keep the Parisians quiet.

GRATITUDE Don't mention it.

GREEK Whatever one cannot understand is Greek.

GRISETTES There aren't any left. You must say this with the discomfited air of a hunter complaining that there is no more game.

GROG Not respectable.

GROTTOES WITH STALACTITES At some time or other a ball or banquet was given there. The stalactites 'look like organ pipes'. During the Revolution, Mass was celebrated there in secret.

GROUP Suitable on a mantelpiece or in politics.

GUARD The guard will die but won't surrender; seven words to stand for five letters [*merde* in French].

GUERRILLA Does more harm to the enemy than the regular army.

GUESTS Hold them up as examples to your son.

GULFSTREAM Famous Norwegian town, recently discovered.

GUNMEN Term used by fierce republicans to denote police officers.

GYMNASE (LE) Branch of the Comédie Française.

H

HABIT Second nature. School habits are bad habits. By dint of habit one could play the violin like Paganini.

HAIDUK Confuse with eunuch.

HAIR (WAVING THE) Not suitable for men.

HALBERDS In Switzerland every man carries a halberd.

HAM Always from Mainz. Beware of it, on account of the danger of trichinosis.

HAMLET A touching noun, which is very effective in poetry.

HAMMOCK Characteristic of creole women. Indispensable in a garden. Persuade yourself that it is more comfortable than a bed.

HAND To have a beautiful hand means to have fine handwriting.

HANDWRITING A neat hand leads to the top. Illegible: a sign of learning, e.g. doctors' prescriptions.

HARD Invariably add 'as iron'. True, there is also 'hard as a diamond', but that is much less forceful.

HARE Sleeps with its eyes open.

HAREM Always compare a cock in the midst of his hens to a sultan in his harem. Every schoolboy's dream.

HARP Gives out heavenly harmonies. In engravings, is only played among ruins or beside a torrent. Shows off the arm and hand.

HASHEESH Not to be confused with hash, which produces no voluptuous sensations whatever.

HATS Complain about their shape.

HEALTH Excess of health causes illness.

HEAT Always 'unbearable'. Don't drink in hot weather.

HELOTS Cite as a warning to your son, though you would be hard put to it to show him any.

HEMICYCLE Admit to knowing of only one, that of the Beaux-Arts School.

HEMORRHOIDS Come from sitting on stoves and stone benches. St Fiacre's disease. A sign of health so don't try to get rid of them.

HENRY III, HENRY IV When these kings are mentioned don't fail to say: 'All the Henrys were unlucky!'

HERCULES All come from the North.

HERMAPHRODITES Arouse unwholesome curiosity. Try to see one.

HERNIA Everybody has one without knowing it.

HEROD To be 'as old as Herod'.

HERRING The wealth of Holland.

HIATUS Not to be tolerated.

HICCUPS To cure them, put a key down the hiccupper's back, or give him a shock.

HIEROGLYPHICS Language of the ancient Egyptians, invented by the priests to conceal their shameful secrets. To think that there are people who understand them! But perhaps the whole thing is just a hoax?

HIPPOCRATES Always to be quoted in Latin because he wrote in Greek, except in the maxim: 'Hippocrates says Yes, but Galen says No.'

HIPPOLYTOS His death the most beautiful narrative subject that can be set at school. Everyone should know this piece by heart.

HOME Always a castle. However, the police can enter whenever they please. Home, sweet home. No place like it.

HOMER Never existed. Famous for his laughter.

HOMO Say: '*Ecce homo!*' on the arrival of any person you are expecting.

HONOUR When mentioned, misquote: 'Honour is a mere scutcheon.' One must always be concerned about one's own, and not greatly concerned about others'.

HORN (HUNTING) Sounds wonderful in the woods, and at night across the water.

HORSES If they knew their strength, they wouldn't let themselves be led. Horsemeat: excellent subject for a pamphlet by a man who wishes to make his name. Race-horses: despise them – of what use are they?

HOSPITALITY Must always be Scottish. Quote: 'Highland hospitality, when sought, is always given, never bought.'

HOSPODAR Sounds well in a remark on the Eastern Question.

HOSTILITIES Hostilities are like oysters, they have to be opened. 'Hostilities have been opened' sounds as if one ought to sit down at a table.

HOTELS Are only good in Switzerland.

HUGO, VICTOR Really made a sad mistake when he went into politics.

HUMIDITY Cause of all illnesses.

HUNCHBACKS Are very witty. Much sought-after by lascivious women.

HUNTING Excellent exercise, which one must pretend to love. Part of the pomp of royalty. The judiciary rave about it.

HUSSAR Pronounce hoozar. Always preceded by 'handsome' or 'dashing'. The ladies love him. Never fail to quote: 'The young hussar, the whiskered votary of waltz and war.'

HYDRA-HEADED MONSTER Of anarchy, socialism and all other alarming systems. We must try to conquer it.

HYDROTHERAPY Cure and cause of all illnesses.

HYGIENE Must always be carefully maintained. Prevents illnesses, except when it causes them.

HYPOTHECATION Use the word when calling for reform of the law on mortgages: very smart.

HYPOTHESIS Often 'dangerous', always 'daring'.

HYSTERIA Confuse with nymphomania.

I

ICE CREAM It is dangerous to eat it.

ICE-CREAM MEN All Neapolitans.

IDEALISM The best of the philosophic systems.

IDEALS Perfectly useless.

IDEOLOGISTS Every newspaperman is an ideologist.

IDIOTS Those who think differently from you.

IDLERS All Parisians are idlers, although nine out of ten Parisians come from the provinces. In Paris nobody works.

IDOLATERS Are cannibals.

ILIAD Always followed by the *Odyssey*.

ILLEGIBLE A doctor's prescription should be. Likewise your signature – it shows that you are swamped with correspondence.

ILLUSIONS Pretend to have had a great many, and complain that you have lost them all.

IMAGES There are always too many in poetry.

IMAGINATION Always 'lively'. Be on your guard against it. When you lack it, attack it in others. To write a novel, all you need is imagination.

IMMORALITY Properly enunciated, this word confers prestige on the user.

IMPERIALISTS All respectable, polite, peaceable, distinguished people.

IMPIETY Thunder against it.

IMPORTS Canker at the heart of trade.

IMPRESARIO Artist's word meaning manager. Always preceded by 'clever'.

INCOGNITO The dress of princes on their travels.

INCOMPETENCE Always 'utter'. The more incompetent you are, the more ambitious you must be.

INCRUSTATION Applies only to mother-of-pearl.

INDIARUBBER Made of horse's scrotum.

INDOLENCE Effect of warm climates.

INDUSTRY See TRADE.

INFANTICIDE Committed only among the lower classes.

INFINITESIMAL Nobody knows what it means, but it has something to do with homeopathy.

INKWELL A suitable present for a doctor.

INNATE IDEAS Make fun of them.

INNOCENCE Proved by absolute calm.

INNOVATION Always 'dangerous'.

INQUISITION Its crimes have been greatly exaggerated.

INSCRIPTION Always 'cuneiform'.

INSPIRATION (POETIC) Aroused by: the sight of the sea, love, women, etc.

INSTINCT Substitute for intelligence.

INSTITUTE The members are all old men who wear green silk eye-shades.

INSTRUMENT If it has been used to commit a crime, it is always 'blunt', unless it happens to be sharp.

INSULT Must always be washed out in blood.

INSURRECTION 'The holiest of duties' (Blanqui).

INTEGRITY Found particularly in the judiciary.

INTERVAL Always too long.

INTOXICATION Always preceded by 'mad'.

INTRIGUE The gateway to everything.

INTRODUCTION Obscene word.

INVASION Brings tears to your eyes.

INVENTORS All die in the workhouse. Somebody else profits by their genius: it isn't fair.

ITALIANS All musical. All treacherous.

ITALY Should be seen during the honeymoon. Is very disappointing, not as beautiful as people say.

IVORY Refers only to teeth.

J

JANSENISM Nobody knows what it is, but it is smart to refer to it.

JAPAN Everything there is made of china.

JASPER All vases in museums are made of jasper.

JAVELIN As good as a gun if you know how to use it.

JEALOUSY Always preceded by 'frantic'. Terrible passion. Eyebrows which meet in the middle are a sign of jealousy.

JESUITS Have a hand in every revolution. Nobody has any idea how numerous they are. Never talk about the 'battle of the Jesuits'.

JEWELLER Always call him Monsieur Josse.

JEWS Sons of Israel. All Jews are spyglass vendors.

JOCKEY Deplore the breed.

JOCKEY CLUB Its members are all gay young dogs and very rich. Say simply 'The Jockey': this is very smart, and gives the impression you are a member.

JOHN BULL When you don't know an Englishman's name, call him John Bull.

JOY The mother of fun and games. Never mention her daughters.

JUDICIARY An excellent career if you want to make a rich marriage. All judges are pederasts.

JUJUBE Nobody knows what it is made of.

JURY Do everything you can to get off it.

JUS PRIMAE NOCTIS Don't believe in it.

JUSTICE Never worry about it.

K

KALEIDOSCOPE Used only to describe picture exhibitions.

KEEPSAKE Should be found on every drawing-room table.

KNAPSACK Case designed to hold marshal's baton.

KNIFE Described as Catalonian when the blade is long; called a dagger when it has been used to commit a crime.

KNOUT Word which offends the Russians.

KORAN Book by Mohammed, which is all about women.

L

LABORATORY Have one in your country house.

LACONICISM Language no longer spoken.

LACUSTRIAN TOWNS Deny their existence, since it is impossible to live under water.

LADIES Always come first. 'God bless 'em!' Be careful how you use the term.

LADS Never give a speech-day address without referring to 'you young lads' (which is tautological).

LAFAYETTE General famous for his white horse.

LA FONTAINE Maintain that you have never read his Tales. Call him 'the good La Fontaine', 'the immortal fabulist'.

LAGOON City on the Adriatic.

LAKE Have a woman beside you when you sail on it.

LAMPOONS Despise them. No need to know any.

LANCET Always carry one in your pocket, but think twice before using it.

LANDLORD The human race is divided into two classes: landlords and tenants.

LANDSCAPES (ON CANVAS) Always so much spinach.

LANGUAGES (MODERN) Our country's ills are due to our ignorance of them.

LATE 'My late father' – and you raise your hat.

LATE NIGHTS Are respectable in the country.

LATHE Indispensable for rainy days in the country. Have one in the attic.

LATIN The natural speech of man. Spoils one's style. Useful only for reading inscriptions on public buildings. Beware of quoting Latin tags: they all have something risqué in them.

LAUGHTER Always 'Homeric'.

LAURELS Keep a man from sleeping.

LAW (THE) Nobody knows what it is.

LAWYERS Too many of them in Parliament. Their judgement is warped. Of a lawyer who is a poor speaker, say: 'Yes, but he knows his law.'

LEAGUE You can walk a league faster than three miles.

LEARNED (THE) Make fun of it. All it takes to be learned is a good memory and hard work.

LEARNING Despise it as the sign of a narrow mind.

LEATHER All comes from Russia.

LEFT-HANDED PEOPLE Formidable fencers. Much more deft than those who use their right hand.

LEGION OF HONOUR Make fun of it, but covet it. When you obtain it, always say it was unsolicited.

LENT At bottom is only a health measure.

LETHARGY Some cases are known which lasted for years.

LIBERTINISM Found only in big cities.

LIBERTY 'Liberty, what crimes are committed in thy name!' We have all the liberty we need. Liberty is not licence (conservative saying).

LIBRARY Always have one at home, especially if you live in the country.

LIGHT Always say: '*fiat lux*' when a candle is lighted.

LIGUE [of sixteenth century] Forerunners of liberalism in France.

LILAC Delights the heart because it means summer is near.

LINEN One cannot display too much, too often.

LION Noble animal. Always plays with a large ball. Well-roared, lion! And to think that lions and tigers are just cats!

LITERATURE Occupation of idlers.

LITTLETON Inseparable from Coke. Nobody knows what they wrote, but no matter. Say to any law student: 'I suppose you are deep in your *Coke and Littleton*' ['Cujas and Bartolo' in French].

LITTRÉ Snigger on hearing his name: 'The gentleman who thinks we are descended from monkeys.'

LOCKET Must always contain a lock of hair or a photograph.

LORD Rich Englishman.

LORGNETTE Insolent and distinguished.

LOUIS XVI Always refer to him as 'that unfortunate monarch'.

LUCKY Say of a lucky man: 'He was born with a caul.' You don't know what that means and neither will your listener.

LUGGER 'Once aboard the lugger and all is well.'

LUXURY The ruination of great states.

LYNX Animal renowned for its eye.

M

MACADAM Has put an end to revolutions: it is no longer possible to build barricades. Is very inconvenient all the same.

MACARONI When prepared in the Italian style, must be served with the fingers.

MACHIAVELLI Do not read him, but regard him as a scoundrel.

MACHIAVELLIAN Word only to be spoken with a shudder.

MACKINTOSH Scottish philosopher; invented the raincoat.

MAESTRO Italian word meaning pianist.

MAGIC Make fun of it.

MAID (THE) Used only to refer to Joan of Arc by adding 'of Orleans'.

MAIDS All unsatisfactory. Servants aren't what they used to be.

MAJORS Now only to be found in quiet hotels.

MAKE-UP Ruins the skin.

MALACCA A walking stick must be of malacca.

MALEDICTION Always uttered by a father.

MALTHUS The infamous Malthus.

MAMELUKES Ancient people of the Orient (Egypt).

MANDOLIN Indispensable for seducing Spanish women.

MARBLE Every statue is of Parian marble.

MARSEILLES (PEOPLE OF) All great wits.

MARTYRS All the early Christians were.

MARY QUEEN OF SCOTS Pity her fate.

MASK Stimulates wit.

MATERIALISM Utter this word with horror, stressing each syllable.

MATHEMATICS Dry up the heart.

MATTRESS The harder the healthier.

MAXIM Never new but always consoling.

MAY-BUGS Harbingers of summer. Fine subject for a monograph. Their total extinction is the dream of every prefect. When referring to the damage they cause in a speech at an agricultural fair, you must call them 'noxious coleoptera'.

MAYOR (OF VILLAGE) Always ridiculous. Thinks he has been insulted when called Alderman.

MECHANICS Lower branch of mathematics.

MEDALS Made only in classical antiquity.

MEDICAL STUDENTS Sleep next to corpses. Some even eat them.

MEDICINE When in good health, make fun of it.

MEERSCHAUM Means 'sea-foam', but found in the earth. Used to make pipes.

MELANCHOLY Sign of a noble heart and a lofty mind.

MELODRAMAS Less immoral than dramas.

MELON Nice topic for dinner-table conversation. Is it a vegetable or a fruit? The English eat it for dessert, which is astounding.

MEMORY Complain of your own, and indeed boast of not having any. But roar indignantly if anyone says you lack judgement.

MENDICITY Should be prohibited and never is.

MEPHISTOPHELIAN Must be said of any bitter laugh.

MERCURY Kills the patient with the disease.

MESMERISM A fine topic of conversation, and one which will help you to charm a woman.

METALLURGY Very smart.

METAMORPHOSIS Make fun of the times when it was believed in. Ovid invented it.

METAPHORS There are always too many in any writer's style.

METAPHYSICS Laugh at it: this is proof of your superior intellect.

METHOD Of no use whatever.

MEXICO 'The Mexican expedition is the greatest idea of the reign' (Rouher).

MIDNIGHT The limit of respectable pleasures; beyond it, whatever is done is immoral.

MIGHT 'Might makes Right' (Bismarck).

MILK Dissolves oysters, attracts snakes, whitens the skin. Some women in Paris take a milk bath every day.

MINISTER The pinnacle of human glory.

MINUTE Nobody has any idea how long a minute really is.

MISSIONARIES Are all eaten or crucified.

MISSIVE Nobler than 'letter'.

MISTAKE 'It's worse than a crime, it's a mistake' (Talleyrand). 'There isn't a single mistake left to commit' (Thiers). These two remarks must be quoted with an air of profundity.

MOB Its instincts are always good. *Turba ruit* or *ruunt*. 'The vile multitude' (Thiers). 'The mob has many heads, but no brains.'

MODELLING In front of any statue, say: 'The modelling has a certain charm.'

MODESTY Woman's greatest jewel.

MOLE Blind as a mole. Yet moles have eyes.

MONARCHY 'A constitutional monarchy is the best of republics.'

MONEY Cause of all evil. *Auri sacra fames*. The god of the day – but not to be confused with Apollo. Politicians call it emoluments; lawyers, retainers; doctors, fees; employees, salary; workmen, pay; servants, wages. 'Money is not happiness.'

MONK Father of a monkey [*moine/moineau*, sparrow in French]. Disciple of St Onan.

MONOPOLY (STATE) Thunder against it.

MONSTERS No longer extant.

MOON Inspires melancholy. May be inhabited.

MOSAICS The secret of the art is lost.

MOSQUITO More dangerous than any wild beast.

MOUNTEBANK Always preceded by 'cheap'.

MURDERER Always 'cowardly' even when he has been bold and daring. Less reprehensible than an incendiary.

MUSCLES The muscles of strong men are always of steel.

MUSEUMS:

VERSAILLES Recalls the great days of the nation's history. A splendid idea of Louis Philippe's.

THE LOUVRE To be avoided by young ladies.

DUPUYTREN Very instructive for young men.

MUSHROOMS Shouldn't be bought anywhere except at the market.

MUSIC Makes one think of a great many things. Softens a nation's character: e.g. 'La Marseillaise'.

MUSICIAN The characteristic of the true musician is to compose no music, to play no instrument, and to despise virtuosos.

MUSSELS Always hard to digest.

MUSTACHIOS Give a martial air.

MUSTARD Good only in Dijon. Ruins the stomach.

N

NAPLES If you are talking to a scholar, always say: Parthenopeia. 'See Naples and die.' (See YVETOT.)

NATURE How beautiful Nature is! Say this every time you are in the country.

NAUTCH-GIRL Word that fires the imagination. All Oriental women are nautch-girls. (See ODALISKS.)

NAVIGATOR Always 'intrepid'.

NECKERCHIEF It is the done thing to blow one's nose in it.

NECTAR Confuse with ambrosia.

NEGRESSES Hotter than white women. (See BLONDES and BRUNETTES.)

NEGROES Express surprise that their saliva is white and that they can speak French.

NEIGHBOURS Try to get them to do you favours without its costing you anything.

NEOLOGISMS The ruin of the French language.

NERVES Blamed every time a disease baffles comprehension. This satisfies the listener.

NERVOUS AILMENT Always an act.

NEWSHOUNDS Journalists: when you add 'yellow', this is the depth of contempt.

NEWSPAPERS One can't do without them, but thunder against them. Play an important part in modern society: e.g. the *Figaro*, Serious Journals: the *Revue des Deux Mondes*, *L'Économiste*, the *Journal des Débats*. You must leave them lying about on your drawing-room table, taking care to cut the pages beforehand. Marking a few passages in red pencil is also impressive. In the morning, read an article in one of these grave and serious journals; in the evening, in company, bring the conversation round to the subject you have studied in order to shine.

NIGHTMARES Come from the stomach.

NINNY Never use this word in the plural when referring to a woman's breasts.

NORMANS Believe that they talk with a broad *a* and tease them about their nightcaps.

NOSTRILS When flared, a sign of lasciviousness.

NOVELS Corrupt the masses. Are less immoral in serial than in volume form. Only historical novels are tolerable, because they teach history. Some novels are written with the point of a scalpel. Others rest on the point of a needle.

NUMISMATICS Related to the abstruse sciences; inspires tremendous respect.

O

OASIS An inn in the desert.

OBSCENITY All scientific words derived from Greek and Latin conceal an obscenity.

OCTOGENARIAN Applied to any elderly man.

ODALISK All Oriental women are Odalisks. (See NAUTCH-GIRL.)

ODÉON Joke about its remoteness.

OFFENBACH On hearing his name, put two fingers of the right hand close together, to guard against the evil eye. This looks very fashionable and Parisian.

OLD Always 'prematurely'.

OLDEST INHABITANTS When discussing a flood, thunderstorm, etc., the oldest inhabitants cannot remember ever having seen a worse one.

OLIVE OIL Is never good. You should have a friend in Marseilles who sends you a small barrel of it.

OMEGA Second letter of the Greek alphabet, since everybody always says: 'The alpha and omega of...'

OMNIBUS Nobody can ever find a seat on one. Were invented by Louis XIV. 'Let me tell you, sir, that I can remember tricycles when they had only three wheels.'

OPENING CEREMONY Cause for rejoicing.

OPERA (WINGS OF THE) Mohammed's heaven on earth.

OPTIMIST Synonym for idiot.

ORATION (FUNERAL) Any sermon of Bossuet's.

ORCHESTRA Symbol of society: Everybody plays his part and there is a leader.

ORCHITIS Gentleman's disease.

ORDER How many crimes are committed in thy name! (See LIBERTY.)

ORGAN MUSIC Lifts the soul up to God.

ORGASM Obscene term.

ORIENTALIST Man who has travelled widely.

ORIGINAL Make fun of everything that is original, hate it, jeer at it, and annihilate it if you can.

OSTRICH Can digest stones.

OTTER Very useful for making caps and waistcoats.

OYSTERS Nobody eats them any more: they are really far too dear!

P

PAGANINI Never tuned his violin. Famous for his long fingers.

PAGEANTRY Lends prestige. Strikes the imagination of the masses. We need more and more of it.

PAINTING ON GLASS The secret of the art is lost.

PALFREY A white animal of the Middle Ages whose breed is extinct.

PALLADIUM Ancient fortress.

PALM TREE Supplies local colour.

PALMYRA An Egyptian Queen? Ruins? Nobody knows.

PAMPHLETEERING No longer done.

PANTHEISM Ridiculous. Thunder against it.

PARADOX Always originates on the Boulevard des Italiens between two puffs on a cigarette.

PARALLELS (HISTORICAL) The choice is limited to the following: Caesar and Pompey, Horace and Virgil, Voltaire and Rousseau, Napoleon and Charlemagne, Goethe and Schiller, Bayard and Mac Mahon...

PARIS The great whore. Heaven for women, hell for horses.

PARLOUR SONGS A man who can sing parlour songs appeals to the ladies.

PARTHIAN SHOT Wax indignant at such a shot, though it is in fact perfectly legitimate.

PARTS 'Shameful' to some, 'natural' to others.

PASS Always mention Thermopylae. The passes in the Vosges are the Thermopylae of France. (This was often said in 1870.)

PATIENT To raise his spirits, laugh at his ailment and deny his sufferings.

PEDANTRY Should be ridiculed, unless it is applied to trifles.

PEDERASTY Disease that afflicts all men at a certain age.

PELICAN Tears its breast to feed its young. Symbol of the paterfamilias.

PERU Country in which everything is made of gold.

PERSPIRING FEET A sign of good health.

PHAETON Inventor of the carriage of that name.

PHEASANT Smart to serve at a dinner.

PHILIPPE-ÉGALITÉ Thunder against him. Another of the causes of the Revolution. He committed all the crimes of that dreadful period.

PHILOSOPHY Always snigger at it.

PHOENIX Fine name for a Fire Insurance Company.

PHOTOGRAPHY Will make painting obsolete. (See DAGUERREOTYPE.)

PHYSICAL TRAINING Cannot be overdone. Exhausting for children.

PIANO Indispensable in a drawing-room.

PIDGIN Always talk Pidgin to make yourself understood by a foreigner, whatever his nationality. Use it also for telegrams.

PIG Its insides being 'identical with those of man', they should be used in hospitals to teach anatomy.

PIGEON Eat it only with peas.

PILLOW Never use a pillow: it will turn you into a hunchback.

PIMPLES On the face or anywhere else, a sign of good health and strong blood. Don't try to get rid of them.

PIPE Not good form except at the seaside.

PITY Always avoid feeling it.

PLANETS All discovered by Monsieur Leverrier.

PLANT Always cures those parts of the human body that it resembles.

PLOT The heart of any play.

POACHERS All ex-convicts. Responsible for all the crimes committed in country districts. Must rouse you to a pitch of fury: 'No mercy, my dear fellow, no mercy!'

POCK-MARKED Pock-marked women are all lascivious.

POET Flattering synonym for fool, dreamer.

POETRY Completely useless and out of date.

POLICE Always in the wrong.

POLICEMAN Bulwark of society. Don't say 'the police' but 'the forces of law and order' or 'the constabulary'.

POLISH PLAIT If you cut the hair it bleeds.

POLITICAL ECONOMY Cold, heartless science.

PONSARD The only poet with any common sense.

POOR Caring for them is equivalent to practising all the virtues.

POPILIUS Inventor of a kind of circle.

PORK-BUTCHER Stories of pies made of human flesh. All pork-butchers have pretty wives.

PORTFOLIO Carry one under your arm: this makes you look like a Cabinet minister.

PORT-ROYAL Very smart topic of conversation.

POST Always apply for one.

POTTERY Smarter than china.

POULTICE Always apply one while waiting for the doctor.

PRACTICAL JOKES Always play practical jokes when you are picnicking with ladies.

PRACTICE Superior to theory.

PRADON Never forgive him for having been Racine's rival.

PRAGMATIC SANCTION Nobody knows what it is.

PRECINCTS Sounds well in official speeches: 'Within these precincts, gentlemen ...'

PREOCCUPATION Is all the more profound in that being deep in thought, one is motionless.

PRETTY Used for whatever is beautiful. 'It's very pretty' is the acme of admiration.

PRIAPISM A cult of ancient times.

PRIESTLY CALLING Art, medicine, etc., are so many priestly callings.

PRIESTS Should be castrated. Sleep with their housekeepers and give them children whom they pass off as their nephews. Still, there are a few good ones all the same.

PRINCIPLES Always 'fundamental'. Nobody can tell their nature or number; no matter, they are sacred all the same.

PRINT One must believe whatever is in print. There are people who commit crimes just to see their name in print.

PRINTING Wonderful invention. Has done more harm than good.

PROBLEM Needs only to be stated to be solved.

PROFESSOR Always 'the learned'.

PROGRESS Always 'headlong' and 'ill-advised'.

PROPELLER The future of machinery lies in the propeller.

PROPERTY One of the foundations of society. More sacred than religion.

PROSE Easier to write than verse.

PROSPECTS Find them beautiful in nature and gloomy in politics.

PROSTITUTE A necessary evil. A protection for our daughters and sisters, as long as we have bachelors. Should be harried without mercy. It's impossible to take one's wife out any more with all these women on the boulevards. Are always working-class girls seduced by wealthy bourgeois.

PROVIDENCE 'Where should we be without it?'

PRUNES Keep the bowels loose.

PUDDING A sign of gaiety in the house. Indispensable on Christmas Eve.

PUNCH Suitable for a stag party. Source of riotous gaiety. Put out the light when setting it on fire. It makes fantastic flames.

PUPPET Grave and impressive insult to fling at a political opponent: 'Sir, you are a puppet of the Palace!' Used only on the tribune of the Chamber.

PURGE Used only with regard to the emotions.

PUS Rejoice when it comes out, and express astonishment that the human body can contain such large quantities.

PYRAMID Useless edifice.

R

RABBIT PIE Always made of cat.

RACINE Naughty boy!

RADICALISM All the more dangerous that it is latent. The republic is leading us towards radicalism.

RAFT Always 'of the Medusa'.

RAILWAYS If Napoleon had had them, he would have been invincible. Enthuse about them, saying: 'I, my dear sir, who am speaking to you now, was at X this morning: I had taken the train to X, I transacted my business there, and by X o'clock I was back here.'

RAILWAY STATIONS Go into ecstasies over them, and cite them as architectural wonders.

REDHEADS See BLONDES, BRUNETTES and NEGRESSES.

REGARDS Always 'kind'.

REGENCY SUPPERS Wit flowed at them even more freely than champagne.

RELATIVES Always a nuisance. Keep the poor ones out of sight.

RELIGION Part of the foundation of society. Is necessary for the common people, but there mustn't be too much of it. 'The religion of our fathers . . .'; this phrase must be uttered with unction.

REPUBLICANS The republicans are not all scoundrels, but all scoundrels are republicans.

RESTAURANT You should always order the dishes not usually served at home. When uncertain just order what the others around you are eating.

REVOLUTIONARY ERA Still going strong, since every new government promises to put an end to it.

RHYME Never in accord with reason.

RIDING Excellent exercise for slimming (all cavalry officers are thin). Excellent exercise for putting on weight (all cavalry officers are pot-bellied). 'He rides a horse like a regular centaur.'

RING Wearing one on the index finger is distinguished. Wearing one on the thumb is too Oriental. Rings deform the fingers.

ROBE Inspires respect.

RONSARD Absurd, with his Greek and Latin words.

ROPE People don't know how strong it is – stronger than iron.

ROUSSEAU Believe that Jean-Jacques Rousseau and Jean-Baptiste Rousseau were brothers, like the two Corneilles.

RUINS Induce reverie; make a landscape poetic.

S

SACRILEGE It is sacrilege to cut down a tree.

SAFES Their devices are very easy to outwit.

ST BARTHOLOMEW'S EVE Old wives' tale.

SAINTE-BEUVE Ate nothing but meat on Good Friday.

ST HELENA Island famous for its rock.

SALON To write a criticism of the Salon is a good beginning in literature; it enables a man to establish his reputation.

SALT CELLAR Upsetting it brings bad luck.

SANGFROID Good form, and also makes you look English. Always preceded by 'imperturbable'.

SAPPHICS and ALCAICS Sounds good in a critical article.

SASH Poetic.

SATRAP Rich man of loose morals.

SATURNALIA Festivals of the Directory period.

SAVINGS BANKS Only encourage servants to steal.

SCAFFOLD When you mount it, contrive to say a few eloquent words before dying.

SCENERY (STAGE) Isn't real painting. All you have to do is to splash paint on the canvas and spread it with a broom; distance and lighting do the rest.

SCHOOLS The Polytechnic: every mother's dream for her boy (*old-*

fashioned). Terror of the bourgeois during riots when he learns that the Polytechnic sympathizes with the workers (*old-fashioned*). Just say: 'the School' and people will think you've been there. At Saint-Cyr: young aristocrats. At the School of Medicine: all hot heads. At the School of Law: young men of good family.

SCHOOLTEACHERS (WOMEN) Are always from good families in reduced circumstances. Dangerous as governesses in the home: corrupt the husband.

SCIENCE A little science takes you away from religion; a lot brings you back to it.

SCUDÉRY Snigger, without knowing whether the name is that of a man or a woman.

SCURF Sign of good health. (See PIMPLES.)

SEA Bottomless. Symbol of infinity. Inspires deep thoughts. At the seaside one should always have a telescope. While contemplating the sea, always exclaim: 'Water, water everywhere!'

SEALED Always preceded by 'hermetically'.

SEASHELLS Always bring some back from the seaside.

SEASICKNESS To avoid it, all you have to do is think about something else.

SECRET FUNDS Incalculable sums with which ministers buy men's consciences. Wax indignant about them.

SELFISHNESS Complain of other people's, and overlook your own.

SENECA Wrote on a golden desk.

SERIALS The cause of our present demoralization. Argue about the way the story will end. Write to the author suggesting ideas. Fly into a rage when you find that one of the characters bears your name.

SEVILLE Famous for its barber. 'See Seville and die.' (See NAPLES.)

SHEEP'S GUT Used only to make toy balloons.

SHELLS (ARTILLERY) Can be used to make clocks and inkwells.

SHEPHERDS All sorcerers. Specialize in conversations with the Virgin Mary.

SHIPS The only good ones are built at Bayonne.

SHOE-POLISHING Only done well when you do it yourself.

SHOTGUN Always keep one at your country house.

SIGH Must be heaved near a woman.

SIGNATURE The more ornate, the more beautiful.

SINGERS Swallow a raw egg every morning to clear the voice. Tenors always have a 'tender voice'; baritones a 'full, pleasing voice'; basses 'a powerful organ'.

SITE Place for writing poetry.

SKIFF Any small boat with a woman in it. 'Come into my little skiff!'

SKULL-CAP Indispensable to the man of letters. Lends dignity to the face.

SLEEP Thickens the blood.

SNAKES All poisonous.

SNEEZE After saying 'God bless you!' start a discussion on the origin of this custom. It is amusing to say that Russian and Polish aren't spoken but sneezed.

SOCIETY Its enemies. What destroys it.

SOIL (THE) Grow tearful about it.

SOLICITOR More complimentary than lawyer. No longer to be trusted.

SOMBREUIL (MADEMOISELLE DE) Recall the glass of blood.

SOMNAMBULIST Walks at night along the roof-tops.

SOUTHERN COOKING Always full of garlic. Thunder against it.

SOUTHERNERS All poets.

SPELLING Like mathematics. Not necessary if you have style.

SPICE [*chacal/shakos* in French] Plural of 'spouse'; an old joke, but still good for a laugh.

SPINACH Acts on your stomach like a broom. Never forget to quote Monsieur Prudhomme's famous remark: 'I don't like it and I'm glad I don't, because if I liked it I would eat it – and I can't stand it.' (Some people will find this perfectly reasonable and won't laugh.)

SPLEEN You can run faster if it has been removed. No need to know that this operation has never been practised on man.

SPURS Look well on boots.

SPY Always in high society. (See CROOK.)

SQUARING THE CIRCLE Nobody knows what it is, but shrug your shoulders at any mention of it.

STACKING ARMS The hardest duty of the National Guard.

STAG PARTY Calls for oysters, white wine and racy stories.

STAGE COACH Look back nostalgically to the days of the stage-coach.

STALLION Always 'fiery'. A woman must not know the difference between a stallion and a horse.

STAR Everyone follows his own, like Napoleon.

STEADY Always followed by 'as a rock'.

STEEPLE (VILLAGE) The sight of it makes the heart beat faster.

STICK More to be feared than any sword.

STIFF Always followed by 'and unbending'.

STOCKBROKERS All thieves.

STOCK EXCHANGE Barometer of public opinion.

STOICISM Is impossible.

STOMACH All illnesses come from the stomach.

STOOL-PIGEONS All in the pay of the police.

STRENGTH Always 'Herculean'.

STRONG As a horse, an ox, a Turk, Hercules. 'That fellow should be strong, he's all sinew.'

STUDENTS All wear red berets and tight-fitting trousers, smoke pipes in the street and never study.

STUD-FARMS A fine subject for a parliamentary debate.

SUBURBS Terrifying in times of revolution.

SUFFERING Always has a beneficial effect. Real suffering is always silent.

SUFFRAGE (UNIVERSAL) The summit of political science.

SUICIDE Proof of cowardice.

SUMMER Always 'unusual'. (See WINTER.)

SUMMER-HOUSE Place of bliss in a garden.

SUPPRESSION Applied exclusively to vice.

SURGEONS Hard-hearted. Call them butchers.

SWALLOWS Never call them anything but 'harbingers of Spring'. Since nobody knows where they come from, say it is 'a distant shore' (this is poetic).

SWAN Sings just before it dies. Can break a man's leg with its wing. The Swan of Cambrai was not a bird but a man called Fénelon. The Swan of Mantua is Virgil. The Swan of Pesaro is Rossini.

SWORD The only famous one is that of Damocles. Look back nostalgically to when swords were worn. 'My trusty blade.' Sometimes the sword had never been used. The French want to be governed by a sword.

SYBARITES Thunder against them.

SYPHILIS Everybody is more or less infected with it.

T

TALLEYRAND Wax indignant against him.

TASTE 'What is simple is always in good taste.' Always say this to a woman who apologizes for the simplicity of her dress.

TEETH Are spoiled by cider, tobacco, sweets, ices, drinking immediately after soup and sleeping with the mouth open. Eye-teeth: it is harmful to pull these out because they are connected with the eyes. Having a tooth out 'is no joke'.

TEN (COUNCIL OF) Nobody knows what it was but it was. Carried out its deliberations wearing masks. Still causes a shudder at the thought.

TESTIMONIAL A safeguard for parents and relatives. Always favourable.

THICKET Always 'dark and impenetrable'.

THINKING Painful. Things which compel us to think are generally neglected.

THIRTEEN Avoid being thirteen at table; it brings bad luck. The sceptics should not fail to joke: 'What's the difference? I'll eat enough for two!' Or again, if there are ladies present, ask if any is pregnant.

THRIFT Always preceded by 'honest'. Leads to wealth. Tell the story of Laffitte picking up a pin in the courtyard of the banker Perrégaux.

TIGHTS Sexually exciting.

TIME (OUR) Thunder against it. Deplore the fact that there is nothing poetic about it. Call it a time of transition, of decadence.

TIPPING (ON NEW YEAR'S DAY) Express indignation at the practice.

TOAD Male of the frog. Its venom is very dangerous. Lives inside a stone.

TOBACCO Government tobacco is not so good as that which is smuggled in. Snuff suits studious men. Cause of all the diseases of the brain and spinal cord.

TOLERATED HOUSE Not one in which tolerant opinions are held.

TOLLS One must try to avoid paying them. (See CUSTOMS.)

TOYS Should always be educational.

TRADE Argue which is nobler, trade or industry.

TRANSFER The only verb known to army men.

TRAVELLER Always 'dauntless'.

TRAVELLING Should be as fast as possible.

TROUBADOUR Fine subject for an ornamental clock.

U

UKASE Call any authoritarian decree a ukase: this annoys the government.

UNIVERSITY *Alma mater.*

UNLEASH Applied to dogs and evil passions.

UNPOLISHED Whatever is antique is unpolished, and whatever is unpolished is antique. Remember this when buying antiques.

USUM (AD) Latin expression which sounds well in the phrase *Ad usum Delphini*. Should always be used when speaking of a woman called Delphine.

V

VACCINE Mix only with people who have been vaccinated.

VELVET On clothes, means distinction and wealth.

VERRES Hasn't been forgiven yet.

VIZIR Trembles at the sight of a piece of cord.

VOLTAIRE Famous for his frightful *rictus*. His learning was superficial.

W

WAGNER Snigger when you hear his name and joke about the music of the future.

WALK Always go for a walk after dinner; it helps the digestion.

WALTZ Wax indignant against it. A lascivious, impure dance, which should only be danced by old ladies.

WAR Thunder against it.

WATCH Good only if made in Switzerland. In pantomimes, when a character pulls out his watch, it must be a turnip: this never fails to raise a laugh. 'Does your watch keep time?' 'The sun goes by it.'

WATER Paris water gives you colic. Salt water buoys you up. Cologne water smells good.

WATERPROOF A very practical garment. A very harmful one because it checks perspiration.

WAVING (HAIR) Not suitable for men.

WEALTH Substitute for everything, even reputation.

WEATHER Eternal topic of conversation. Universal cause of illness. Always complain about it.

WHATNOT Indispensable in a pretty woman's home.

WHITEWASH (ON CHURCH WALLS) Thunder against it. This aesthetic anger is extremely becoming.

WINDMILL Looks well in a landscape.

WINE Topic for discussion among men. The best is claret, since doctors prescribe it. The worse it tastes, the purer it is.

WINTER Always 'unusual'. (See SUMMER.) Is healthier than the other seasons.

WIT Always preceded by 'sparkling'. 'Better a witty fool than a foolish wit.'

WITNESS Always refuse to be a witness. You never know where it may lead you.

WOMAN Member of the fair sex. One of Adam's ribs. Don't say 'the little woman' but 'my good lady', or, better still, 'my better half'.

WOODS Induce reverie. Well suited for the composition of verse. In the autumn, when walking through them, say: 'There is a pleasure in the pathless woods.'

WORKMAN Always honest, unless he is rioting.

WRATH (OF THE VATICAN) Laugh at it.

WRITING 'In haste.'

WRITTEN 'Well written': a hall-porter's phrase to describe the newspaper serials he finds entertaining.

Y

YAWNING Say: 'Excuse me, it isn't that I'm bored – it's my stomach.'

YOUNG GENTLEMAN Always sowing wild oats. This is as it should be. Express astonishment when he doesn't.

YOUNG LADY Utter these words diffidently. All young ladies are pale, frail, and always pure. Prohibit, in their interests, every kind of reading, and all visits to museums, theatres, and especially the monkey-house at the zoo.

YOUTH What a wonderful thing it is! Always quote these Italian verses, even if you don't know what they mean: 'O Primavera! Gioventù! Primavera della vita!'

YVETOT 'See Yvetot and die.' (See NAPLES and SEVILLE.)

Printed in the United States
by Baker & Taylor Publisher Services